BRANDED

978-1-955729-00-0 (Cloth Hardcover with Dust Jacket)
978-1-955729-01-7 (Paperback)
978-1-955729-02-4 (E-book)
978-1-955729-03-1 (Audiobook)
978-1-955729-04-8 (Case Laminate Hardcover)

THE FORGOTTEN SERIES: BOOK 1

BRANDED

JOSEPH T. HUMPHREY

INTREPID PEN PUBLISHING, L.L.C.
UNITED STATES OF AMERICA

For Melissa – beautiful wife,
encouraging inspiration,
and best friend.

PROLOGUE

"I can't run this fast after giving birth. I don't have the strength."

Thom turned around. His face was covered in sweat. He squeezed his wife's hand.

"I know, Dawn. I'm sorry." His eyes looked to the horizon behind her. The sun was descending in the west, falling into a murky grave of black. Or darkness was rising to swallow the sun. He wasn't sure which one.

"The world is dying," Thom said. He looked down to the baby in his arms. "But I won't let either of you die with it."

Thom gently handed the swaddled newborn back to Dawn in a mound of blankets. She pulled the child close to her chest. Thom bent over and scooped Dawn up in his arms.

"I will be your strength," he said.

Her eyes glistened with tears. She leaned her head forward to his and sighed. The moment hung in the air—the baby in Dawn's arms, and she in Thom's.

"Why now?" Dawn asked. She looked down and wiped her tear away. "We didn't even get to celebrate his birthday."

"We will. I promise."

Her eyes searched for his. "Is this the end?"

He stared at the horizon. The sky grew darker and the air colder by the moment. It wouldn't be long now. Thom turned back to the east, to the unknown before him.

"Never."

He bolted forward. Stride after heavy stride, he held all that mattered in his arms. The world swirled before him and coaxed him to collapse. He couldn't stop.

Run.

A few miles later, he slowed.

"We're here," Thom said in between breaths. He placed Dawn on the ground.

She pulled back the blankets and peered at the baby. "He's sleeping," she said. "So peaceful. I wish that could be us again."

"Me too. But not after today. Today of all days." Thom leaned forward and put his hands on his knees, panting. He looked at Dawn. "One of them found it."

"But you went after him. You stopped him, right?"

"He was the only one."

"You took him out?"

Thom looked back to the horizon. He closed his eyes and nodded. "A scout. On the way back with the information. I took it from him. Now, I'm the only one who knows."

"Thom, if the Nekura got their hands on that . . ." A shudder raked through Dawn's body. "All life would be bound beneath them. It would be unending enslavement."

Thom sighed. "I know. A nightmare come alive. The Nekura have set themselves up as gods—and now their unholy fury is at our backs. They will never stop until they get it. We have to go to the other side."

Dawn's eyes flashed. "Thom, is this right? If we leave, who will stand against them?" Suddenly, she clenched her chest with a frantic hand. She doubled over and fell to a knee, hardly breathing, but clung to the blankets in her arm.

"Dawn! Are you alright?" Thom dropped next to her.

"Thom, it's coming . . . I can feel it. The darkness . . ."

"Dawn, you won't survive if we stay. If we jump to the other side, we can hide. We can blend in. Others already have."

"We won't be as strong there." She gritted her teeth in pain.

"Neither will the Nekura."

"But they will be harder to recognize. Their deception will be more insidious." She spluttered the words out.

"We'll take precautions. But I can't protect us now if we fall asleep. With what I know, I can't afford to dream. Maybe ever again." He nodded at the delicate bundle in Dawn's arms. "And if we jump, it will give Henry a chance to live."

"I'd give everything for him." She looked up at Thom with glassy eyes. "I'd give everything for you. The Nekura will try to break us, tear us apart . . ."

"They can never tear us apart. I promise, Dawn, whenever you call my name, I will find you."

She nodded. "Okay. For all of us. Let's jump."

CHAPTER 1

The thick walls muted the thunder outside but held the reverberating scream inside.

The walls weren't padded.

Maybe they should've been. For people like that.

The thunder raked through the sky again. Rain pounded the windows with unforgiving force, tossed in sheets by the wind. The echoes of the fading scream snapped Henry out of his drifting thoughts. He stiffened up.

The rain clouds rolled in quickly from the west, carrying dark cover and dropping temperatures. It was unexpected.

The screaming more so.

He heard it a second time, this time more distant—now only a harsh whisper hung in the air. As quickly as the sound started, it dissipated—like a flame from an ember that flared and vanished. He stared at the door.

The large man at the front of the room jumped at the sound and spilled his coffee, which now dripped from his shirt. He shook the hot liquid from his hand with a grimace, but his eyes were fixed on the door also. He didn't move, unsure if he should open it to whatever lay on the other side. He paused, then walked over and opened it.

Everything stood strangely still outside the room.

"Hello?" he called down the empty hallway.

No one answered. No one was there.

The shrill voice had traced an icy finger up Henry's spine and nestled at the base of his skull. The sound had been awkward and throaty, not like the typical rambunctious yelling. Everyone else in the room whispered in hushed tones.

The man shut the door and relaxed into his natural, slumping posture and tried to corral everyone. His sigh of relief betrayed the cigarette smoke on his breath. He pushed his gray palette of hair across his head in a futile attempt to cover his baldness, trying to regain composure.

"Finished before Monday," he said, "and no exceptions."

The reminder of homework pulled everyone back into the classroom with a collective groan.

The bell rang.

The other students packed up their bags and Henry did the same, mimicking their actions. The feeling at the base of his skull remained, but he had other things to worry about. Besides, the scream was somebody else's concern. He'd spent a long time steeling himself against the craziness of high school life and didn't need this.

He tried to forget about it.

Like he tried to forget about his canceled baseball game. His mind drifted to the baseball diamond, thinking of the boggy moat it was becoming. There was one spot by second base that was probably a small lake by now. He really needed that scholarship. How was he supposed to get it if he couldn't even play?

He tried to think back to before the scream. He hadn't been paying attention anyway. Daydreaming again, he missed out on most of his trigonometry class. He had no idea what had to be finished before Monday.

He groaned but caught himself and slapped his hand over his mouth. His eyes widened and he glanced around to see who had heard.

The rest of the class was already gone.

Hoisting his backpack over his shoulder, he raced toward the door. One class left for the day. He had to hurry. His drifting thoughts had already cost him.

"And Mr. Murphy . . ." the teacher said. Henry stopped and turned around. With a sideways nod of the head back into the room, the teacher signaled to the textbook on Henry's desk. "You might need that if you're going to do any of the assignment."

"Oh, thanks."

The teacher rolled his eyes.

Henry offered a sheepish smile in return. He ran back in and stuffed the textbook into his backpack. He just wasted valuable seconds. He had to get to his locker before the next class. Without a game today, he needed his practice clothes instead of his uniform.

Playing a game would have been far better than practice. Games were fun, practices were grueling. Wind-sprints replaced homeruns. And the standing rule for practice was being late meant missing playing time when the games actually happened.

He sped to his locker and spun the tumbler on the lock. He opened the door and stuffed his books inside the locker, but they fell backward to the floor in an ungraceful cascade. He rushed to pick them up and grabbed everything he would need for his last class. The mental checklist was long: biology textbook, bag of baseball equipment, practice clothes, ball cap, cheese sandwich . . .

Was that everything? He glanced at his watch.

He had to hurry.

He slammed the door shut on his locker and turned, then jumped in surprise.

Someone had been hiding behind the locker door, only a few inches away. A girl. His backpack fell off his shoulder with a thud and his whole armload went to the floor again.

"Charley, don't do that!" Henry said. The adrenaline still laced his veins from the strange sound that had filled the hallway.

Charley smiled in return. "You're right, Henry, I should have told you that I was standing here. Like I did a minute ago when I walked up and stood here talking to you."

"Oh." He stared at her.

"You didn't hear me at all?"

"No. You were like a ninja or something."

"Ugh, don't give me that because you weren't listening. Okay, I'll start over. Did you hear that scream?"

"Yeah. Who didn't?"

"What do you think it was?"

"I don't know, Charley. I'm just trying to forget about it."

"Why? Aren't you concerned? Just curious?"

"Why? It's somebody else's issue. I've got other things I'm worrying about."

"That's right," came a voice from several lockers down, "you should worry about other things." It was condescending, and Henry gritted his teeth with frustration.

Trevor.

CHAPTER 2

"Coach will bench you if you're even a few seconds late," Trevor taunted. He flashed a smile. "But you'll be benched anyway. You're overrated. You're just second string. Maybe third."

Henry stared back and didn't move, his gear still piled at his feet. "Don't worry," Henry said, "I'll be there. We'll just see what happens."

"I already told you what's going to happen."

The muscles in Henry's neck clenched with frustration. Trevor always had that effect on him. He was so enamored with his own ability and loved to flaunt it, if nothing more than to remind everyone else of how great he was. A love affair with himself.

Trevor was chunky, but the extra weight served him well for generating power on the diamond. A scraggly beard covered his thick chin and made him look older than a high schooler. It also made him look fatter. His thick lips and tongue were always getting in the way of his breathing, so he breathed through his mouth while licking his lips. He looked like a cosmic baker had injected too much frosting in his face and his lips were going to burst with buttercream. A cherry fritter—chunky, red, and bloated.

"Don't spend too much time with the orphan, Henry," Trevor said. "She'll make you lose that scholarship."

Henry's gaze shot to Charley. Her face had already fallen and she looked at the floor. She didn't make a sound. She looked like a wounded dove.

Henry's blood boiled. "Back off her, Trevor!" He stepped over his gear and strode up to Trevor. He pointed his finger right at the buttercream. "Don't you call her that."

"What? Orphan? That's what she is."

Henry seethed and the hair bristled on the back of his neck. "I said don't call her that!"

A crowd quickly formed around them, watching with wide eyes. Trevor didn't budge, but the new unwanted attention only added to the problem. A menagerie of cell phones emerged from pockets and were already recording. Henry had to rein in the scene. He turned away.

"Stop being such a pretentious jerk, Trevor. If you even know what that means."

"If it means 'late to practice,' then don't worry about me."

The crowd dispersed as the promise of a fight flitted away. Henry walked back to Charley. "Hey, you okay?"

She nodded.

"Don't worry about him, Charley. He's an idiot."

"He's also right," she said, "you're going to be late for practice if you don't get your gear to the gym before last class starts."

It wasn't fair. She was right about Trevor being right. Henry snatched up all his belongings with a large scoop.

Charley reached down and tugged at the baseball cap crumpled under Henry's foot, and he moved back.

"Oh, thanks," Henry said. "I didn't even realize . . ."

She laughed at him and shook her head. The hat was smashed down in the center with his large footprint, but she didn't bother to undo it. She placed the soiled hat on his crop of shabby reddish-brown hair, where it fell sideways, the bill dipping over his left eyebrow.

"Look at you, Henry Murphy. You're a mess!" Her face softened.

He smiled back at her.

"Yeah," Trevor said, "you're a mess."

His voice felt like a jagged piece of metal in Henry's ribs. Trevor still leered with a smug grin, licking his lips.

"Don't you see," Charley said, "he's trying to make you late. He's goading you."

He wanted to stand up to Trevor. No one should be allowed to say things like that, just mowing people over. Fire burned in Henry's chest. But Henry also wanted to lead Charley away from the situation. She was always so sensitive about the orphan thing. And seeing her tears had unbridled him. But he also needed to get his gear to the gym to play ball. He had to get that scholarship.

His thoughts circled again in his mind, eyes sweeping back and forth. Trevor picking a fight. Charley's crying. And all the stuff he held was getting heavier.

"Gagh!" he groaned and squeezed his eyes shut. The emotional yanking was paralyzing. He was being drawn and quartered by all the sudden claims on his life.

He couldn't deal with any of this right now. He heard the call in his mind.

Let go, Henry Murphy.

"Go, Henry, I'm fine," Charley said, straightening up. "Really, I'm fine. You need that scholarship."

"But are you—"

"Go!"

A brief pause as he searched her face.

He ran away clutching his bags in his arms. Like a maddened and half-blind ostrich, Henry Murphy bounded down the hall, long legs scrambling, colliding into other students whom he didn't see beneath the brim of his cockeyed ball cap, mumbling sincere apologies along the way.

CHAPTER 3

Charley watched Henry sprint down the hall. She had told him to go.

She wished he would have stayed.

She didn't know why she was so sensitive. She just was. She hated when her emotions overtook her like that.

Charley navigated through the crowds toward her locker and heard indistinct conversations float around her about the complications of teenage love and the latest gossip. She wasn't interested. The scream from last class had piqued her concern and curiosity, but now it felt dampened and surreal after Trevor's barb.

Maybe whoever screamed did it because they finally had enough of Trevor. He drove someone to insanity.

She smirked at the thought.

At least Henry stood by her—for the moment. But ultimately, he ran off to baseball.

Again.

He was after a scholarship. She knew—she had read the news.

Henry Murphy was forgetful, and she toyed with the idea that he was even a bit of a klutz, but something transformed when he got onto the baseball diamond. She even saw him play in a couple games. He was a full head taller than his classmates, and with his baseball skills maturing, he filled out to a strong, lean frame, even if he was still a little lanky and unorthodox.

The news article, which was only from the school paper and brief, said he could pound the ball when he swung and had an electric throwing arm. Now he was in his senior year, and the article praised him as a phenom at Middleton High. Colleges, maybe even professional scouts, were looking at him.

But for all his athletic prowess, he tended to get lost more in the mundane than in the sublime. He could listen to his coach about the subtleties of his baseball swing, but Charley had a hunch he didn't even hear the assignment from the trigonometry teacher. Which he had repeated three times.

She opened her locker door and her books welcomed her, arranged by height on their familiar white-wire shelf. An array of highlighters in a plastic bin sat on top with a giant stockpile of index cards filled with neatly written notes.

Simple practicality. It made her feel like she at least had control over something. Some other girls had mirrors affixed to the inside of the door and an arsenal of lipstick, mascara, and glitter-laden eye shadow. Others had oil diffusers or popping colors or school-spirit banners. The inside of the high school locker was sacred.

Charley fingered the curved edge of the worn newspaper clipping neatly stuck with small magnets at its four corners on the inside of her locker door. The picture was modestly faded and some of the letters were rubbed out from the text after so many years. She had already read it twice today.

She sighed. It would have made today a lot easier if she could have changed it.

She grabbed her book and shut the door to see Henry bounding down the hall toward her. He exhaled a triumphant breath.

"See?" A couple more large breaths. "I made it, right?"

"Uh-huh," she said. "You're right. I'm impressed. Kind of."

"So . . . what did you think of the scream last class?"

"Not now, Henry. You don't have to make up for ignoring me at your locker."

"Okay, okay! Just trying to talk . . . since now I don't have to run all over the school."

"Let's just get to class. I'm ready for this day to be over."

CHAPTER 4

Henry walked into biology class behind Charley, and they made their way to their seats. Biology class allowed lab partners, and their teacher, Mrs. Ball, a lingering hippie from decades ago with long blonde hair and a silk flower headband, liked to give them the freedom to choose their partners. Sometimes she spent half of the class recounting stories of her former glory days and how she learned to "walk with the breeze," as she would say. Then she would stick them with homework anyway.

"Sit down, sit down," Mrs. Ball said. She reclined in her chair, feet crossed on the desk, showcasing her bargain-value white sneakers from underneath her ankle-length denim skirt.

Henry sat down and stretched out his long legs. The tension unwound from his spun muscles. His head lolled back over the seat and he groaned.

"Made it. Whew!"

The three electronic tones of the bell resounded off the cinder block walls in the small classroom. Mrs. Ball ambled toward the door in her sensible sneakers and shut it.

"Hey, where's Rachel?" Henry asked.

Charley looked around the room. "I was thinking the same thing."

"We need her to complete our assignment."

"I know. She's the reason we haven't killed each other yet over this thing."

"Did you see her today?"

"I talked to her right after lunch." A quizzical look appeared on Charley's face. "It's not at all like her to skip class."

"Do you think she's okay? You don't think the screaming was her, do you?"

"No, way! She looked fine. I told her I liked her new frock sweater and her topaz necklace."

"What's a frock?"

Charley sighed. "Never mind, Henry."

Silence for a few moments.

"Something's not right," Henry said.

"Maybe."

The class started with its normal drone, with Mrs. Ball at the white board reviewing basic anatomy. It sent Henry into a stupor, the kind where he couldn't focus on the material but couldn't muster intelligent thought about anything else. He leaned over.

"Charley . . ."

No response. Automation had taken her over, and she was lost in thought.

Henry tipped his chair to the side and whispered louder.

"Charley! Hey, do you know what the trigonometry assignment was?" Henry mumbled to hide his need for help.

She popped open her binder with the flip of a finger and slid it in front of him, pointing at the assignment she had scribed into her assignment log.

"Thanks," Henry said. He found his own loose paper and scrawled down the notes.

Charley continued following Mrs. Ball's haphazard trail through the anatomy of the human body. She was focused. He wanted to unearth her from the emotional trench Trevor had dug but he didn't know how. "Do you have gymnastics today?"

She shook her head.

He wished she did. Gymnastics became the way for her to channel her emotions when they began to stew, when the hopelessness began to open its mouth, hungry, and wanting to swallow her whole.

She was only four years old when she started. It was something her parents had wanted her to do. Henry had baseball, Charley had gymnastics, and they only ever spent time together for schoolwork. Except for the rare baseball game Charley attended just because she couldn't study with him.

"Ugh," Henry said and rubbed his sleepy face. "I wish I could take my eyeballs out and put them in my pocket to rest."

Charley shook her head and continued writing.

Henry slumped down in his seat.

A faint sound echoed outside the room. A long, drawn tone, muffled and distant.

He lifted his head up. His ears tingled. He was certain the sound was the same, just far off. He sat up, looked at Charley. She hadn't moved.

"Charley . . ."

She put her finger up to her lips to silence him. "Not now," she said. "Pay attention!"

He looked around the room. No one else seemed to notice.

Panic rose inside him. Should he say something? What if it was nothing . . .

Again the sound came, this time closer. Like the dying call of an albatross as it falls from the sky before it lands lifeless on the shore. The icy grip squeezed at Henry's neck again and rose into the base of his skull.

"Charley!" He was insistent. "Listen! Do you—"

The door flung open.

CHAPTER 5

The classroom door whipped inward as if a grenade had exploded on the other side. It crashed into the wall with a bang, nearly unseating it from its hinges. The door stopper shattered.

Henry jumped and knocked Charley's note cards to the floor. His nerves shivered, and he gawked at the open door.

What could make such a force?

The thunderous boom rang in his ears. The door swung like a pendulum, hanging from damaged metal brackets. Everyone froze and stared at the gaping entrance.

A girl burst into the room.

Screaming.

She looked familiar, yet wrong. Very wrong.

Was that . . .

Rachel?

Her mouth hung open in a terrified, unapologetic scream. Her voice radiated through the room and stung Henry's ears with its reverberation. He squinted his eyes at the pain.

The same scream . . .

She looked bedraggled, like she had just crawled through the razor wire of a foreign battlefield. Her new sweater hung in tatters, white wool pills falling off in streamers and already giving a threadbare appearance at the shoulders. Her hair, normally full and pulled back into a conservative bun, was disheveled into a soiled brown mess and teased out—or maybe ripped out.

Her eyes were wide with horror. The panic emanating from her felt tangible from across the room. The air became thick and heavy.

She drew a large breath and glanced past everyone. She was looking for something. For someone.

Her eyes locked with Henry.

Or was it Charley?

She stilled for an instant and gazed at them through the chaos she brought with her. The moment froze in time.

She screamed again. A word, long and loud, dripping in urgency, rang through the room.

"RUN!"

She only had time for one word.

Arms reached from behind her with grabbing hands. Men with blue vests were quickly upon her and subdued her. They held her back while she fought against their pulling arms. She was no match for them, and they dragged her out of the classroom, thrashing, still screaming.

Mrs. Ball stood up and watched, transfixed. One man with dark, slicked-back hair leaned in, donning a pair of wire-rimmed glasses with brown lenses. He hovered at the door as the other men carried Rachel away in their arms, still wildly fighting. He inclined his head and with a disproportionate look of triviality he shrugged his shoulders and puckered his lips.

"Nervous breakdown," he said. He gave a quick chuckle and closed the door.

The room hung in stunned silence. The walls quieted the screams again and the echoes died, strangling the spectacle as if it was a fleeting apparition.

The whole episode took only a few seconds. Henry shot a look at Charley. The same disbelieving look filled her face. They ran to the door and flung it open.

Everything on the other side was still. More than still.

Muted.

The men and Rachel were gone.

"Where did they go?" Charley said.

"They were just here . . ." He didn't need to complete the sentence.

Mrs. Ball spoke up from behind them. "Stranger and stranger." With a shake of her head and heavy sigh, she resigned the event to the past. "But that is why we have professionals. Henry, Charlotte, come back now. We shouldn't poke our noses into other people's problems."

The use of Charley's full name snapped her attention back into the classroom. Incredulity flashed on her face, and she stormed in like an obstinate toddler. She walked within a foot of Mrs. Ball.

"My name is Charley," she said and paused to make the point, muscles already tense.

Henry hadn't moved. He stood outside the room in the eerie silence, observing. He felt like something more should happen, but nothing did. The screaming was gone, but the uncomfortable shiver that had wrapped around his neck still held tight. His gaze remained locked down the empty hallway.

"Okay, Henry," Mrs. Ball called. Henry acquiesced and came back inside. He tried shutting the mangled door. The damage was impressive on closer inspection.

How did Rachel do that?

"We need to trust our staff that they know what they are doing," Mrs. Ball said, "and what is best for Rachel."

She flapped her arms toward herself like a mother hen calling her chicks close. Henry looked back over his shoulder through the broken doorway.

The other students had already returned to their lab tables, using the interruption as an opportunity to pull out their cell phones and send a flurry of messages about what just happened. It was tantalizing to talk about someone else's problems. With the hall monitor's declaration of the event as a psychiatric occurrence, the strange nature was smoothed over in a matter of moments, except that it made good social media fodder. It would be the talk of the school out of novelty rather than concern.

"Let's just mind our own business," Mrs. Ball said. She was eyeing Henry and Charley directly.

Just like Rachel had.

"It seems like Rachel needs some professional help," Mrs. Ball said. A segue into her repetitive opinions was coming. "This is why I say people should walk with the breeze, because people are too anxious these days and they have these breakdowns! There are just all these mental health problems in the world, and they're beginning to affect everyone. When I used to . . ."

Henry didn't hear another word.

His mind was far away. Wherever Rachel was.

CHAPTER 6

When the last bell of the day rang, Henry and Charley sprinted to the school office.

"Was that Rachel?" Henry asked. He had never imagined Rachel like that. It was like something had broken inside her—snapped right off.

"I don't know," Charley said. The same urgency filled her voice.

In a couple minutes they arrived outside the principal's door.

The principal's secretary, a woman in her mid-sixties with a brown beehive hairdo and too much hairspray, sat behind a high wooden desk. There was no one else in the room. The principal's desk sat in a small room adjacent to the secretary's desk and was also empty. The door was propped open, and the room was immaculate and undisturbed.

"Ms. Prang, where is Rachel?" Charley said.

The woman gave an absent smile and scrunched her forehead. "Who?"

"Rachel! Rachel Morgan! Senior, in our biology class, the sweetest person you'll ever meet!"

"Rachel Morgan?" Ms. Prang paused and looked thoughtful. "Doesn't sound familiar. She must not be a regular troublemaker. What did she do?"

"Troublemaker? No, no, it's not that. She's the one who just transferred to Middleton High last year after being homeschooled. Do you remember her?"

The gears began turning beneath the beehive. "Ah, yes. Rachel Morgan . . . I remember now. Messy situation." She scanned their faces. "What do you want with her?"

Charley surged with frustration. "We were just in class when she burst in screaming and was taken out by the hall monitors. They said was having a nervous breakdown. She looked awful!"

Ms. Prang gave a surprised look and sat upright, cocking her head to one side. "I don't know what you're talking about," she said. "I haven't heard of anything like that."

"Where would they have taken her?"

Ms. Prang emitted a mild laugh of tolerance. "There's nowhere else. If a student had an issue like that, they would certainly have come here. And I certainly would have known about it."

Henry stared at the secretary. It didn't make sense. Where was Rachel?

"But wait, we saw this happen," Charley said. "And she yelled at us to run! I don't know what's going on, but I think she's in trouble."

"Who escorted her out," Mrs. Prang asked. "The hall monitors?"

"Yes. They were wearing the blue vests."

"Okay, let me make a quick call." Ms. Prang grabbed the radio scanner and clicked a button. "Hello, this is Ms. Prang in the administrative office. I have two students here who are concerned about one of their friends. Miss Rachel Morgan?" She made eye contact with them, and they both nodded their heads. "They said she made quite a scene last period and had to be escorted out of class."

Static came back on the receiver with a man's voice a few seconds later.

"No, sorry. Nothing happened. I just checked with the other hallway staff and they said they've had a quiet day. We will check more into it. Are the students sure about it?"

The seedling idea landed in the secretary's brain and took root. She faced them full on. "Young lady, young man, is this your idea of some kind of game?"

"No! It really happened!" Charley said.

"Mrs. Ball was there, too," Henry said. "She saw it also."

"Well," Ms. Prang said, "if Rachel told you to run, maybe you should."

Charley's mouth fell slack and her eyes went wide. She turned white as a ghost. "What?"

"Run, little children."

Henry took a step back. His skin turned to goose bumps. "Ms. Prang . . ." The words fumbled in his mouth. "What do you—"

She threw her head back and cackled like a witch. After a few seconds, she leveled her eyes and looked at Charley.

"See, I can play your little game, too. Look out for the boogeyman!" She raised her hands above her head and made her voice shrill.

Charley grabbed Henry by the wrist and turned around. Her fingers were slick with sweat and cold as frost. "Come on," she said. "We're leaving."

She stormed out of the office. Henry looked down. Her hands were shaking.

Ms. Prang called after them as they walked away, her voice a fading echo intertwined with her cackling laughter. "Run! Run! They are coming for you."

CHAPTER 7

The hall monitors' room was just a few doors down from the administrative office. Charley charged forward with Henry in her grip.

The room was relatively small, with only five people inside. A few staff members lounged on old-fabric sofas with coffee stains. The fresh cups of coffee they held in their hands were waiting to tip and stain the couches again. A vintage tube television broadcasted commercials in the corner of the room. In the center of the room, two of the staff sat at the table writing on clipboards.

Charley barged in. "Where is Rachel?"

No one answered her. The hall monitors looked at her and then back at each other. One larger man with extra weight, a furry mustache, and a bald head sat on the couch with a disposable coffee cup. He looked at her and leaned forward.

"There is no Rachel that works here, young lady."

"No, not works here! Rachel Morgan! The student you dragged out last period!"

A shocked look settled over the faces of each staff member. They looked around the room, one to the other, shaking their heads and mumbling.

A short elderly female with bluish-gray hair sitting at the table stopped filling out reports. "I'm sorry, sweetie, nothing like that happened today."

Charley placed her hand on her forehead and began breathing faster. She took a step backward and leaned against the wall.

The picture of Rachel screaming in tattered clothes and with disheveled hair rose in Henry's mind. Nothing was making sense. The only thing she'd said was . . .

Run.

The word echoed in his mind. One ominous word.

But who was she talking to?

Henry took a step forward. "Where is the hall monitor with the slicked hair and the brown-tinted glasses?" Looks of confusion passed over the staff's faces.

"We don't have anyone like that," said the man on the couch with the caterpillar mustache.

"No one?" Henry's voice pitched higher. "But he was wearing one of your vests!" He shot an accusatory finger at the rack of blue vests hanging in the back of the room.

Charley put a hand over her stomach and groaned. She staggered and hit the wall. "The room's spinning," she said.

"Look," the man with the mustache said. He stood up from the couch and pointed at Charley. "She doesn't look too good." He squared his shoulders and put down his coffee cup.

"Maybe we should call somebody to come get her."

Come get her? Henry took a step back. What did he mean?

The man took a step forward and reached out a large, fleshy palm toward them.

Henry's eyes drew wide with apprehension.

"She needs help," the man said.

"Yes, get her some help," replied the others. Nods all around.

"Stay back!" Henry yelled.

He stared at the man's hands. Meaty hands. Good for grabbing. For restraining.

He heard the woman with the blue-gray hair speak. "It's okay, sweetie, we just want to help." She reached out her hands also.

"We don't need your help!" He backed away, grasping for Charley. She leaned against the wall, half-aware. She swooned under her hyperventilating dizziness and took a staggering step. He shoved her toward the door while he kept his eyes on the staff.

Each staff member stood up. They inched toward him. They spoke gently to him.

They reached their hands toward him.

Henry put up his other arm defensively and shuffled backward, eyes darting. His breathing was shaky. In his mind, he heard his own scream lifting into the same forgotten realm as Rachel's.

"It's okay, son," the man said again. "Maybe you need some help, too."

"No!"

He pushed Charley out of the room. She was barely aware of what was happening.

Henry put his arm around her and they ran—down the hall, away from the office, Charley's feet following with meager effort.

They ran, like they were told.

Charley stammered out the words in between gasps. "Who took Rachel?"

CHAPTER 8

Henry and Charley slowed down when they reached Mrs. Ball's classroom.

Henry's skin crawled. A shudder went from the top of Henry's spine all the way down his sweaty legs. He looked behind them. No one followed them. For the moment.

Charley stood up straight. "Mrs. Ball saw it and she's school staff. Maybe she can help."

They needed an adult. As teenagers, they were mostly considered imperceptive and incapable of responsibility. They were caught in a decade of hormones and emotional upheaval so memorialized across the culture that they were considered not insightful, poised, or capable of constraint. The idea of a young adult had been obliterated from most adults' mindset and replaced by the notion of a precocious child who had nothing more than the abilities and desire to drive a car and reproduce.

Mrs. Ball sounded off a recycled version of the same assumption.

"I'm sure Rachel will be fine," she said, sitting at her large gray metal desk, hardly making eye contact. Her hands flew over her paperwork, making slash marks and circles in red pen. "I think that the hall monitor was right. It seemed like a nervous breakdown to me."

"But that's what we're trying to tell you," Charley yelled. "They weren't hall monitors! The hallway staff doesn't even know who those men were. Ms. Prang at the principal's office doesn't know anything about it!"

Mrs. Ball paused and looked up with an exasperated expression. "I'm sure that somebody knows something." She went back to grading papers but continued in a soliloquy. "People can't just walk into school and take people. They could have been medical professionals—our hallway staff aren't the only ones in the world with blue vests. She obviously needs some help. Was the principal there? In the office?"

"No." It pained Charley to admit it.

"There, see? He probably knows, but you just didn't have a chance to ask him."

"But wouldn't Ms. Prang know?" Henry asked.

"Probably not," Mrs. Ball said and laughed. "The principal told me that she has been going to the doctor for the last year for the early stages of dementia. She's been here for so long that he doesn't want to let her go. She knows her job like second nature. I wouldn't worry about Rachel. I'm sure she is fine. She's so painfully quiet, I'm sure all that emotion just wound up inside her and exploded."

"What do you mean?" Charley said. "Don't you care about her? She looked like she had just fought a gang of pit bulls!"

Mrs. Ball folded her hands and leaned across the table. "Have you ever seen a person with schizophrenia? Or a psychotic break? Have you ever seen someone go off their medications? Have you? When I was a kid, you couldn't imagine what I saw kids do when they would 'experiment' in their teens." She made air quotes with her fingers.

Henry was surprised at the assertion. "You think Rachel's on drugs?"

"I can't believe you would even say that!" Charley was shouting, and her voice quivered. "She's one of the brightest, dearest, calmest—"

"And also one of the most private," Mrs. Ball said. "I don't put anything past anyone anymore. Walk with the breeze, that's what I always say," Mrs. Ball said to herself. She stood up and gave them her back. "I bet tomorrow she'll be fine. You'll see."

Mrs. Ball grabbed a stack of papers from her desk and walked toward a filing cabinet. Something glinted on her desk, under where the papers had been stacked. Charley's breath caught in her chest, and she raised a silent, accusatory finger.

"That . . . that's Rachel's necklace."

Mrs. Ball snapped her head up from the filing cabinet and stared at Charley. "What?"

Charley's finger hovered over the silver chain with a topaz gem. "Why do you have Rachel's necklace? Why is it on your desk?"

"Oh," Mrs. Ball said. She never broke gaze, never blinked. "It must have fallen off when she ran in here. I'll give it back to her tomorrow."

Henry felt cold goosebumps cover his skin. He stared back and shook his head. "It didn't fall off. We all saw it." His stomach began to somersault, and his voice pitched low. "How did you get it? And why were you hiding it?"

Mrs. Ball slammed the filing cabinet closed. She took a step back toward the desk. She reached out her hand. "Let me just explain."

Charley grabbed the necklace from the desktop. She backpedaled.

Mrs. Ball surged forward and reached for the necklace, but the desk acted as a large barricade. She doubled over the desk and sneered. Charley turned and sprinted out of the classroom.

"Run, Charley!" Henry said. He turned to follow and saw Mrs. Ball in the reflection of the broken door's glass. She overturned the desk, and the remaining papers launched into a flurry. He sped down the hall, chasing Charley as fast as he could.

"Henry, Charlotte, that's not yours!" Mrs. Ball shouted. "Don't you run from me!"

CHAPTER 9

Charley stopped when she reached the other end of the school. Henry came up behind her.

"Is Mrs. Ball involved?" she said. "Do you think—"

"I don't know, Charley. I don't know anything. I'm scared right now, too, but let's try to think logically about this." The mental picture of Mrs. Ball throwing the desk stained his mind, but he couldn't share that with Charley. It would only add to the problem. He had to try to be level-headed.

Henry pulled out his cell phone and tried to call Rachel. He wasn't hopeful, but it was worth a shot. The phone rang without answer. The familiar voicemail began and he hung up. Not a time to leave a message. He turned back to Charley. "We need to do something. We should call the police. Or we could look for the principal."

"They won't help us," Charley said. "What if the Blue Vests come after us, too?"

"Now you're sounding paranoid."

"And you're not? Were you even with me five minutes ago?"

"Everyone's not after you, Charley."

"How can you say that?"

"Because they took Rachel, not you. You would be gone if they wanted you instead."

Charley hit Henry on the arm. "You are so insensitive." Her voice cracked and a wave of fear washed over her and made her tremble. She wiped away a tear.

The tears again. Just like earlier. Seeing her tears reminded him of the jab from Trevor. That had been enough stress for her, but now this incident with Rachel was crushing Charley. Rachel was probably Charley's closest friend and she had made the transition to public high school with some difficulty. Rachel was as wholesome as they come—straight as an arrow, modest in dress, never too much makeup to suggest glamour. She was quiet and reserved, which made it difficult for her to meld into a young adult's world built on clamor and bravado. In a generation where attention is the currency of the modern market, if it wasn't demanded, it wasn't given. Rachel was too gentle to flaunt her personality or demand the commodity of attention, so she mostly went unnoticed. Until today.

So why her?

If people came in easily to take Rachel, they would leave even easier. They would allocate a mental health crisis, and there would be no further questions.

"I think we should go home," Henry said. "I don't want to stay in this school any longer."

"Me either."

"I'll talk with my parents. Maybe we can try to call Rachel's parents. I don't know where she lives or else I would drive there."

Charley gave a heavy sigh. "Okay. I'll try to study tonight while we wait. And speaking of, I think we still need to study tomorrow night for the history test."

It was an abrupt change of thought, but Charley was trying to compartmentalize. To cope. Retreat into something familiar.

She leaned in and pointed her finger at him. "The library is only a couple minutes from your house, so you're going to be there." She pointed back at herself. "And I'm going to be there. And then you and I will fight. And I will accuse you of being a forgetful slack-off who doesn't care."

"And I'll accuse you of being an anxious and overbearing fear monger."

"And Rachel will be there to referee. Just like she always does."

He nodded. Charley made it sound like it was going to be true.

He hoped it would be.

CHAPTER 10

Really, Henry didn't need to go home.

He needed to get to baseball practice.

His concern for Rachel was real enough and it outweighed the need to go to practice. That's what he told himself. But he needed that scholarship. He sprinted down the open hallways to the gym.

Forty-five minutes late.

"Why didn't you just skip practice altogether?" Coach Barnhard said. Henry stood opposite of him while he hit balls to the players who had already devolved into sweaty messes. "You could have hung out with your friends while all of us are training."

"Coach, please, a friend of mine came into class and she was—"

"Screaming and yelling?" Coach Barnhard interrupted.

Henry gaped in disbelief. All his thoughts tumbled and his tongue stuck in his mouth like thick taffy. How did Coach . . .

"Had to be escorted about by the Blue Vests?" he continued.

Thwack. A ball jumped off the coach's bat. He kept talking while swinging. "Did you go to the school office about this?"

Henry scrambled to recover. "Yes, I did."

"Well, what did they say?"

"They wouldn't listen. They said that nothing happened. But I think she's in danger!"

Tha-Whack!

A ball screamed through the gymnasium, sailing over the heads of the defenders and ricocheting with a deafening bang. The players covered their heads as the ball bounced downward.

Coach Barnhard slammed the barreled end of his bat on the ground and leaned over the handle to give Henry his full ire.

"Look, Murphy, I heard about it."

"How did you—"

"See, I've got a group of ballplayers over there," the coach said, pointing to Henry's teammates, "and they were in class today, too. You're not the only kid in the school. Trevor told me all about it. Said it was a nervous breakdown."

Trevor.

A torrent of rage silently racked Henry's body. He glowered at Trevor with sideways eyes. What an opportunistic, insensitive . . .

"But look at him, Murphy," Coach Barnhard said. "He's out there." Trevor posed with his hands on his hips, sweating like a hog. He knew what was happening. The smirking beard was obvious from across the gym. "He made it to baseball practice on time." Coach Barnhard lifted the bat again and put it over his shoulder. "Let the professionals handle it from here, Murphy. Now get out there unless you want to lose more playing time."

Henry didn't say another word.

He was thankful when practice ended. He ran into the locker room to get changed and leave the horrible day behind.

Coach Barnhard turned the corner of the lockers while Henry was changing out of his sweaty gear.

"That's forty-five minutes off the next game, Murphy," he said. "You sit the bench for the first half because you showed up late to my practice."

It felt like he had been cut down by an axe, rived right through. "But the scholarship! If I don't play, I might not get it. Coach, please, there might even be professional scouts there."

"You'll play. Just forty-five minutes late."

"But they're not interested in second-stringers. They won't care about who is coming in halfway through!"

"Then you shouldn't have missed practice."

"But, Coach Barnhard, it was an emergency! Isn't there an emergency excuse or something?"

"That comes from the office. They can give you an excuse. But you said they don't believe you."

Henry hung his head.

There was nothing left to say.

Coach Barnhard softened his tone. "Look, Murphy. You're a good ballplayer. But I'm a man of principle. And if you're starting to go off the deep end, then I've got to make sure you know that I won't stand for it."

"Go off the deep end? What do you mean?"

"Whatever you're mixed up in. You almost get into a fight in the hallways. Your friend loses her mind and has a nervous breakdown. You show up late to practice. Then one of them Blue Vests comes here looking for you."

"A Blue Vest was looking for me?"

"Yeah, some guy. Hair slicked back, brown glasses. Never seen him before."

The cold sensation played on the back of his neck—dancing, spinning.

"He said you had something to do with the whole thing. I told him you should've been at practice but I didn't know where you were. But I'm not going to be party to you dodging authority."

Henry could barely breathe. If he had shown up on time to practice . . .

"You can't be like that, Murphy, not on my team."

"Yes, Coach."

"You've got to dig down deep inside for something else."

"Uh-huh."

"Be something different."

"Okay."

"You even hearing me, Murphy?"

"Yes, Coach."

"Okay, well, get out of here. And try to get your head on straight."

Henry sprinted out of the school.

CHAPTER 11

Henry sped out of the student parking lot as soon as the murky copper-brown car roared to life. The engine obeyed the mashed accelerator and Henry tore down the open road.

He opened the windows in his car. He needed the fresh air. Normally, the crisp fall air was exhilarating—the slight nip, perfect for baseball.

Except the fall air wasn't the reason for the chill that enveloped his spine.

He kept his eyes on the rearview mirror until the school disappeared. He released a long groan and leaned his head back on the headrest.

The gentle hum of the well-worn motor soothed his frayed nerves with a sweet, monotonous lullaby. The auburn-speckled hills with left-over cornstalks and harvest-ready apple trees filled the outskirts of the suburban cityscape. Everything glowed with an infused radiance from the recent lush rainfall. The freshly fallen leaves made a beautiful mosaic of debris on the road, but enough colors still clung to the trees to form a painted tapestry when the sun finally emerged, bright in the sky from behind the clouds.

He took a long, dragging breath through his nostrils and exhaled. He smelled the tingle of burning leaf piles. Autumn made him feel good for some inexplicable reason, all the way down to his core.

Maybe it was the harvest foods. Pumpkin pie, fried cinnamon donuts, fresh cider. He could taste the tart hit on his tongue. It lightened his heart as he drove through the scant traffic of the back roads.

He sighed.

Maybe he had been overreacting.

It seemed like everyone else thought he had been.

Maybe he was.

He pulled into his driveway. All the lights were on, and relief mixed with familiarity inside of him.

Home.

He walked in to the aroma of sautéed chicken with spices and the sound of a sizzling stir-fry coming from the stovetop. His mother stood in front of the oven, working the skillet over the heat.

"Hey, honey!" Her smile was full and warm. "How are you?"

"Meh." He slid his backpack and baseball equipment bag to the floor just inside the front door. He worked his feet to pull his shoes off, grabbing the edge of each shoe with his other foot.

"What's meh?"

"I've got a lot to tell you, Mom."

"Sure, what's up?"

It made Henry feel good. The constancy—his mother at home, her simple compassion, dinner on the stove, like she had always done for as long as he could remember—it was a concrete moment in his otherwise vaporous day.

Something was right.

Maybe he wasn't going crazy.

The sound of footsteps came up from the basement stairs, followed by a voice. "Dawn, I don't want to fight about this any longer. I just think—"

"Thom," Dawn interrupted, "Henry's home."

"Henry's home?"

The last few steps were hurried and thunderous. Thom turned the corner of the basement doorway and smiled.

"Hey, slugger! How's it going?" he boomed, all elation, casting his arms wide. Sometimes the demonstrativeness made Henry feel embarrassed in public, but in the secret world of his own home-life, he drank it up.

Maybe he felt that way because he was their only child. His parents tried having more children for a long time after Henry was born but gave up. As long as Henry could remember, their family was just the three of them.

"Hold on, Dad," Henry said, as if talking to an eager puppy, "I haven't even said hi to Mom yet."

Henry walked around the kitchen island and hugged his mother around the waist, careful not to disturb the frying pan. "Love you, Mom." Then he walked back to his father, who still stood with arms out, and received the broad embrace.

"How was school?" Thom said. "How was baseball practice?"

Henry looked up at him. "Were you guys fighting again?"

"Fighting? No, we were just having a conversation about something that got a little . . ."

"You were fighting."

"Sometimes we have disagreements."

"You've been doing it a lot more recently."

"Hey," Dawn said, "our problems can wait. Thom, why don't you leave behind all that tinkering on the basement remodel. Dinner is almost ready and Henry said he's got a lot to tell us."

Thom and Dawn both turned to Henry and waited.

That was all he needed.

The words came like a waterfall—pouring out of him. His father with-drew his arm to sit down and he offered a chair to Henry when he heard the sobriety in Henry's voice. His mother's tone, too, also changed from pleasant to concerned. She'd always contended for him, like a mother lioness for her young cub.

"So, you think she was abducted from class?" Dawn's eyebrows creased together. Her eyes narrowed to thin triangles. She was the first person to actually empathize with Henry. "Thom, what do you think?"

Thom sat in the chair across the round glass table from Henry. His hands were still speckled in sawdust, his hair was sweaty and matted down, and he leaned hard against the back of the chair, his head cocked to the side. He looked exhausted.

"That is quite disturbing," Thom said. "And you said that the office staff and the Blue Vests knew nothing about it."

Henry nodded his head.

"The man who took her said she was having a nervous breakdown," Thom said.

"Right."

"But you don't think so."

"No way. Not at all."

"Okay."

And that was all.

Thom stood up and went to the kitchen drawer full of pencils and papers. He pulled out a school brochure with directions on how to access the parent-teacher association from his cell phone. The encrypted website held phone numbers for any family who opted to be in it. It was meant for this reason—to link parents together in case they ever needed to contact one another. He scrolled through the numbers until he found the Morgans' name.

He dialed the number and waited. Henry watched in silence. Dawn worked the skillet on the stovetop with a steady rhythm and listened. In the growing tension of the moment, she scoured the surface of the pan harder and harder with the spatula.

"Ah, yes, Mr. Morgan? Hey there, this is Thom Murphy, Henry's dad. Do you have a minute?"

It seemed so.

"Henry just came home from school and was troubled that something may have been bothering your daughter. He wanted to make sure she was alright." Thom's wording was euphemistic, but it was better than saying he was fearful that she was abducted and fighting for her life.

Henry looked at his mother. She stared at Thom. The skillet was taking a beating.

Henry looked back at his father. Thom kept his eyes averted, down at the ground.

Henry couldn't sit still. He stood up.

Thom reached his hand over and held out a quiet finger. He kept his eyes down.

Henry sat down again and ran his fingers through his soiled hair.

Did Rachel's parents even know something happened this afternoon? He could just imagine what Rachel's father was saying— "She hasn't come home yet. We were just getting worried about her. Does Henry know anything that could help us find her? When did they—"

"Okay, thanks," Thom said, "sorry to bother you at dinner, Mr. Morgan. Good-bye."

Henry jumped to his feet. "Well, what is it?"

Thom set the phone down on the countertop. Dawn stilled the spatula and turned down the heat on the burner. The moment spun into quiet absolution.

"She's at home, Henry. He said she got home a little late but other than that everything has been normal. She's fine."

CHAPTER 12

Henry was dumfounded.

Everything was normal?

"Dad, seriously, something was wrong! I saw it. I saw—"

Thom stopped him. "Henry, I believe you." He walked over to Henry and grabbed him by both shoulders to get eye to eye. A somber expression crossed his face. "You've always told me the truth. You've earned my trust. Whatever happened with her, I'm just glad she is home safe now."

Earned my trust. The words sated Henry's quivering emotions.

His dad was right. All that matters was that she was home safe.

A sigh of relief escaped from his lungs. He unwound and slouched into his chair. He hadn't perceived the spring that tightened inside him again while reliving the details.

Maybe Mrs. Ball was right. Maybe Rachel really did have a nervous breakdown. From all Mrs. Ball's stories, it sounded like she had a wild adolescence herself.

And maybe Mrs. Ball had a breakdown when Charley stole the necklace.

His family believed him, and there was repose in that. After talking to Ms. Prang, the hallway staff, Mrs. Ball, and then his baseball coach, Henry didn't know if he trusted himself anymore. His dad always said that trust is a funny thing—it takes a long time to build but can be broken in an instant. He learned early on that lying to his parents only hurt that trust and ultimately hurt himself worst of all. His continual truthfulness garnered him more freedoms—including his own car, even if it was a couple decades old with rusted side panels.

"Alright, wash your hands!" Dawn scooped the skillet off the stovetop and plopped the stir-fry onto their plates. Henry's appetite instantly rose to critical.

A return to normal was the best medicine.

He was glad his father was home tonight. As a doctor, Thom sometimes worked crazy hours. Some evenings he had to stay at the hospital late. Thom liked his job and made a decent salary, but he would also say that he wished they had more time together. But then again, Henry figured, which family didn't?

"So, studying again with Charley?" Thom asked.

"Not tonight. I need a break."

"She's a nice girl, Henry."

"Sure."

"What does that mean?"

"It means I guess so."

"You don't think so?"

"I don't know. Everything's just really complicated with her."

"Are there any girls who aren't complicated?"

"Mom."

A superior smile appeared on Dawn's face. Her large hazel eyes flashed at Thom. Without another word she had just seized the victory banner from their fight.

Thom chuckled and bobbed his head down. He poked his fork into the chicken on his plate. "I am defeated," he said. He lifted the sautéed piece and inspected it closer, then showed it to Henry and shook it at him with flair. "Do you see this? This could have been me. I could have been on the receiving end of that spatula."

Dawn stood up to clear the table. She grabbed a stack of dishes and walked behind Thom. She leaned over his shoulder. "That's right. You just be careful."

She bit the piece of chicken off Thom's fork. Her head snapped away, tossing her hair.

Henry remembered when she decided to let her gray hair grow out. It was prematurely gray, but not completely—wisps of rich brown came through underneath. The gray gave a shimmery look to her hair, more reflective than muted. She had tried coloring her hair for years, but the chemicals were harsh on her scalp. Painful, too. So, she gave it up and decided to "go gray," as he'd heard her say.

Henry got up from the table and walked to his mother at the sink. "Thanks for dinner. Can I help clean up?"

"You're welcome, and no, we've got cleanup tonight. Go take a break."

Henry rocketed to the couch and flung himself on to it. He landed on his back with remote in hand. The television flickered to life, and he changed the station to the baseball highlight reel.

Baseball.

He hadn't told his parents yet about missing playing time.

One thing at a time.

He would forget about it for now.

CHAPTER 13

Baseball highlights flashed before his eyes on the screen.
One more thing to do.

He dug into his pocket, grabbed his cell phone. He needed to call Charley with the good news. Then the day could be over.

"Hello?"

"Charley, it's Henry. I've got great news!"

"You found Rachel?" Anticipation gushed in her voice.

"Yes! My dad called her parents. She came home right after school. Sounded like everything was okay."

Done. Back to baseball.

"What?" She sounded confused.

"She's home."

"She's home? But what happened earlier?"

"I don't know. My dad talked to her dad."

"But that doesn't make any sense! She looked horrible. And why would she scream at us to run?"

"Sure." Homeruns and strikeouts were rolling in glory.

"Henry, do you actually believe that?"

"Sure."

"Did your dad think Mr. Morgan was telling him the truth?"

"Uh-huh." Terrible pitch.

"All this is not okay. She will tell us herself at our study group tomorrow."

He had pleasantly forgotten about the study group, but now it sizzled in his ear. The reminder was imposing. "Come on, Charley, we just had a big day. I'm still feeling twitchy from it all. I don't want to do a study group tomorrow."

"But you said you would."

"I know. It's just that things got mixed up today. Besides, haven't you read everything like three times already?"

"What does that matter?"

"I mean, do you really need to study? Can't you just rest a little bit?"

"No."

"Why not?"

"Because no. That's why."

"You need to just stop freaking out all the time about class. Or gymnastics. Or even this Rachel thing. Everything's fine now. Take a break. You're driving me crazy with this anxious load you make me carry with you."

"You just don't care as much as I do."

"I care about it!"

"You think I'm anxious, but I think you're just unconcerned. You've got it so easy that you can remember this stuff, but some of us have to work hard to get good grades."

"I didn't say to slack off."

"Close enough. You would like it if I didn't worry so much—you wouldn't have any competition!"

"That's not true. Look, I just can't study tomorrow night. I showed up late to baseball practice today and I have to focus on. .." He closed his eyes and put his hand to his head. He regretted the words the moment he said them.

"You went to baseball practice?" She yelled through the phone. "When Rachel was missing and all but dead?"

"She's fine and back with her family. It all worked out."

"I can't believe you, Henry Murphy."

"Charley, I need that scholarship! I'm not going to get any government aid to go to college, not as the son of a doctor. But that lawsuit put our family in a hard position and if I can't get it, then I'll never—"

"Don't you talk to me about having it hard."

"I'm not comparing, I'm . . ."

"You're what?"

"I'm saying it's not easy for me either."

"You have no idea."

"I'm not comparing!"

"You used to be loyal, Henry. You've changed."

Henry jumped up from the couch and snarled. He spluttered. He held the phone within an inch of his mouth.

"I'm just trying to forget everything else right now and focus on what's important!"

A pause.

"Is that really what's most important to you?" Charley said.

He couldn't respond.

"I'm going to bed, Henry."

She ended the call.

Henry dropped into the couch again with all his weight and bounced on the cushion. He leaned over his knees and rubbed his forehead with his hand until it hurt.

How could she say he wasn't loyal? He'd stood with her—stood for her—against Trevor. Just this morning! Wasn't that loyal? He groaned and flopped backward onto the couch. He stretched his long legs out and stared at the ceiling. The words spun in his head.

Wasn't loyal.

Changed.

"Was that Charley?" His mother called from the kitchen.

"Yes."

"Is everything alright with you two?"

"I don't know, Mom. She can just get so . . . ugh!"

Dawn waited for him to continue.

"She wants to study tomorrow, but I missed so much of practice today that I've got to make up for it."

"Are you going to tell her?"

"I tried to! She just jumped all over me. She won't listen."

"Just be patient with her, Henry. She's been through a lot."

"I know, I know."

"Okay. But remember that tomorrow you'll have to fend for yourself for dinner. Your father has to work late and I have the benefit dinner for human trafficking awareness."

"Yeah. Uh-huh."

"Henry. Henry . . ." She waved and waited for him to look at her again. "Just make sure you get to bed at a good time tonight. None of this staying up 'til midnight watching baseball again."

"Okay, Mom."

"Goodnight."

Wasn't loyal.

Changed.

CHAPTER 14

Ten minutes before midnight.

Baseball played on the television before Henry's vacant eyes. His brain boiled. His mind sizzled.

How could Charley say that?

He'd just risked everything today. Everything. For her, and for Rachel.

Charley had asked if the scholarship was important. Of course it was! The lawsuit was gripping their family tighter and tighter. If he didn't get the scholarship, everything would just . . .

He felt betrayed.

Stand up for somebody, then they cut you down at the knees from behind.

How else was he supposed to feel?

He knew Charley was sensitive about being pegged as an orphan. He knew it! And he sensed it. He jumped in front of the mud Trevor slung at her. Didn't that mean he was the one who was sensitive?

Well, he jumped, and look at what that bought him.

She skewered him for it.

Wasn't loyal.

Changed.

Henry put his hands to head again and rubbed. His thoughts ran in circles, round and round, trudging a ditch in his mind.

He didn't want to feel this antagonized toward her. But that simple accusation—it electrocuted his defenses like a lightning strike on a downed power line—snapping and sparking already, the new searing bolt overloaded him to high voltage.

He hated when he felt this way, when he felt overcome by the insanity inside him. He wanted to let it go, but there was a deep part of him that soaked in the anger. He used to be able to control it, but could never cure it.

Why did her accusation enrage him so much? It made him sad that he was so unbridled, which further compounded his guilt. Charley was hurting also. The day had been bizarre and confusing. He should be able to talk himself out of his inflamed fit. Do the mature thing. It wasn't a big deal.

But as much as he wanted to dislodge himself from the anger, he felt bound, given over to an intoxicating fury inside him. The emotions imprisoned his mind, and he felt like a different beast controlled him, drove him forward. He felt duplicitous, like two different men trapped inside the same body, switching between them. He wished he could speak to the monster inside himself, reason with it. Or carve it out. But it was too late for that. The thing had awoken again.

How could he let it go? The ruminations consumed him.

It wasn't fair.

She was the one who wasn't being loyal.

How would she feel if he . . . ?

He was going round and round again.

He had let the worries drift away earlier. But Charley's insistence unearthed all the unpleasant, gnawing thoughts. He had been content enough to forget it.

Now he couldn't.

CHAPTER 15

Henry looked over the bookshelves in his dad's office. Although he wasn't a doctor, one lived in the house. He held a list in his hands with words he scrawled down—words like *schizophrenia* and *psychotic*. Words Mrs. Ball had said. He didn't know exactly what they meant.

He intended to find out.

He suddenly felt less convinced that everything was alright.

A horrible shudder raked through him as he remembered the man with the blue vest and glasses. And that he was looking for Henry. The sweet, alluring effect of forgetfulness fled from Henry's mind.

He traced his fingers over the various books, shaking his head no at most of them. He wasn't sure how to begin, but if he could find some answers—something that could prove the incident was beyond psychiatric—he could show proof to the school administration. Then he would have authority on his side, not the other way around.

He moved his hand to the end of the shelf. One book was tucked behind the edge of the bookcase, hidden from view. He could only feel its leather binding. He shoved the other books to the side to give room. He tugged at the book and felt the bottom stick. The leather casing molted into flakes, breaking from its fusion with the shelf underneath.

The massive book felt like a brick of pages. It was also dusty and made him sneeze. There was no name on the book, but a symbol of a hammer in silver foil was embedded into the cover. The hammer had a square head with beveled edges, equal on both sides, like a spike maul from old railroading days. An intricate crest with intertwining lines decorated the book's spine. An attached brown bookmark, wide and long, sat in the center of the book, sticking out from the pages.

He looked at the cover again.

It seemed like it was—glowing.

Then it stopped.

He rubbed the foiled hammer on the cover, but nothing happened. He squinted at the book and put it on his father's desk.

Nothing happened.

What was he thinking—that the book was actually glowing? It had been a long day. Lots of strange things had happened.

Then he had an idea. He turned off the lights.

The room went dark. The book lay dull and still, like every other book on the shelf.

He needed to go to bed. But he had been sure that—

A clear, faint shaft of light shone in through the window from the darkened sky. The silver hammer on the cover of the book illuminated in response, faintly, quietly, like candlelight hidden beneath linen cloth.

Henry walked back to the desk and stroked the illuminated cover. The shimmery silver foil slipped beneath his fingertips. It still felt the same. He walked to the window and looked up.

The moon pierced the dense rainclouds that still cluttered the night, gleaming like a solitary beacon. The clouds pushed back and swallowed up the moon within moments. The glowing hammer quieted.

Henry's attention was rapt. He looked back at the book and stared, eyes wide. The hair on his arms stood on end. He reached for the book with tentative, trembling fingers.

He opened the cover.

The wind leapt in the treetops outside, a furious gust that whistled with violent force. It sounded like the long howls of distant wolves that called and answered from lonely hills hidden deep in the forest.

The sky responded in anger, cracking with thunderous force. It ripped through the quiet, like the fabric of the night had been torn apart.

CHAPTER 16

Henry jumped back from the desk. He never heard such a haunting mixture. He panted. His muscles tensed and coiled. Silence.

He ventured a glance out the window at the quieted night sky.

Fog.

Thick and dense, it surrounded the window and muted the night.

No more moon. No more trees. No more sky. Just fog.

It hadn't been there a minute ago.

"Thom . . ." His mother called from the bedroom.

In that one word, her voice rose with eerie insistence, building like a giant wave of the ocean that swelled just before it hammered down upon the jagged rocks of the shoreline.

She never sounded that way.

"Thom!" She called again, this time louder, more demanding. Her voice pitched higher.

The storm that enveloped and shook the house had awakened her. She was probably only half awake. The sudden thunder and wind must have startled her with . . .

"Dawn!" Thom yelled back.

Their yelling was bizarre and pressured. It didn't make sense.

Henry tucked the book under his arm and leaned out of the office doorway to look at his parents' bedroom. Their door was closed, and both voices came from the other side. They were in the same room, but they shouted with throaty voices like they were lost and couldn't find each other.

He tiptoed closer, now only a few feet away.

"Thom! Find me!" Another cry, loud and forlorn, shattered the silence.

"Dawn!" This cry was booming, urgent.

Their voices sounded like children's in a pool calling to one another with their eyes closed, arms out, reaching blindly, hoping some way their calling would make them stumble into each other. In the middle of a thunderstorm. Under a wrap of swirling, blinding fog. Amid the baying of imagined wolves on the wind.

Henry played that game before. His parents were not playing a game— there was no fun in their voices.

He put his hand on the door handle and felt the smooth, cold metal under his fingertips. He felt like he had switched roles—he, the parent, checking on his children who were thrashing in the grip of clinging nightmares.

He pressed down on the handle. Before the latch disengaged, he heard it. Crying. Bitter and cathartic.

"Thom, Thom," Dawn said. Her voice was soft. "What has happened?"

"I'm here. I found you."

Henry eased his fingers back from the door handle. He listened.

Just crying.

CHAPTER 17

Henry backed away, holding the book under his arm. He wasn't sure what had just happened with his parents, but it seemed like the panic had gone. He retreated.

His bedroom was at the top of the stairs. The room was large, with a small couch. He liked having friends sleep over and he had an extra bed that his friends used. He even had an extra dresser that he used for some older clothes that he had outgrown.

He flopped in bed and turned on his nightstand lamp.

The book was ancient with worn pages. It carried the smell of must from sitting undisturbed for too long. As he flipped the pages, he saw various texts and pictures strewn together in collections. It seemed like an anthology.

He read a couple of short stories. The really short ones. He felt exhausted and only read for a couple minutes. He devolved into just looking at pictures.

There were pictures of pretty scenery and fancy scripts. He flipped through them but then stopped. In the center of the book he saw a man standing on a plot of land that extended far behind him with mountains and water and rolling hills. The man took up most of the page, cloak hanging low over his face, shadowed and indiscriminate, with the cloak's tail falling to the back of his knees. In his hand he bore the same hammer that was on the front of the book, stem planted into the ground like he was claiming the land. It was as tall as the man and the hammer head looked even bigger than the cover suggested. The title of the picture read "The Hammer of Andelis."

"Easy for you," Henry mumbled to himself. "You don't have my problems."

Henry's eyes were heavy and it was past midnight. At least he could say he listened to his mother and hadn't stayed up this late watching baseball. The book had done its job and sent him to the edge of slumber. He closed the book and hit the lights.

The hum of the heater occasionally clicking was the only sound. A blue nightlight by the doorway was on, something he turned on each night since his mother and father gave it to him when he was just a toddler. He never went to sleep without it on. It was partly nostalgia and sentimentality, but he also relied on it when he got up in the night for the bathroom.

The faint blue peaceful light was the last thing he saw before his eyelids closed.

. . .

His cell phone rang.

It buzzed on his nightstand and lit up with the incoming call. The clock read a little past one in the morning. Sleep still clung to his brain. He reached for the phone.

Rachel's name lit up the screen.

Henry's eyes snapped open. He answered the call.

"Hello, Rachel?"

Nothing.

"Rachel, are you alright? Rachel?"

Eerie silence filled the other end. Henry heard a low rumble, indiscriminate and distant, with the sound of hushed, deep voices that spoke words he couldn't decipher.

"Rachel!" Henry yelled.

The phone call ended. The call timer on his phone mocked him.

Alarm flooded Henry. He tried calling her back.

"Come on, come on!" he said into the phone. "Answer!"

The phone rang until her familiar voicemail played. Henry ended the call and tried calling again. And again.

He got the same result each time.

Ice draped his neck.

Sleep evaded him the rest of the night.

CHAPTER 18

The alarm rang with annoyance. Henry mashed at it with his fingers until he found the snooze button. He opened a bleary eye and looked at the clock. He didn't remember hitting the snooze button that many times. He groaned and rolled over in bed.

He felt terrible.

What had happened last night? The haunting phone call still toyed with his mind, but the morning light made the event seem surreal, almost dream-like. He tried calling Rachel again, but the same voice-mail message still disregarded his attempts.

At least it was Friday.

He sat up on the edge of the bed and rubbed his eyes. A big yawn came next, and as he finished, he noticed the book on the nightstand. He grabbed the book under his arm and walked downstairs. He placed it in his backpack.

In the kitchen, Dawn was making batter for pancakes. "Good morning. Did you sleep okay?" she asked.

"No."

"Why? Were you worried about Rachel still?"

"She called last night, Mom, but it was just silent on the other end. Then she hung up. I think something is still wrong."

Dawn's face furrowed. She looked down and shook her head.

"What are you going to do?" she asked.

"Go to school," he said with a forced smile, "and make sure she's alright."

"Well, hurry up and get ready," Dawn said. "These pancakes will be ready soon and you know that your father will want some, too."

Thom, on cue, came out of the master bedroom. He walked up behind Dawn, put his arms around her and held her for a moment. He kissed her on the cheek. "Good morning."

"Good morning, sir."

"Is that bacon available?" he said, reaching in to snag a piece next to the griddle where the pancakes were frying.

"I'm sorry," he whispered in her ear, "about, you know . . ."

Dawn closed her eyes and nodded her head in his embrace. "I know."

"What were you two yelling about last night?" Henry asked. "Were you arguing again? You sounded . . . weird."

"You heard that?" Thom said.

"It was hard not to. You were screaming each other's names. Like you couldn't find each other."

Dawn and Thom quickly shot glances at each other, then back to Henry.

"Henry, we need to talk." Thom said.

"About what?" Henry shoveled pancakes into his mouth as he spoke.

"About a lot."

"Okay, like what?"

"First of all, wear your watch. Don't take it off. Second, always keep your nightlight on. You have—"

Thom's phone started to ring in the bedroom and cut him off mid-sentence. Thom moved quickly toward the door. "I need to take this. I need someone to cover my shift tonight at the hospital. Things have suddenly changed. I'll be right back."

"Thom," Dawn said and followed after him into the bedroom, "we need to finish talking with Henry."

Henry watched his dad through the open door, pacing back and forth.

Henry was running late because of snoozing too long. Besides, why weren't they talking about last night? Nightlights and watches seemed trivial right now. He wished he could linger, but he had to check on Rachel. And he had to make it to practice. Saturday was the last game.

He was proud of himself. He was being diligent. Prioritizing. His dad would be proud.

Henry grabbed his bags and bolted out the door. He jumped in his car and drove back to school, tearing through the new leaf piles on the way.

He noticed the four missed phone calls from his father after he got to school. But it was too late to talk. He walked inside, hoping for a better day.

CHAPTER 19

No Blue Vests were waiting at his locker. No shrieking classmates were in the hall. Friday started like a regular day.

The only stressor other than Rachel was Charley. She stood beside Henry's locker again. Tapping her foot on the ground.

"How could you be so insensitive? You said you were going to go home and work on trying to find her! Instead, you just went to baseball practice?" The conversation picked up right where it left off—roiling and indignant.

"But everything is fine now," he said. He wished it was. Now was not the time to tell her about the strange, absent phone call last night.

"That's not the point!"

"Stop being so dramatic, Charley! Rachel's fine, I went to baseball practice. You're the only one who's not fine."

"How do you know she's fine? Have you seen her?"

"No, because her dad told us she was fine. Why, have you seen her?"

"No," she shot back. "Stop being so argumentative."

"Me being argumentative?" Henry guffawed. "You're the one having the conniption."

"Just, shut up!" she said, then she stormed away.

He didn't even believe himself that Rachel was fine. But he liked throwing large vocabulary words back at Charley.

They were all going to have history class together in a couple hours, and for now the distance between him and Charley was best.

Charley's turmoil felt excessive, but it was close to her operating baseline. She became a foster child at only five years old when her mother and father died in a terrible car accident. Like Henry, she was an only child. There were no surviving relatives. There was no will. Charley quickly became a ward of the state.

She had been whisked from foster home to foster home every few years, some of them good while many of them were bad. She'd been living with her current foster family, the Hellens, for about the last year. She confided to Henry and Rachel during their study group that she didn't like living there. Both foster parents worked at the university in town and were more concerned with their professional careers than about establishing a home environment. They had no other children. To inherit a sixteen-year-old girl with deep psychological scarring and complex social needs, they frankly had no idea where to begin.

Being foster parents was a modestly noble effort on the part of the Hellens. They liked the idea of helping but didn't know how. The reflex for the Hellens was often to retreat, believing that Charley needed space to do her own thing—to process things her own way. They didn't want to impose. The truth was that she was not as emotionally mature as she was emotionally bruised—she longed for more than the niceties of the cell phone they paid for and an abstraction of a family.

So, she glommed on to gymnastics. It was her parents' desire to start her early in training, and that was the only thing she really knew of them. She soaked in it and became convinced that gymnastics was the only way to attune herself to her parents. She would go to the gym to perfect her routines at odd hours, sometimes late at night and other times painstakingly early.

Those who knew her saw intense dedication.

Those who knew her better saw loneliness.

It was aimlessness rather than freedom, a festering ennui that wouldn't be silenced in a parentless world.

Charlotte Scott had become an anomaly. A diligent student and an accomplished gymnast, she lived in constant apprehension of her own shortcomings. The pang of never being good enough was the fear that drove her.

Sometimes Henry wondered if she even liked gymnastics. To put forth so much effort for something unenjoyable made no sense to him. She practiced relentlessly, studied incessantly, and was rarely ever home. The Hellens thought she liked it that way.

Things were only magnified with Henry and Rachel in the fold. Their presence added to her fear that someone would be able to keep pace with her. Henry found the fear insufferable—he tried to be a good friend but he desired distance from her.

It wasn't that Henry found Charley unattractive. She was pretty but preferred practicality in her clothes rather than try to be fashionable. Gym shoes and never heels, work-out tops and never blouses. She wore her hair up in a ponytail every day, dirty-blonde hair stringing down in long natural curls that kept her hair out of her textbooks. She had a slender, muscular frame from years of gymnastics and had a graceful neck with soft cheeks—all behind a large pair of awful pink-framed plastic reading glasses that sat on top of her nose.

Henry was biased and he knew it—but his father had always told him to look for a woman like his mother.

He mulled the two over and juxtaposed them in his mind. He suddenly realized that his name was being called.

"Mr. Murphy!" the literature teacher said. "Any thoughts on the poem?"

"Uh, I don't think so." He scrambled to see the paper in front of him. He tossed papers on his desk, his hands a sudden flurry to find the poem. He had drifted on an imaginative jet stream again, somewhere far away. He looked up and gave the teacher a blank stare.

"Very insightful," his teacher said. "Would anyone else like to comment?"

A few minutes later, the bell mercifully rang.

On to history class.

And to see Rachel.

CHAPTER 20

Rachel sat in her chair, hair pulled back into a workable bun. The normal conservative clothes. The same quiet demeanor. No tatters. No yelling.

He had to see it to believe it.

"Rachel!" Charley yelled. She pushed past Henry with a shove and hustled across the room.

Rachel looked up, smiled a polite smile, and grabbed her books out of her bag.

"You're alright!" Charley still bordered on shouting, though now she had closed the gap to within a few inches. Henry walked up also and stood behind Charley.

"Hey!" Rachel said and stood up in reciprocity. Hearing her voice validated her presence—she was here, in one piece.

Charley eyed her from head to toe, sizing her up like she was an apparition that would vanish in any moment. She gaped with mouth open, arms extended. "Look at you!" she said.

Rachel smiled and looked at the ground. "Let's not make a big deal of it." She rubbed her feet with nervous movements.

"What happened yesterday?" Charley demanded.

A little sheepish, with an upturned corner of her mouth and a sideways glance, Rachel muttered. "Nervous breakdown. I think it's from us moving to a new house a few days ago." She brought her eyes forward again. "But I'm better."

She looked better.

"I didn't know you were moving," Charley said. "But who were those men?"

"Medical staff. I felt the breakdown coming and called my medical team. It's a new mobile response unit that the psychiatric hospital is trialing. I think it worked. My parents came also."

Charley exhaled. Maybe for the first time since yesterday. She visibly unwound.

Then Charley started the cascade.

"Why did you look like you had escaped a pack of wolves? The Blue Vests told us that . . . Wait a minute, why did the medical staff have the same vests as the hallway staff? What about the—"

The bell rang and the history teacher directed everyone to their seats. Henry and Charley were ushered away from Rachel's desk.

The questions had to wait, and there were many to ask. Henry wondered how many other students had already asked them, but if his history class were any sort of a poll, he didn't think so. There were only a few awkward waves from afar and mutterings of "glad you're back." For those like Rachel who flew under the radar, anything strange about them pushed them further under.

When class was over, Charley waited to catch Rachel. Henry sat at his desk in the back and didn't get up. He tapped his pencil rhythmically and stared ahead, grinding in thought.

Rachel's sensationalism was over. The food for social media junkies was spoiled. Everyone else would nurse a sense of relegation now—don't need to know all the details, might be private, shouldn't go nosing into other's personal business, let the professionals handle it—but Henry didn't have that sense. He'd heard those excuses before. They were simple aphorisms that never answered anything. Don't poke the sleeping bear, water under the bridge, walk with the breeze.

Those were for Mrs. Ball.

He continued to grind.

What if . . .

What if he did need to know all the details?

It's where they say the devil is.

"So, nervous breakdown was all. You're sure you're alright?" Charley sounded like a court stenographer reading back a legal defense.

Rachel spoke with flat affect. "Why wouldn't I be?"

"Well, alright. If you say so."

She at least looked alright. But something felt wrong. Henry wasn't sure what it was.

"Maybe," Charley said, "we could talk more about it later? We could . . . catch up!" She gave a feeble attempt at laughing and squeezed out a smile, like squeezing a bottle of wine from a single grape. "Are you still able to do our study group tonight for the history test? I mean, I don't want it to stress you out or anything."

"I don't know. Maybe. I'll check with my parents. They told me to take it slow. Where is it again?"

"At the library. Like always."

Rachel scooped up her books in her arms and walked toward the door. She didn't seem like the wide-eyed maniac from twenty-four hours ago.

She turned to leave when another question burst out. Henry had awoken from his statuesque slumber. "But why did you call me last night?"

Rachel gave him a funny look. Charley did also, leveling her sight at him with demanding eyes.

"Oh," Rachel said, "I must have just accidentally dialed your number." She gave a forced chuckle.

Henry shook his head. His frown deepened. Then, with jarring realization, he knew what bothered him. "Why did you tell us to run?"

She smiled back, the wholesome white teeth and the winsome smile flashing. "Oh, never mind."

Then she walked out.

CHAPTER 21

Never mind?

Henry drove home from baseball practice, mulling it over. He was angry.

He had been apt to believe Rachel initially—that everything was copacetic. He wanted it to be, maybe to a fault. But seeing Rachel did not validate his reassurances. Seeing her disturbed him.

Why never mind? She made it their business when she tore into the classroom like a shrieking banshee yesterday. He couldn't never mind.

He shook his head and squeezed the steering wheel.

Everyone told him things were just fine, from his biology teacher to Rachel's dad and even Rachel herself. But something gnawed at him. When she walked out of history class, he realized it.

Why did she yell to run?

They didn't need to run if she was the one with the nervous breakdown.

And who was she screaming at? Charley and Rachel were close friends. Was it just Charley? The whole class?

Then the Blue Vest had come looking for him.

Baseball practice went longer than normal, and the sun had already set. He pulled into his driveway. The craftsman house had an inviting, covered front porch and sat nestled between trees in the sprawling wooded countryside. Neighboring homes speckled the countryside on the outskirts of Middleton and gave a feeling of peaceful seclusion. Henry's mother loved to plant flowers in the garden, but at this time of the year much of the flowering had faded, except for a few brilliant and hardy marigolds that refused to give in to the changing of seasons.

Home. It was a welcome relief.

Henry parked the car and strolled up the winding walkway of paver stones and onto the front porch. With a quick turn of the key, the front door opened.

The lights were off. No one was home.

He remembered something faintly from last night. He looked at his father's schedule on the refrigerator and saw he was at the hospital again. That one was easy to figure out. His mother, however, said she had something else. Some dinner.

He threw his keys and cell phone on the counter in the kitchen and went to find something to eat.

He felt exhausted. The extended practice had been grueling, but he had to make up for the missed practice time. The need to sit down beckoned more than hunger. After a few minutes he left the kitchen with his backpack and went upstairs. He checked his matted hair in the mirror at the top of the stairs. He was a mess.

He went into his bedroom and closed the door. He flipped on the blue nightlight as he always did and turned on his lamp that cast a soft glow. Throwing his feet up on the bed, he reached down to his backpack on the floor and pulled out his trigonometry book. He missed hearing the assignment yesterday but Charley had—

Charley!

"Oh, man!" he said aloud and put a hand to his forehead, rubbing his face.

He forgot. Their study group at the library. She was going to kill him. He looked down at his watch. It was already 7:30. They were supposed to meet thirty minutes ago. He silently pleaded with the watch, begging it to stop for a little bit so he could rest.

His father had given him the watch and told him it was an heirloom. It had a large brown face bound to a leather strap with fancy stitchwork. It had never even needed a battery change. Thom always said that he should wear it every day. He made it sound like it was tantamount to committing treason if he didn't. "It's not good to be late," he would say.

So much for that.

The watch arms moved without hesitating. He would have to pack up, clean up, get changed, and drive to the library.

But he was so tired.

The library was only a few minutes away.

Ugh.

He would deal with Charley tomorrow. Just let it lie for tonight.

He swung up his textbook into his lap. He wrestled with the numbers and graphs on the page, but exhaustion took over. His eyes drifted. He couldn't do much more.

He closed the math book and went to grab the large leather-bound book from his backpack. Maybe he could read a short story before going to sleep. He looked in the bag, pushing aside the schoolwork.

"Oh, come on!" Another thing he forgot. He had taken out the book and placed it in his locker to make his backpack lighter. Resignation flooded him. He lay down and closed his eyes.

Sleep came quickly.

CHAPTER 22

Henry bolted up in bed, startled awake by loud clanging.
It was still dark. He looked down at his watch.
8:30. He'd only slept for an hour.
From downstairs came the sounds of pans banging. The sounds subsided and everything was quite for a moment. Then, some shuffling footsteps in the kitchen beneath him.

His mother must be home, probably getting something ready for breakfast in the morning. He started to slouch in bed and drift toward sleep again. His sprung muscles unwound.

The second, thunderous crash disagreed with him. It was loud and cacophonous, an assault on the quiet of the night.

That noise wasn't his mother. It was the sound of things smashing.

His clinging sleep instantly fled. Apprehension swelled.

Someone was in his house.

On the tail of the thought came another loud crash. This one was closer. The floorboards shuddered under the legs of his bed. The intruder was moving quickly through the house with no desire for being secretive. He was rifling through the house.

Henry lifted himself off the bed and set his feet onto the floor. He walked on his toes toward the door and cracked it open.

The mirror at the top of the stairs hung cockeyed from the vibration of the intruder's smashing. Henry tried to still his breathing. A vacant, still image of the base of the stairs reflected back at him.

Then, a shadow of midnight black trailed across the bottom of the mirror.

It was enormous.

Henry shut his bedroom door without a sound and locked it, but with the way the intruder was decimating the house, the door handle could easily be smashed off. He had to do something more. He could move the dresser in front of the door. That would create a barricade.

No, too loud. It would give away his presence.

He glanced around the room. He had left his baseball bat downstairs.

He had nothing to defend himself.

Another crash, this time on the stairs. Heavy trodding footsteps, each one shaking the house's frame. By the sound, the intruder was massive. He had never heard anyone thunder up the stairs like that.

His escape was cut off. He was trapped.

He looked at his front window. It led to the shallow-pitched roof of the covered front porch. He could make a break for it.

Henry glided on the floor, thankful for his thick baseball socks that muted his footsteps. He had to be quiet. The intruder didn't know he had a victim captive in the house, and Henry would use that momentary advantage. He moved to the window and unlocked the latch. He lifted the pane.

The night became easier to see. Henry looked up and saw the moon escape from the corner of a cloud. It stood full and bold in the night sky, the light brilliant among the darkness of the surrounding woods.

As soon as the last of the cloud rolled away, a long, drawn howl filled the house.

It was the same sound from last night.

Wolves baying at the moon.

But he thought it had just been the wind whistling . . .

Now it was in his house.

Ice seized his neck like a furious vice and nearly dropped him to his knees.

He looked up through the window.

A small wisp of cloud passed the moon again and dimmed the light. It sped away in a flash and the moon shone full again.

A second raging howl followed. It gurgled and filled the house with baying.

It sounded like the intruder was not just howling toward the moon, but was howling at it. It sounded angry, defiant.

A stream of thudding sounds came from outside Henry's bedroom. The bookshelf outside the room—the books were being thrown to the ground. The far wall shook under its force.

He had to get out.

He tried to dislodge the screen out of the window, careful to be quiet.

The screen was a snug fit. It resisted his pushing.

Then the door flew open.

The mangled door handle clattered to the ground. The lock hadn't done a thing.

The breath caught in Henry's lungs, and he couldn't breathe. He felt asphyxiated.

A massive, shadowy frame filled the doorway.

In the deep fears of his mind, his wild thoughts told him the shadow might be a werewolf.

The truth was worse.

The shadowy creature was hulking and blotted out the light. It had a rock-formed frame with a rough, thickened surface of charcoal and deep crevices. Large protrusions jutted out at strange angles. The creature looked like living volcanic rock. Its head was flat and low, like a dome, looking like a creature robbed of its mind. Where there should have been eyes set deep in the dome, there were none—just a large mouth that slowly parted into a wicked smile, baring rows of razor-sharp teeth.

With fright fueling him, Henry turned and smashed against the screen in the window, but his hand went through the delicate wire mesh. He pulled his hand out and looked back. The creature pushed into Henry's room and its shoulders tore the door frame away.

Henry tore at the screen in a wild panic. The creature closed the gap with slow, heavy footsteps.

Henry's attention suddenly split.

A blue light glowed from behind the creature. The light from Henry's little blue nightlight was growing exponentially in intensity. The creature stopped and turned its low, dome-like head to the side, away from Henry.

The room lit up with brilliant blue color, too bright for Henry to see. As the brilliance faded, a projection of light remained in its place—another creature. It looked like a huge dog or even a bear. The creature was outlined in blue light with a hazy, translucent center. It was made of light and air itself, wisps of blue slowly rolling inside its outline. It regarded Henry with only a glance—its focus was on the rock creature.

The dog's hair stood on end. Then it growled in a long, low drone.

The rock creature turned to face the animal that materialized from the nightlight. It extended its arms for a fight, massive black hands open in defense.

Henry used the moment to finish ripping away the screen. He clambered out of the window onto the roof.

He looked over his shoulder. The creature of blue light pounced upon the rock monster and knocked it down. It growled and snapped its teeth at its prey underneath. The rock creature put up its large, volcanic arm and flung the other creature across the room. The dresser splintered into wooden carnage beneath it. The rock monster stood up again and faced the window. It looked at Henry with eyeless perception. It bounded for the window.

Henry yelled and ran to the roof's edge.

The animal from the nightlight snarled with hair flared and teeth showing like a wolf. It crashed into the side of the rock creature and knocked it down again.

Henry jumped down from the roof.

He heard howling, he wasn't sure from which creature.

He didn't have his keys to his car. Or his cell phone. Or even his shoes. They were all inside the house and so was that black rock creature. It was certain doom to go back inside.

He remembered a word.

Run.

CHAPTER 23

The wind sprints that Coach Barnhard had forced him to do were paying off.

Henry ran uptown, mind awash in abject terror. He had just seen something . . . his mind searched for the word and couldn't come up with it. Instead, his mind insisted on fleeing. Fear fed the muscles in his legs. He looked over his shoulder.

He couldn't see anything following him. He descended the sloping road and his house disappeared behind the cresting hill as he ran away. Nothing pursued him.

Yet.

He had to think of something. He didn't have his phone. There was no traffic on the road in the rural wooden landscape. He needed someone close by, someone who could help.

Then he remembered.

He knew exactly where someone was—Charley would be at the library until it closed. Rachel might be there, too! The library was close enough, just a few minutes away. He tore down the road, regularly glancing over his shoulder.

Still nothing followed him.

This had something to do with Rachel. He was convinced of it. She had told him to run and now he was doing just that. But she tried playing that off in class today. If there really was a reason to run like Rachel had warned, then why try to cover it up? She became unhinged yesterday, and it seemed like there was good reason to be.

Had she seen what he saw? The same rock creature?

No one was supposed to be home tonight, including Henry. But he had skipped the study session. Did the creature know that no one was supposed to be home?

The clouds descended denser onto his brain, questions swirling.

He couldn't focus. For now, he took Rachel's advice to run. Chest burning, legs flying without breaking stride.

The lights of the library parking lot appeared through the dotted trees. Charley's car sat in the parking lot and Henry felt a spark of hope.

The library door flung open with Henry's momentum. It made a clamorous sound in the quiet lobby, and the lady behind the counter turned and gave him a scornful look. He disregarded her and ran through the entryway sensors.

The library held a smattering of small tables scattered throughout the interior. He rifled through the library and spotted Charley sitting at one of the tables. A large stack of textbooks towered in front of her with a display of note cards arranged around her.

"Charley!" He yelled across the library.

Charley's head snapped up. Large pink-frame glasses encompassed most of her face. She glared as he closed in.

"Henry! You might as well have—"

"We have to go."

"What?"

Henry reached across the table and grabbed her large backpack and unzipped it. With one large scoop of his arm across the table, he swept all the note cards into the bag. She flared with indignation.

"Hey! What do you think you're doing?"

Henry, unfazed, grabbed the textbooks and shoved them in also. She stood up and grabbed control of her backpack.

Suddenly, he realized. "Where's Rachel?"

"She didn't show up. I was stood up by both of you."

His voice rose. "She's not here?"

"No. And what's wrong with you?" She looked at the jersey he was wearing. She leaned forward and sniffed, then pulled back with a horrible face. He smelled like sweaty adolescence. "You ditched me so you could play baseball? This is getting really old, Henry."

"Charley, listen, you're going to think I'm crazy, but I just saw something." He paused to try to sound sober. He looked back at the library entrance. The doors remained closed. He looked back at her. "I just saw a monster in my bedroom."

It sounded crazy as it came out.

"Henry, how dare you!" Charley said. "How dare you make up something like this after what we've just been through! You're trying to play my fears so you can have an excuse to miss our study group and play baseball. You promised that—"

"Charley!" His voice boomed in the small library and he grabbed both her wrists.

She froze and looked at him. His hands were cold on her warm skin. His eyes darted over his shoulder, looking at the door again, checking. She looked up and saw he didn't have his baseball cap. His face was flushed and wet. She looked down and saw he wasn't wearing shoes.

"Did you just run here? Without shoes?"

"Yes, that's what I'm trying to tell you. We have to go. Now!"

He grabbed her backpack and started heading out. He spoke without looking back. "I'll explain in the car."

CHAPTER 24

Henry bolted out of the library. He turned and saw Charley lagging too far behind. It wasn't fast enough. Henry doubled back and yanked her by the arm.

"Hey!" she said. "What are you doing?"

"Leaving."

He led her forward like a reluctant toddler to her car and he looked through her backpack.

"Where are your keys?" Henry asked. He piqued with frustration. Some of the spare note cards fell to the ground as his hands rummaged through her backpack.

"Henry!" Charley yelled to get his attention. She reached in her sweatshirt's pocket and held up the keychain. He paused to look at her. Her mouth was open in bewilderment as she held the keys up with her two fingers. "What's gotten into you?"

He ignored the question. He ran to her and reached to take her keys.

"No, no way," she said, shaking her head and pulling the keys back. "You start talking first. Where are we going?"

"I don't know. Somewhere else."

"What are you trying to do?"

"I don't know."

Henry rubbed his forehead, and the effort to think forced him to stand still. It was all so much to process. He knew he needed to get to the library, but now that he was here, he wasn't sure where to go next.

"Henry?" Charley asked.

He didn't notice her anymore. Instead, he noticed a large, obtuse shadow that moved of its own volition against the light from the streetlamps, darting through the tall evergreen bushes at the edge of the parking lot. Faint hints of white appeared in the black mass. A crescent-shaped smile.

Instant terror surged through Henry's body and his breath seized in his chest.

"Charley!" he screamed and his voice cracked. He snatched the keys dangling from her hand. He sprinted the rest of the way to the car. He ripped open the door after fumbling the keys in his hands and jumped into the driver's seat, smashing the keys into the ignition and sending the engine of the small car roaring to life. "Get in!" he yelled and closed the door.

The panic in his voice was enough to mobilize Charley. She ran the last few strides to the car and jumped into the passenger's seat.

Henry peeled out as the rear tires grabbed traction while Charley still tried to close her door. He flew down the road hyperventilating.

"Henry, what are you doing?" She yelled at him and buckled her seatbelt. "You can't just take my car like that! Start talking right now." She folded her arms in defensive posture. "And start making sense!"

Henry didn't talk. He was frozen.

After some time passed, he spoke in a low voice.

"I saw it," he said. His voice trembled.

"Saw what?" Charley said. "Saw your closet-monster in the library parking lot?" Her tone was mocking.

He looked at her, face pale, his eyes as big as saucers. He was sweating again, but it was not from running.

"Yes! It was *right there*. It . . . followed me."

"There was nothing there, Henry!"

"It was there, Charley," he replied. His tone was somber. "That means it got away . . ." He looked back to Charley, frozen again. "I'm really scared."

CHAPTER 25

Charley gazed at Henry and thought about what he said.

He had never said he was scared before.

Whatever he saw had rattled him. The longer they rode together in the car, the more she perceived it. Henry was a bit of a clod sometimes but he was an honest clod. He wouldn't turn the episode yesterday with Rachel into a twisted game to be endured. She knew that.

His muscles twitched and his eyes darted from the road to the rearview mirror incessantly.

His mind had been riven.

Her next thought frightened her.

She had been willing to stave off the outlandish sightings with disbelief like any rational person would. She could call him crazy and disregard what he said. But if she took a step forward—if she chose to believe him—a great abyss of fear and the unknown lay before her. To believe it as rational, to cede any resolve that it was only a delusion, would be an unraveling of the fabric of her self-controlled world.

First Rachel, now Henry. Her friends.

Worlds collided. No, worlds were breaking.

She took a breath and committed.

"Henry, what did you see?"

He told her the whole thing—the thunderous sounds in the house, the giant creature of black volcanic rock that chased him, and how another creature appeared out of his nightlight and fought against it. He ran, leaving his shoes, keys, and phone in the house.

The picture of Rachel from the day before screaming to run was etched into Charley's mind with an indelible imprint. Charley might not have believed a word of Henry's story on any other day, but her reality was suddenly twisted by strange irregularities.

Rachel.

"We have to find Rachel!" Charley said. "She might be in trouble."

"I know," Henry said, "but remember her telling us they just moved? We don't know where her new house is."

Charley picked up her phone and called Rachel. There was no answer on the other end, and the same sublime voicemail message was ever cheerful. She hung up, rankled.

Charley turned and looked out the back window. She could no longer attempt denial. Her skin crawled under the hair that stood on end.

"Pull in here," she said and pointed to a small coffee shop with a sign made of old pallet wood. "I can't think straight—I need caffeine."

CHAPTER 26

Charley and Henry switched seats in the drive-thru. She waited for the car in front of them to finish up.

Henry still looked unwell. He was strung out on fear. "We shouldn't have stopped," he said.

"Henry, we've driven five miles from the library. We can stop for five minutes."

"How do you know?"

"Whoa, don't snap. I just need some caffeine. One of us needs to be in our right mind."

The caffeine would help to align her thoughts. It was getting late and she contemplated what to do. Henry's head spun on his neck like a swivel, darting this way and that every few moments, gazing out the windows. He had not calmed down.

"What do you think the deal is with the two creatures?" Charley said.

"I don't know," he said. He was distant.

"And why were they fighting?" She was musing aloud, halfway hoping for a real answer. Something bizarre was happening, but she also hoped it could be solved with rational thought. So, she got to analyzing. "What would the black monster want with you anyway?"

Mentioning the creature again made Henry twitch in his seat, and he wiped his brow with a shaky hand. He grabbed Charley's phone from the center console and dialed numbers again, leaving sweaty smears on the surface of the phone. He sat, waiting. After unending ringing, he ended the call. "I wish someone would answer!"

Henry had tried calling his parents six times but to no avail. He left voice messages pleading with them to call back and he sent text messages as well. Their phones were silenced, no doubt. His dad asked for someone to cover his shift at the hospital tonight, and his mom was somewhere he couldn't remember. He couldn't go to them.

"What if they come home? What if that thing goes back there? I've got to warn them!"

He called his parents again. Still nothing.

"You can't go back there," Charley said. "Not yet."

He lowered his head. "I just don't know what to do." He gave another quick glance through the parking lot. Nothing moved except an occasional passing vehicle on the road. The night seemed quiet here.

The car in front of them moved up and Charley inched her car forward. "No police, right?"

"They're not going to listen to me. If they go to the house they will see the destruction—but they won't believe that it was two freakish creatures sparring in my bedroom. I wish I could get a hold of my parents! I can't imagine what would happen if they go home now."

The barista opened the window and handed Charley her mocha.

"What about Mr. Hellen?" Charley said. "My foster dad is working late tonight at the university. We could go talk to him." Mr. Hellen was an upstart biochemist that had garnered professional spotlight and just received a federal grant for his lab. He often worked late into the night with post-graduate students.

"Really?" Henry asked. "Do you think he'll listen?"

"I don't know. He's pretty caught up in his experiments in the laboratory, which is why he's still there. But I bet he would know what to do next."

"He won't think I'm crazy?"

"Henry, I already think you're crazy. That's not something to worry about."

"Charley, come on! I really need help."

"I know, I know. Let's just see if we can get a few more answers, and maybe he will also have access to the parent-teacher website with Rachel's family's phone number."

It was the best option they had.

"Okay, I guess so," Henry said. "But we have to go. We can't just sit here anymore. That thing followed me once already."

They sped away.

CHAPTER 27

Ten minutes later they pulled into the parking lot of Middleton University.

The science building rose several stories in front of them, sprawling across the campus with a few lights emanating from the windows. The building was much longer than it was tall, with a bridge running to connect divided segments of the building. Charley turned the engine off and exited the car, stuffing her keys into her pocket.

"Come on," she said and began walking. "His lab is this way."

Henry followed her on the sidewalk that led up to the entrance on the left side. Except for the sparsely lit windows, the campus landscape looked abandoned. Only a few cars remained in the parking lot and no students walked the sidewalks. He sped up his pace and came alongside her.

"I came here before when I needed to talk to Mr. Hellen," she said. "I had to get a signature from him as my foster parent that was due at school the next day. I had to come all the way out here!" she said with grandiose intonation. She was trying to lighten the mood. It didn't help.

They came to the security call box and she hit a button. An awkward electronic sound buzzed within it.

"The security guard is nice. We just wait for him to buzz us in."

There was no answer on the call box.

They stood outside the door and the wind picked up, gusting them under the awning like they were in a wind tunnel. It chilled Henry through his lightweight baseball jersey.

Charley hit the button again and the same static sound came back. They waited, but still no answer.

"That's odd," she said. "There's supposed to be campus security staff that guards this building because of all the expensive science equipment."

She reached down and tugged on the handle of the door. It was locked.

Undeterred, she reached for the sister door and it swung open.

"Good, we can go find him ourselves." She let herself in.

"Charley, are you sure . . ."

"It's fine."

It felt cavalier to go in without notifying security. It also felt cavalier because she had not seen what he had seen at his house.

They walked into the foyer and turned the corner. They could now see the campus security guard's circular desk. No one was there.

Charley peered at the desk as they walked by. A coat was draped over the back of the chair and a cup of coffee sat on the desk, still steaming.

"There, see?" She pointed to the desk and turned her head around to look at Henry. "He's here. Looks like he just poured himself a cup of coffee. I bet he just went to the bathroom or something." The conviction in her voice wavered.

Charley walked past the desk and pressed the button to call the elevator. The doors opened and they went inside. She pressed the fourth-floor button. The doors closed and the elevator lurched upward, numbers also moving upward on an electronic display.

"This will only take a moment," she said, "then we can figure out what to do."

Henry stayed silent.

Once the elevator signaled the number four, the doors opened to a hallway that extended to the right. Charley led the way, looking at the laboratory entrance doors, mumbling the names on the placards. "I just have to remember which one it is, exactly."

The hallway was empty and long with several fluorescent lights burnt out in the drop ceiling grid. Mute-colored, sterile cinder blocks interlocked together to form the walls.

The long hallway yawned in front of Henry. He needed to make a pit-stop. A bathroom was adjacent to the elevators.

"Charley, I've got to use the bathroom. Just give me a minute and I'll be right out."

"Okay," she said over her shoulder.

Henry disappeared into the bathroom.

CHAPTER 28

Charley kept walking and kept searching. The names on the lab placards were unfamiliar. Maybe Mr. Hellen's lab was on the third floor instead. Maybe she could—

Something clanged in one of the labs several doors ahead.

She snapped her eyes from the placards to the hallway.

No one was there. However, one door stood open further down. If someone were there, she could ask where Mr. Hellen's lab was. That would solve the wandering.

Moving forward was the best course of action. Maybe the noise was from the security guard. He might get mad because he should have authorized them to enter, but he could at least help them now. She walked to the open door and went in.

The room was dark. The only light was the casted glow of the campus lights from outside the windows and the reflected moonlight. Her fingers reached for a light switch but couldn't find one. Her eyes began to adjust to the dimness.

"Hello?" she called, confused. No one answered.

A series of black metallic filing cabinets stood between her and the windows. Lab tables filled the room at regular intervals and the room stretched toward the right side. She stepped into the room and saw the faint glow of a chemical hood to the right, nestled into the same wall as the door. The blue light of the hood showed a series of small beakers and flasks sitting undisturbed.

Charley frowned. She surveyed the room again. What had made that noise? There were no chemicals bubbling under the hood, there was no object on the floor. Apprehension crept up her spine and the hair on her neck tingled.

She walked to the filing cabinets and looked on the other side of them. Nothing there. She touched the filing cabinets and ran a finger over them. She considered how large they were and how much information they must have, and then had a realization. Curiosity played at her like a kitten with a ball of yarn.

She grabbed the handle of one of the cabinets and slid the drawer out. Manilla folders populated the drawer with random papers of technical data. She pulled the drawer back and shoved it closed.

A loud clang shook the room, the same sound from only moments ago. Someone had just closed the drawer, but there was no one in the—

"Hey!" A voice sounded from the shadows.

Charley whirled around. A figure stood in the far corner of the room, unmoving. She was on edge instantly and her eyes widened.

Nobody had been there a moment ago. She was sure of it.

"What are you doing?" the person asked. It was a male voice, but Charley could see no other distinguishing features. He was only a silhouette, hidden from the moonlight in the corner of the room.

"Oh, sorry," Charley said, fumbling. "I didn't see you. How did you get—"

"What are you doing?" the voice asked again.

"I was looking for my foster dad, Mr. Hellen, and I heard something in here so I was going—"

"Mr. Hellen isn't here." The shadow started to move out of the corner.

"I just thought someone would know where he was."

"He's gone." It was a slow, deliberate statement, filled with awkward inflection. There was something familiar about his voice.

The aggressive tone was offsetting, but she needed answers too.

"Are you the security guard? Who are you?"

The light from the lampposts outside the window caught the face of the man as he walked forward and reflected off the wire-rimmed glasses on his face. The light fell upon his slicked-back hair. He wore a blue vest.

Charley gasped.

CHAPTER 29

The man moved out of the corner with slow precision, shuffling around the lab tables along the edge of the room, taking care to avoid the beams of moonlight blanketing the center of the lab. The moonlit tables separated him from Charley.

Charley started to hyperventilate and backed up, forgetting about the filing cabinet and stumbling into it. She fell to the floor, and the sharp corner of the cabinet ripped her shirt and gouged the skin over her ribs. She let out a small yelp and grabbed her side.

Charley clambered to get up. She needed to flee, but something else screamed to be recognized and would not be silenced. The gears spun quickly in her mind like an untethered flywheel, and she needed one thing.

"What did you do with Rachel?" She snarled at him, accusation pointed like arrows.

"Don't worry about her," the man replied. His steady, slow pace was undeterred. He had crossed from the back to the front of the lab in the shadows and walked toward the chemical hood. The same blue vest that he wore yesterday at the high school hung open, draped from his shoulders.

Charley turned and looked at the door. She looked back toward the man. He walked by the blue light of the chemical hood.

She couldn't look away.

The silent blue light crackled and shone on his features as they suddenly changed. The combed hair and metal glasses disappeared.

Something horrible replaced them.

The light displayed a creature with a bulbous head on a disproportionately smaller body. There were no eyes in the large head, but rows of triangular teeth were fixed inside its open mouth. The creature's skin was oily and molting, hanging off its body in peels, like a wet mummy or a sickly walking birch tree. After it walked past the light of the hood, its visage changed back to the man with the glasses and vest.

Charley's momentary fixation was gone.

Charley ran through the doorway. Fear seized her heart in a new intensity she had never dreamed possible. She ran as hard as she could down the hall and screamed, her shrill voice echoing through the empty corridor.

"Henry!"

She hoped that the creature wouldn't pounce upon her at any moment.

She barreled into the men's bathroom at the end of the hall by the elevators. Henry stood at the sink, washing his hands. He jumped with her sudden entrance.

Charley grabbed him, tearing at his frame with wild hands. She gushed words.

"Henry, there's something here, it was the hall monitor that took Rachel, but it walked by the blue light and it turned into a creature and it's coming after us! We have to get out of here!"

She ducked behind him, putting him between herself and the door.

She saw her reflection in the mirror. She was pale as the white on his jersey logo, the blood drained from her face. Tears streamed from her eyes.

"I don't want to die," she said.

"It's here?" he asked. His face went slack. "The black monster?"

"No, it's not that! It's something else. It looked like an oily mummy with a really large head, like a rotten watermelon. It had wet peels coming off. But it was the man from school at the same time!" She felt hysterical, angry that he didn't understand. The fear pitched her voice an octave higher.

"It's a different one?" The fear that rose in Henry was tangible, pouring off emotion and validating her own fear.

They needed to get out.

CHAPTER 30

Henry walked to the bathroom door and put his ear against it. He didn't hear anything.

He cracked open the door just enough to peer with one eye down the hall.

Nothing.

Charley stood in the back of the bathroom, up against the wall, watching.

He dared to open the door a little further. He looked as much as he could in each direction. Still nothing. He turned back to Charley and silently waved toward her to come. She barely moved.

He walked into the hallway for a better look down the long corridor of lab spaces.

Just the abandoned hallway with poor lighting and austere decorations. He called over his shoulder.

"Charley, which one were you . . ."

She was no longer in the bathroom. She stood at the elevator, pressing the call button furiously.

The elevator was still in the same spot from their trip up. The doors opened and Charley flew inside. Henry had no other choice. He ran inside the elevator. She pressed the close button as fast as she could.

"I think we should have taken the stairs," Henry said as the doors closed.

"I just want to get out of here," Charley shot back. "I'll feel better when I get in my own car and I'm miles away from here."

The elevator began its descent.

"Do you believe me now?" Henry asked. She looked at him with saucers for eyes and, holding her side, she nodded.

"You're bleeding?" he said. "What happened?"

"It's nothing," she said. He tried to get close to look but she shooed him away.

The elevator dinged for floor three.

"I just scraped it on a filing cabinet."

"It . . . it wasn't from that . . . thing, was it?"

"No!" she said. Fear electrified her answer.

Floor two.

"My dad can help you. Once this is over, we've got some bandages and stuff—"

The elevator seized with a jerk and stopped moving. The lights all went dark except for the elevator indicator light that still displayed a red digital two.

They both looked around in silence.

The elevator was frozen.

CHAPTER 31

"No no no no no . . ." Charley's voice rose as she spurted out the words. She assaulted the control panel, mashing the buttons with renewed vigor.

"I told you we should have taken the stairs! What were you thinking?"

"Don't yell at me!"

"Okay, what should we do?"

Charley pressed an array of buttons without success. The elevator refused to move.

"Isn't there an elevator phone?" Henry asked.

"I'm not going to sit here and wait. Besides, what if the man with the glasses is the one who shows up?"

"Okay, I'm just thinking. What about an access panel in an elevator, like in the movies?"

"I don't know. Look around!"

Henry looked up and pressed on one of the decorative suspended panels in the ceiling. It retreated and gave way to the metal encasing behind it. There was a faint outline of light shining through the cracks of an access panel. "There's one here. Come on."

Henry stood on the arm rail of the elevator. He reached up and unfastened the latch. He flipped the panel open and clambered up into the bowels of the elevator shaft. It was dark except for the emergency light, hung high at the top of the shaft. The doors for the elevator exit for the second floor were right in front of him. The elevator had only moved a couple feet down from the second floor before stopping.

He stuck his head down into the elevator. "Charley, we can get out here."

"Then pull me up!"

She stood on the elevator arm rail and Henry yanked her up through the access grate at the top of the elevator. She winced and grabbed her side when she stood up.

"Did you scrape your side again?"

"You did, Henry!"

"Does it hurt?"

"What do you think?"

"Sorry," Henry mumbled. She pulled her arm back from him.

He turned to look at the inside of the second floor's door.

"There must be a latch or something," he said. He searched to find something that would give. He found a lever and moved it. A metal mechanism popped and he grabbed the center of the doors. He pulled them open with a tug. They stepped out of the elevator shaft onto the second floor. "Okay," Henry said, "we made it down two floors. We just have to get down one more." The sign for the accompanying stairwell was just a few feet away. "Let's get downstairs."

Charley nodded and fled to the stairwell door.

Henry went to pull the door open, his hand a few inches from the handle, and froze.

The stairwell door banged and shook. The small vertical window into the stairwell was filled with black obscurity, and a small droning sound came from the other side.

Charley backed away, eyes on the door, unwavering.

"That's not good," Henry whispered. "I don't think we should go in there." He backed away from the stairwell with quiet steps. He breathed slowly, as if his breathing were too loud and would give away their presence.

Another few steps backward. Still nothing—the stairwell door stayed closed, but the droning sound became louder.

They started to pick up their pace, moving further away. Henry broke his gaze from the stairwell door to the other end of the long hallway. There was a door at the end, like a mirror image of the one ahead of him, and he figured it must be the stairwell for the other end of the building. There was no window on the door to tell if the lights were on or off. They would have to chance it—the first stairwell they already knew to be compromised.

"Look, there's a—"

He didn't have time to finish.

The door of the unlit stairwell creaked open. From out of the shadows there came a chattering sound, like someone snickering at a joke. The tone was mocking, and the snickers called and answered like the voices of hyenas. Henry felt the terror play on his ears and the meaning sunk into his mind.

There was more than one.

CHAPTER 32

Half a dozen creatures burst out of the shadowy stairwell in wild commotion. They were smaller than the rock-like monster—strange creatures with smooth gray skin, slanted red eyes, and sharp pointed ears like Dobermans' on each side of their triangular heads. Each of their fingers ended in a knife-life talon and opened and closed like scissors. Their heads, along with their hands and feet, appeared large compared to their small frames. They were half as tall as Henry but they created the same fear within him as the larger black monster. And there were six of them.

The creatures charged down the hall.

"Run!" Henry cried.

Henry and Charley sprinted away. The six Gremlin creatures cackled as if the chase were a game.

"Head to the last door, it's the other stairwell!" Henry shouted. He started behind Charley but his long strides gained ground on her.

Henry looked behind him at the creatures.

Their shorter legs made the creatures slower, and Henry and Charley gained some distance. The creatures' skin was wrinkled in small heaps at their joints and at the base of their necks and their chattering sounds increased with the excitement of the chase. Two bounded sideways, galloping with limp legs, using arms for support like a monkey. One ran in the center of the hallway, arms spinning in large circles with talons in whirlwind arcs. Others bounded off the wall to get to the front of the pack.

Henry overtook Charley and got to the end of the hallway first. He seized the metal door latch and pressed down. He threw the door open. It was dark inside.

He couldn't look for a light switch. No time for it. This stairwell was their only option.

"Go downstairs!" he yelled at Charley. He propped the door open for her. "I'll meet you at the car!" Charley ran through and disappeared into the dark.

Henry went in behind her and slammed the door shut. He threw his back up against it. A fire door for a stairwell wouldn't have a lock. He would have to barricade the door. That would at least allow Charley a chance to get to the car. She could pick him up—maybe even run over some of the creatures.

"Henry!" Charley cried, right next to him. Her voice was forlorn.

"Why didn't you go downstairs?" he said. Instant frustration surged through him at her refusal to cooperate. She just blew their one chance to get away.

His eyes adjusted to the darkness. His heart sank into his stomach.

"This isn't a stairwell!" she cried. Fear emanated from her voice. "It's a maintenance closet!"

Metal racks with cleaning chemicals came into view, and a few mops were propped up against the side of the wall. The room was small with no windows.

He just sealed their doom.

"We're trapped!" she screamed.

CHAPTER 33

Henry looked around, panicked.

He didn't know what to do. He grabbed a large broom and wedged it behind the exposed metal frame of a mounted shelving unit to barricade it closed. He retreated to the back of the small room where Charley stood, trembling.

There were a few moments of stillness, of watching the door in fear, of waiting for their inevitable end. Henry grabbed a spare mop and held it in his hands. The creatures could rip him to shreds with their sharp talons while his wooden stick would do no good. He couldn't defend against six of them.

Bang!

The door vibrated against the barricade. Charley jumped at the sudden sound and grabbed Henry, yanking at his baseball jersey. She clung to him and tears streamed freely down her face.

Bang!

It sounded like a giant was on the other side. Henry grew nauseated and his knees nearly buckled. His palms were slick from sweat, and it was difficult to even hold the mop up.

He was going to die.

Bang!!

The sound was monstrous. The broom splintered into pieces and flew across the room. The door swung open.

The Gremlin creatures crowded the door's threshold. Some dangled from the sides of the door frame and hung suspended in the entrance. The largest one surged forward with talons extended. It leaped into the air.

Charley cringed and buried her face in Henry's shoulder. He held out the mop in a meager effort.

A loud blast rang through the small room. The Gremlin suddenly exploded in a burst of blue and vibrant light. The blue light consumed the creature in midair, and the creature evaporated. Its scream was silenced in a decrescendo, like a brilliant firework explosion snuffed out.

The other Gremlins reeled, and their strange language suddenly became cacophonous and angry, like agitated chimpanzees before an overpowering predator. They looked around in a frenzy.

Suddenly, another boom.

A second Gremlin burst into blue flame. It screamed as the light enveloped it. In its smoldering place was only a plume of black smoke coming up from a small pile of charcoaled ash.

The Gremlins scattered and ran back through the doorway, but their vicious tones still echoed in the small maintenance closet.

The thunderous sound came again, and in a split second a Gremlin flew back into sight. It was thrown up against the wall in violent force, a burning blue crater in its chest. The blue fire encompassed the whole creature, and ash clung to the wall in its place.

A man in a long black coat ran into the maintenance room. The coat broke at his knees and shrouded most of his frame. He spun around and gave his back to Henry and Charley. In the dark of the room, his face was unrecognizable. His arms were extended, pointing at the door. The faint reflection of light from the hall showed two large pistols in his hand with long, flared muzzles. They looked like relics—each like a blunderbuss gun found in a museum, fused with steampunk flair.

The man waited.

At once the remaining three creatures charged through the door with nimble speed. They jumped on the man and clawed at him with eager talons. One hung on the back of his neck, one crawled on his left arm, and the other clung to his leg.

With a quick retraction of his right arm, the man pulled back his gun and fired a shot behind his head at the creature on his neck. He dispatched it with a shot of decimating light from the blunderbuss, and the echo reverberated in the small room. The Gremlin hanging from his other arm reached for his free hand and lurched toward the man's face. The man bent backward suddenly, like doing a limbo, with his coat dragging on the floor, and the Gremlin flew over the top. The man bolted upright and fired both guns downward. The light turned the Gremlin on his leg into blackened dust.

He spun around and his coat flew open in the small room. The man's face flashed before Henry and Charley. He extended both pistols and unleashed a succession of a dozen shots. The room exploded in blue light and the shots riddled the last creature against the wall. Ash fell with each round until there was nothing left of it but smoke snaking upward.

The man lowered his pistols.

Henry stood and gawked. Relief and confusion mixed inside him. The bizarre monsters that pursued him without reason had strangled his heart in fear. But the man before him only added to the crushing load.

Henry couldn't believe it.

"Dad?"

CHAPTER 34

"Come on, we have to move," Thom said.

It couldn't be.

"Dad?" Henry asked again.

"Yes, it's me," he said. He wore a black zip-up ribbed sweater underneath his long coat, zipped up all the way to the neck. He had on dark jeans and a pair of black boots. Henry had seen him wear those clothes before, but he never looked the way he did now. He looked like a phantom undertaker. "We can talk later but for now we have little time."

He took a step closer to Henry and Charley.

"Charley, do you have your phone?"

"Yes." She reached in her pocket and handed it to him.

"Are you going to call—"

"Henry," he said, cutting her off, "You wore the watch like I said. Good work. Can I have it?"

Henry nodded. "Of course. You told me I should always wear it."

Henry unfastened the clasp on the watch's brown leather band. Thom took the watch with the phone and walked over to the metal shelving. He placed the phone and watch on the shelf.

"Now, I just need to find something," he said. He opened a toolbox lying in the corner of the room and pulled out a carpenter's hammer.

"Dad, what are you doing?"

Thom brought the hammer arcing down on the face of the watch. It shattered, and glass shards flew across the room.

"Dad, that was your heirloom watch!"

He brought the hammer high again and smashed the phone into electronic pieces.

Charley barely moved. Her mouth hung open. When she spoke, she sounded as shattered as the phone itself.

"Why? Just . . . why?"

Thom put the hammer down and left the broken phone on the shelf. He picked up the watch.

"It's how they were tracking you. The Gremlins, and the man with the glasses and vest."

A deep shadow settled over Henry's brain.

"Tracking us?" He barely stammered out the words. He was silent for a moment. "But how do you know that?"

"Because it's how I was tracking you."

Thom stuffed the fractured watch into his pocket then walked toward the door and looked out. He held his pistols ready, checking. "I planted a tracker in the watch years ago in case this ever happened. It's why I've always made you wear it."

Charley trembled. She cocked her head forward. "You mean you knew about these things? These . . . these . . . monsters!"

"Like I said, I'll explain later. Follow me."

Thom moved out of the maintenance closet. Charley and Henry ran to keep up. Outside the door, a stairwell stood ten feet away. They had missed it earlier, on their frantic run down the hall. Thom descended the stairs with his guns out, sweeping. He moved with urgency. They didn't speak another word until they were in the parking lot.

Outside, Thom started to run to his truck. Henry ran afterward but then looked behind him midstride. Charley had broken away and was running toward her car on the other side of the parking lot.

Henry stopped. "Charley, wait! Where are you going?"

She didn't answer. She kept running. The quiet, heavy night betrayed her sobbing on the wind. She didn't speak until she had safely opened the door of her car.

"Just leave me alone!" Her voice cracked in the still air. "I don't want anything to do with your monsters, or your tracking, or your family! This is your problem, not mine."

She slammed the car door behind her.

Henry planted his foot to run after her but felt a hand on his shoulder. "Let her go, Henry," his dad said. "She's right—it doesn't involve her."

She tore out of the parking lot.

"This is our fight."

CHAPTER 35

C harley hammered the accelerator.

Sixty-five in a thirty mile-per-hour zone. It didn't matter.

She had to get away—flee into solitude. Somewhere hidden from those creatures and everyone else.

That was the best thing to do—separate herself from the Murphys and their world of nightmares.

The roads were empty and she turned her car hard around the corner. The wheels squealed with velocity. She pulled into her driveway and the car lurched to a sudden stop.

The familiarity of her house was welcome. Even the security bars over the windows gave a sense of warm invitation, like if she could just get inside she could bar out the darkness. When the Hellens had installed them, they said the bars were for her safety. She needed that safety tonight.

Charley ran through the front door.

Mr. and Mrs. Hellen stood in the small kitchen.

"Where were you?" Charley demanded. She slammed the door behind her.

"What do you mean?" Mr. Hellen said.

"You weren't at the lab!"

"No, I went home early tonight. Why, did you go to the lab?"

"You never go home early!"

"Tonight I did."

"Charley," Mrs. Hellen said, "we've been wondering about you. The library closes at nine. It's past eleven. Where were you?"

"We were worried sick," Mr. Hellen said. "We tried calling you. Don't you have your phone anymore? You need to tell us everything!"

"Everything," Mrs. Hellen said.

Curiosity poured off them, and some of Charley's tension unknotted. At least Mr. Hellen was home tonight and not at the lab. It was better this way. For him, and for her.

"I don't know what's going on," Charley said and paused. She felt confused. The story sounded crazy in her mind. And to speak it out . . . she felt like she wasn't just losing her sanity, but that she had thrown it out like a piece of useless clutter she no longer needed. Would the Hellens even believe her? "I saw something," she whispered. "Creatures . . ."

They didn't move. They waited. Like they hadn't heard what she'd said. Then Mr. Hellen spoke. "Go on."

"They were at your lab. I went there with Henry because we—"

"Henry? Henry Murphy?" Mrs. Hellen said, her voice rising. "Is that boy still going to your study groups with Rachel? I don't like him. He's irresponsible."

"Why would you say that? I thought you liked him. Didn't you say that you were glad he was in our . . . okay, whatever. We can talk more about him later. Anyway, we went to the lab and I was looking for you because you're always there late with your grad students. Do you remember the man I told you about yesterday, the man who took Rachel?"

"Yes."

"He was there! And then—"

"Was Henry with you then?" Mr. Hellen said.

"Yes, I told you he was there. But, well . . . no, he was using the bathroom so he didn't see the man. So as the man walked toward me I—"

"Where is Henry now?" Mrs. Hellen asked.

"I don't know!" Charley yelled and threw her hands into the air. "His dad came to pick us up and I just came home. Can I finish? Why are you so concerned about Henry anyway?"

"Henry's dad was there?" Mr. Hellen said.

"Are you even hearing me? Yes, that's what I said."

Mr. Hellen walked over to Charley from the kitchen.

"Then you had better call them. They may need help."

"Yes, we need to help them," Mrs. Hellen said.

CHAPTER 36

"I don't have my cell phone," Charley said. "I left it at school."

It was easier to lie. Better than saying a gun-wielding maverick smashed the several-hundred-dollar phone the Hellens had bought her.

"Charley, we need to find them," Mr. Hellen said.

"Why?" Charley's eyes went large. Realization dawned. "Did you already know about those creatures? Are Henry and his dad in trouble?"

"Like you said, we can talk more about Henry later. For now, just call them and find out where they are."

"How am I supposed to call them? I don't have my phone."

"Use the landline."

Charley snatched up her backpack and walked to her room at the end of the hall. She sat down on the chair in front of the small desk. She reached up to grab the phone mounted on the wall, yellowed from age. Mr. Hellen still thought a landline was important because he still thought faxing was important.

She stared at the keypad.

It stared back at her.

She had no idea what Henry's phone number was.

His number was saved into her shattered phonebook in a laboratory maintenance closet. She had never memorized his number. She could search the drawers for the printed phonebook that Mr. Murphy had used to find Rachel's family's number but . . .

Charley tapped the phone with her finger and wrinkled her eyebrows.

Why did it matter if she called them anyway? It seemed like Mr. Murphy could take care of himself and Henry. Besides, she had just recited the reasons why she needed to run away from them, not to search for them like lost toddlers in an amusement park.

She looked up and caught a glint of light dangling from the neck of the desk lamp on a silver chain. A teardrop shaped blue gem hung in the center.

Rachel's necklace.

Charley had draped it there after she stole it off Mrs. Ball's desk. She forgot to give it back to Rachel today. She fingered the blue topaz amulet, thinking about the day's abrupt changes.

The phone beeped in her hand with the expired dial tone. She hung the phone back on the wall.

She only knew one phone number. She had called it enough times. Rachel.

She grabbed the phone again.

Rachel's enigmatic change stung Charley's mind. The last few hours rewrote everything Charley had experienced at school. The fear from Rachel's disappearance now clung to her psyche again. Everything was cast in a different light . . .

Cast in a different darkness.

She pressed the numbers on the keypad with trembling ceremony. She felt like she was calling the underworld itself, seeking to speak with apparitions of a lost realm. She—

"Charley?"

The sudden answer snapped Charley out of her circling thoughts. Rachel's voice was worn and gravely. She sounded like she had screamed for hours.

It wasn't the voicemail.

"Rachel?"

"Yes, yes!" The crazed voice surged through the phone.

"Rachel, what's going on?"

Mumbled, pressured static came back.

A stroke of entitlement surged in Charley's core. She never played the entitlement card. She never asked anyone for anything. She never asked for her parents to die and leave her to the jaws of the government and the foster home system. This was her life now that was being vacuumed away into a black abyss. If Rachel knew anything, she owed it to Charley.

"You need to tell me what's going on!" Charley held the phone and yelled into it.

Broken, analog sounds, hazed and out of focus wafted into Charley's ear.

She only now realized that Rachel was yelling also. The unhinged voice, the same one from yesterday, shook the small phone receiver in Charley's hand.

"Charley . . . run . . . not me . . ."

Charley pressed the phone to her ear.

" . . . can't trust your . . ."

The phone went dead.

CHAPTER 37

Cold fear and sweat still clung to Henry's brow.

"Dad, what is going on?"

Thom's truck barreled down the road and the scenery sped by in a blur. Henry's chest still heaved with rapid breaths. He turned and looked out the rear window. The landscape retreated into the night behind them.

Thom gripped the steering wheel and snorted. He shook his head.

Thom's coat fell open and a glint of light reflected off the pistol holstered next to his chest.

"Dad, when did you get those pistols? I never . . ."

The words stalled on his tongue. The thought echoed in his mind.

He never saw any of this before.

Everything was shifting.

Coils of apprehension constricted like bands around his heart. He threw his back up against the side of the door and faced Thom, scrambling backward.

"Wait, you're not one of those . . . shape-shifters . . . Charley was talking about, are you? You're trying to trick me! You—"

"Henry! No, it's me." Thom reached his hand out and tried to calm Henry. "Settle down. It's me. I've been with you since day one—since you were born. I delivered you. There was so much blood. You nearly killed yourself and your mother. You were a miracle baby."

Henry unwound. Hearing the familiarity of the story soothed his tension. This was really his dad. He relaxed into his seat and put his head in his hands.

"I'm sorry, Dad. I had to be sure."

Thom's hand squeezed Henry's shoulder. His grip was firm and strong. "They found us, Henry. That means everything's changed."

"Dad, when I was at home, one of those things—"

"I know," Thom replied. "I know what happened at the house."

"But what about Mom? Where is she? She can't go home either. We have to tell her!"

"She already knows."

"She already knows? But I tried calling and texting her and I never got ahold of her. Are you sure she's okay?"

"She's fine. She turned her phone off. It's our contingency plan—to go dark. No cell phones. We'll try to disappear again." He shook his head. "We were invisible for years. We were living normal lives." Thom snapped out of the moment. "But why were you at the university? You said you were going to the library. I would have never found you without the watch."

"I didn't know what else to do. It was Charley's idea."

"Why?"

"Her foster dad works there. She said that—"

The brakes screeched with wild grinding and the seatbelt locked under the weight of Henry's body. The large truck squealed to a stop. Thom turned to Henry. "He works there?"

"But he wasn't there tonight."

Thom spun the steering wheel in mighty circles and Henry's seatbelt locked again as the truck tore through the gravel shoulders with a large U-turn. The truck nearly tipped over.

"We have to fly. Charley's in danger."

CHAPTER 38

"Who was that, Charley?"

Charley jumped out of her chair and fumbled the phone. It fell to the floor. She hadn't heard anyone walk down the hall.

Mr. Hellen stood in the doorway, arm propped on the doorframe. His jaw was set.

Charley put her hand over her chest. She slumped back into the chair. She scooched forward to place her legs back under the desk, like she always did when studying.

"I'm really jumpy tonight," she said.

"Who was that?"

He didn't move. He stared at the phone receiver on the floor. She bent down and snagged it.

"It was Henry. You told me to try calling him." She hung up the phone with finality. "He didn't answer."

There. He couldn't disprove the lie. She had hung up the phone. There was no caller ID on the landline.

Mr. Hellen gave a slow, disapproving shake of his head. He looked up from the floor and his face darkened. "You shouldn't lie."

Charley squirmed in her seat.

"I'm not lying," she said. "I tried calling Henry."

"You called Rachel. She's . . . busy. You shouldn't talk to her either."

"I didn't call Rachel."

Mr. Hellen smiled wickedly. "I can taste your deception, Charley. It's delicious."

Mrs. Hellen walked into the doorway from the hall. She held a cluster of phone wire and her hand was coated in white drywall powder and frayed threads of yellow insulation. She cocked her head to the side with a taunting smile, like she was demeaning a child.

"Did the phone just go dead?" she asked.

Charley leaned back from the door in fear. "Did you just rip the phone wires out of the wall?"

Mrs. Hellen threw the fractured phone wires at Charley's feet. "You can't deceive the deceivers, Charley. You're speaking our language."

Fear gripped Charley's heart like a giant hand, wringing the life out of her. She pleaded with staring eyes, wishing the nightmare had not followed her home.

Triangular teeth flashed on the Hellens' faces.

Charley shot a look toward the window. It was her only way out.

Security bars stood erect over the window, like the house was a garrison for a prison. The bars that she'd thought would protect her now held her captive.

"For your safety," Mrs. Hellen cooed.

Charley was cornered.

CHAPTER 39

Charley's legs were pinned under the desk. She shoved hard against the wall and the chair fell over backward. She landed on the floor with a thud. Her backpack fell with the push and spewed its contents on the ground and knocked over the study lamp. The blue topaz necklace dislodged and landed on the carpet an arm's reach away.

The blue gem inside started to glow.

She recognized that light.

She looked up at the Hellens, and in the new blue light their appearance changed. The withering, gaunt appearance of the shape-shifting creature she had seen at the science lab now replaced both of her foster parents. Tattered peels clung to them like soiled remnants of broken straitjackets.

They stepped into the room toward her.

The light grew brighter with their approach.

The creatures raised emaciated arms to shield their eyeless faces from the light.

Charley looked back at the necklace and grabbed it.

It was hot to the touch and burned inside her hand. She reflexively threw it and it landed at the feet of the approaching creatures.

The topaz gem exploded into a torrent of blue light. Flames ruptured out of the necklace and the entryway burned with peals of blue fire licking upward, a sudden impassable barricade. Charley crawled backward.

She barely felt any heat from the large, violent flames that stretched to the ceiling. The fire raged, as if a bottle of lighter fluid exploded from the piece of jewelry.

Wails of frustration echoed from the other side of the blue fire. The creatures swatted at the flames with claw-like hands in futility. The fire singed the ends of their hanging peels, and the creatures moaned in gruesome cries.

Charley clambered back to her feet. The strange fire gave her a moment of relief. She looked around.

The knotted pull-cord dangled from the attic door in the corner of the room.

She had no other option.

She ran to the corner and yanked down on the cord. The wooden panel levered open. A rickety ladder descended from the opening that betrayed its old age. Charley climbed up the precarious ladder as fast as the aging wooden steps allowed her.

"You can't escape!" The creature's cry echoed through the room.

Charley yanked up on the ladder, and the access panel closed, sealing her inside.

She had never been in the attic before. The room swam in darkness. She had no idea what else could be inside.

Her hands fumbled for a light switch. Her fingers found a rafter, and she felt an electrical socket with a light bulb. She tugged on its thin rope and the light turned on.

The attic was small and confining. Wooden rafters and columns of insulation muted the sound beneath her. A few heavy boxes stood next to the closed-up entrance. Charley shoved the boxes over the entrance. She had no other way to barricade herself inside.

It was a terrible idea to go into the attic. She knew it. But what else could she do? Stay in the room and watch those things try to assail her?

Her mind reeled. She second-guessed. If they could rip through walls just to grab phone wires, what prevented them from tearing through the ceiling to get to her?

This was a bad idea. But she couldn't go back down there either. The anxiety strangled her, choked her neck like a leather belt. She whimpered and stared at the meager barricade of boxes.

She waited.

Darkness was coming to claim her, just on the other side of those boxes.

How was she going to get out?

She hadn't figured that out yet.

CHAPTER 40

*B*ang.

The sounded reverberated the frame of the Hellens' house.

A second bang. Then a third one, louder, closer.

Charley didn't move.

"Charley!"

The voice was familiar.

"It's me, Thom!"

"Mr. Murphy!" She felt herself breathe again. The feeling of the belt around her neck loosened.

"Where are you?"

"I'm in the attic."

She walked toward the stack of boxes and moved the first one to the side. She nearly had the second one moved when she thought of it.

Shape-shifters.

"No!" she screamed and shot back. She stumbled over the joists of the floor and fell onto a piece of plywood. "No!" she screamed again at the attic door, even louder, the cramped-attic echoing painfully in her ears. "Not again! You will not trick me!"

Another bang. The boxes burst apart under a blast of blue light. It ripped open the attic entrance. Papers with cardboard fragments flew everywhere.

Charley stood up. She inched closer to the gaping hole that had replaced the wooden panel. She peered over the edge.

Thom Murphy stood with his pistols out.

"How do I know you're not one of them?" Charley asked.

Thom pointed the pistol toward two piles of ash just outside her bedroom. The blue fire was gone. So was the necklace.

"It's me," Thom said. "Do you think you can let yourself down?"

Charley leaned over the edge and studied the piles of ash. She dropped her legs down and jumped.

"Charley, when I got here, there was a blue fire at your bedroom door. How did it get here?" He sounded surprised.

"I don't know. Rachel's necklace fell to the ground and it just burst into flames."

Thom squinted his eyes. "The flames disappeared as soon as I shot those two."

He bent down and ran his hand over the carpet.

Charley bent down also. There was no sign of fire, or charred carpet, or anything. Including the necklace. The only thing on the carpet was Charley's pink glasses that had fallen out of her backpack. They looked like they had been burned by the fire, with bluish streaks across the lenses. She snagged them and put them in her pocket.

Thom ran out the front door with pistols out and Charley followed him.

She didn't want to be alone anymore.

CHAPTER 41

Henry slouched in the truck so he couldn't be seen from the outside. He had moved to the back seat—more room to hide. He wrung his hands together with nervous agitation. He crept up and ventured a glance toward the house.

Thom had said Henry would be safe in the truck.

He didn't feel safe.

His dad was inside the house, rescuing Charley.

He was inside the truck, cowering in fear.

He hated that.

He wanted to do something to help.

He wanted more to do nothing and just run away.

The conviction of his cowardice stung and made him feel worse. It accused him.

And his mother was still missing.

That was the part that bothered him the most. Instead of going to find his mother and protect their family, they were spinning their time away here. They needed to get going! He couldn't imagine a world without his mother.

The bleak insanity of the night bathed his mind.

Pulling Charley into this situation had turned out to be a mess. She had led them right into a hotbed of whatever those things were, and now the car sat idling in her driveway. He regretted even going to the library. Everything was a lot more complicated with her involved. He and his dad didn't have time to just—

The truck's doors ripped open and Henry leapt in fear. Thom and Charley jumped into the truck, Charley going to the backseat.

She jumped also, seeing Henry lying on the floor of the truck. "Are you okay?" she said, slamming the door closed.

Henry got up silently and buckled his seatbelt. He couldn't admit how terrified he felt.

The truck roared out of the driveway.

"So, how do we get a hold of Mom?" Henry asked.

"We don't," Thom said. "Tomorrow night we will meet up. It's been arranged ahead of time—what to do if this happened."

"But Mom will be in trouble by herself!"

"Ha!" Thom sounded amused. "Your mother can take care of herself. I'd be more concerned about the three of us than her." Thom let out a sigh. "They'll try to follow us but without the tracker in the watch, it will be a lot harder. We need to stay on the move."

Quietness ensued.

Charley gazed out the window, periodically trembling. She was deeply rattled.

With Thom's arrival, Henry felt some stress pour out of him and onto the shoulders of his father. He was happy to have his father in this uncharted debacle. But Charley . . . Charley had no one. An absent look hung on her face. She had retreated to an inner sanctum of seclusion and rumination, a dark abode where dark thoughts come and go at their leisure.

The bleak insanity of the night had captured her, too.

CHAPTER 42

C harley finally spoke. It was a mousey voice, defeated and frightened. It squeaked from the back seat.

"What . . . what were those things?"

Thom drew a breath through his nostrils and exhaled. He looked in the rearview mirror.

"They are called the Nekura." He frowned as he said it and nearly spat. "The name is Japanese in origin. It means 'dark-natured.' It's the only name I have ever heard them called."

The name tingled in Henry's ears and made his brow sweat. To hear their name was to validate all the uncanny events as real and not just a maniacal dream. The dark creatures, the oppression, the fear—it was all real.

Thom continued. "I'm glad you turned on the nightlight, Henry."

"Then you know about the blue creature from the nightlight?"

"Yes. The watch, the nightlight—they were failsafes."

He heard it then, the soft whimpering from Charley. It was bitter, lonesome weeping. She leaned against the window and held her lacerated side. Henry reached out to touch her arm but she pulled away harshly.

The heavy atmosphere of the inside of the truck breathed sleepiness over them as Thom drove down random streets. Charley cried herself to sleep.

Henry toiled through nagging thoughts of Nekura chasing him, asking himself why, to no avail. A fractured sleep came upon him, one that swept him away from consciousness but refused to let him rest.

CHAPTER 43

Henry snapped awake when Thom hit the brakes. He was still on edge. Residual adrenaline clung to the inside of his veins. Thom pressed the brake pedal but the truck barreled forward in momentum. Henry looked out the front window.

An unmoving black object stood ahead in their highway lane. A solitary, black monolith.

Henry leapt up from the seat and pointed. "That's it! That's the black rock creature from my bedroom!"

The creature held out its arms. It looked like it was going to catch the truck with its bare hands.

Thom lifted his foot from the brake and hit the accelerator. He threw the steering wheel and the truck swerved to the side. The back end of the truck fishtailed wildly. Thom dropped the transmission into neutral and yanked hard again on the wheel. The truck spun around one hundred eighty degrees, and started going in reverse through the oncoming lane. The truck flew backward toward the creature.

The stunt surprised the creature. It was too slow to move over to the other lane and catch the careening vehicle. Henry realized the point of the daredevil move—the truck would rocket past the creature in the other lane, and it placed the gun-wielding driver immediately next to the monster.

The scene unfolded in slow-motion. Thom kept one hand on the wheel and grabbed the large percussion pistol in the other. He only had one shot.

A massive discharge of blue light erupted from the end of the gun and rocketed through the air.

The shot was off target.

It caught the upper right torso of the beast, splitting its shoulder and rending the arm halfway from the chest. The arm slumped partway, but the monster was unfazed. The car sped by and the monster began to chase them, using its half-dangling arm like a grotesque pole vault. It worked with its new incapacitation, leaping forward in bounds.

"Hang on," Thom said and flung the steering wheel again, working the floorboard pedals in unison. The truck went into another skid and then back out of it, going forward. The wheels caught the pavement again and Thom dropped the transmission back into drive and hit the accelerator. He looked in his rearview mirror.

"I only wounded it," Thom said. "It will come after us even though it's maimed."

"Dad, that was it. That was the thing in my room." Henry turned around to look out the rearview window. "So that's a Nekura?"

"It's called a Bludgeon," Thom said. "Yes, it's one of the Nekura."

"A Bludgeon?"

"Yes."

"Why didn't you run it over?" Charley asked. She had awoken with the swerving.

"You can't."

"Why not?" She sounded indignant.

"Because you can't. There not vulnerable to attacks with physical weapons."

Henry looked at the pistol lying in the front seat. "Then what is that?" he said, pointing.

"Later," his father said.

Charley leaned over and whispered to Henry. "That was the monster in your bedroom? It looks too big to have fit in your room!"

"It didn't."

"We need to get off the roads," Thom said. "We've shaken most of the Nekura with the tracker disabled."

CHAPTER 44

Thirty minutes later, Thom pulled into a shabby hotel's parking lot beyond the city limits of Middleton.

Henry got out of the car, exhausted and with frayed nerves, and walked into the hotel.

In the lobby, a fancy chandelier hung from the ceiling and wood paneling with ornate carvings and trim decorated the walls. The floor had circular tile in the center beneath the chandelier and resembled a ballroom. It didn't appear as shabby on the inside.

Thom approached the desk.

"One room for the night, please. Two queens. We'll pay in cash."

The concierge behind the desk took the payment and gave them the room keys. They went to the elevator and pressed the button. The elevator dinged at the second floor.

Any niceties of the hotel were left in the lobby. The hallway to their room showed old stained carpeting with drab paint that was a dingy, parchment white. The sign for the elevator was caved in, the remains of someone putting a fist into it. Thom was unfazed by the dilapidated appearance and went to their room.

The room was also worn and weary. The same old carpeting continued into the room and the air conditioning unit was loud and obnoxious. Wallpaper edges curled on the wall and the bed linens were frayed. A funny smell of bleach and mildew permeated the room. Thom walked in and threw his keys onto the television stand.

"Charley, listen—Henry and I will take the bed closest to the door. You take that one." He waited until she acknowledged him, and then he looked at Henry also. "I'll stay up so you two can get some rest."

He went to Henry and pulled him close. Henry smelled Thom's cologne, and the soothing familiarity of it calmed his anxiety. "I'm glad you're alright," Thom said. "Good thing you listened to your father about the watch and nightlight."

He walked over to Charley. She sat on her bed and wore a frown. She looked away to a random object in the corner of the room. He crouched down to meet her at eye level.

Henry recognized the posture, the tone. As Thom's son, he had been on the receiving end many times before.

"Hey, Charley, you're not alone in this. I don't know what has happened to Mr. and Mrs. Hellen. You might think you're in free fall right now, but I promise I'll get you through this. And I don't make promises lightly."

His words sunk home. She broke gaze from the random object and looked at him. She nodded.

"Now let me have a look at your side."

The cut was long but mostly superficial, coursing its way up from her waist all the way to her shoulder blade. Thom found some first-aid supplies buried in the top of the closet and cleaned the wound with some rubbing alcohol. She winced, but allowed him to continue.

"It will heal. It's not deep into the dermis. It will take a few weeks." He turned back to Henry. "Sleep for now. Tomorrow morning I'll tell you everything. And if this hole-in-the-wall of a hotel has room service, then we'll have breakfast in bed," he said with a smile.

Henry nodded in agreement. It was a tiny spark of something pleasant in an otherwise dreadful night.

With Thom as a sentry, Henry indulged in the moments of safety. Thom sat in a chair by the television stand, leg up on a table and holding his pistol, lost in thought. Charley fell asleep in minutes, breathing rhythmically. Henry drifted to sleep, only after his mind had tumbled with the thought that his father was much different than he knew.

CHAPTER 45

Henry awoke the next morning and saw Thom leafing through a folder.

"I can't believe it," Thom said. "This shabby hotel actually has room service." He tossed the menu on the bed and Henry looked it over. It wasn't grand but it was more than he anticipated.

Charley stirred and Henry walked over to her.

"Hey," he said. He sat on the edge of her bed. "How are you feeling?"

She grimaced some and sat up. "A little better." Henry handed her the menu and she looked it over. Thom called to the hotel concierge and placed their order.

They had slept through the rest of the night. Right now, they were safe. Henry didn't want to go anywhere else. He would stay here and eat room service for the rest of his life.

Thom turned his chair around to face the bed. "Thanks for your patience with me," he said, "but I think everyone needed the rest."

He sighed and paused.

"Have you read Descartes in school?" Thom asked.

"Yes," Charley said.

"Who?" Henry asked.

"He was a French philosopher," Charley said. She shot a look of frustration at Henry. "If you hadn't been so concerned with—"

"Okay, okay," Thom said and put his hands out to try to calm the situation. "It's called methodological doubt. Descartes came up with it. He wanted to prove what was true around him. What was really real. So he doubted everything—everything he saw, smelled, touched. He wanted to make sure it wasn't all illusion. So to be sure, he took a final position—he would consider that an evil entity was actively trying to deceive him. To trick him into believing something else."

Henry nodded. It sounded familiar.

"What if . . ." Thom paused and looked at each of them, "Descartes was right?"

CHAPTER 46

"The Nekura have been around for as long as anyone knows," Thom said. "When they came into control of our old world, it began to die. I don't want to talk about them too much. To talk about them is to validate them. To give them a corner of attention. The story that you need to hear—the real story—is the one of the Salients, the children of the Celestials.

"The Salients are a special breed, of rare lineage," Thom said. He continued with slow cadence. "The Salients were commissioned to be stewards of the Light. Henry, your mother is one of them."

Henry didn't know what his dad just said. It sounded unbelievable. "Mom is a Salient," he said. He felt like a dimwitted parrot, repeating the statement in disbelief. "How do I not know this?"

"Well," Thom said, "it's because of something your mother did."

Thom stood up and took off his long black coat, which he had worn through the night. He said no more. Charley took advantage of the quiet moment and slipped into the bathroom.

Thom unzipped his sweater and lifted off his shirt. Charley walked out of the bathroom and looked away nervously.

"It's alright, Charley," he said. "I should have warned you."

Henry had seen his father with his shirt off plenty of times before—at the beach, changing from a basketball game, running out of the bedroom half-dressed to get food on the mornings he overslept—but he never saw him like this before. Long curving lines draped around Thom's neck and came down his shoulders like decorative bands with detailed markings, wrapping around each arm like a constricting snake. The markings came down in the center of his chest to end in a small circular pendant.

Henry touched the area on Thom's arm where the corded line wrapped around it. The markings were more in his skin than on it, tattooed beneath his finger's touch. The lines were a translucent blue that ebbed and flowed, like gentle water rolling in channels that cascaded down Thom's arms from his torso.

"Whoa," Henry said. "How did you get this?"

"This," Thom said, pointing at the inscribed pendant in the center of his chest, "is from your mother. It was her gift to me on the day we married." He touched the center of his chest as he said it. "My heritage is . . . not Salient. This gift is the spark of the Salient. Your mother gave up her heritage to be with me." He said it in an awed tone. He looked up. "She can never return to her true Salient form without this. Now that I have it, I will also always be something else." He smiled and pulled his shirt back over his head.

The romantic tale sparked Charley to life again. "Wow, this is so . . . crazy! So, what about Mrs. Murphy?"

"She leads her life as a regular human, although her true Salient blood is still noticeable. Her hair is a dead giveaway with the silver in it."

"Her hair?" Henry was confused. "I thought Mom went prematurely gray."

"What?" Thom sounded appalled. "Prematurely gray? Ha! No way." He shook his head and snorted. "There is a big difference between gray hair and silver hair. Most people in the world have gray hair, but silver strands are the mark of a true Salient. Look for it and you will notice it. It is the lifeblood of the Salient begging to break out. Your mother certainly does not have gray hair."

Henry was checked by the difference. He had always figured his mom was just unfortunate to have gray hair, but Thom was resolved that it was the manifestation of hidden prestige. "Silver hair," he said under his breath.

There was a knock at the door and everyone startled. Tension surged in the room. Thom grabbed his percussion pistol but stayed poised. He reached out his hand, fingers extended, coaxing them to be calm.

"It's okay," he said, "it's probably just breakfast."

He got up and walked over to the door. He kept one hand on the pistol cradled in the small of his back.

He opened the door.

A smiling male hotel attendant stood at the door holding a large tray of food with several plates covered by silver dish toppers. The attendant was young and probably only a shade older than Henry.

"Room service," the attendant said.

Thom broadened a smile and grabbed the tray. He thanked the attendant and closed the door.

Small victories.

CHAPTER 47

"But what about that blue thing from the nightlight?" Henry shoved his mouth full of cafeteria-grade scrambled eggs. "Did you put it there?"

Thom leaned back in his seat and felt the uncomfortable pistol in his back. He set it on the table next to the other one and nodded. "Ever since your mother gave me the Salient's spark I've had this new, strange connection. I've been able to make those pistols and even invented the nightlight."

"You made that creature?"

"Ha, no," Thom said. "I made the nightlight, not what came out of it."

"What was that thing?"

"Probably the closest way I can describe him is a guard dog. The nightlight was set to activate if Nekura came into your room. I placed him there to protect you. It was the reason we turned your nightlight on every night when you went to bed."

"But the Bludgeon got away! That means that the blue creature . . ."

"Don't worry about Phred," Thom said with a smile, "he'll be fine. He can retreat into the nightlight if he needs to. It's kind of like his dog-house."

Charley ate her fruit cocktail of cantaloupe and strawberries, listening until now. "You're saying Henry has an otherworldly guard dog named Phred that lives in the nightlight of his room?"

"Pretty much," Thom said.

She shook her head and took another bite. She looked down. "I wish I had something like that."

Henry sat in silence and picked at his food. The answers only led to more questions. Why did he have a guard dog made of blue light in his room for years without his parents ever mentioning it? Why did his mother have a secret origin that he didn't know about? Why were the Nekura after them now? Henry's mind rolled through the questions. He kept orbiting around one thing.

"Dad," Henry said, "why didn't you tell me any of this?" He looked at his father dead in the face. He felt betrayed—first it was Charley, now his own father. Betrayed by the secret agenda of keeping quiet something so monumental and dangerous. That betrayal nearly killed him! The tears welled up in his eyes. "Don't you trust me enough to tell me?"

Thom hung his head and grimaced. He took a moment before he spoke.

"Henry, I love you. And I trust you. It wasn't that at all. It's just . . ." He sighed. "We hid from them. But in our hiding, we allowed ourselves to forget. We became too comfortable."

Thom stopped and sat in pained silence.

Henry expected more, needed more. That didn't sound like a good justification.

"How could you forget something like that? You have a blue living tattoo on your body! There's a blue guard dog in my nightlight! There are dark creatures that—"

"I know!" Thom yelled and stood up, his voice strained, "I know! Believe me, I know. I can't believe it either." He buried his head in his hands. Hair stuck through his clenched fingers. "We were carried away by parties and traveling baseball teams and oil changes and paying the mortgage. Our vigil just became less of a priority, little by little, day by day, until it faded out of consciousness. The important bowed down before the immediate.

"Cell phone not working? Have to get it fixed today. Kitchen sink is broken and it needs to be repaired now. Urgent emails and twenty-four-hour sales and expensive hobbies and movies at the theater. And you know what? It all fooled me. I thought I wanted it, needed it, for me to be whole. I had to be able to talk about cars with the mechanics and guns with the shooting club. I had to know who the best players were for any sport, and then I had to know who the best players were going to be. The newest, the latest, the most up and coming! I was pulled away and lost in a whirlwind of insignificance."

Thom stopped and sat down. His muscles went lax.

"The more I lived for myself, the less I had of myself. I just forgot. That's what people tend to do. It's our nature. Marriages end in divorce because people forget the love that bound them to each other. Friendships are lost because people move on with their lives and forget all the memories of those good friends. Love grows cold and people grow faint at the bewitching of time."

Thom paused again, then looked back up to Henry's face. "I'm sorry. I forgot. I forgot it all. That's why you never saw the pendant on me before. It faded away."

It was a moment of transparency that Henry had not seen before. His father was usually decisive and strong. He was jovial and humorous. But this . . . this was a side of him that Henry had not seen—a raw, abraded man, filled with regret over his sweeping failure.

Thom spoke again. "But when everything started—the nightlight, the tracker in the watch, and everything with Rachel—I began to remember. You helped me to break free."

Henry nodded and felt like he understood, partly if not all the way. In Henry's mind, he pictured a rusty key in an ancient door lock that finally moved enough to release the door's latch, breaking open to an old musty room filled with memories long forgotten and stowed away in disregarded corners of the mind.

"But now," Thom said, "I know that there are pieces missing. I remember some, but not all. What scares me most is that now I know that I don't know. Like why we were hiding in the first place."

Charley got up and walked over to the miniature coffee maker in the room. "I need an extra cup after all this," she said. She looked around, but there were no coffee grounds. "I can't believe it! They have a coffee maker but no coffee? This is a crummy hotel and I don't think I'll ever stay here again." Henry smiled and nodded. The lighthearted moment was needed after the heavy heart-rending. For a moment, life felt livable.

The door knocked again.

"Coffee refills." It was the voice of the hotel attendant that had brought them room service.

Charley let out a sigh of relief. "Well at least the attendant is back. And perfect timing with the coffee!" She walked to the door.

The smiled wiped clean from Thom's face. "Charley, no! Don't open it!" It was too late.

CHAPTER 48

The Nekura lurched through the door and jumped in the air. It landed on top of Charley and knocked her to the floor.

Henry hadn't seen this kind of Nekura before—the one Charley had described from the science building. It was hideous with a bulbous head and oily, molting skin. His heart pounded in his chest, beating out of control. Fear immobilized him.

Charley screamed and thrashed, but it was like fighting the air. She couldn't make contact. When she did, she only grabbed the creature's peeling skin that came off in flakes.

The Nekura savored the moment. It indulged in Charley's overwhelming panic as she fought against it. The Nekura opened its mouth garishly wide, dislocating its jaw like a snake. The inside of its mouth was cavernous.

Charley hit critical mass. She tried to get up, to move, to do anything other than scream but she was completely impuissant.

The Nekura bent to bite.

The creature suddenly burst in a concussion of blue light above her, rupturing open with smoke and ash. The slick secretions of the Nekura coated her skin and the falling ash clung to her and stuck.

Thom stood in the back of the room holding the blunderbuss. The whole event took only a matter of seconds but that was nearly all the Nekura needed.

Charley lay on the ground and screamed. The Nekura was gone now, and she thrashed freely. Fear had given way to protest.

Henry rushed over to her. She lay on her back, kicking and punching the air wildly.

She looked like she had been tarred and feathered by the darkness.

"Charley, it's okay, it's gone," he tried to soothe.

She refused to stop. She took a large breath and screamed again.

Thom frowned at the back of the room. He tucked the pistol in the small of his back and reached for his sweater. He put it on as he shook his head.

"Filthy Shades," he said. Disgust filled his voice. He zipped up his sweater.

Henry looked back at him. "Shades?"

"They're shape-shifters. Deceivers. They're some of the most difficult to deal with."

The thought settled in Henry's mind. Shades. Shape-shifters. The Blue Vest at school, at the science lab—it was the same one. Or was it?

Thom walked over to Charley and knelt.

"Charley. Hey . . . hey . . . hey," he said, drawing out each word. He placed his hands on her wild arms. "It's gone. You're alright. Try to calm yourself." He reassured her to the point that she stopped screaming. She put her arms down to her sides. She stared at the ceiling, transfixed. Suddenly, she got up without saying a word and stormed into the small bathroom and slammed the door.

The shower turned on.

Thom sat down in the chair again by the doorway. "I shouldn't have spoken so freely about all of it," he said. "Not here at least. Even the walls have ears."

They sat and waited while listening to the rhythmic fall of the shower.

After five minutes, Thom got up and spoke through the door of the bathroom. "Charley, we have to get going."

Agitated, her voice came back through the door. "I can't get this oil off my skin!"

He sat back down.

Ten minutes.

"Charley, we need to go!" Thom called through the door. She didn't bother to respond.

Fifteen minutes.

Thom got up and walked to the door. He opened it without knocking. He reached his arm into the shower and turned off the water.

"Hey!" she cried.

Taking care not to betray her modesty, he reached out and grabbed the edges of the shower curtain. With a step forward, he wrapped the edges around Charley like the curtain was a giant blanket. Thom tugged on the curtain and it ripped down from the shower rings. With Charley wrapped up in the curtain, he picked her up and lifted her out of the shower.

"What are you doing?" she yelled.

He set her down in the center of the bathroom.

"I told you I don't make promises lightly. We have to leave. Now!" Thom reached back and grabbed a couple towels and shoved them at her chest, and she grabbed them through the shower curtain. "For your safety—for all of us—we need to leave. They know where we are and this is not a safe place. They will come after us. We leave now."

"But I can't get this oil off! I don't have any clothes! And I—"

It was going nowhere. She was trying to scrub away the indelible imprint on her soul rather than the oil on her skin.

Thom threw on his coat and grabbed his other pistol. He took a small wad of cash out of his wallet and threw it on the table. Then he walked back to Charley and scooped her up in his arms, still wrapped in the shower curtain like a cocoon.

They sped out of the room and down the hall to the stairwell. They descended the stairs and with a quick glance around, they hurried to the truck. Thom lifted Charley and placed her inside. She sat in the backseat of the truck in her shower-curtain swaddle, hair sopping wet, colicky as a newborn baby.

CHAPTER 49

Thom drove down the road a few miles and stopped at the first megastore they saw. Mid-Mart, a local chain store burgeoning in Middleton and its suburbs, was busy.

He left the car running while he ran inside. Henry remained quiet while Charley sulked. Thom came back within a few minutes with a bag.

"Charley," Thom said, "I'm sorry that I needed to pull you out like that. I'm sure it was . . ." He stopped when he saw her glare. "Just—I'm sorry. But here, these are for you."

He handed her a bag of newly purchased clothes.

"You can go inside and get anything else," Thom said.

Henry walked away from the truck with Thom while she changed. In a couple minutes she emerged, dressed in her new clothes. "Thanks," she murmured.

"You get five minutes," Thom said to Henry and Charley, "then we're gone."

They went into Mid-Mart, glancing around in suspicion every few seconds.

Henry had never been so happy to buy shoes. He wasn't even sure that he was allowed in the store wearing only socks. He grabbed a shirt and a jacket to replace his grubby baseball jersey while Charley grabbed another change of clothes. They hurried through the checkout. Henry and Thom began loading the truck.

"Hey," Thom said, "where's Charley?"

"I don't know, she was just here."

Henry looked around. Charley walked out of the store a moment later. She held an oversized coffee cup in one hand and a king-sized candy bar in the other.

What was she doing? She was jeopardizing everything for coffee and—

Thom reached out his hand over Henry's chest, as if intercepting his thoughts. "I wouldn't," he said. Thom looked back at her and chuckled. "Let her be."

They set back out on the road.

"We're heading toward our safe house," Thom said.

Thom drove the car northward without stopping. The mindless hum of the engine and the gentle rumble of the road made good fodder for mind numbing.

Thom exited the highway and got onto the side roads. The landscape changed from the sprawling suburbia of Middleton to dense forest. Rolling hills with large deciduous trees decorated the landscape for miles. As they rolled along, the amenities became less noticeable. A few meager restaurants and even more meager gas stations with dilapidated signs decorated the landscape.

The area felt abandoned. They drove away from the Nekura, but they also drove into the wild unknown.

"Dad, where are we?" Henry asked.

"It's Brainerd County. It's mostly unincorporated. We're several hours north of Middleton here in the woods. We've got one hundred twenty acres, too. I haven't been here in ages." After a pause, Thom continued. "The cabin has been imbued with light, similar to Henry's nightlight. It will be a safe haven . . ."

Thom paused mid-sentence and considered what he just said.

"At least from what I remember. I wish I could remember more."

It was the end of the afternoon and the sun dipped low in the sky. The high ridgeline of the forest canopy met the sun quicker than in the city and cast long shadows on innumerable unmarked back roads.

Henry rolled down his window and smelled the air. The clean air smelled great in his nostrils. It was crisp and cool here, further north— uncomfortably cool for this time of the year. He rolled up his window again.

Thom pulled the large truck into a winding gravel driveway that bore no markings. The long, lonely driveway ended at a cabin.

CHAPTER 50

The cabin was old and ominous. It felt strange to Henry to have a small house in the center of forsaken woods. A large stone-worked chimney rose from the center of the roof.

"Is Mom here yet?"

"No, I don't think so. I don't see her car here."

Thom led them up the stairs to the front door in the center of the house. From there, the stairs became an elevated walkway, adjoining the house to a patio, with sliding glass doors on the left.

Thom spun the key in the lock and opened the door. He turned on the light switch and the dim furnishings came to life under the light. A large fireplace stood in front of them and the floor was made of beautiful, rustic maple planks. A balcony from the upper level overlooked the main area, with vaulted ceilings displaying the height of the fireplace.

"There are two bedrooms upstairs," Thom said. "The main level has the master bedroom and a couple other rooms."

Charley ascended the stairs to explore the bedrooms.

Thom looked at Henry. "I need your help."

"With what?"

"I got a few groceries from the store. Can you grab them from the truck?"

Henry walked outside to the truck. Periodic gusts bent the trees and rustled their leaves like bursts of anger from the wind. It felt like the forest was protesting their presence.

As Henry walked toward the truck, he heard a voice call from over his shoulder. "Hi, honey."

Henry whirled around.

His mother stood by the side of the house.

"Mom!" Relief flooded him. The crushing weight of worry and dread lifted from his chest. "You're here!"

He hadn't seen her car or even heard her come up.

"Yes! I just couldn't get in, I didn't have a key. I was waiting for you!"

He started to jog toward her.

She reached out her arms and smiled.

A thunderous boom echoed through the quiet forest, assaulting the evening.

Then she screamed. A loud, piercing scream.

Henry leapt back.

She doubled over, holding her stomach.

She collapsed to her knees.

"Mom!" Henry cried

"Henry . . . I can't breathe . . ."

She spluttered on her words.

She was dying.

CHAPTER 51

"Help me . . ." Henry's mother said.

She was turning gray.

Henry bolted forward. He couldn't have come this far, hoping to be reunited, only to watch his mother die in front of him.

"No! Don't touch her!" another voice said. A woman's voice.

The new voice came from around the corner of the cabin, hidden among the heavy shadows. The muzzle of a black shotgun emerged first, locked on to Henry's mother, still kneeling on the ground in pain. The fading sunlight glinted off the polished barrel. The gun-wielder walked out with careful steps.

She was also Henry's mother.

He was seeing double.

"Just stay there, Henry," said the one holding the gun.

Dawn held the shotgun and pointed it at the other Dawn, still clutching her stomach. Faint threads of black smoke billowed from under her arms. When she pulled her hands away, blue light chewed away her abdomen, and chunks of ash fell to the ground. She continued graying until the form of a Shade appeared in her place.

The Shade shrieked and dove forward at Henry.

Dawn leveled the shotgun at them both.

She was going to shoot him with the Shade!

Henry closed his eyes. His hands flew over his body in defense.

The sound was like a cannon. He felt the warmth of the scattershot on his skin.

But there was no excoriating pain. He cracked his eye open. There was no Nekura either. He looked down at himself. Nothing looked different. He felt for wounds, but there were none.

The explosion of light hadn't harmed him.

He looked up. Dawn smiled and lowered the shotgun.

Henry ran into her arms and squeezed her tight.

"Good to see you, too," she said. "Come on, we should get inside."

His heart ached for her. Even though he saw the false persona of Dawn turn back into a Shade, seeing the image of his mother in such awful pain had been unspeakable torment. He watched her die! He couldn't get the image out of his mind. It indelibly stained his soul.

"Mom, I can't ever lose you. That Shade . . . it just seemed so real."

"It wasn't me," she said, and she ran her fingers through his crop of auburn hair. Her gentle touch soothed him. "I'm here. You know, that Shade told you the truth. It couldn't get in, it didn't have a key, and it was waiting for you. It's strange—spilled from their mouths, even the truth can be used for deception."

She pulled back to arms' length to look at him.

"It's just a good thing I was waiting for you, too. I saw that Shade crawl out of the covered bed of your dad's truck right after you arrived. That was the only one. With it gone, our safe house should still be safe."

Henry nodded. Dawn ushered him back toward the front door.

It was good she was a Salient.

Whatever that meant.

CHAPTER 52

"You've lost your edge, babe," Dawn said.

"What?" Thom turned around from where he stood in the kitchen and saw Dawn and Henry walk in the door. "Dawn! Good, you're here."

"Yeah, it is good. A Shade lifted up the bed cover on your truck and popped out."

"A Shade? Out of my truck?"

"Did a pretty terrible impression of me, too."

Thom glanced at Henry. "Are you alright?"

Henry nodded.

Dawn embraced Thom and her face fell. "I can't believe this is happening."

"Me either," Thom said.

"What are we going to do?"

"I don't know. One step at a time. Let's start with dinner."

Twenty minutes later, they sat around a microwaved dinner at the small kitchen table.

"Hopefully, that's the last Nekura for a little bit," Dawn said. "I think we could use the breathing room." She passed a hot container of instant mashed potatoes to Charley.

"I'm glad you're with us, Charley. We wouldn't want you anywhere else."

Charley bit her lip and tried to smile. It looked painful.

Henry harrumphed. He wasn't so sure he was glad about it. He wanted his mother's attention. Time for an intercept.

"Mom, since when do you carry a shotgun?" he said with a wry smile and a mouth filled with mashed potatoes.

She smiled and reached for her cup of coffee. The smile failed. Her eyes flittered quickly, batting away tears, and she looked at Thom. He frowned and nodded his head in somber reflection.

"It's a long story," she said, "but it involves change." She sighed and looked out the windows, mind going to another place. "The strongest, most jagged rocks become smooth and compliant stones with time. Nothing is immune to change. But we can work with it, and I chose to change for your father." She reached out and squeezed Thom's hand.

"You were a Salient," Henry said.

"Yes. Was." Her tone changed, and tears flooded her eyes again. "But time fooled me. When I gave my spark to your father, I thought it was happily ever after. But the breakers of time continued to wash over me and I changed more, further and further away from who I had been."

Dawn's voice rose. "I didn't throw away who I was. But I no longer felt the height of it. When something is out of sight, you have to commit to remember or else it's out of mind also. The Light, our heritage, our mission—it became old history, and it tarnished. The modern—that's what is traded in the marketplace of relevancy. Every news channel flashes their breaking news. It is the currency of the day. Nobody wants old history."

Dawn wiped tears away with her hand and her mascara streaked. She pushed her coffee cup away. "Soon, without even realizing, I was swept away. I needed to be modern, too! What was important was replaced by what was new. But then that became old, and I needed something else new. I could never really capture 'new.' It always deceived me. And that's how change shackled me—it bound me when I didn't know I had provided the chains."

Her countenance was downcast. Thom had burst out in frustration in the hotel room, but Dawn let the words slip out in melancholy. They were her confession.

"That's what happens," she said. She sniffed and couldn't look at Henry. "People change and people forget—even the most important things."

"But what about the Nekura?" Charley said. "Isn't it their fault? Didn't they deceive you?"

"Yes, but deception and forgetting are two sides of the same coin. As much as the Nekura have exploited us, we allowed it. It's not that we let the Nekura get a foot in the door. It's more like we just left the door wide open and walked away. In a way, we invited them in."

The words hung in the air.

"Henry, that's what you really meant when you asked about the shotgun, right?" Dawn said.

Henry fidgeted in his chair.

"I'm so sorry, Henry," she said.

"I am, too," Thom added.

Nobody spoke.

CHAPTER 53

It was late, but the lamp in Henry's room was still on.

He sat on his bedside, mulling through thoughts. His mind tumbled with a mix of questions, speculations, and fear in a blend that would not allow him to sleep.

The door opened with a quiet knock.

Charley walked in. "Are you still awake?"

"Yeah. Couldn't sleep."

"It doesn't look like you're trying to sleep," she said.

"Oh, yeah." He adjusted, straightening upright.

"Can I come in?"

He waved her in and she sat down on the edge of the bed next to Henry. There was awkward silence.

"I think it's really great that your parents have this place," she said.

"Hm." The words stung. They reminded him that he hadn't known any of this alternate life that had been kept secret from him.

"I mean, they even have three bedrooms here! It's like they were expecting to have someone stay with them."

More silence.

"Look, Henry," she continued, "I really think I should . . . apologize. I've been a little, I guess . . . out of my element."

She hung her head.

The image of the wounded dove returned, the same way she had looked with Trevor. Her contrite posture softened Henry.

"It's alright, Charley," he said. "I bet it's not easy. I mean, I have my family right with me, but you . . ."

He paused. Any wrong words would make her spiral further down.

"Like you said, you're really out of your element."

It struck a chord. Just showing he was listening became balm for her. She quickly turned her face away, trying to wipe a tear from her eye.

"The craziness of the last twenty-four hours doesn't negate the girl you are. It was just the strange, frightening nature of the situation. You're still strong. I can see it."

She turned back to Henry and showed her tear-stained face. She looked down at the bed and then back at him.

"Thank you, Henry."

"For sure."

She got up and let herself out of the room.

It felt good to be civil again with her. After juggling all the emotions in the last few days, they enjoyed a conversation that didn't leave them embittered.

As she walked out, she looked stronger than when she had entered.

CHAPTER 54

"Good morning," Charley said.

Thom sat at the table, dressed and brooding. Henry and Charley walked downstairs and sat at the table with him.

"Oh, hi. Good morning. I didn't even hear you come down."

"You look lost in thought," Henry said and pulled a milk gallon from the refrigerator.

"I guess I am. I've been lost all morning."

Henry reached for the cereal box and grabbed a bowl from the cupboard. He searched through the drawers for a spoon.

"Where's Mom?"

As if on cue, the front door opened. Dawn walked in, shotgun in hand, and shut the door behind her.

Charley gasped.

Henry nearly dropped the milk on the floor. "What happened?" he said.

Dawn was covered in soot, with large smears from head to toe. She looked like she had just finished a day's job as a chimney sweep. She smelled of sulfurous smoke, and small plumes evanescently rose from her shirt into the air of the house. She brushed her sleeves off at the door.

"I need a shower."

She tossed her shotgun on the couch and walked into the bathroom.

Thom, Henry, and Charley dug into their breakfast. A while later, Dawn walked out, clean and drying her hair. She wore a change of clothes stashed away in a dresser from years ago.

She pulled up a chair.

"So much for secrets," Dawn said. "The Nekura are more aggressive and pursuant than ever. I've never seen them like this before. We need to figure out something. The protection of the safe house will only last so long." She reached for the bunch of bananas on the table.

"Really," Thom said. He gazed away, back into his reverie.

"They are after something," Dawn said.

Henry felt panic rise. He read between the lines. They are after something—or someone.

"Do you think they're after me?" Henry's mind flooded with dark thoughts.

"I'm not sure," Thom said. "I've been trying to figure it out all morning. Why now? And why is Charley involved? Even more—why is Rachel involved?"

Henry didn't feel any better.

"All these years of silence," Dawn said, "and it seems like now the Veil has been ripped wide open. The Nekura are more numerous and brazen than I have ever seen them here."

Thom stood up and went to the door next to the kitchen and opened it. Stairs descended.

"Then we need to do something," he said. "The watch, the night-light—I put failsafes in place. Maybe there's something more. Let's start by looking in the basement."

CHAPTER 55

A set of simple, roughed-in wooden stairs descended to a concrete floor. They went down in single file.

Thom flipped a light switch that lit up the basement. The space
was open with concrete walls and metal beams supporting the weight
of the upstairs. An old tube television sat in the corner like a relic, and
bookshelves were filled with various clutter. There were old metal desks
and a workshop in the corner, with fluorescent lighting suspended above
a wooden workbench. Various tools and bizarre gadgetry were strewn
on top of the bench.

"Look around," Thom said.

Henry walked around the basement and leafed through the various
piles of junk on the desks. Everything was a mess.

He walked over to the bookshelf and traced his finger on the ledge.
He thought about the large book he had found on the shelf back home,
hidden behind the edge of the bookcase. He had felt the book more than
he had seen it.

He wondered.

He ran his finger to the end of the shelf, the same way he had done before. Something was there, tucked away from sight. He paused and swallowed hard, then moved the other books out of the way.

A blue clamshell case of plastic peeked out from its hiding place. It looked like an old video-cassette case. Henry grabbed the case and pulled it out. He gasped when he read the label.

On the spine was a white peeling sticker with marker scrawled on it. It read: *The Forgotten*.

"Dad!"

Thom looked over. "What is it, Henry?"

"I found something."

Thom walked over to Henry and looked at the case. "You found this on the bookshelf?"

"Yep."

Thom raced over to the old television and threw aside piles of junk. Underneath a stack of magazines and a blanket of dust was a video-cassette player. He grabbed the video cassette and shoved it inside. The television flickered to life and a grainy image appeared on the screen.

"Thom," Dawn said, "do you recognize this video?"

"No, but I hope it will help us."

"I hope so," Henry said. "I'm waiting for someone to give us some answers."

An empty chair appeared on the television screen.

"Let's see what you've got to tell us," Thom said to the screen. A man walked into the picture and sat down in the chair.

It was Thom.

CHAPTER 56

Thom stared at the younger version of himself. He was strong and lean, only a few years older than Henry.

"It has only been a few months," young Thom said, "since we crossed the Veil. I'm recording this video as a safety precaution. I already feel my memory slipping. Things are less clear, becoming more nostalgia than the details themselves."

Silence hung in the room.

Young Thom smiled. "We fled from the other side of the Veil after I stole something from the Nekura on the day of Henry's birth. They found something, and if they got their hands on it, it would have been the end for all of us. I couldn't let that happen. They found the furnace."

"The furnace?" Henry asked the television screen.

Young Thom seemed to intercept the question. "Some said it was all Salient lore—a legend of a perpetually burning, self-existent source of the Light that swelled like a furnace's fire. But it's true. And when the Nekura found it, I took out the one person who knew about it."

Henry looked at his father. "Took out?"

Thom drew a large breath and said nothing. He stared at the screen.

"If the Nekura can deceive us now," young Thom said, "imagine how they could butcher our minds if they had a source of endless power. It would be slavery without a fight—the slaves would never know any better. How do you quell uprisings? By convincing the people that what they have is all there is. Take away their hope and their foresight for anything greater than what they already have. Life becomes only what they see. That's how power is consolidated forever—it is willingly given, and people become voluntary servants when their birthright should be freedom."

Young Thom frowned. "The Nekura would've chased us forever, so we had to disappear. We had to leave. After that, we—"

The screen glitched into obscurity and young Thom's voice distorted. The grainy screen lasted half a minute, then the picture came back. The setting was the same, but the Thom that walked onto the screen looked older, with a faint beard on his face. His brow was furrowed. He looked weary, like he had just finished a hard day of labor.

"I should have done this regularly," young Thom said, "and now there's so much more that I can't recall. I've been hesitant to record anything. It's another way the Nekura could find out about us. But the past is becoming more obscure, with holes I can't fill."

Young Thom stared into the camera, seemingly lost for what he was going to say. He shook his head. "I hid the information about the furnace in a place that the Nekura would never look. I had to make sure they would never find it. It had to be somewhere that could easily move, that I could always watch over. Something I could track, something I could set failsafes around."

Track. Failsafes. The words echoed in Henry's mind.

Young Thom stared at Henry's family from the other side of the screen. "I hid the secret of the furnace in—"

The screen scrambled again and young Thom's voice disappeared into analog chaos.

"Come on!" Thom said and hit the video player with his hand. "Not now!"

The screen settled, and the familiar setting of an empty chair appeared again. But the Thom that ran onto the screen had changed again. Longer hair, bedraggled and soiled in mud, he appeared frantic. He came in close to the camera and his face filled the whole screen.

"I can't remember. I can't remember!" He spoke in between broken, labored breaths. "The past is gone, it's all open to re-interpretation. I keep saying two words to myself, over and over. I can't them slip." He pressed the words out, like if he paused the words would be lost forever. "If all is lost, if we disappear into the Forgotten, these two words— furnace . . . and . . . and . . ." Young Thom searched for it, clawing to remember. He went into a distant stare, then his gaze snapped up and he grabbed the camera. The video camera shook as he shouted at them. "Henry! It's Henry!"

Then the screen went black.

Everyone turned in unison and looked at Henry. He stood under their heavy stares like a convicted man.

"Henry," Thom said, "you wanted to know who is going to give us the answers?"

Henry shifted on his feet.

Thom nodded. "You are."

CHAPTER 57

"Me?" Henry said. He panned across their faces. "But I don't know anything!"

It must be a mistake.

Thom's unbroken stare dug into Henry's core. "It's you, Henry. That's why you had the watch. It's why the nightlight was in your room, not ours."

"I only found out about the Nekura a few days ago. Now you're telling me that I know more than you?" Henry's arms were in the air and he was yelling.

"No," Thom said. "Not more. Only one thing."

"Which is?"

"How to find the furnace."

"I've never heard of any furnace."

"Henry," Thom said, "I hid the information in you. I implanted it in your memory by the power of the Light. Remember me saying I could do new things with the Salient's spark? Like I said in the video, I had to hide it somewhere the Nekura would never look."

"And that's inside me?"

Thom frowned. "Not under a rock. Not in a lockbox. Not buried in the ground. I thought they would never find it if I hid it inside a person. And especially a child—my own, that I could always watch. Who would think something so incredible was hidden inside a baby?"

"But," Charley said, "they did find out you hid it in a child." She put her hand to her head and staggered backward. She looked like she been punched in the stomach. Her mouth hung open, and the implications wormed their way into her psyche. "That's why they went after Rachel. And me."

The thought of the man with slicked-back hair passed through Henry's mind. The man had been looking for him also. The Nekura were after all of them.

After children.

"We can no longer run or hide to protect the furnace," Thom said. "We have to find it ourselves. So, Henry, what's our next move?"

Henry felt like screaming. He had no idea.

Then suddenly, he did.

Vague images and hazy words floated through his mind like the lyrics of a tune that he could never recall but somehow knew. He was drawn to something, a fraction of a memory hidden beneath baseball statistics, social media updates, and trigonometry equations. Like his dad looking for the video player, Henry threw the mental junk aside and dove behind the curtain of cobwebs.

One word surfaced.

"Book," Henry said, eyes wide, surprising himself. He dug further through the memories. "I remember a stanza, something about a fire."

Thom's mouth fell open. Silent gears spun in his mind. Dawn shook her head, like waking up from sleeping. "The book," she whispered.

"The history and lore of the Salients," Thom said.

"I found it on the shelf at home," Henry said, "hidden like the video was here."

"Henry," Dawn said, "where's the book now? Is it still at home?"

"No, I took it to school to read it. It's in my locker."

"Then we have to go get it," Thom said, "at once. What happened with Rachel means that the school has already been compromised." He glanced at the workbench in the corner and smiled. "And I just remembered something else."

CHAPTER 58

"The history of the Salients and the Nekura are recorded in the book," Thom said, "but it's not straightforward. It's written in legend and poem, but that doesn't make it any less true. It just makes it less blatant to the uninterested."

Thom walked up to one of the metal desks. "The Nekura are made up of animated smoke and ash, but their life is from the other side of the Veil. That's why there are piles of ash left when they are destroyed. However, because they are ash and smoke, they still must play by the physical rules of the world. Things like gravity. They can't pass through walls or anything. But here's where it gets dicey."

He made a fist and hit the top of the desk with a forceful wallop. The strike was unexpected and startled Henry. Thom swooped his arm off the desk and a great plume of dust came up.

"Go ahead, punch it."

No one moved. The dust tumbled in the air and danced beneath the speckling light.

"No, seriously, punch it! Or kick it. Or shoot it. Or cut it with a knife or run it over with a truck or smash it with a piano." Thom coughed with the amount of dust he stirred up. "You can't. That's the point—you can't kill smoke and ash. The Nekura can't be hurt with any physical attack. Charley, that's why you couldn't get the Shade off you in the hotel. I watched your arms pass right through the dark thing."

"But they can hurt us!" Charley said. "The Nekura knocked me over! How can they do that to us but we can't fight back?"

"But we can," Thom said, "and we do. The one thing we have—the most important difference—is that the Salients are the stewards of the Light."

"What is the Light?" Charley asked.

"It's that stuff that came out of your pistols and the shotgun, right, Dad?" Henry felt confident. His mom was a Salient.

"It's more than that," Dawn said. "Way more. The light from the guns is not just an ultraviolet light. No naturalistic law of this world can explain it."

"It is of different substance," Thom said, "than anything else in this world, just as much as the light of the stars is different than the light of that single household light bulb." He pointed at the solitary bulb of the stairwell. "It is more alive than a heartbeat, more tangible than the concrete we stand on, and more permeating than the sound of a thousand drums reverberating together in the ears and chest of the listener."

"Is this like a cosmic energy field?" Charley asked. "Something that weaves through all life and binds the whole universe together?"

"No," Dawn said, "it's not that. We don't make it and we are not a part of it. You see, the Light is much more penetrating than that. It is the reason for the animation of life, the song in the breast of the bird that bursts forth, the strength of the towering mountains, and the joy of an innocent child. But it is not all these things in summation—it is the cause of it all."

Henry didn't understand. They were beautiful words, but his analytical mind wished for numbers and formulas. This was abstract. He looked at Charley. She looked transfixed.

"It's difficult to compare it to anything because nothing is like it," Thom said. "But if you had to compare the Light to anything, it is more like a personhood, an identity beyond all the cosmos that yet somehow is inside the world and sustains it. It is because the Salients have been the bearers of the Light for this long that there is a special connection between the Light and them. With your mother's pendant, I was given a connection to the Light also, to help fight the Nekura."

Charley shuddered. "The Nekura . . . they're just plain evil," she said.

"Evil is a funny word," Thom said. "The Nekura don't love evil for the sake of being evil. No one is ever like that. Think about it—every crime, every disgraceful deed, every shocking act on the news—no one revels in the darkness for the sake of the darkness. No. There is a pleasure that is taken through those deeds. There is pleasure in power over others. Self-ishness, greed, indulgence—things are done for twisted pleasures. People kill because it puts them in power over another. People steal because it consolidates their power while mitigating someone else's.

"Evil, then, is a way of justification. It is a way to have power over the powerless without ever needing to defer to a greater purpose other than one's own lusts. The Nekura are evil for their own autonomy and justi-fication. They may do as they desire without any constraint to the Light or anyone else. Their power gives them meaning, their own twisted form of significance."

Henry scratched his head.

What was his dad talking about? He sounded like a philosophy pro-fessor. Henry wanted to elbow Charley to see if she understood any of it, but she was still rapt.

"Mr. Murphy, you sure know a lot about the Nekura," Charley said.

"Hm," he said, "I've spent a lot of time dealing with them." He walked over to the wooden workbench. "Follow me. We're going to need these for what's coming."

CHAPTER 59

C harley was entranced.

Thom moved a few random items on his desk and grabbed a pair of metal arm braces. Exposed wiring and rivets coursed up the sides of the metal braces. They looked complimentary to the percussion pistols.

"These," Thom said, "are the gauntlets."

Charley squinted and walked closer. They looked interesting, wrapped in wires and metal bands. They also looked archaic and meager, a drop in the bucket of force needed to beat the Nekura.

But she was willing to try anything. Everything had been taken from her. Everything destroyed. No home. No parents. No safety.

She was at the suffocating bottom.

Thom took off his sweater and laid his pistols down on the workbench. He put a gauntlet on each arm. The metal-braced exoskeletons held closely to his skin. They encompassed the back of his hands and traveled up to his elbows. He moved his hands and fingers freely.

"Here," Thom said. He held out another pair of gauntlets to Charley and a pair to Henry as well.

"There are three pairs here," he said. "Your mother can't use them because she is of full Salient blood and already has a unique connection to the Light. The gauntlets would be redundant. So, we have an extra pair."

"How do they work, Mr. Murphy?"

"Charley, it's okay. Call me Thom."

"Okay, Thom, how do the gauntlets work?"

Thom turned away and extended his gauntleted arms in front of him. He pointed away at a pegboard on the other side of the room. He slowly pulled his right arm back.

An archer's bow of dancing blue electric light appeared in his hand with increasing intensity. The more he pulled back, the more manifest it became. An arrow appeared, notched in the bow, held by his other hand. Thom released the blue arrow and it flew through the room, singing in the air, and penetrated a printed target hung on the pegboard. The arrow instantly vanished.

Charley's mouth gaped open.

Thom chuckled and looked back at them. "What do you think? I made these gauntlets because of my connection to the Light. That is what they do—they allow a connection to the Light."

Charley walked to the pegboard and Henry followed. There was no hole where the arrow pierced.

"That's like yesterday," Henry said, "when Mom's shotgun didn't hurt me but destroyed the Shade."

"Exactly," Thom said.

"Remember," Dawn said, "that the Light is more than physical but is not less than that. It operates in a different way, because it is of different fabric. But it can still affect material things."

Thom turned around and drew back in the empty air again. The bow of blue light appeared, and he loosed another arrow toward the pegboard.

This time, the arrow embedded in the pegboard with a large hole, the arrowhead deep into the target.

The shot was deadly accurate.

Thom smiled. "It's all in how you use it."

CHAPTER 60

Charley eyed the gauntlets in her hands. "Could I try them on?"

Dawn smiled. "Remember, the gauntlets are not about power. Lust for power is the Nekura. The gauntlets are a way to channel a connection with the Light. The connection is different for everyone. The relationship to the Light is not standardized. The Light lives and manifests differently for each person."

Charley slipped the gauntlets over her arms. They fit snuggly.

"Charley, do you want to be connected like that?" Thom asked.

She looked down at the thin metal strips on her hands, at their exposed filaments and wires.

It was what she always hoped for, what she always dreamed of—something more. For her identity to finally be determined by something outside of herself. To no longer have to generate her own value and meaning by toiling with no end in sight, except for the constant reminder of her failures. To stop scrounging for significance but to be given it freely. She breathed out the answer, and with it she breathed out the anvil that had weighed on her chest for years.

"Yes, I want that."

In a flash, a living whip of blue light appeared in her hand, extending down to the floor in a long, prehensile coil. It slowly curled and unwound on the concrete. The whip was like a live electric cord, severed and sizzling.

"It's amazing," Charley whispered.

She wasn't looking at the whip. She was distant, in an altogether different place.

"Well, aren't you going to try it, Charley?" Henry asked.

She looked down at the whip. It danced for her like she was a snake-charmer. She picked up her arm and snapped it with meager effort. The whip recoiled with a vicious snap and a crack that echoed in the workroom.

Dawn grinned. "It is yours. It is the power of the Light more than your own effort or ability. It is channeling through you."

"I feel it. I can't describe it."

Something more. That was what she had needed. She looked down and smiled.

Finally, it had come.

CHAPTER 61

Henry had enough.

He was eager for his turn. Thom and Charley both had amazing weapons of blue light. He wanted that too! It was amazing that a weapon would just appear out of thin air. This was going to be awesome.

He strapped on his gauntlets and waited.

Nothing happened.

An awkward silence hung in the air.

He extended his arms in front of him. He pulled one back to form a bow, just like his father had done.

Nothing happened.

He frantically started punching the air in front of him.

"What's wrong with these stupid things? Why aren't they working?" He waved his arms in the air, flapped them, and hit the gauntlets together.

Nothing happened.

"How come she gets something and I don't?" he pointed at Charley.

She hung her head. The whip in her hand dematerialized. Only evanescent vapors hung in the air where the whip had been.

"Henry," Thom asked, "are you ready to be connected to the Light?"

"Of course I am!" Henry yelled. He felt hurt and embarrassed. He'd just discovered that his mother was a Salient, and that meant that he had some of the same blood in him. Yet he might as well have been wearing metal coat hangers twisted around his arms rather than the gauntlets. They were useless. "Are you sure they're not broken?"

Thom watched Henry fidget with the devices on his arms and frowned.

"Honey," Dawn said to Henry, "I don't think you quite understand. I don't think you perceive what is being asked of you."

"I was asked to put on the gauntlets and I did that." He shook his head. "Charley didn't have to do anything else." He frowned and took off the gauntlets. He tossed them back on the workbench. He walked upstairs.

He stayed in his room until dinner.

Henry walked downstairs and found Thom reclining on the couch. A fire roared in the fireplace. Dawn worked over the stove. Charley was with her.

Laughing.

Envy smoldered in Henry. The monster was awakening inside him, the poison for which he had no remedy. He felt himself being given over to it.

Dawn was his mother, not hers.

The laughing stopped.

He tiptoed down the stairs to listen.

" . . . the Nekura are more active at night . . ." Dawn said. Henry couldn't hear the rest, so he went closer. " . . . we don't want the Nekura to know that you are now attached to the Light. Any surprise we have is in our favor. A lot of old instincts are coming back to me, like muscle memory. We are being hunted. We must remain wise, concealed, and only strike when ready."

Dawn put her arm around Charley.

Familiar feelings of competition with Charley burbled forth in him—this was a fight with the prize as his own mother.

Would Charley inherit Dawn's heritage instead of him?

He would have none of this nonsense.

The monster inside took over.

He walked away without saying a word. He went down to the drab basement and flipped on the lights. He walked to Thom's workbench and looked at the gauntlets. He thought for a moment about trying them on again.

Then he noticed Thom's percussion pistols.

Thom said the gauntlets worked differently for each person, but Henry wasn't sure how to use them.

He might not know how to work the gauntlets but he knew plenty well how to shoot a gun. Just point and pull the trigger.

If he would've had these pistols at the science lab, he could've defended himself instead of running in fear. He wouldn't have lain down in the truck at Charley's house like an opossum, playing dead just to survive.

His mother had said they were being hunted. He would not sit sidelined while everyone else fought back. He was tired of running, of being scared, and of feeling completely helpless.

He grabbed the pistol from the bench and pointed it toward the target on the pegboard.

He didn't think he even pulled the trigger.

A massive round of light discharged from the pistol, like dynamite exploding in his hand. It ripped the target to shreds with loud cracks and jagged splinters.

Henry screamed.

CHAPTER 62

The pistol fell to the floor with a clang.

Blistering pain.

He looked down at his hand. It was completely seared from the explosion. He gripped his burnt hand with his good one and yelled in a tight voice.

The burnt skin spread from his hand up past his wrist. The singeing intensity played upon the nerve fibers. The burn was unlike anything he had ever seen. The under-the-skin quality looked eerily similar to the amulet around his father's neck, but instead of being beautiful and intricate, a jagged scar had already appeared—a muddy blue that looked more like deep bruising.

Henry gritted his teeth as another wave of pain rolled through his body.

Thom rushed downstairs with Dawn and Charley. They saw the target blown apart and Henry half on his knee, half lying on his side, screaming and gripping his hand that had turned midnight blue.

"What were you thinking, Henry?" Dawn said and ran up to him. She went to her knees and placed her arm around him. His hand was swollen, and when she touched it, he yelped in pain. "You weren't ready for this. You did something foolish, Henry, trying to manipulate the Light to your own ends."

The Light hadn't burned him when Dawn shot him. Why the difference now? It felt unfair.

He had dabbled with something far beyond himself and was paying a painful price. Henry felt the sting of regret and he couldn't handle his mother's reprisal. He got up and ran out of the basement.

Charley stood on the stairs as Henry ran by.

Dawn looked back at Thom. He wrinkled his brow and grimaced.

"Was I wrong?" Dawn asked.

"No. No, you were right," Thom said. "I think he knows it."

Henry slammed his bedroom door shut. He sat on the edge of his bed and scowled. In a few minutes, Dawn let herself in and held a coffee mug.

"Does it hurt a lot?" she asked.

Henry nodded.

She set the mug down. She moved to the small bathroom and returned with a white plastic container of first-aid supplies and a metal bowl.

"Here," she said. She set down the bowl on his nightstand and filled it with cool water and a small packet of powder from the first-aid box. She helped him lower his hand into the bowl. The cool water was soothing to the sensitive skin. "There, does that help?"

Henry nodded again.

"Do you want to tell me about it?"

He didn't say anything. He was in the wrong and didn't feel like reliving the details, but the confession was needed. "I tried firing the pistol."

"Honey, I'm sorry for you." She was sensitive in her tone. "I'm also sorry for yelling at you afterwards. But I still stand by what I said." She took his hand out of the water and dried it off with a clean towel. She started to wrap his hand in a roll of gauze. "To manipulate the Light is dangerous and, more importantly, shows you don't understand."

"But Mom, you don't understand! That's my pitching hand! My chance at the scholarship is gone!"

Dawn sighed. "I don't know what to say, Henry."

"I'll never be able to play again!"

He started to cry. His hand throbbed. He couldn't pitch with a maimed arm. The chance at a scholarship had received his devotion while he rationed out scraps of himself to everything else. All the hard work, all his hopes—burned away.

His life was ruined.

Charley poked her head around the corner and saw the wound before it was fully wrapped. His hand was more swollen and angry than only a few minutes ago. She winced at the sight.

Henry burned inside as much as his hand did outside. The wild, irrational fury howled in his chest. He tried to smash it down but he was already inside the cage of his own emotion, pleading with himself to not say the words that flew out.

"I don't understand how she gets to come in here and instantly be the golden child," Henry said. "She suddenly has this Light connection, more of a connection with you, and now she's more of a child to you than I am."

"Henry, I just—" Charley said.

"Don't even bother."

"But Henry, you're still their son! I wish I still had my parents."

"Well, congratulations, now you have some."

"How dare you . . ." she started, but something caught her tongue.

He had played this game with her before. He was ready for it. It was the satiating need to cut each other down and then outdo the other. Curse back three times more. Don't just get even but inflict pain seven times greater. He waited for her to peddle it back to him.

She just hung her head and walked out.

"Was that really necessary?" Dawn said.

"Mom, she's always got to try and be the best at everything! The best at school, the best at gymnastics, and now she's the best at being in my own family!"

He wanted sympathy. He wanted to be placated and hear his mother coo over him with sweet condolences.

She didn't.

"Your misery is not license to incite the same on others," she said.

He frowned.

"Henry, you are loved," his mother said, "but these dark things have gotten a foothold on you. Sometimes, the darkness of the Nekura also has a corner in our own hearts." She leaned forward and kissed him on the forehead. "Try and get some rest. You're going to need it."

The nightmares came easily.

CHAPTER 63

Henry slept fitfully, fighting against unseen apparitions. His mind sowed fevered visions that he fought helplessly against. Darkness surrounded him on every side. He spun around and looked every way, but his vision was obscured by dense fog, the kind that descended on his house when he had opened the book. Out of the heavy clouds he saw the large, toothy smile appear—the same one he had seen that first night in his bedroom. There were no eyes, just the haunting smile of the Bludgeon.

It mocked him. He backed away, and it instantly vanished. Another one appeared behind him, picking up the chorus of the same mocking laughter. It vanished again and Henry spun in circles. He became dizzy and couldn't stand. He collapsed to the ground.

He still heard the laughter. It grew in haughtiness but he couldn't see the smile anymore.

Louder, it was closing in on him.

He still couldn't see anything—until he looked down.

The smile of the Bludgeon was on his stomach, laughing at him. It was derisive and crowed.

Henry scrambled in horror and clawed at it. He tried to wipe it away with furious hands, but they brushed uselessly over it.

He punched at the awful smile. He struck himself in the belly and knocked the wind out of his lungs. He doubled over and vomited on the misty floor of his dream world. But the laughing smile still remained.

He looked up from his vomit and saw a new vision. It was his father and mother. They walked away from him with Charley in between them, their arms around each other. They were carefree and laughing as they walked away. Henry called to them with a weak voice, but they continued walking, backs turned, ears deaf to his pleading.

Ash fell from the sky like volcanic rain, landing in circles around Henry. Dense charcoal smoke descended upon him. The ashes fell on him with heavy thuds and smashed him to the ground like falling anvils. Their weight was crushing. He couldn't stand up.

The smoke filled Henry's lungs and it stole the air from his chest. He couldn't breathe. He tried to cry out but couldn't. His vision began to fade. The only thing he could see were three people, happy and united, walking away from him, unconcerned. They didn't hear him or care.

Please, no . . .

He struggled, but the ash pinned him.

Don't leave . . .

The smoke forced its way down his throat.

Help . . .

His vision dimmed. He couldn't see them anymore.

One final scream . . .

Death drunk him up.

Henry bolted up in bed, shrieking. The small bedroom reverberated under his terror-filled shrills.

Or maybe not. The room was quiet, like the room had been watching him in silent horror. He wasn't sure what was real. His scream lingered in the world of nightmares and his consciousness teetered on the brink of reality.

His sheets were soaked. He'd poured sweat through the night and the same vomit from his dreams coated his pillowcase and sheets, spilling off onto the rug. He felt faint.

His hand stung.

A sudden gust of wind shook the trees outside and pushed on the timbers of the cabin. Even the wind carried malice on its gusts for the little house and the ones who slept inside.

The faint linger of his dream whispered in his ear, singing.

"When the wind blows, the cradle will rock . . ."

Was he still dreaming?

"When the bough breaks, the cradle will fall . . ."

He looked around the room, but no one was there. The voice played on his ears.

"And down will come Henry . . ."

Dizziness overtook him and he passed out again.

"Family and all."

CHAPTER 64

Silence.

He awoke again. It was still night.

The night felt abnormally long. How long was this night going to last?

His hand pounded with immeasurable pain.

Henry stood up from bed and felt woozy. He needed pain medication for his hand. He hoped there would be some in the cabinet downstairs.

His stomach grumbled. He had missed dinner. Maybe a glass of milk would help.

He walked to the stairs and tottered down, leaning on the banister with legs ready to betray him.

He made it to the kitchen. The coolness on the inside of the refrigerator felt good, and he stuck his face inside and closed his eyes. He grabbed the milk gallon and poured a glass. The creaminess helped his parched tongue. He set his glass on the countertop.

A hand wrapped around his mouth.

Panic instantly piqued. He wriggled underneath the strong hand but was too weak to break free. His hand throbbed as he grabbed the assailant's arm. He couldn't wrench free with the intense pain in his hand.

Another arm wrapped around Henry's chest and lifted him off his feet. He squirmed to no avail. The assailant and Henry quietly moved backward and dropped into the recliner chair. He heard a whisper in his ear.

"Shhhhh . . ." The voice was strong and directed.

Henry smelled his father's cologne. The strength of the arms comforted him and he sunk into them. What little strength he had left was now spent.

But why grab him like that?

Thom extended his arm, pistol in hand, toward the sliding patio doors.

A large, fleeting shadow moved on the back porch. It darted with quiet and swift movements. A familiar mouth glinted inside the shadow in the shape of a large Bludgeon underneath the haunting moonlight.

Henry squirmed. It was looking right at them.

The Bludgeon sized up the house but acted like it couldn't see them. No longer interested, the Nekura jumped over the edge of the railing and landed on the ground. It fled to the forest and disappeared into the tree line.

It felt like an eternity before Thom released Henry from his grip and Henry slid sideways.

Thom set his pistol down. "The imbuement of light on this cabin will only keep them away for so long," he said. "How long it will last, I don't know." He embraced Henry again. "You were shaking so much," Thom said. "I don't think it was just from fear. That fever is burning you up."

"It was the Nekura from my bedroom," Henry said.

"No," Thom said. "This one was different. It didn't have a half-severed arm."

"How many are there?"

Thom paused. "Many."

Henry moved over to the couch next to the chair. Thom got up to retrieve pain medicine from a cabinet. "I can always do a little doctoring away from the hospital."

He brought Henry a couple capsules and his glass of milk.

"But, Dad, why were you awake?"

Thom looked out the window again at the still landscape. "I never sleep."

Henry tracked him with weary and sick eyes.

Thom sat down on the couch next to Henry. "Someone's got to keep watch. That's why we had the nightlight at home. Your mother will do the early-morning perimeter sweep."

"You're sending Mom out there?" He tried to stand up but felt woozy again. He collapsed into Thom on the couch. "That thing is out there!"

"Yes, it is. And there are probably a lot more of them, too."

Henry felt lightheaded, almost delirious. He barely heard what Thom had said. "I just wish we had the nightlight here, with Phred," Henry whispered. "We need some help."

"Don't worry," Thom said.

Thom ran his fingers through Henry's hair and felt the sticky sweat from his fevered struggle. He gazed away into the bleak and forlorn night.

"We have help. We have your mother."

CHAPTER 65

Henry felt barely alive.

". . . not sure what to make of it," someone said.

Fragmented, difficult to decipher. Scattered. Couldn't tell what was being discussed.

"What do you think we should do?"

"I'm not sure . . . increased Nekura in the woods this morning."

"We'll have to move on. We can't wait here!"

Voices, from the kitchen. Mom and Dad.

Rolling over, he moaned. He felt terrible.

"Is he awake?"

Another wave of nausea. Henry moaned again.

"He looks awful!" His mother's voice.

Heat poured off his body from his fever. She unwrapped the bandage around his hand. The scarring had coiled up to his elbow. His skin appeared blistered, and she ran her fingers along the deep blue contours.

"Thom, these blisters are under the skin. His wound is much worse."

"This is no earthly wound." His father's voice. "It's beyond my scope."

A minute later, a cool wet rag mopped his head.

A gasp.

"What happened?" Charley's voice. "All his color is gone! It looks like he's been bleached out."

Henry knew it. He moaned, opened his eyes, then closed them again.

"What do we do, Thom?" Dawn said.

"I don't know."

"Should we take him to a hospital?"

"No. I wish that we had somewhere we could take him."

Time passed in gallops.

"The center room," his father said, like a dawning revelation.

"Yes! Good idea."

Strong arms came underneath him, lifting him up.

A door opened in the center of the house. Henry cracked an eye open.

Modest, simple room. Small bed in the center with tight linens. Nightstand with a small candle. Nothing more.

Laid him on the bed.

His death bed.

CHAPTER 66

Charley followed Dawn into the center room. "Why here?" she asked.

"Certain items or places may be imbued with light," Dawn said. "The whole house is protected, but this is the center. The Light is exponentially stronger here."

She stopped.

"It was my responsibility to remember," Dawn said. Emotion tightened her voice. She sniffed. "There is more to remember. But there is no benchmark for how much has been forgotten. What else did they make us forget?"

Charley looked back at Henry.

He looked like all the color had moved out of his body and concentrated in his hand, a stark contrast of dense blue against ghastly white.

"He'll be safe here," Thom said. "Right now, we need to go get that book."

Dawn's mouth fell open. "And leave him here? You can't be serious."

"Yes, he'll be safe."

"I'm not going to just leave my son! He's dying!"

"Dawn, if we don't get that book, we're all dead. You know it's true. You've been a guardian of the Light for years. You know he is safe here under the Light."

"He's going to be safe here?" Charley asked.

"Just like Henry's nightlight," Thom said. "the shroud of Light here will protect him."

"But what kind of a mother am I to just leave my son?"

"This is not the time to try to live up to a standard that someone else has imposed about being a parent," Thom said. "We're not judging your motherhood. We can do nothing more for him regardless of whether we are here or somewhere else. He's under the covering of the Light, now. And that's the best place for him to be."

Thom walked close to Dawn and put his hands on her shoulders. "But what you can do is help all of us. I need you, Dawn. I can't do this without you."

"And he's supposed to go through this without me?" She shot daggers with her eyes.

"It's not up to you! You can't heal him. Only the Light can. You could be in Middleton with us or sitting here, right next to him, and it wouldn't make a difference." He took a breath and slowed down. "Please, Dawn. It's out of our hands."

Charley grimaced. She bent down to Henry's ear, close and gentle.

"Henry, I need your lock combination."

His lips were parched. He spoke out the first two numbers. He couldn't get out the third. His head lolled to the side and he said nothing more.

His life was being siphoned away.

"It's enough," Thom said. "We'll just have to spin the tumbler for the third number."

Dawn leaned over Henry and embraced him, tears falling upon him.

Charley hugged his limp body where it lay on the bed. "Please pull through, Henry."

Thom leaned over the nightstand and eyed the candle. He held up his arm, donned in a gauntlet, and snapped his fingers. A small spark of blue light appeared over his finger, and he tilted it toward the wick on the candle. The blue light eagerly drank up the wick and the candle soon burned with a soft, steady blue glow. The candle filled the room with a peaceful fragrance of lavender and field lilacs.

"There's nothing more we can do now," Thom said. Tears stung his eyes, and his mouth turned down. "We're all helpless to do anything more. Right now, the only thing we can do for him is get that book back."

CHAPTER 67

They were close to the school.

The familiar subdivisions came back into view.

Except they weren't familiar.

Not anymore.

The town and everything else crawled with Nekura. The school. The university. The hotels. Their homes. Charley had never known they were there. Now, the town welcomed her with a gaping mouth, excited to swallow her alive with its false promises of serenity and modern living. She had lived in a debauched reality of balance beams and algebra quizzes.

The hair on the back of her neck stood straight and tingled. Goosebumps covered her arms.

Everything looked the same.

Everything was different.

She hoped Henry was still alive.

The Light that powered the gauntlets was the thing that both burned Henry and yet now protected him. A modest fear came over her; one born out of sobriety rather than terror.

She couldn't imagine what Dawn was going through.

"Charley," Thom said, "Nobody here knows what's happened with you or Henry. You've disappeared for several days. Try to be quiet."

Thom turned to look at her. "It has to be you who goes into the school," he said. "The Nekura don't know about your connection to the Light. You can slip through. We can't. Just grab the book and get out."

She nodded. She needed to get the book before those hideous creatures did. If she didn't, the whole world would turn to smoke and ash.

They parked several hundred feet from the school's front door and waited.

The brown metal doors opened, and students ran down the stairs in usual riotous fanfare.

"Charley, you're up."

Her heart quickened with anxiety. She slid on her sweatshirt, and it covered the gauntlets. She opened the door of the truck and walked toward the front of the school.

It was completely unlike any other time going to school. Inside was a deadly new world where black-hearted creatures lurked.

She inhaled through her nostrils. The cool air was biting and helped her to focus. She glided up the stairs and through the school's doors.

Around her were the same familiar hallways, the same familiar faces. Students walked by laughing and carrying on, unaware. Nothing looked different—but she couldn't shake the feeling like she was an imposter. Like someone was going to find her out.

Sweat trickled down her head. But she couldn't take off her sweatshirt.

Just grab the book and get out.

CHAPTER 68

Charley kept her head down. Maybe no one would notice her. Her feet shuffled through the hallway and she slipped the hood of the sweatshirt over her head.

She hurried toward Henry's locker.

She made it halfway there.

"Charley!" a voice said behind her.

She tried pressing on, acting like she didn't hear.

"Hey, Charley!" It was a male voice. It was closer to her this time.

She squinted her eyes. She couldn't make a scene by running. She turned around.

Trevor.

Her heart sank into the soles of her feet. She couldn't deal with him now.

He was breathing harder than normal through his thick lips. Small beads of perspiration clung to the scraggly beard and the brown curls beneath his baseball cap.

"Charley, have you seen Henry? He's been gone for days! The coach is freaking out right now. We really need him for the last game—it was rescheduled for tomorrow!"

"Um . . . I don't know. I've been really busy."

"You don't know? You always study together! He needs to talk to Coach Barnhard and get back to practice!"

"Yeah, sure."

She turned to leave.

"Wait a minute," he said. "The school staff said that several students went missing, and said they might need help. I thought it was just Henry . . ." He opened his mouth and pointed his finger at her. "You've been gone, too! I don't know what you two are doing, but the school office needs to know."

He turned around and ran away.

Anxiety squeezed her lungs. It became hard to breathe.

It was only a matter of minutes before she would be found out. She had to get to Henry's locker.

She turned a corner and walked down the next hallway.

Mrs. Ball talked with another teacher outside her biology room. She saw Charley from a distance and stopped mid-sentence. Confusion knotted her eyebrows and she gawked. She watched Charley walk by in quick strides.

Normally, Charley would be carrying a backpack. She was also wearing different clothes from Mid-Mart. She would never wear a hood up in school. She hoped her appearance was different enough for her to escape notice.

Mrs. Ball held up a hand to say something, but the other teacher put her hand on Mrs. Ball's shoulder and continued talking. The distraction was enough.

Charley turned around another corner. The last hallway. Straight ahead from here.

She reached Henry's blue metal locker.

Her nervous fingers twitched as she spun the dial on the lock.

"Thirty-five," she said aloud. First number in. She hesitated. A funny feeling washed over her. Someone was watching her.

"Charley?"

Rachel Morgan stood next to her.

CHAPTER 69

"Rachel!" Charley said. "Wait. Prove it's you. When did I talk to you last?"

"When you called me the other night from the Hellen house."

Charley relaxed her posture. "Good, it's really you."

"Where have you been?" Rachel asked.

Charley wasn't sure what to say. "I was out of town," she said. She still felt the need to be cautious.

"Out of town?"

"Yes."

"But everyone's looking for you!" Rachel said. "Everybody here has been worried about the missing students!"

Charley was taken aback. For all her years, she was a nameless person among a sea of faces, swimming among people of greater value than her and carried away by the torrent of insignificance. She felt validated by their concern, like she had gained some form of collective approval from her peer group.

"Really?" She liked the idea of being missed.

"Yes! I've been coming here to your locker every day!" Rachel said and pointed up at the locker number. "Didn't you get any of my text messages?"

Charley shook her head.

"All my phone calls?"

That jogged something inside her. She remembered more of the phone call with Rachel.

"Yeah," Charley said, "what exactly were you trying to tell me?"

Rachel appeared perplexed, like she hadn't expected Charley to turn back the questions to her. Rachel was trying to press the conversation to keep Charley off balance and from noticing the holes in her story. Anxiety gripped Charley's chest again.

"And this isn't my locker," Charley said. "Why are you coming to this one every day?"

Rachel glared back.

With a sudden burst of anger, Rachel slammed her hand on the locker door to hold it shut. Her hand smashed the lock tumbler, the lock still engaged. The metal door crumpled like she'd made a snow print with her hand.

Charley leapt back.

"You're not getting anything from in here," Rachel said.

Then the fire alarm went off.

CHAPTER 70

Loud sirens blared down the hallway with uncomfortable reverberation. Lights flashed from small red boxes mounted on the walls near the ceiling. An automated voice projected from the speaker.

"Fire alarm. This is not a drill. Evacuate immediately."

The hallway filled with clamor and everyone fled outside.

Except Rachel. She stood in front of the locker like a sentry with an unwavering gaze. In a matter of a few moments, they were alone in the hallway.

"What did you do with Rachel?" Charley yelled.

Rachel smiled, but this time the distinctive smile of a Shade, with its sharp teeth, replaced Rachel's delicate mouth.

The Shade leapt forward.

Charley underestimated its speed.

The Shade grabbed Charley's wrist, and wet shreds of peeled gray skin wrapped around her arm like a tightening noose.

Rachel's appearance continued to change until all that remained was the Shade with its swollen head.

"Where's Rachel?" Charley screamed again, voice cracking and straining.

But she already knew.

Rachel was gone.

She pulled back against the wraps, but she was bound. The wraps wound up her arm and encased her like a mummy.

Anxiety clouded her mind. She couldn't think.

The stairwell doors at the end of the hallway burst open. Dawn sprang in with a shotgun leveled at the creature.

The Nekura yanked Charley close and held her hostage. It wrapped one oily arm around her chest and arms and held her subdued. At the end of the other arm, the Nekura extended a smoldering finger, glowing like a burnt orange knife toward the edge of her neck.

"Put your gun down, Salient," the Nekura said.

Dawn held aim steady at the bulbous head that protruded behind Charley. Its smoldering finger burned brightly, hovering only inches away from the flesh of Charley's neck. Dawn took a breath and didn't move.

If she took the shot, Charley's neck could be filleted before the creature disappeared.

Dawn grimaced and set her gun down on the floor. She put her arms up in the air and took a step backward.

"No tricks," the Shade said in a sing-song tone. It wagged its glowing ember finger at her like a parent scolding a child.

The Shade slid its arm up to Charley's neck and held her in a headlock. It backed away from Dawn.

Charley was being pulled by it, but could not do anything back.

Her fear came again. The same overdrive panic that she'd felt before.

At the science lab.

At the hotel.

After her parents died.

She couldn't help it—it overwhelmed her faculties and beat her into submission until she was an apoplectic nuclear storm. She tried to claw frantically, but she was bound.

The Shade pulled her around the corner, out of sight from Dawn.

CHAPTER 71

Charley sat in a chair, in a room of midnight black, bound by oily bandages from the Shade, swaddled like a mummy's daughter. The Shade wrapped its bandages around her thicker, denser. They cocooned her in. The molting skin reeled off the Shade like it was alive, spooling off a fishing reel, eager to encase her.

Her mind was chaos.

Her sweatshirt felt wet from the Shade's oils that soaked into her. She swooned.

She felt like passing out, but the layers of dead peels held her to the chair. Her head fell forward.

"When you emerge, you'll be different," the Shade cooed in her ear. "You'll be as black-hearted as I am."

Different.

The word meant something to her.

Thom had said it.

But it was hard to think.

Something was different, different than anything else. Of different substance.

What was it?

Her arms stung, like metal was cutting into her skin. Why did they hurt so bad? It was like she had braces on both arms that—

Gauntlets.

The memory flooded back.

The Light.

The memory was nearly taken from her. So quietly, without notice.

She remembered. Her mind screamed it.

The living blue whip exploded out of the gauntlets and ripped open the strips that held her. She leapt to her feet, free.

She saw the Shade's severed hand fall to the floor with the oily peels. The orange burning light faded from its finger.

The whip lit up the room. She could finally see.

Three Shades stood with her.

One Shade grasped its severed arm in agony, hissing in pain as smoke and ash bled onto the floor. Its taunting smile was gone.

Everything felt different. But the change wasn't the whip or the deadly wound it made on the Shade. It was her fear. It felt less overwhelming, less primary, less ultimate. All her emotions had suddenly been aligned appropriately—not that the fear had disappeared altogether, but she saw it for what it was—unnecessary.

She didn't need to be afraid anymore, and that thought drove the fear away. It was a blissful awakening to the reordering of things that she never before realized she needed.

It was a compass finding magnetic north.

In a graceful move like a ribbon dancer, she threw her arms above her and spun in a circle. The whip followed the circular motion and spun around her waist like a blue snake. She stepped toward the Shades, and with a simple throw of her wrist, the whip flew into a devastating arc. She landed the death blow with a graceful follow-through, incising them. The Shades split in two, severed at the waist, and they fell apart and decomposed.

The move came as instinct.

Every remnant of the Shades had burned off her with the Light. No oil or ash clung to her anymore.

She looked at the whip. It still danced on the floor, eager to drink up more smoke and ash.

She promised not to forget again.

CHAPTER 72

C harley burst into the hallway and ran back toward Dawn.
"Charley!" Dawn called.
"I'm here!" Charley yelled. She ran toward Dawn's voice.

Dawn saw Charley charging around the corner. Her shoulders relaxed and she allowed her gun to rest downward.

"Oh, Charley! I looked everywhere for you. I'm so glad you're safe."

"Me too."

Dawn smiled and nodded toward the whip in Charley's hand. "I was so scared that you would forget everything you learned. The power of the Nekura is strong."

"I nearly did."

"Looks like you didn't. Come on, let's hurry."

They rushed back to Henry's locker. Dawn saw the destroyed lock that refused them entrance.

"Stand back." Dawn pointed her shotgun at the lock. A buckshot pattern of blue light erupted from the gun and blasted the door open.

The large, leather-bound book sat waiting.

Dawn opened the satchel she brought and stuffed the book inside.

"That fire alarm wasn't an accident," Dawn said. "It was supposed to get you alone with the Nekura, I'm sure of it. But it also warned Thom and I that something was wrong."

Dawn started heading for the stairwell doors she had come through.

Charley followed, then stopped. "Wait, I need to get something."

"Charley, we don't have—"

Charley didn't hear the rest. She ran the other way.

Just one more thing.

She could never live life without it. She needed it—needed to remember it always. This was the start of her promise to never forget again.

Charley ran through the abandoned hallways until she got to her own locker. She madly dialed her locker combination.

She swung the locker door open and breathed a sigh of relief.

The newspaper clipping still hung from its magnetic perch. She was careful not to tear the memento more than it already was. Dawn ran from around the corner.

"Charley, come on! We need to go!"

The alarm still wailed, but in between the individual blasts of the siren the distinctive chattering sound of Gremlins filled the hallway. Shadows fleeting among the flashing lights started to live and move on the walls.

The Nekura were coming for them.

"Come on!" Dawn yelled again. She took off toward the back door.

They flew through the hallway. Charley couldn't see the Nekura yet. She didn't need to. Their noises were incessant. They grew in sound and filled the air with anticipation of overtaking their prey. They were closing in.

"Thom is out back!" Dawn yelled over her shoulder.

Dawn barreled into the stairwell entrance and sent the storm doors flying. She looked up to see a Gremlin jump down from the stairs to try to land on her. In a blur, she ripped the shotgun upward and dispatched the creature into nothingness.

"Get in the car, I'll hold them off!" Dawn yelled. A growing flood of Nekura appeared from around the hallway corner. Charley ran past the stairwell door and Dawn railed off rounds of her shotgun to hold back the Nekura tide. If Dawn stopped firing, they would overtake Charley. "Hurry!"

Charley ran out the second set of doors. Thom's truck was parked at the base of the stairs.

"Get in!" he yelled. "There are more on the way!" He unleashed arrows of light that flew through the air over Dawn's shoulder. The assistance gave enough buffer for her to back out through the doors to get outside. She turned and ran the last few feet and dove through the open door into the back of the truck. The Nekura charged toward them.

"Go!" Dawn yelled.

Thom hit the accelerator. Dawn's legs still hung out of the truck as they sped away.

CHAPTER 73

Thom said they needed to make one more stop. They needed to stop at home.

Charley didn't like that idea.

Instead of Thom and Dawn going home with their whole family, a different teenager rode in the back seat. She wondered how Henry was.

Dawn sat in the back seat with Charley and looked out the window. She had not said a word since they left the school.

The upper level of the Murphy house appeared above the cresting hill in front of them. The lower level was still hidden. In a few hundred feet they would—

Dawn suddenly clutched her chest and struggled to breathe. Charley leapt at the sight.

"Dawn? Are you alright?"

Dawn clenched her shirt with white knuckles.

Thom slammed the brakes. He looked back at her. "Dawn?"

Her breathing was labored.

"What's wrong?" Thom said.

She shook her head. "No, we can't go back there," she said and pointed. "It's in there . . ." Dawn whispered. She stared unblinking ahead, eyes wide and voice hushed, " . . . the darkness . . ."

Charley strained her eyes to see the house in the distance. There were long shadows, now in the middle of the afternoon, that hung over the house, the kind that seemed out of place because the sun was still high above the trees. Fleeting visions went by the windows, nearly unperceivable shadows. Their movements were sudden and swarming, like a fog of mosquitoes hidden in the night that is only seen through the light of a lamp.

"I haven't seen you do that since we crossed the Veil," Thom said. Worry permeated his voice. "I didn't know the situation was this bad." Thom backed the truck down the road and into a neighbor's driveway. Then he sped the other way. "I wish we could have gotten Phred back. We could've used him."

"I know," Dawn said. "Phred will have to wait. He'll be safe inside the nightlight."

A few moments later, Dawn released the death grip over her chest and relaxed into her seat.

"How long is it to the safe house?" Dawn asked, looking at her wrinkled shirt where she had clenched. "That feeling—it's been a long time since I felt it. There is something more to this, more than we know."

She clutched her chest again. She snapped her head up and looked at Thom with realization and renewed fear. "Thom, get us back to the safe house. Henry's in trouble."

CHAPTER 74

Thom rocketed the truck north.

Charley needed to think of something other than Henry. There was nothing more she could do for him right now.

"How much longer?" Dawn asked again.

"I'm trying." Thom said. He gritted his teeth and turned on the radio. He settled on one station reporting the local news.

" . . . was concerning. The fire burned Middleton High completely to the ground. Firefighters arrived quickly after the alarm was pulled, but the blaze was out of control. Authorities believe the fire started from a school prank, with a report of some seniors burning fireworks for Homecoming Week. However, the end result was devastating, with one student perishing from the fire. The deceased body of Rachel Morgan, a student at Middleton High, was discovered—."

Thom snapped the radio off as soon as he heard it.

Charley's heart sank into the depths of her stomach.

Was Rachel really dead? The Nekura's deception was so deep, she couldn't trust anything. The only thing she could be sure of was the Nekura's craziness—they'd burned down the whole school.

The more she thought about the radio report, the more she was incensed by it. That wasn't Rachel's body the firefighters found.

But no one knew any better. Rachel could still be alive, but the news report would allow Rachel to completely disappear. There would never be anything more to it. How long had Charley lived like that—oblivious to a world that now dictated her every action?

She thought of her own life. She remembered the fear, the glowing finger of the Shade held close to her neck like a burnished scalpel waiting to incise.

"I nearly died," she said.

"Hm?" Dawn said. "What did you say, Charley?"

"Sorry. I was just thinking about what happened at the school. Sometimes, I mumble out loud to myself when I'm nervous. It's a habit."

"Well, what did you say?"

"I said that I nearly died."

Dawn straightened up. "They don't want to kill you Charley. If the Shade wanted you dead, it would have done it. It was trying to take you."

An icy chill shook through Charley.

"Take me?"

"Yes. The Nekura are evil, but it doesn't mean that they are ignorant. To truly defeat someone is to not just destroy them, but to take them—to make them one of their own—so that their lives become as dark and black and soulless as their own. Their victory is to add the deluded recruit to their ranks."

"Can they take people already connected to the Light?" Charley asked.

"No, they can't destroy your connection. They will instead try to convince *you* to destroy it."

"Will the Nekura go after others not connected to the Light?"

Dawn frowned. "Not necessarily. You have to see that most of those people walking around your schools, shopping at the mall, the people you ride the bus with, the man who serves you ice cream at the ice cream shop, the woman who bags your groceries at the market . . . so many around you are already gone. They are unwittingly instruments of the Nekura and already lost in a game played from behind the Veil—all because they are unaware. Why do you think those seniors claimed responsibility for the fire? We both know it wasn't them. Those who are unaware of the Nekura are not their enemies. They are pieces on the Nekura's chessboard and become their feet and hands . . . and fists.

"They can kill easily enough, Charley, but that's not what they want. They want to take, and to take as much as their dark souls can devour. The biggest mockery of all is when they steal and destroy without killing, when they make their victims live in voluntary, unending darkness."

What Dawn described sounded worse to Charley than dying.

"Now you see, Charley, what happens when people forget. How easy it is to be carried away. How devastating the results . . . and how it happened to us."

It felt good to talk and listen. It was the spark of courage Charley needed. She needed to ask the question that burned within her.

She leaned forward in her seat.

"Thom, why didn't you come inside the school?" Her emotions betrayed her. Hot tears stung her eyes. She wanted vindication.

He saved her at the science building. He saved her at her house. He carried her out of the hotel. He was like the father she had longed for—but then he sat in the car and sent her into the school alone! Abandonment was a constantly re-injured wound. Jostled from one foster family to the next, receiving some scraps of affection only to be jettisoned away somewhere else.

"Why did you just leave me?" Charley said. It was the question she wanted to scream out to the world, to everyone, to anyone who would listen, to echo through the stitches of time to her parents years ago—"Why did you just leave me?"

Thom looked in the rearview mirror at her and kept driving. He let the question linger. The air felt stunned with his silence.

"The Nekura were going to go for the vehicle," he said finally.

"What?"

"They were going to stop us at our getaway. That's how they do it. You said it yourself, you were surprised at how much I know about them. It's why I had to stay with the truck. And it's why Dawn couldn't stay with Henry."

"How do you know that?"

She could see the pain rise on Dawns' face. This was sacred territory.

"Years ago, Dawn and I had some friends that also connected to the Light. They fought the Nekura with us. We were on a mission together. The Nekura sabotaged their vehicle at the last moment. They surrounded our friends, and then finished them off."

He turned his head sideways and glanced through the corner of his eyes at Charley from the front seat.

"Their car was wrecked," Thom continued. "We never saw them again. And if the Nekura realize that they can't take you, that's when they finish you off. I stayed with the truck because I needed to protect our getaway. I wish I could've driven the truck right through the center of that Nekura-infested school. The same way I didn't want to leave Henry alone, I didn't want to leave you alone. But you had Dawn, you had your gauntlets, and because I wanted to protect you I stayed with the truck."

She wiped a tear away from her eye.

Someone finally answered.

CHAPTER 75

The safe house appeared out of the trees as they careened up the driveway.

The cabin sat still in eerie darkness, a glob of black in the shrouded night.

"The lights aren't on," Thom said. "That's not good."

Dawn flung the truck door open and sprang out before it stopped moving. She gripped her shotgun with iron fingers. She bounded up the stairs with Charley and Thom behind her. At the top of the stairs, she froze.

The front door was mangled. The center was shattered open, an array of jagged wooden fibers with excoriated paint. The door swung from its lowest hinge, the others broken away completely. A massive hole of blackest night stood on the other side, the frame ripped into splintered submission. Looking through the doorway was like looking into the mouth of a giant Bludgeon, hollow and hungry.

"Henry . . ." Dawn said.

The mother lioness came out.

Dawn charged through the center of the broken doorway and into the mouth of the darkness.

Cold fear gripped Charley. Something had ravaged the door. And it was inside the house.

Thom bolted through the doorway also.

Charley stood alone outside. The wind howled in the trees like lost banshees of the forest. It pressed hard against her skin and bit her ears.

She couldn't stay outside. She had no other choice.

She jumped into the hornets' nest behind Dawn and Thom.

Charley heard the sound of scratching and gouging. She'd heard those sounds at the school.

The lights turned on. Thom was at the light switch.

A dozen Gremlins filled the hallway. They clawed at the door to the center room in a wild frenzy, with two giant Bludgeons behind them. The door to the center room, despite the scraping, stood firm and without a mark.

Charley was transfixed. The moment felt surreal. The Nekura outnumbered them. Charley reached to create the whip of light, but something happened before she could.

Dawn's silver hair began to glow. Her hair became brilliantly iridescent, changing from muted silver to white-hot sterling. Her hair raised from the back of her neck as if alive, and light beamed from the end of each strand. It flooded her eyes and poured out of her mouth. Her core became a flooded combustion chamber of light. She threw her head back and lifted off the ground.

The Nekura watched and recoiled. They no longer scratched at the door to the center room. They watched Dawn Murphy become a living paragon of the Light. They growled and cried before her presence.

She looked at the Nekura through lustrous, glowing eyes.

Then she surged forward.

Dawn lunged with the velocity of a cannon shot. She struck with the precision and speed of an incensed viper, body-checking the first Bludgeon into the second with a crushing shoulder charge. Even with her small frame, she threw the two massive beasts backward against the wall with incredible force. She leveled her shotgun in a single swoop, and light exploded out of the end of the gun. The massive burst of light ripped them apart, and their hard stony exteriors shattered throughout the room. The pieces splintered into flying shards that decomposed into ash before they hit the ground.

She spun around and grabbed a Gremlin by its spindly arm. She launched it into a group of three others and brought up the shotgun again. Another large, wide-mouthed blast devastated the four Gremlins, with evaporating smoke and murky ash smeared on the wall.

Like a dancer in choreography, she flipped the shotgun in her hands and held it by the barrel. She swung the stock of the gun as a club, which connected with the remaining Gremlins. They were crushed backward, and all landed in the corner in a heap, each falling on the other and clamoring to get away, screeching in terror at the Salient's wrath and light-filled body.

She flipped the shotgun in her hands and pointed the barrel at the teeming mass of Nekura. Three scatter-shot rounds ripped into the heap, and their moving stopped. The Nekura decomposed into a common black mass. All that was left was unmoving ash and wafting smoke.

The light pouring from Dawn's eyes began to dim. She settled on her feet and no longer walked on the air. Her hair settled on her neck, and its color changed back to its quiet, suggestive silver with faint glints of sparkling. Her hazel eyes returned and her posture relaxed.

She turned and gave Thom a silent, glaring look.

She walked up to the door of the center room and opened it easily.

She let out a sigh.

Henry lay in the center of the room, safe and undisturbed, still unconscious, with the small candle beside him burning soft blue light.

CHAPTER 76

Charley looked to Thom. "Whoa. Did she just become Salient again?"

Thom shook his head. He walked into the center room and Charley followed.

Dawn stood over Henry. She leaned over and felt the warm, rhythmic breaths in his chest rising and falling. She gave a gentle kiss to Henry's forehead.

Thom placed his hand on Henry's head. He was no longer dripping in sweat like earlier in the morning. "He still has a long way to go, but his fever has broken."

Dawn walked away without saying a word.

Charley looked back to Thom. "What was that back there? Does she always do that? The Nekura wouldn't stand a chance against her!"

Thom gazed at the floor. A stunned silence filled the room. "To see her do that again . . ." He didn't finish his thought. "I've only seen her do that once before. It happened when she was pushed to the edge. It's like her survival mechanism."

"When was the other time?"

"Remember the story of how the Nekura killed our friends?"

Charley nodded.

"Then."

These were painful memories. There had been a lot of that recently. The things that were stolen from the Murphy family by the Nekura's deception—she understood why Thom and Dawn had blocked them out of their minds in the first place. It seemed like the more they dove into the black sea of the Nekura, the more they drowned. Charley wished for a bright spark, a glimmer of . . .

Hope.

Charley smiled and looked out the open door.

Hope—she stood in the other room. And her name was Dawn.

"I wish she could do that all the time," Charley said.

"Yeah, me too," Thom said, "but she gave her Salient spark to me. She can't."

He shuffled his feet and stared at the wall, like he was looking through it to the distant starry horizon beyond.

"I remember her as a Salient, full and undiluted. The most beautiful creature I ever saw. That's why I married her. But that was years ago, before she selflessly gave me her spark." His voice choked, his eyes glistened. "And look what I've done with it. I nearly lost Henry." He hung his head.

Charley felt her connection to the Light. But what Thom was talking about was different. Thom wasn't experiencing a reconnecting to the Light—he was undergoing a reckoning with it.

"But if you have her spark, how could she do that?"

He wiped a sleeve over his eyes. "She is connected to the Light on different terms. Without the Salient's spark, she will never be able to manifest her true form. But there are moments like these that show something powerful remains in her."

He laughed.

"What's so funny?" Charley asked.

"You're going to think I'm crazy."

"A week ago I would have. Not anymore."

"Well, that's true."

"So, what is it?"

"I think it's kind of like drinking a milkshake."

"What?"

"Dawn's connection. It's like a milkshake."

"Okay, you're right. That is crazy."

"Hey, you asked! Just hear me out. You know when you're drinking a shake and you get to the bottom and you think it's all gone? But if you hold the cup just right and move the straw, there's still a big glop at the bottom. That's the best part because all the chocolate sank down there. Dawn gave up her Salient spark, but she's not empty—the best of the spark is deep down inside her. That's what I think."

Charley laughed. "Okay, I get it. Some. It's still a weird analogy."

He sighed and his smile vanished.

"I look forward to the day I can keep laughing." He shook his head and looked back at Henry, comatose on the bed. "One day. But not today."

Then he walked out of the room.

CHAPTER 77

Thom, Dawn, and Charley sat together at the kitchen table. And an empty chair.

No one said a word.

Charley poked at a frozen instant meal thawed by the microwave. It was painfully quiet.

She should try saying something.

"Thom, I'm sorry you had to rip up the floors to barricade the door. The wood was nice."

Thom looked over his shoulder to the broken door. A dozen foot-wide floorboards were nailed over the broken entrance in a rushed, cockeyed manner.

"Thanks, Charley. I'm just glad we had some wood to use."

She looked back to the family room. The plywood subfloor peered out from under the edges of the rug like a moth-eaten cloth. He had torn up half the floor to get boards big enough to barricade the door.

The house felt vandalized, like a hurricane had thrashed through their home.

More silence.

Thom spoke up. "Honey, I can help clean up from dinner."

"No." Dawn shot the words more than spoke them.

"I think I'm going to get ready for bed," Charley said.

She walked upstairs. A moment later, she heard Thom speak to Dawn.

"What's up? Are you mad at me?"

"You made me leave him!" Dawn shouted. It was immediate and livid. Charley couldn't ignore it. She peeked over the edge of the stairs and saw Dawn standing, glaring at Thom. "He almost died!"

"I know, Dawn. I'm sorry. I don't think—"

"What if we had been just a few minutes late?" Her voice quivered. "He would have been dead. Or even worse, they would have taken him."

"I couldn't remember, Dawn! I forgot that the protection of Light on the house needs you for it to be at its strongest. It needs the Salient's connection. We're safe now that you're here."

"For now."

"Now is all we have. It's the same reason why the Bludgeon got into our house in Middleton—because you weren't there."

"Are you accusing me of being responsible for the attack on Henry?"

"No! No. I'm saying we're both responsible."

Dawn walked away from the table. She paced the room, arms folded.

"You feel it, don't you?" she said.

Thom nodded in a solemn gesture.

"The curtain of the Light on this house," she said, "the protection—it's failing, even with me here. I hope Henry wakes up."

"I don't know if I made the right decision or not leaving him here," Thom said. "But he's fine. The Light protected him in the room."

"He's fine because we showed up before the Nekura broke down the door."

"The Light protected him, Dawn. Just like we trusted it would. The Light just used you to do it."

She collapsed onto the couch with her back to Thom. She buried her face in her hands. Her chest rose and fell with her crying. "I should have never left."

Thom walked to the couch and eased down next to her. He placed a gentle hand on her back.

"It's all been stolen from us. But we need to keep fighting for what was lost. Henry's safe. The Light protected him in that room. He was safer in there than he would have been anywhere else with us. It's why the door wasn't damaged despite all the clawing. And now, we have the book."

Thom stretched his arms toward her, inviting her, asking her. She looked at them, unsure.

She paused.

Then she fell into his embrace.

He wrapped his arms around her with giant strength. He swallowed her up in a silent promise.

Charley watched from the balcony. She smiled.

It felt good—the reconciliation.

"I'm so sorry, Dawn," Thom said. "Many years ago, I promised to never leave you nor forsake you. Do you remember that?"

She reached her hands up and pulled his arms further around her. "I remember."

"We have something the Nekura don't. We have love." Thom kissed her on her forehead, long and lingering. "Love is on our side."

CHAPTER 78

Henry moaned and cracked open an eye. His vision was bleary. A blue candle burned faint light next to him. It looked new. No wax had melted, no wick was exposed.

Must not have slept too long.

He rolled his head. Charley sat in a kitchen chair on the other side of the bed, slumped over, asleep. A novel was in her lap called *Mildred the Magnificent*, a tale about a talking rabbit and her adventures on her motorcycle.

"Henry?" She startled awake and knocked the book to the floor. "Henry! Are you awake?"

"Ugh. I think so."

"He's awake!" Charley turned her head and called through the open door.

"Charley, not so loud, I just woke—"

He was interrupted by a thunderous flurry of footsteps. He tried sitting up as Dawn ran into the room.

"Henry!" Dawn cried.

She bowled him over with her embrace and wept and buried her face in his hair, kissing him and smelling his own unique smell.

"Hey, Mom. Is everything okay?"

Thom followed through the door.

"Henry!" He threw his arms around the two of them. "How are you feeling?"

Henry lifted his arms out of the embrace and above his head for a large, long stretch. Stretching felt pretty good. Actually, overall he felt pretty good.

"Better."

The large discoloration was a permanent, intense navy color under his skin that burrowed up to his elbow. His arm looked like he had submerged it in a giant vat of indigo ink that splashed up his skin.

He flexed his fingers. They felt normal.

The normalcy surprised him. "It doesn't hurt at all."

"I'm just so happy that you finally woke up," Dawn said.

"Wait, what do you mean?"

"Henry," Thom said, "you've been asleep for four days."

That surprised him more.

"Four days?"

"We debated if we should stay here or try to take you somewhere else," Thom said. "It seemed like you were safest here. With your mother."

"We didn't know if you would ever wake up," Dawn said. She pulled him close again.

Four days. That explained why his stomach roared inside.

"What happened?"

Charley smiled. "There's a lot to tell you."

"Now that Henry's awake," Thom said, "we'll leave at sunrise. Every night, I feel the hot, dry breath of the Nekura down my neck. They are close. But tonight we celebrate! And I've got just the thing."

CHAPTER 79

They sat at the kitchen table, four people filling four chairs. Charley's eyes sparkled as she talked.

"Seriously, Henry," Charley said, "the Light is amazing—how I've connected to it. I felt like I was thinking fifty thoughts all at once. My mind was on overdrive."

Henry gulped down his root beer float. It was his second one. A third one wouldn't hurt.

"But your mother," Charley said, "she turned into a reaper of the Nekura just outside your door."

The image sounded amazing. He wished he'd seen it.

Henry reached for the large soda bottle. He drenched his generous helping of vanilla ice cream in a river of root beer.

"You're lucky," Dawn said. "It's only because you almost died that I'm letting you polish off a third."

Henry smiled and drank merrily. Root beer floats were always a favorite. They had become a staple in the Murphy household as a way to celebrate. In their escape from Middleton, Thom had grabbed those groceries at the stop at Mid-Mart. Henry had carried them in from the truck.

Henry paused and considered it. Buying root beer and ice cream while running away from the Nekura? It seemed trivial, even frivolous.

But it also seemed like Thom trusted that everything was going to be okay. Like he knew it. That there was a guarantee of a celebration to come.

It spoke volumes.

Maybe things would be alright after all.

CHAPTER 80

"Dawn," Thom said, "have you seen the dental floss?"

Thom rifled through a grocery bag in the kitchen while Dawn placed a teakettle on the stovetop. Charley walked downstairs and turned to look at Dawn.

"Could we talk?" Charley asked.

Thom looked up from the bag. "Who, me?"

"No!" Dawn scolded. "She doesn't mean you."

"Oh, I didn't know."

Dawn shook her head. "Femininity he does not get," she said and smirked. She walked over to the stairs and took Charley by the hand. "Come on, we can have some tea and sit down." She led her to the box of teabags in the cupboard.

Dawn turned back to Thom, who continued rummaging through the bag. "Honey, why don't you just take the whole bag into the bathroom to find the dental floss? Really, that garlic from dinner is not sitting well with you. You should probably spend some time in there fixing it."

She lilted a pandering smile and walked toward him.

"Really?" Thom said. "I didn't know—"

"Just go fix yourself," she said. She spun him around and pushed him forward.

"But why do—"

"Good night, honey." She shoved him into the bedroom and shut the door.

"There," she said, "with Henry asleep already, the boys have been removed."

Charley giggled. The corralling was quite the spectacle.

"I tell you," Dawn said, "he's brilliant. A doctor, those gauntlets—but he still can be completely clueless."

They laughed together.

It felt good to laugh again.

They selected orange-spiced herb teabags, and the teakettle whistled within a few minutes. They poured the water into their mugs and Charley took a sip of her tea. She didn't realize how chilled she had become, being in the north woods in late fall. The hot drink felt good.

"Here, follow me," Dawn said and went upstairs.

Dawn led her to a small observatory with two leather chairs, a modest wooden desk, and a bay window with a cushioned bench. Above the bench, a large round pane of glass overlooked the blackened forest. The edge of the tree line retreated as it sunk along the course of the hill away from the house.

"I love it," Charley said. "It's so peaceful. I didn't know this room was here."

Dawn smiled and shut the door behind them. She walked over to the bay window bench and sat down on the soft cushions. She patted the cushion and Charley sat down next to her. The evening light of the silver moon cast an evanescent shimmer on Dawn's hair that seemed to make it live again.

"Dawn, what I saw you do the other day, it was amazing. What was it like?"

Dawn took a minute and looked out the windows at the tranquil night scenery. "I was terrified for Henry. Then suddenly, I wasn't. It felt the way a bullet must feel being shot out of a gun—feeling all the wind around me, able to touch and feel while spinning through the air, all the while knowing that something else blasted me forward."

Charley nodded.

"I felt something like that at the school," Charley said, "but I still remember being at the hotel with Thom and Henry. There was a Shade there that mimicked a room attendant and it jumped on me and nearly . . ."

Dawn placed her hand on Charley's to still her anxious movements.

"I never want that to happen again," Charley said. "I couldn't touch them, but you did. You smashed two Bludgeons into a wall, and just one of them is five times your size! How were you able to stop them?"

Dawn smiled. "A remnant of my Salient spark still smolders inside. Because the Salients have been the stewards of the Light, we can physically engage the Nekura on their plane."

"Thom said it was like drinking a milkshake."

"What?"

"I know," Charley said and smirked. "I said the same thing."

"A milkshake?" Dawn raised her eyebrows.

"The way you were able to light up and take down the Nekura. He said it's like drinking a milkshake."

"Really?"

"Yep. Like your smoldering spark is a big glop of chocolate at the shake's bottom, after you think the cup's empty."

Dawn shook her head. "Of course he would say that. He has such a sweet tooth! You know those root beer floats tonight were just as much for him as they were for Henry?"

These were the family trifles, the kind of things that are usually kept hidden from strangers to preserve social appearances. Charley was becoming privy to the dynamics—the gears and underpinnings of how these people interacted—to which she was previously uninvited. It was subtle, but she was being let in.

Into a family.

CHAPTER 81

Charley watched Dawn sip her tea. She understood Henry's sentiment.

She was also drawn to this woman.

Maybe because Dawn was the only other female in the house.

Or maybe because Dawn could dismantle ash monsters with her glowing hands.

"Dawn, do you think Rachel is really . . . dead?"

"It's hard to say, Charley." Dawn looked back out the window at the night landscape that rolled away before her. The stars twinkled in the cloudless night with invitation to the greater unknown, to the promise of something more, cast beyond the scope of the darkened forest. "Do you see those stars shining up in the sky?" she said. She pointed to a bright cluster in the lower horizon.

Charley nodded.

"See that large one?" Dawn said. "If there is no star there, then of course there would be no light in that empty space. But what if that star exists—and take up its place in the night sky—and does nothing? It becomes an obstacle for other stars to cast their light around. In fact, to be a star and not to shine is even a worse fate than to have no stars at all. It's the great undoing—to have the chance to shine and not."

Dawn looked back to Charley. She continued.

"There are always fates worse than death, and the Nekura do not prefer death. Rather, they want to exploit life through their deception. They want you, me, Rachel, anyone on their side. It's rare to find Nekura just killing someone off. They would rather poison people to the point that they become one with them. They do not want your death but your agency. It's all about agency. In death you're simply no longer a factor. In life you can still fight and shine, or your life can be squandered without dying. That is what the Nekura celebrate."

"So, you think Rachel's still alive?"

"Probably."

Charley wasn't sure if she should be relieved or even more scared.

"Is Henry going to be alright?" Charley said. "Really alright?"

"Yes, I'm convinced of it. He had quite an ordeal trying to tamper with the Light on his own terms, but I think he understands something from it. I think there's something more to all of this."

"Well, what do we do now?"

"Look through the book and see what Henry finds."

"Have you looked at it yet?"

"No. I couldn't. Every time I tried, I thought of Henry. Thought he was the price I paid to get it back. It made me nauseated. Now that he's better, I'm better. Have you looked at it?"

"No. I didn't know if I was allowed. It's your book. I didn't want . . ." Charley shifted in her seat. "I didn't want to get burned. Like Henry."

"That won't happen," Dawn said. "I'm sure of it."

"You'll let me look at it?"

"Absolutely. And the book should tell us where the furnace is."

"I hope you're right."

"I better be, because we must leave quickly. The imbuement of the Light on this house is falling."

"I know. I heard you tell Thom."

Silence crept in, but they lingered and looked at the stars. They were beautiful and opulent in the north, where the sky was hidden away from the ambient lights of the bustling Middleton cityscape. The stars declared their stately presence with intensity. The sky glowed with a vivacity that Charley never knew, like a cosmic painter had spilled his white paint over the stretched canvas of the night sky, leaving streaks and splotches and whole galaxies of brilliant light.

She looked back to Dawn.

Her next thought struck her as odd at first. The night's light made Dawn's hair shine, but at the same time, it seemed more that Dawn herself made the night sky brighter. It was as if the stars had been muted, silenced and strangled in darkness, but had awoken with Dawn, the natural outflow of it all, the return of things to their intended way. The stars had been held captive but now celebrated in glorious display the Salient's awakening.

Nature itself had sided with them against the darkness.

Although Charley had never seen stars like this before, they had been there all along. The stars hadn't changed—she had.

Funny, change was happening a lot lately.

CHAPTER 82

Charley flopped onto her bed.

Time for some homework.

This was her element.

She grabbed her pink-framed reading glasses from her bag. She tried cleaning the lenses again, but the stubborn blue streaks remained. The blue fire had made the streaks permanent.

She turned on her bedroom lamp and lifted the cover to the *Book of the Salients*.

No burning.

She wasn't sure where to begin. How should she start looking for the answer to an ancient mystery? Henry had said something about a stanza with fire.

She started flipping pages.

Charley glanced through long sections of prose of an epic story and then through poetry. Scattered among the writing were various pictures of lands with lush landscapes and waterfalls. Other pictures had fore-boding castles with jagged spires shrouded in darkness.

One picture made her pause. A man with a cloak took up the center of the picture, face obscured, and a hammer in his hand that appeared to match the one on the cover of the book. The hammer was larger than the cloaked man and its head rose high, like an oversized spike maul for driving railway nails made for giants. In the background lay rolling hills with wheat fields bending in the wind, stars that twinkled and called to each other, and bodies of water that rippled and coursed. The picture nearly seemed alive—a mosaic of life behind the faceless man. At the top of the page was inscribed "The Hammer of Andelis."

She took off her glasses and rubbed her heavy eyes. So tired.

When she looked back at the book, the colors were muted. Every-thing looked still. The picture was no longer infused with the life that had jumped off the page a moment before.

"That's funny," Charley said.

She put her glasses on again. The colors sprang back. They rolled and tumbled on each other, a heartbeat giving life to the picture.

What was happening? Her eyes moved to the page on the other side of the book and found a short stanza.

> *Not burnished bronze nor smelter's ore*
> *Is the fire's blazing core*
> *In weathered lands on distant shore*
> *Fire reaches, wanting more*
> *From dancing flames, the skies adore*
> *The rising fire they implore.*

The verse stood alone on the page, a solitary description surrounded by empty space.

The stanza made no sense. It felt cryptic, backwards. Is the sky on fire? That wouldn't be good.

But this might be what Henry talked about. Maybe he would remember more if he saw it.

She ran downstairs.

"I found something!"

CHAPTER 83

Henry snapped awake.

The voice sounded like Charley. Why was she yelling?

He walked out of his bedroom. He felt groggy. He staggered downstairs. Each step took monumental effort.

He didn't feel like he had slept for four days. Maybe he could use another four.

Charley stood between Thom and Dawn. They all leaned over the dining table, around the open book.

Charley was pointing and speaking without pausing to breathe. "With my glasses on, the picture seems to be alive. The background is moving and changing. It's amazing. But when I take them off, everything stops."

"Are you okay?" Henry asked. He stood behind Charley and looked over her shoulder down at the page. "I've seen this picture before. It's never—"

Charley thrust the pink-framed glasses over her shoulder and onto his face.

He looked down and his mouth fell open. He reached past Charley to touch the picture. He fingered the page with a new reverence.

It was amazing.

"This is totally different," he said. Wind blew through the wheat field in the picture, sending waves of glinting amber colors, and the background rolled behind the cloaked man holding the hammer.

Thom and Dawn looked at the picture and then both tried on Charley's glasses. Dawn sat down in the dining chair with slow, aching movements. Thom pulled up a chair and sat next to her.

"Look! That's it!" Henry said. He pointed at the text. Charley read the stanza aloud.

Not burnished bronze nor smelter's ore
Is the fire's blazing core
In weathered lands on distant shore
Fire reaches, wanting more
From dancing flames, the skies adore
The rising fire they implore.

"What does that mean?" Henry asked. But he was supposed to be the one who knew. Why couldn't there just be a map? It would be a lot easier.

"I haven't heard that in years," Dawn said. "I don't think I would have ever remembered without hearing the lines of that song."

"It's a song?" Charley asked.

"My father used to sing it to me when I was a little girl. I once asked him about it. He said it involved a legend—a legend of a perpetually burning, self-existent source of the Light that swelled like a furnace's fire."

"The furnace!" Charley said.

"It doesn't sound much like a song," Henry said. "It sounds like long division in math class."

Thom took Dawn's hand and they looked at each other and nodded. They timed their breathing.

Then they started to sing.

Thom started by humming. His voice swelled in baritone, deep and rich. Dawn followed and chanted in alto with an otherworldly elegance. The rhythm was slow, steady, and enchanting. The song was a dirge, complex in harmony but simple in melody. Dawn sang the lyrics and the words were no longer words—they transformed into threads, weaving their way into and throughout their souls, tempered by minor chords and a creeping fugue.

The song was brief and over too soon. A hallowed silence lingered afterward.

"I . . . I've never heard anything like that before," Henry said.

"It was the most beautiful thing I've ever heard," Charley said. "Could you teach it to me?"

Dawn smiled. "It's from long ago. I don't exactly know when."

Henry didn't hear anymore. He had an idea.

The center room was where the Light was the strongest, right?

So, he got up from the table and walked toward the center room. He opened the door and lay down on the simple bed. The candle still burned, undaunted, emanating its light and scent, as if in perpetual motion.

He could do this. He had to figure out what the song meant.

"Weathered lands on distant shores" didn't narrow the search any. And the lyrics said what the furnace is not, rather than what it is. He felt a familiar frustration grow inside him, but this time he was able to check it. The song was not something to become frustrated about—it was certainly more than that.

He couldn't help thinking about his hand. He looked at his arm and traced his finger along the deep colors that scrolled up his forearm. The song confused him, but at the same time, some of it made sense. The pain he'd felt certainly was like fire when he shot the pistol and the

Light unfurled up his arm. The nerve fibers reminded him of the intense burning. If there was a furnace of Light out there, it certainly would have a blazing core. He could see why the Nekura would want to own it—and manipulate it.

An idea struck him and he bolted up in bed.

"Dad! We have to leave. I think I've figured it out."

CHAPTER 84

Twenty minutes later, the truck barreled away from the cabin.

"I'm glad we didn't stay there any longer," Dawn said.

"Why?" Thom said. "Did you feel the protection was going to fall tonight?"

"Yes. But also my garbage can was so full of ash that I didn't have room for any more Nekura." Dawn smiled and looked out the window at the passing scenery.

"Henry," Charley said, "where are we going?"

"To a volcano."

"A volcano?"

"Yep."

"Why a volcano?"

"Think about it. The 'rising fire' could be lava on the inside and it would come from a blazing core. I think there's something to it."

"There's a town called Superior," Thom said. "It's a few hours away. A volcano erupted there many years ago and made national news. But there was a lot more happening behind the Veil when it did. I think we should start there. It should be dormant now."

"You mentioned the Veil before," Charley said. "What is it?"

"It's the dividing wall between our world and theirs," Thom said. "It is the curtain that separates us."

"It's another world?" Henry said.

"Sort of, Henry. But this is not a multiple-universe scenario. There is no multiverse here. The other side of the Veil is still our same world, but we see it from two different vantage points. It's like when you look at water in the ocean. Things look differently whether you look at it from the shore or you're submersed in it."

"So, which one is the real world?" Charley asked.

"They both are. This side of the Veil, the world you know, might appear to you as more tangible but it is also more insipid. This world is a reflection of the realities of the other side—and in a sense, that is the more real one." Thom grabbed a small black duffel bag and tossed it behind him into Henry's lap. "I brought these for you."

Henry zipped open the bag. A pair of gauntlets lay inside.

Henry threw his arms into the air and recoiled.

"They won't bite, Henry. You can still have your own connection to the Light."

He reached out a tentative finger and brushed one of the gauntlet's side.

Nothing happened.

He picked up the bag and placed it on the floor next to him.

"I think things will be different this time, Henry," Thom said.

Henry looked at his arm with the deep discoloration. He would carry the mark forever. "I don't know if I'm ready."

"The Light is not something to be trifled with or manipulated, but neither is it to be disregarded. Both are just as wrong."

Henry took off his shoes and stretched out his long legs as much as he could. He looked out the window at the changing landscape. The hills had grown into mountains, and evergreen forests with cliffs of shale rock rose along the edge of the road. The green luster of the trees remained despite the chill that crept into the air with the changing of seasons.

"Do you think you might try the gauntlets?" Charley asked.

Henry detached from his window reverie. "I don't know."

"You don't have to use them but maybe you could put them on, just in case."

"Charley, the Light nearly killed me. Why would I mess with it again?"

"Because it's your heritage, Henry. Because the Light is amazing, when you approach it on its terms. And because the Nekura are trying to destroy you more than the Light is."

"I don't know."

"Just think about it."

"Okay, okay. I'll think about it."

CHAPTER 85

A lofty precipice rose in front of them, magnificent and power-ful. A wooden sign painted brown with blue letters heralded the entrance to Superior National Park.

Thom pulled the truck into a small, single-lane parking lot.

Henry slid out of the truck.

The air was brisk and cut at him. He put on his jacket and zipped it upped to the top. Charley grabbed her hoodie and leapt out of the truck.

"Dawn," Thom said, "how do we conceal your shotgun? You can't carry it in a national park. We don't need that kind of publicity. Do we saw off the barrel?"

"Don't you touch my shotgun," she said. "Would you ask a painter to saw off his paintbrush?"

"Oh," Thom said with a surprised laugh, "so you're an artist, now?"

"You're just noticing?" Dawn racked the slide of her shotgun.

"I have been a fan of your work for years."

Dawn smiled, satisfied. She took a scarf from the truck and wrapped it around her neck and under her right arm like a holster. She twisted the scarf to form a loop and slid the shotgun down into it. The shotgun dangled by its stock, high up in the armpit.

"Hopefully, we won't have to fight," Thom said. "We stick together, get the furnace, and get out."

"We didn't get in and get out at the school," Charley said.

"I know," Thom said, "but now we're together."

Thom wore a heavy tweed jacket and Dawn put on a long duster coat that stretched to her knees and concealed the shotgun. Thom grabbed a backpack from the covered bed of the truck, and they set out toward the hiking trails.

Henry had no idea what he should be looking for. No one else did either. What does a furnace even look like? Trying to find it was like the blind leading the blind, but he was supposed to be the one who could see. Even so, they had to press on. The Nekura had to be stopped. His life had been shattered. He didn't want that to happen to anyone else.

Blind? Yeah. But onward. Onward until his eyes were opened.

CHAPTER 86

The trail wound deep into the evergreen woods. The trees stood tall and their massive arms created a sanctimonious feeling like a cathedral. The trails wound upward over innumerable exposed roots that coursed through the earth like the veins of creation. The spruce trees thrived in lush greenery. Many of the other trees had already lost their leaves, except for the stubborn oaks that refused to release theirs to the changing weather. The leaves that had fallen made a variegated color carpet, fit for the treading of royalty.

Thom led the expedition forward. A few straggling hikers hailed him with polite greetings along the way.

"There are not many people hiking," Charley said.

"Most people have resigned from hiking the trails by this time of year," Thom said. "Many of the leaves are already down."

"There were no other cars in the parking lot," Dawn said.

"What does the furnace look like?" Charley asked.

"I think I'm going to grab a hunk of lava right out of the mountain-side," Henry said. "I'm just going to go with that. Couldn't hurt any worse than what I've already felt."

Charley began to sing the chorus that Dawn sang from the book. She tried to mimic the same inflections, but it didn't have the same haunting quality as when Dawn sang. Still, Charley tried.

"If I were a furnace," she said after she finished, "where would I be?" She hummed the tune to herself.

There was no snow at the top of the mountain but in a couple weeks there would be plenty. Natural springs curved next to their path, and with the promise of snow the streams would find renewed vigor. The trail rose in areas of steep incline that required extra effort, but they clambered up and pressed on. Except for a few sparse areas of difficulty, it had been a refreshing walk in the woods.

Henry chuckled. "Everyone else is in school. I'm hiking a volcano."

"I haven't missed a day of school since second grade," Charley said, "and now I've missed over a week!"

"I hope things will be able to go back to normal, though."

"I'm okay with a little abnormal."

"You want things to stay this way?"

"It's better than how they were. Go back to living a dull, ignorant life? No thank you."

He didn't know how to answer, so he didn't say anything. He didn't feel like fighting.

"We have a little way to go," Thom said. "We have to go to the top because that is where the fire reaches to the skies like the song says. We are going to the mouth of the volcano."

CHAPTER 87

As they continued upward, they entered a thick fog, and visibility decreased. At first the fog was faint haziness, plumps of gray suspended in the air. It rolled on the mountain, moved by the wind. The further they ascended into the density, the more the fog tumbled in strange ways, like it moved of its own volition. The wind stilled but the fog didn't. It seemed to be alive. A feeling of ice tingled on Henry's neck.

Henry could not see past the immediate tree line surrounding them. The sky and mountaintop disappeared from sight. The scenery felt dizzying. Still, Thom led on as the trail wound its way among an increasing sparsity of trees.

Henry glanced all around. Something didn't feel right.

"Dad, why are all the trees without leaves?"

"It's the fall, Henry. This far north, most trees lose their leaves earlier."

"Dad, that's not what I mean."

Henry pointed at the trees. The maple and ash and birch were vacant of leaves, but those weren't the trees Henry was pointing at. He was pointing at the evergreens.

All the evergreens were without needles. They were completely barren. Their branches looked like barbed wires spun into a cocoon that exploded outward into tangled disarray—bony fingers reaching out at the intruders. What used to be hearty spruces and firs were now stark and empty.

Everything looked dead.

Dawn looked where Henry was pointing. She backpedaled and shook her head with rising tension. "No . . . no no no!"

"Dawn," Thom said.

She looked at him and bent over with arms outstretched, pleading. "We aren't ready for this! They . . ." she pointed to Henry and Charley, "they aren't ready for this!"

"What's going on?" Henry said.

"They're just kids!" Dawn said.

"No, they're not," Thom said and shook his head. He turned in a circle and looked at the lifeless surroundings. "Not anymore."

Thom gave a pained sigh. "These are the Wastelands," he said. "At some point on the trail, we crossed the Veil."

"We haven't been back across the Veil since we fled, and we go first to the Wastelands! The Nekura will find us soon," Dawn said. "They fill this place."

"We just walked right out of our world and into theirs?" Charley said. "We're on the other side of the Veil?"

Dawn's eyes darted to Thom. "We have to leave."

The foggy mist that surrounded them grew denser and darker. It swirled around them and felt heavy on Henry's skin, like it was pushing him. The mist seemed to resemble—

Smoke! Like in his dream . . .

Henry gasped and looked at Dawn. "Mom! Can you do the thing, where your hair lights up?"

"No, I can't just do it whenever I choose!" She spun around in a circle. "I never came here even when I was in my full Salient form. The Wastelands are too dangerous."

Henry looked down at his feet.

The trail had disappeared. He had no idea where they came from or where they were going.

Dawn noticed it, too. "We're lost."

CHAPTER 88

H enry must've been hallucinating.

The dead trees moved. He knew it.

The movement was unperceivable at first. They glided through the ground, and the smoky mist moved with them. Henry turned around and saw the faint, halting motion of the trees. He whirled around, and the trees on the other side were closer. Their branches touched each other, like hands held in a circle of death.

He spun around again. The knotty arms of the trees wove together to form a jagged mesh that held his family captive.

"Mom, Dad, the trees are moving!"

The trees slid along the ground in slow menace. The dead branches inclined forward. The limbs stretched from the trunks and grew with slow creaking, their bark cracking and falling to the ground in ashy piles. The forest had become a mangrove swamp of encroaching death.

Dawn reached for her shotgun inside her coat. Her hand grasped at air where the stock should have been. "Where is my shotgun?" she said and spun around.

The last part of the shotgun was being pulled into the ground by black roots.

She had been pickpocketed.

"Thom!" Dawn cried. "I don't have my gun—the roots are coming out of the ground!"

A blackened tree root grew over Henry's foot and held him down. More roots rose up and wrapped around his leg. His shoe sunk into the ground.

He tried to yank his foot upward, but the ground was like quicksand and he only sank further.

"Dad!" His voice cracked. He was already covered to his knee.

Thom threw his tweed coat on the ground and the gauntlets showed on his arms. The markings on his arms and chest glowed, and an arrow formed in his hands.

The trees halted before the Light. Henry stopped sinking into the ground. An arrow pierced the base of the roots around Henry's leg. The hungry vines released Henry and the roots sizzled under the blue light. Henry yanked his foot out of the mud.

The terror paused in his heart. He could move again.

Thom picked a spot in the tree line and pointed another arrow toward it. He walked forward.

The trees moved backward with reluctance. Their crooked arms released and opened a way out of the grove. The arrow of blue light in Thom's hands stayed steady. Thom led the way out of the mangrove trees, and when Henry turned around, the trees descended into the ground, like melting black wax. The dense mist swirled around the remaining tree stumps, which evaporated into the fog.

"Dad, what was that?"

"Stay close," Thom said. He walked forward.

"Do you know where we are going?" Charley asked.

"In the Wastelands, everything is manipulated," Dawn said. "Salients never manipulate the environment like this. Time and space are twisted here. It is a signature of the Nekura. A day can stretch on for weeks with the sun in the sky. You can walk in circles for hours and have never moved a step. It is living vertigo here."

"Okay, so . . . no. The answer is no, you don't know where we're going," Henry said.

"But if we find the furnace," Thom said, "all this will be over. We could end it now."

"Thom, we have to figure out how to leave. That is now priority number one," Dawn said.

"But if we see something that looks blue," Thom said, "anything at all, that could be it. Keep looking while we search for a way out."

CHAPTER 89

The mist retreated before Thom's arrow and showed a path downward into a small crater. Henry followed Thom into it.

"We're at the top of the volcano," Thom said.

In the center of the volcano's mouth, Henry saw a faint glimmer. A glint of blue light flashed again behind the curtain of the swirling fog.

Henry pointed. "I think I see it!"

"Follow me," Thom called over his shoulder as he dashed forward. The fog instantly swallowed him up.

"Thom, wait!" Dawn launched after him.

Henry couldn't see the blue glimmer anymore.

Or his parents.

Charley and Henry stood alone in the dense, curling fog.

"Did you see which way they went?" Charley said.

"No."

"What do we do?"

"I don't know!"

"Thom! Dawn!" Charley yelled.

"Mom! Dad!" Henry called.

They yelled over and over. No reply. The fog suffocated their cries for help and drowned them out.

Charley turned to Henry. "Don't you leave me!"

"I won't."

She grabbed his hand and squeezed until his fingers bulged with the pressure. "We have to stick together."

Sure. Tell that to his parents.

CHAPTER 90

Thom slowed when he got close to the glinting blue light.
The fog in the volcano's mouth swirled and Thom crouched on his knees to see the source of the light better. It was a stone, the size of a baseball. Blue crystalline flecks were embedded inside, like a piece of blue amethyst had been ground up and mixed throughout it. Thom reached down and pulled back on the stone. It felt stuck.

He dug his fingers into the dirt around the stone, feeling the gritty hard flecks of volcanic rock under his fingernails. The stone refused to move.

Dawn stumbled through the mist behind him and tripped on his leg. She landed on the ground with a thud. Thom jumped.

"Thom!" She clambered to her feet and let out a sigh.

"Dawn?"

"I was calling for you but you never answered!"

"I didn't hear you."

"I'm just glad I found you. I couldn't see you in this accursed fog. Where are the kids?"

"They're not with you?"

Dawn's face went white with fear. "No, I thought they were with you."

"No, they were with you."

"You were the one leading!"

"They were following you!"

Dawn grabbed Thom's shoulder. "We have to find them. Come on!"

Thom didn't move. His eyes were locked on the stone in front of him. "Go look for them. I need to get this stone out. If this is the furnace, it will set everything right."

"No! Are you crazy? I'm not leaving you again. I only found you because I tripped over your leg."

Thom said nothing.

If this was the furnace, then if he could just get it out—

"Thom! We have to go." Her voice was urgent.

He drove the blue arrow downward underneath the rock and levered back on it. The rock still clung to the earth in protest.

Dawn put her hands up to her mouth. "Henry! Charley! Where are you?"

Nothing.

"Dawn, we need the Light's power to clear this fog and find them. Come on!"

Dawn shook her head, then bent over with a huff. "You were wrong about the safe house," she said. "It nearly cost Henry his life. You'd better not be wrong about this, too."

She grabbed the end of the arrow next to Thom. When her hand touched it, the arrow grew in Thom's hand until it became like a giant crowbar.

"On three," he said.

"Just hurry!"

"One . . . two . . . three!"

They yanked back on the arrow. The stone dislodged and flew away into the mist.

"Follow me," Thom said.

Dawn held the end of Thom's large blue arrow and they raced forward like runners in a baton exchange.

The glinting stone was only a few feet away. When they reached it, Thom bent down and his fingers brushed the edge of the stone.

Instant pain. His temple felt like it had exploded from the impact of a mortar round.

He was airborne, arms flailing. He felt like he was tumbling through a vacuum.

He landed hard on his back, and the jagged rocks dug into his spine. He forced his eyes open.

His vision was blurry. and the world spun.

A massive onyx Bludgeon stood next to him with its teeth bared. Its arm looked like a giant club.

Unconsciousness swept him away.

CHAPTER 91

"Thom?"

He was just there and then he vanished. A giant black shadow suddenly overtook him and he disappeared.

Dawn looked down at her hand where she had held the blue arrow. The arrow was gone. She uncurled her fingers and faint wisps swirled out of her hand.

"Thom!" She snapped her head all around but saw nothing.

The blue light from the small stone had also vanished.

She was alone.

Hazy gray fog swirled around her like a sandstorm of volcanic ash.

She didn't have the furnace.

She didn't have her shotgun.

She didn't have her family.

She felt it. The overdrive. It wanted to come out. But it was a simmering fear rather than a florid panic sending her to critical mass. She wanted her inner spark to light up the mountain.

It stayed stuck inside.

She couldn't allow herself to be captured. She knew what the Nekura would do if they caught a Salient.

The dense shadow lurched out of the mist before she had time to react. A giant Bludgeon smashed into her and she flew backward into the unknown.

Her head hit the ground with a bang and blackness washed over her.

CHAPTER 92

The earth began to shake. It was a slow grumbling, like the earth growled at them.

"What's happening?" Charley asked.

The vibrations traveled through the soles of Henry's shoes all the way up his body. His bones shook.

The ground was getting warmer. Pockets of steam drifted upward from cracks in the surface. The swirling mist grew darker in color. The blackening air carried a choking smell. Henry coughed as smoke poured into his nose.

The realization swept over him.

"The smoke, Charley! It's not just mist from the Wastelands, it's smoke from the volcano! It's getting ready to blow!"

"Oh, no!"

She let go of Henry's hand. She snapped her hand down toward the ground and a second later she held the whip. The blue cord encircled her feet and the smoke retreated from her.

"Charley!" Henry reached to grab her arm back.

It was too late. The smoke enveloped him and shut him out.

She did the one thing she made Henry promise not to do—let go of his hand. She had the Light, but he didn't. The smoke picked him off as soon as she let go.

The smoke swirled around him and pressed against him. It clogged his nostrils. He felt like he was spinning in circles.

Living vertigo . . .

He swam in disorienting fog and it dove under his feet. He couldn't see the ground anymore. Every direction was cold, heavy, living fog. He wasn't sure which way was up. He couldn't see or hear anything.

CHAPTER 93

Charley let go of his hand to make the whip.

She turned around and he was gone. How was he gone that fast?

She made him promise not to let go. But then she did!

Henry wasn't connected to the Light. But Thom and Dawn were. They could fight back. And it would be easier to look for two people instead of one.

Charley didn't want to abandon Henry. But standing in indecision would forfeit them all.

She charged ahead and the smoke parted for the Light. Find Thom and Dawn. Then, with the furnace, they can get Henry back.

Her gut churned with the decision of what she should do, and she tasted bile rise in the back of her throat.

She had to be fast. He would be dead within minutes without the Light.

But she couldn't fight alone.

Hold on, Henry.

CHAPTER 94

The grumbling volcano shook. Small rocks vibrated loose and fell into crevices in the ground. Charley had a hard time maintaining her footing on the crumbling surface beneath her. The heat was becoming intense. Then, the shaking subsided.

Faster. She had to move faster.

She didn't have time to—

She screeched to a halt.

A giant Bludgeon of shining black onyx appeared before her, birthed out of the dense volcanic mist. It threw its arms upward in the air and the ground shook in response. The Bludgeon was somehow controlling the volcano, coaxing it to explode.

The Bludgeon was of beastly proportion. Large, rocky protrusions jutted out from its head like a helmet plume of sharpened stone. The Bludgeon was gladiatorial, larger than the ones she had seen before, empowered from its presence in the Wastelands.

It snarled with bared teeth. The Bludgeon lowered its arms and the shaking ground settled.

Charley steadied her feet. If she didn't stop this creature from calling forth the lava deep inside the mountain, the volcano would erupt in minutes.

Two more giant Bludgeons materialized out of the mist, one on each side of the gladiator. They were suddenly there, like the ash in the air had summoned them into existence.

Three against one.

The blue whip twitched with anticipation to lash out at the Nekura. It cracked and snaked on the ground, eager to drink up the darkness.

The muscles in her legs tensed.

CHAPTER 95

Henry tumbled through the mist. The ocean of smoke spun him like a lost swimmer in a twisting vortex.

It was hard to think.

Where were his parents? He needed them. He needed to ride their coattails out of this mess—the fog, the volcano, the Wastelands. Everything.

Nausea washed over him.

They had the Light. Not him.

Charley said to wear the gauntlets. Just in case.

What good would they do? Burn him alive? At least that would end things faster than being lost forever in the Wastelands, behind enemy lines.

The whole mountain was spinning.

He was fighting for his life. And failing.

He was being swallowed alive.

He was alone. Defenseless. Save for the scarring, searing Light.
He had nothing to live for anymore.
Everything was lost. He was undone.
Wasn't loyal.
Changed.

CHAPTER 96

Charley pounced forward like a jaguar. She leapt toward the gladiator Bludgeon in the center.

The Bludgeon on the right was equally fast. It struck her with a large, sweeping arm and knocked her off course. She landed on her side to the left of the creatures.

The intercepting Nekura charged at her as soon as she landed. It held its jagged arm in the air and howled as it barreled forward.

Instincts fired and Charley sprang to her feet with the momentum that had carried her into the gymnastic tumble she had practiced for years.

The Nekura couldn't stop in time.

Charley ripped the whip downward with an arcing crack that severed the giant Bludgeon in two from top to bottom. The smoldering halves fell apart and the creature dematerialized, uniting with the swirling, smoke-filled air.

She looked for the other two.

She saw only the gladiator. It raised its arms in the air and the mountain rumbled.

Charley staggered. It was difficult to see.

Where did the other—

Giant, rocky arms wrapped around Charley's chest. She was lifted off the ground, and her arms were held down at her side immobilized. She thrashed against the Bludgeon, but its massive strength was unbreakable. She couldn't get her whip up—her arm was pinned against her body inside the Nekura's grasp.

The whip dove for the feet of the Bludgeon but flickered when the Bludgeon squeezed Charley. Its grip crushed her chest and pushed the air out of her lungs. The gladiator put its arms down and the eerie calm returned. It sauntered over to Charley.

The gladiator bent down and leered in her face with an eyeless visage. Its voice was low and gurgled, like its throat was a cauldron filled with cooked bile.

"Death to the Light," it said.

The acerbic breath choked her. The Nekura that held her squeezed again. The remaining air fled from her lungs. Dizziness pressed down upon her. The whip in her hand faded out of existence.

Her vision went black around the edges and her hearing became muffled. Her head fell to the side and she began to slip into unconsciousness.

The last thing she saw was a faint blue light in the distance, like a light at the end of a tunnel. She heard its call.

Move toward the light.

CHAPTER 97

Move toward the light.

That's what people say when they're dying.

Or maybe the light was moving toward her.

Hard to tell.

The mist parted.

The blue light in the distance came closer, closer.

The tunnel of smoke separated. It cascaded to the sides of the approaching blue light like water breaking upon rock. The light flew upward like a flare into the night.

It grew in size, brightened in intensity.

Then, it fell back down like the remains of a shooting star.

It was going to overtake her.

But what came down was not a star.

A brilliant blue light came down in a thunderous, concussive blast on the head of the Nekura holding Charley. The Bludgeon collapsed into a heap, like an overripe pumpkin.

Charley fell to the ground on all fours and sucked in large, gasping breaths.

It never felt so good to breathe.

What just happened?

Her vision filled again. The cracked ground of the volcano filled her sight. It ran with faint rivulets of orange lava and was hot on her hands.

The volcano was going to erupt soon.

Something had saved her. A blue light.

She looked up.

She saw it again, bobbing and dancing.

The mist vanished before it. Her vision sharpened.

Disbelief washed over her.

CHAPTER 98

Henry felt like the gauntlets had exploded.

But the feeling was different this time than when he shot the pistol. It wasn't searing pain that he felt. It was a feeling like warm water running on his hand after being outside in the cold.

The connection happened when he finally bowed before it. The Light. When he had nothing left to give, he gave it up. An inner genuflection.

Then the gauntlets activated and a bo staff of blue light exploded into his hand. The weapon was a simple, straight rod, but it looked as alive as Charley's whip.

The first Bludgeon was no match for the attack. Jumping in the air had given Henry momentum, and when he brought the staff down the creature crumpled under the blow.

Charley was free. He was almost too late.

The second Bludgeon was bigger. A row of sharpened stones rose from the creature's head. It looked like a Nekura mercenary in battle attire. It roared at Henry's sudden presence and his weapon of Light.

The staff vibrated in his hands. It tugged him forward with subtle insistence. It wanted the Nekura's ash.

The Bludgeon charged forward and struck at Henry with a massive fist. He dodged and parried with the bo.

He didn't know what a parry was. How did he just—.

The Bludgeon struck with a sweeping hook of its other arm, and Henry blocked it again and sidestepped with a leap.

He didn't know how to move like that. He just did it. Something new awoke inside him.

The Nekura shot its arms up and the ground trembled. The volcano shook and Henry staggered on his feet. He shoved the staff in the ground and held on.

But planting the bo also made him . . .

A stationary target.

He ripped the staff out of the ground and looked up.

The Bludgeon had paused for a moment with its target unmoving. It took a large breath and reared back.

Henry had a split-second advantage.

He sprang forward before the Nekura could react.

A quick jab to the low, wide forehead with the bo made the Bludgeon stagger back and it couldn't exhale.

Henry cracked the creature's leg with the other end of his staff. It fell to one knee.

One hit after the other, each end of the staff gouged the Bludgeon's rocky shell. Henry pummeled it with a chain of rhythmic hits like he was beating a drum.

Henry thrust the bo forward into the Nekura's belly. It doubled over, and smoke rose from its mouth. The staff infused the creature with a flood of light that poured into the Nekura's abdomen. The Bludgeon groaned and its toothy mouth twisted downward. The deep crevices of the creature's exterior glowed blue. The monster swelled and stretched until it was taut, then exploded into a shower of ash and blue light.

CHAPTER 99

Henry ran over to Charley and dropped to his knees.

"Charley! Are you alright? Charley!"

She coughed. "I think so." She sat up and leaned back on her arms. "Look at you! You wore the gauntlets."

"Are you injured?" He looked over her arms and legs, then looked at her back. He tried to assess her how his Dad had done in the hotel room.

"I'm fine, Henry." She nodded, held his gaze. "Thanks."

He broke away and stood up, then looked around.

"Charley, just stay on the ground for a second. I think I've got a way to find Mom and Dad."

Henry held the bo staff at its end and lifted it above his head. He spun it like the rotor of a helicopter.

The smoke swirled into a dense cloud like it was an injured animal. It recoiled into a twisting vortex and lifted off the mountain top. It dissipated into a ceiling of cloud cover.

"That is no ordinary volcanic smoke," Charley said. "That's evil." Charley squinted her eyes and surveyed the landscape. "I can see easier now. Look over there!"

Charley pointed to where Thom and Dawn lay on the ground thirty feet away. Charley and Henry ran over to them.

"Mom! Dad!" Henry dropped down on the ground. He grabbed their arms and shook them. Their skin was still warm and they were breathing.

"Ugh," Thom said. He put his hand to his head. "What happened?"

Dawn sat up with a start. She looked at Henry and the staff of light in his hand. Her mouth fell open.

"Henry," she said, "you did it."

He was abashed about his new connection and how he had muddled it the first time. He released the staff into evanescent air.

Dawn pulled him close in an embrace. "Henry, I'm so proud."

"Yes," Thom said and stood up. "We would have been toast for sure." He placed his hands on each of Henry's shoulders. "Something is different now."

"Yeah, I can feel it," Henry said. "But we never got the furnace." He looked around again. No glinting blue light remained in the mouth of the volcano, but the amount of orange lava was increasing. The trembling surged under their feet.

"The Bludgeon did enough to wake the volcano," Dawn said.

"There!" Thom said and pointed. The rolling mist no longer hid their exit. He shot a blue arrow toward a small path that led out of the volcano's mouth. "Run!"

The mountain shook violently with another quake.

Thom crested the mouth first and ran down the path. Dawn, Charley, and Henry sprinted right behind him. They ran down the trail until they started to see trees again.

They were nearing the exit of the Wastelands, the same place that the trees had tried to ensnare them when they first—

Thom tripped on a root that rose out of the ground and he tumbled down. Dawn collided with him. Charley swerved, but Henry barreled into her and they collapsed into a pile.

CHAPTER 100

The sun shone through the windows of the truck when Henry awoke next.

They'd made it out.

Henry looked out the window of the truck. A few big-rig trucks had parked next to them. The rest-stop appeared large and clean. Vendors and restaurants were advertised on the exterior wall. His stomach growled.

Dawn poked Thom in the ribs. "Aren't you going to take a girl out for something to eat?"

"Come on," Thom said. "Let's get some food."

They got out of the truck. The sun was warm and the breeze felt invigorating. It was a beautiful day in late fall.

"Hey, where are our gauntlets?" Henry asked.

Charley looked at her arms and patted them. "I don't have mine either!"

"Don't worry," Thom said. "We're fine. Let's eat."

"But Dad!"

"I'm hungry," Dawn said. "We'll worry about them later."

Thom and Dawn said nothing more. They walked away toward the building.

Henry looked inside the truck and checked under the seat, then got out and looked in the bed of the truck. Nothing. He looked up. Thom and Dawn had already disappeared.

"Why aren't they concerned?" Charley asked.

"Come, on Charley. We can't lose them, too."

They walked toward the rest-stop. Charley leaned in. "What happened? How did we even get here? Did we fall asleep?"

"I don't know."

"It's really warm and sunny. This weather is totally different than before."

"That's a good thing," Henry said.

"Is it?"

"Why not? Better than that volcano."

"Something just feels off."

Henry grimaced. His hand hurt again. It had felt better at the volcano, even when he held the bo staff. But now it stung again.

They entered through the rest-stop's glass doors and saw Thom and Dawn. They sat alone in the center of a cafeteria, with metal wire chairs neatly arranged around long white tables. Everything gleamed in immaculate cleanliness. Two red trays with food on them awaited Charley and Henry's arrival.

Nobody else was inside. Familiar food-court restaurants decorated the rest-stop's inside. There was a small Mid-Mart store, too. But there were no patrons, no employees, no drivers for the trucks outside. Just Thom and Dawn, sitting in the middle of a ghost town of convenience stores.

The *Book of the Salients* lay in front of them.

"That wasn't the furnace," Thom said. "Here, maybe we can find out more from the book."

"Yes," Dawn said to them. "Maybe you can help."

CHAPTER 101

"Aren't you hungry?" Dawn asked. A large hamburger filled a plaid paper boat on the red tray. A mountain of fries spilled over the edges of the tray and steamed with invitation.

Henry's stomach growled again.

"Here, look at the book," Thom said.

Henry sat down and Thom pulled the food away. He pushed the book in front of Henry. "This is more important," he said.

"I can't eat?"

"We don't want you smearing the pages with mustard, Henry," Dawn said and smiled. "Just help us first. Consider the food a reward for a job well done."

Henry didn't know if he could eat anyway. With each pulse of pain in his hand, a new wave of nausea washed through him.

He groaned and flipped the pages. He stopped again at the picture of the man with the hammer. The man held the hammer like it was a flag and he was claiming a new land. A long thin banner of red with silver edgework hung from the hammer just beneath its head, with the same symbol as the emblem on the book's spine. It looked like a coat of arms.

"Do you think it means something more?" Thom asked.

"Well it must, if we were wrong about the volcano."

It was hard for Henry to focus. His hand throbbed with pulsating rhythm. The intensity was distracting.

"I don't have my glasses," Charley said and snagged the book. "They're in the backpack in the truck."

"Do you need your glasses?" Dawn asked.

Charley turned down the corner of her mouth. "I guess I remember it well enough without them. I just won't be able to see all the colors."

Henry paused and sighed. He snatched the book from in front of Charley. He rubbed his burned hand and tried to focus. It was up to him—the secret was locked away inside his mind.

"Colors . . ." he said.

He read the inscription again.

Not burnished bronze nor smelter's ore
Is the fire's blazing core
In weathered lands on distant shore
Fire reaches, wanting more
From dancing flames, the skies adore
The rising fire they implore.

"Not burnished bronze," Henry said. He nodded and looked back at the picture. "The hammer has more details compared to the man in the cloak. And yet . . ."

He tapped his finger on his chin. Inside his repressed memories, he was bulldozing a path to find the answer.

"The hammer—the bronze handle, the head made of metal ore—is not the point of the picture. Something else is. The lyric is telling the reader to look past the man and his hammer. They are the obvious attention-getters, but also a distraction." He traced the next line with his finger. "In weathered lands."

Charley looked over his shoulder at the picture.

Even without Charley's glasses, Henry saw some of the details, but they were more subdued. On the left in the deep background, a small coastline of water snaked in from the side of the page. The sky held smudges and splotches of light gray that foretold coming rain. Shadows were cast on the land below. The dark clumping clouds obscured any of the sun's attempt to—

"The sun!" Henry said.

CHAPTER 102

Henry jumped up. Charley's chair teetered and she nearly fell to the ground.

"What?" Charley said.

"The sun, Charley! It's the sun!" The answer rang inside him like a struck gong. He grabbed her by the arm and yanked her closer.

"But the sun isn't in the picture, Henry."

"That's the point. Look!" He pointed again.

Realization crossed Charley's face. "It's a cryptogram," she said. "It's meant to dissemble!"

"Dissemble?"

"Yes, Henry," she sighed and rolled her eyes. "It means to have a misleading appearance, to conceal the truth. You know, false on the surface?"

"Oh, sure," Henry said. "Obviously."

"Look at the last line," Charley said, "about the rising fire. What fire rises? The rising sun! Henry, you're right!"

"And the sun rises—"

"In the east," Charley said and threw her hands up. She grinned. "We have to go east. As far as we can. To the distant shore."

Henry nodded. That resonated inside him. They found the answer!

Dawn smiled. "That's great, you two."

Thom nodded.

"Now we eat," Henry said. He reached across the table and snagged the burger. A job well done. It was a double patty, too. Oh, he was so hungry. He would fight through the nausea.

He took a massive bite.

The burger turned to ash inside his mouth.

CHAPTER 103

Henry spat.

Smoke plumed out of his mouth. He spluttered, but the taste clung to his tongue.

His hand pounded.

He should have listened to Charley. She recognized something was wrong when he didn't.

Charley reeled back. She snapped back to Thom and Dawn. They smiled and twisted into circling pools of smoke, like dirty water draining out of a bathtub, and disappeared.

The scenery faded and drifted away. Light vanished and the rest-stop receded into the void. A canopy of darkness descended from the sky and threatened to swallow them.

Everything was vanishing. Henry looked to the only thing left he could see.

"Charley! Grab my hand!"

He thrust his hand out to her. She was going dim. She was being swept away.

Charley stretched her hand back toward Henry. Their fingers barely touched.

The darkness yanked at her. It pulled her. Yawning, hungry darkness.

He stretched. Every finger tingled, ligaments taut, near breaking with the effort.

She clasped her fingers around his.

The pain seared through his hand with her grip. The same burning, fire-filled pain soaked his senses again, like when he had shot the pistol and experienced his scorching introduction to the Light.

He staggered. He felt his senses fade. The only thing left was indescribable burning.

But this time, he would not let go of Charley's hand, like she did his.

He squeezed. Despite the raging pain, he had to hold on.

He would not let go.

The pain knocked him unconscious.

CHAPTER 104

Henry's hand didn't hurt anymore.

Was he dead?

He opened his eyes. He was on his back. A thicket of woven tree branches encased him a few inches from his face in an enormous, mutated spider web of charred ash. He looked toward his feet.

The branches were close. But they didn't bind him like they had when he first entered the Wastelands. But why not? He looked to his right.

Charley lay next to him, unconscious, branches encroaching but not touching her. He looked down at their hands.

They held together.

The pain in his hand didn't incapacitate him. It hadn't knocked him unconscious.

It had knocked him conscious.

Back to the real world. The rest-stop was another fevered dream, sewn by the Nekura.

He looked at Charley's other hand. The whip glowed in her grip, and he traced the course of it with his eyes. It encircled the two of them completely.

That was it. The whip was the reason why the trees could not touch them.

Time to get out.

A blue staff surged into Henry's hands and pierced upward like a giant needle. The tree branches creaked and an eerie moaning filled the air. The branches fell away and the cocoon opened.

Henry stood up and swatted the branches with his staff. The branches retreated and coils of black withered into atrophy. Large chunks fell to the ground and disintegrated.

"Charley. Charley! Wake up."

Charley's eyes shot open. "Henry!"

"I'm here."

"Where are we?"

"Still on the volcano. Those trees were trying to get to us, but your whip protected us."

She looked down at the blue line that circumscribed them.

"We have to leave," she said. "I can't take this place any longer. I just had the most horrible dream."

"Me too."

"I dreamt that we were at a rest-stop and your mom and dad were there. They were really insistent that we needed to find the furnace, and I told them, but then they just disappeared."

Dread nestled down into Henry's mind.

"And I was the only one concerned about not having the gauntlets?" he asked.

"How did you know . . ."

Charley put a hand over her open mouth.

"It wasn't a dream," she said.

"Not exactly."

"But how did we share the same dream?"

"I think it's because we were holding hands, inside the circle of your whip. And when I grabbed your hand in the dream, I woke up."

"Why didn't it wake me up?"

Henry rubbed his scarred hand. "Let's just say that waking up is hard to do. I know." He pulled Charley to her feet. "We have to find my parents."

CHAPTER 105

Henry barely saw his parents through the thicket that acted like twisted prison bars.

Thom and Dawn were bound tightly in a thatch of mangrove trees. They hung suspended in the air, dangling from the trees like bodies hanged from gallows.

The vines slithered around his parents and constricted tighter around their necks, giant anacondas growing out of the trunks.

Charley wrinkled her nose and snarled.

She dove into the thatch and snapped the whip down in her hand. It incised the snaking limbs and moaning flooded out of the trees.

She tore into them like a woodchipper.

Smoke billowed into a great cloud. The branches released their grip on Thom and Dawn. They fell forward to the ground.

Charley moved onto the roots, and they dissolved before the whip. The roots released Dawn's shotgun and expelled it out of the dirt.

"Mom! Dad!" Henry rolled Thom to his back and Charley helped Dawn sit up.

"Ugh," Dawn said. "I'm tired of this." She rubbed her face and then saw her shotgun at her feet. She snagged the weapon from the ground. "I'm glad to have you back," she said to her gun.

The mountainside shook again. It trembled in agitation, and then a loud explosion ripped through the air.

Thom was already on his feet. "The volcano just erupted!" he said. "We've got to move."

Thom ran forward with wobbly knees on unsteady ground. He nearly fell again but held an arrow of blue light in front of him. The trees pulled their roots away and the path became clearer.

He stopped and turned his head.

Everything was still.

Henry looked back up the trail from where they came. It wound up the mountain in a long, twisting course hundreds of feet behind them. Clusters of evergreen spruces, full of lush green needles, decorated the pathway. Two squirrels scampered along the path in a flurry of activity, chasing each other up a tree.

Dawn looked back, too. "We made it back through the Veil," she said. She let her shoulders slump in relief. She stowed the shotgun insider her coat again. "Let's get out of here."

The sun was low and the air was cold. Thom no longer had his tweed jacket, so he wrapped his arms around himself to stay warm.

"Oh, wow, I feel so hungry!" Henry said. The hunger caused him physical pain that ravaged his stomach. "I'm starving."

"Me too," Charley said. "I'm so wiped out right now. I could sleep for as long as you did, Henry."

In the parking lot, one other vehicle was parked next to theirs—a small, white pick-up truck with the symbol of the Superior National Park painted on its side. A park ranger stood at the base of the trail with his back to them.

Thom closed the gap until he was nearly upon the ranger. "Excuse me, sir."

The ranger turned around and jumped in surprise. "Oh! You startled me."

"Has there been any activity in the volcano?"

The man stared at Thom like he was an alien who had landed from the distant horizons of another galaxy.

"Of course not," he said. "There hasn't been anything for two decades." The ranger furrowed his eyebrows. "Look, is this you?" he said and pointed to Thom's truck.

"Yes. Why?"

"Park rules say that you can't stay overnight in the preserve. I don't even know where you would stay up there since there's no camping site." He looked at each one of them. "And you don't have any gear either? Really tried roughing it, I see."

"What are you talking about?" Dawn said. "We didn't go camping up there. We went for a short hike up the mountain."

"Lady, this truck has been parked here for three days. I don't call three days on the mountain a short hike."

Henry's eyes widened in disbelief. "Did you say three days?"

"Did you get lost or something up there, like altitude sickness? Not the first time I've seen something like this. This truck has been parked here, unmoved, for the last three days."

Thom walked toward the truck and everyone followed. Nothing more needed to be said.

The park ranger called after them. "Do you all want to go to the hospital? If you've been up there for three days without food or water, I think you should get checked out. That altitude sickness can make people crazy. Makes people see things. Some people talk about seeing weird creatures."

"No," Thom said. "I think we'll be good."

"What are those things on your arms?" the ranger called back.

Thom smiled and patted the gauntlets. "My gear."

CHAPTER 106

The sun shone through the windows of the truck when Henry awoke.

They'd made it out.

This time, hopefully their escape was real.

He looked up at the clock on the dashboard. It was noon. He had slept sixteen hours. He craned his neck. He felt stiff from the way he had slept.

He was getting tired of sleeping so much.

Getting tired of sleeping?

That didn't even make sense.

Ugh. Can't even think right.

He heard Charley stir next to him. "Hey, how did you sleep?" he said.

Charley groaned and stretched her arms above her body. "Decent."

"Sixteen-hours decent."

"I feel so disgusting. The ash, the smoke, sleeping in a truck. I've been wearing the same clothes for four days without showering." She raised her arm to her face and sniffed. "I smell terrible."

"You're not the culprit, Charley," Dawn said. She turned around and looked at Henry. "But we probably all smell."

"Where are we?" Henry asked.

"Driving east," Dawn said. "It's the only word Charley said before falling asleep."

"In the dream," Charley said, "the Nekura were convinced the furnace was somewhere else. We told them how to find it. We figured it out for them!"

Henry's heart sank to remember. They'd given the Nekura the answer. Things were going to get a lot harder.

"It's not your fault," Dawn said. "It's the Nekura's deception. And using dreams is their specialty. However, now we are on the clock. Our enemies know as much as we do and have a head start." "How long will that clock run?" Henry asked.

"Maybe twenty-four hours. Or less."

"How long have we been driving?"

"I'm not sure," Thom said. "I pulled into a secluded area outside of Superior. I needed a moment of rest. The Wastelands did a number on me."

"Did you sleep?" Henry asked.

"Like I said, I never sleep. Somebody's got to keep watch. I just pulled into the rest area and started driving again when I felt better." Thom reached a hand inside his backpack. "Okay, next topic. What do you think this is?" He pulled out the stone from the volcano and passed it to Dawn. The noonday sun played off its surface and illuminated the flecks of deep blue embedded inside.

"It's beautiful," Charley said. "It looks like the blue flecks are alive." The light of the stone ebbed and flowed as if a whole sea of blue colors lived inside.

"Hm," Dawn said. "I think that the furnace should be more . . . fiery."

"But why would the Nekura fight for it?" Henry said. "I felt like we had to go to the volcano to get it."

"It seemed more like a trap to me," Dawn said. "Those Bludgeons were waiting for us to take it."

"I think Dawn's right," Charley said. "Weren't there more Nekura at the school? And at the cabin trying to break in to get to Henry?"

That didn't help Henry feel secure.

"Thom," Dawn said, "you remember the great battle of the Salients?"

"Yes."

"All those Nekura? That's the Nekura fighting back. There's a big difference between then and what we saw on the volcano."

"Great battle of the Salients?" Henry asked.

"It was the last time I saw your mother in her true Salient form," Thom said. "I'll never forget it." He shifted in his seat. "At least never again. That battle is what allowed her the freedom to come to this world without being captured."

"How's that?"

"The Nekura put up the Veil as a way to control from the shadows. It was their grandest scheme—to convince the people of this world the Nekura didn't exist. Just like a ventriloquist, they became a voice without an identity. But the victory of that war opened up the Veil."

Dawn placed the stone into the backpack. She zipped up the bag and stuffed it down at her feet.

"If that stone isn't the furnace," Thom said, "then what is it?"

"I think it's just a pretty paperweight," Dawn said. "We'll know the furnace when we see it."

CHAPTER 107

Thom pulled off the highway at an exit-ramp and headed to a well-lit gas station.

"I'll refill and you all take a moment to recharge," Thom said.

Good. Henry was sick of driving.

"But don't take long," Thom said. "We can't linger."

In a few minutes, Dawn returned with a couple pieces of fruit and some protein bars, sipping on a giant cup of coffee with extra creamer. Under her arm, she carried a large bag of potato chips soaked in sour cream and cheddar cheese. Thom raised an eyebrow.

She gave a sideways glance back at him. "What?"

"Do you think—"

Henry grabbed his arm and interrupted. "I wouldn't," he said to his dad. "Let her be." He smiled and wagged his finger.

"That sounds familiar," Thom said.

"It should."

"Hey now, you can't use my own wisdom against me."

"Shows I'm listening," Henry said and climbed in the truck.

Thom's mouth fell open. He shook his head and laughed.

Thom ran inside and grabbed a tall can of carbonated elixir with a guarantee on its side to keep him awake for twenty-four hours. He chuckled and grabbed two.

It was going to be a long night.

The truck shot back onto the road, heading east. The evening landscape stretched before them while the daylight disappeared into the west. Dusk soon gave way to night and the passing scenery retreated into a shroud of darkness.

The darkness reminded Henry of the smoke and ash of the Nekura. They were enigmatic, but he surprisingly felt okay now.

"Do you feel different?" Henry asked Charley.

Her eyes were closed but she nodded her head. "Absolutely. I didn't even know how fretful I was before I connected to the Light."

"I hear that," Henry said. He looked back out the window.

It was a short conversation, but a lot had been spoken.

The moon peeked out from behind the cloud cover for a few moments and the landscape breathed easier under its quiet illumination.

Henry looked at his mother. The moonlight shone through the glass moonroof of the truck. Her hair dazzled with the reflection of celestial light and glinted with silver sparks. Her hair was beautiful. How had he never noticed it before? He couldn't believe he'd ever thought it was gray hair—it was brilliant, rarefied. It was her inescapable branding as a Salient, the daughter of the Celestials.

He looked back to Charley. She had fallen asleep. Her head had fallen backward and her face pointed at the truck's rooftop. Her position looked monumentally uncomfortable.

Henry grabbed his jacket and scrunched it up. He lifted her head and slid it under. He set her head back down and the curls of her hair fell between his fingers. They were long and caressed his hand as he drew it back.

Her curls were insufferably soft.

"Thank you," Charley said. She smiled and adjusted in her seat.

Henry was startled. "I thought you were asleep! I, uh, I wasn't using it and I thought you could use it. Not that I'm trying to give you stuff I don't want, like leftovers or garbage or something. Everyone just needs a pillow, right? You just looked so weird that I—no! I don't mean you look weird. I just was . . ."

He stammered and looked at her.

She looked like a dove—but this time, not wounded.

The hole he was digging with his words was only getting deeper. He felt jittery.

Best to just stop talking. He looked back out the window.

He saw her smile widen in the reflection.

CHAPTER 108

Midnight. The truck barreled on.

Charley and Dawn were fast asleep. Still recovering from the volcano, probably.

Henry unbuckled his seat belt and leaned forward. "How's it going, Dad?"

"Oh, hey, Henry."

"Are you making it? We all sacked out but you're still driving."

"Ha! I know. I guess these things really work," he said. He lifted up a large aluminum can with flames tattooed on its side. "You're not sleeping?"

"I've been doing a lot of sleeping recently," Henry said. "It's nice to be awake."

They rode in silence for a while. The road steadily appeared out of blackness as the headlights beckoned to it with each mile.

"It's nice to have some conversation," Thom said. "It's been a long haul today. I've been lost in my thoughts up here."

"What were you thinking about?"

A heavy sigh. "We always hoped we could leave the Nekura behind. We wanted to forget about them. We talked about the Light and when to tell you, but you were doing well with baseball and school. Life was going so well that we just never brought it up." He bit his lip. "Funny how bumps in the road can bring about truths you hid away."

"It's okay, Dad," Henry said and placed a hand on his shoulder. "Know what I think?"

"Hm? That we failed you? I regret it so much."

"No. That I still want to be great. Like you."

Thom grimaced and shook his head. "How can you even say that? That's not the right word for me, Henry. Great wouldn't forget. I think a better word is—"

"Reclaimed," Henry said. The word just came to him. "You've been reclaimed. If you were that same person as before, you would still be unaware, sitting at home. All of us would be. That's what I think."

Thom scrunched his eyebrows. He looked like one of his arrows had pierced his own heart. "Wow, that's quite an insight." He glanced into the rearview mirror and caught Henry's eyes. "Thank you."

CHAPTER 109

Thom jerked the wheel. The truck swerved.

The abrasive movements ripped Dawn and Charley back to consciousness.

"What happened?" Dawn asked and sat up. "Did you hit something?"

"Flat tire," Thom said. He pulled the truck to the side of the road. "I saw something like a raccoon. I think I hit it."

He pulled the truck over to the shoulder of the road and put the transmission in park.

"Where are we?" Dawn said.

"I don't know. I think my eyes were drifting. I didn't see any road signs." Thom picked up the energy drink next to him and looked again at the inscription on the side of the can. "Not living up to its advertising," he said. "I'm going to have to get my money back."

Thom opened the door and got out.

Curiosity toyed with Henry. He had to see also.

He opened the door and hopped out.

The night was quiet, other than the wind. The air flew like darts and rustled the trees, gusting between the branches like they weren't there. The cold air drilled Henry and made him gasp. He wished for something more to let him know that life still existed around him. But no cars appeared. No streetlight shone. Just cold, violent winds.

Thom crouched next to the front tire on the passenger's side. He ran his fingers over the tire's large treads.

"The tire's fine," he said. "I wonder what it was."

Dawn and Charley also exited the truck. They left their doors open and walked over to Thom.

"Do we need to change the tire?" Dawn said.

"I'm not sure what happened," Thom said.

"Can we leave then?"

"Maybe."

Dawn leaned close to Thom, her lips a few inches from his ear.

"You remember, don't you," she said. "It's why you've been so quiet."

Thom huffed.

"After passing out on the mountain," Dawn said. "You remember it."

"Yes." His voice was gruff.

"We need to tell them."

"Don't you think I know that?"

"What's stopping you?"

"This tire."

"Before we forget again."

"I just wish I knew—"

Thom straightened up in midsentence. His eyes were no longer on the tire.

Henry felt the change, too. Maybe it was the dimming light of the moon. Maybe it was the vanishing forest line. Maybe it was the smell of smoke that drifted into his nose.

"The fog . . ." Charley whispered. The faint mist swirled over her feet like diseased rodents flooding out of a sewer.

"Back in the truck!" Thom yelled.

They rifled through the open doors of the truck and slammed them shut. The mist swirled outside and pressed against the windows. It clawed against the glass like it was trying to get in.

Thom started the engine and hammered the accelerator down, and the truck leapt forward, showering gravel behind it as it tore back onto the road.

"Dad, are we back in the Wastelands?" Henry clenched his fists. He thought of the blue staff.

"Wherever we are, we're leaving."

Henry looked over Thom's shoulder out the windshield. The dense cloud of twisting smoke obscured everything outside the truck. Still, Thom pressed on. The speedometer accelerated past eighty.

"No more," Thom said. "We have to get out of here."

CHAPTER 110

The fog started to thin.

Henry slumped in the back seat. He sighed in relief.

Charley slouched back also. She looked at Henry and smiled. "Better than the volcano."

Henry nodded.

Thom reached up and opened the moonroof wide. "I need to get that smell of smoke out. It sickens me to smell it." The cool air dove into the truck, but the freshness was a relief.

Charley reached into the side of the door and pulled out a book, then placed it in her lap.

"Hey," Henry said, "I remember that book." He smiled. "That doesn't look like studying."

She smiled back. "Nope. A little light reading. It feels good."

"You do that?"

"I do now."

"*Mildred the Magnificent?*"

She smiled and put on her glasses. The blue streaks on the lenses contrasted the pink frame.

The smile fell from her face. She bent forward and raised her hand. Her fingers brushed the seatback in front of her.

"What are you doing?" Henry asked.

Her fingers lingered on the seatback. "There's a large splotch of black in my vision. I can't seem to touch it." She turned her head from side to side. "And it's staying right in front of me. It looks like a giant scribble, like a toddler went crazy with a black crayon."

She leaned to the side to peer past the seat.

Her mouth opened. She lifted a shaky finger and pointed in front of Dawn.

"Dawn, I think the black is coming from there."

The backpack at Dawn's feet leapt of its own accord. It moved violently and crashed into the side of the door. Dawn jerked her feet up to her seat.

"Mom," Henry said, "what's happening?"

Thom looked over and kept the steering wheel straight with one arm. He reached the other arm down to grab the bag but couldn't.

The moving stopped for a moment.

The backpack ruptured open. A small Gremlin jumped out. In its hand was the blue, baseball-sized stone from the volcano.

It sprang up and slashed with its sharp claws at Dawn. She grabbed the chair-release lever on the seat's side and flew backwards. The chair leveled out and the seatback landed on Henry's knees, pinning him down. The Gremlin swiped at the air where Dawn's face had been a split-second earlier.

The Gremlin landed on the center console. Dawn tried to grab the creature with her hand but its smoky frame passed through her grasp. It cackled and jumped through the open moonroof.

"Don't let it get away!" Thom yelled. He mashed on the brakes but couldn't stop the truck that quickly.

Henry was pinned under Dawn's reclined seat and couldn't move. Dawn fumbled for her shotgun.

If the Gremlin got out of sight, it would be gone for good.

The Gremlin landed on the back of the truck. It took a few scampering steps and leapt for freedom toward the tree line with the blue volcanic stone in its hand.

It was nearly gone.

CHAPTER 111

The Gremlin never landed.

Its momentum suddenly ceased, like it hit a brick wall.

The Gremlin snapped backward in the air, bound by a tight tendril of blue light lassoed around its leg.

Charley was leaning out her window, the wind tossing her hair. An electric whip of blue light extended from one of her gauntlets.

She had caught the Gremlin with deadeye accuracy. Henry didn't even see her move.

She snapped the whip backward and the creature sailed through the air, returning on a round-trip flight toward the truck. The Gremlin screamed in helplessness. The stone came out of its grasp and flew backward into Charley's open hand.

She snapped the whip forward again. The whip tightened around the Gremlin, and the beast emitted a falsetto cry. It flew away from the truck, discarded like a piece of dismembered trash. It started decomposing in midair from its fatal wound.

Thom kept the truck straight but his eyes were fixed on the rearview mirror. He breathed a sigh of relief.

Charley eased back into the truck with the stone. Her whip dissipated into the atmosphere. There was a stunned silence in the car.

"That was fierce," Dawn said. "Nice job." She pulled on the seat lever and lifted the back of her seat off Henry's lap.

"That was the coolest thing ever!" Henry said to Charley.

"I think I'm getting the hang of it," she said. "Each time the whip appears, I feel something new." She eyed her gauntlets, then shifted her focus to the stone in her hands. "Maybe this is important after all."

"How did the Gremlin get into the backpack?" Henry asked.

"When we stopped," Thom said. "Maybe, maybe not. The Gremlin could have been hiding in that backpack since we left the gas station or even earlier, biding its time. But Charley saw it."

"I'm still not convinced that rock is that important," Dawn said. "The Nekura will do anything to propagate lies if it fits their ends. I believe the Nekura would stage a recovery effort only to confuse us, just like they did on the mountaintop. The Nekura thrive on manipulation, anything that would allow them advantage and keep their enemies unsure. Sending one of their own to keep up a wild-goose chase, sacrificing, even devouring their own—it would be just like them."

"You still think it might just be a fancy doorstop?" Charley said.

"Well, at least it's a pretty one," Dawn said. "The furnace should be more alive from the perpetual burning of the Light. This stone just doesn't seem to be it."

"Is it always going to be like this?" Henry asked. "Nekura at every turn?"

"I've never seen it like this," Dawn said.

"We had a false sense of security," Thom said. "We thought things might finally be over. Something significant is taking place because the world behind the Veil has exploded with new activity."

Henry didn't like the rising stakes. He trusted his parents. But he didn't trust anything else. He felt like he was doubting everything.

Descartes would be proud.

CHAPTER 112

The clock crept past two in the morning.

The moon bobbed back and forth from cloud cover to open sky. The winds rolled the clouds through the sky on an endless, invisible conveyor belt.

Henry felt anxious and his legs were restless. He wished to use his muscles. He would even do wind sprints from Coach Barnhard's practice right now.

They were nearly there. At least that's what his dad said.

Henry was going to burst. He needed to do something other than sit in a truck.

He looked down and saw Charley's book from the safe house.

Even reading *Mildred the Magnificent* would be better than waiting. He snatched it off the floor. A piece of worn newspaper stuck out of the book halfway through.

"Looks like you're about half done," Henry said. "I remember—"

Charley ripped the book out of his hands and held it close to her chest. She stared back at him.

"Whoa," Henry said. "I didn't realize that you were that into *Mildred the Magnificent*."

She paused and looked away. "It's not the book." She clutched the book tighter.

"Then what is it?"

CHAPTER 113

Henry wanted to know what was in the book.

Charley wasn't sure if she dared to say.

For the next few moments a debate raged in Charley's mind. She had never let anyone get too close. Her reaction was instinctual—she had to protect herself. Let someone in, get injured. That was the way of things for her. The last people she had truly loved were her parents, and when they died, she told herself she wouldn't be wounded like that ever again.

But things were different with the Murphy family. They had already demonstrated warmth and acceptance. Charley had been living like she was one of them.

Her heart recoiled at the thought of her vulnerability. This was a look into the most protected corner of her fragile and inconstant life.

She opened the book, with turmoil raging inside her. She begged not to be hurt. Any mockery, any insensitivity, would close her up like a dying tulip in an unexpected frost.

She let her arms relax. The pages of the book rolled beneath her fingertips until she stopped at the book's center.

The bookmark was an article cut out of a newspaper. The edges were rubbed smooth and the ink was fading, but it still appeared crisp and unwrinkled.

The picture showed a terrible car accident, a mid-size gray sedan crushed and nearly ripped in two. The front half of the car was mangled, with no room for anyone inside. At the top of the article, the headline was large and bold: "Terrible Accident Kills Young Couple."

Henry read the article while Charley held the book.

"Those were your parents," he said.

She wiped a tear from her eye. She was desperately trying to hold her composure.

She nodded.

Henry looked again at the picture.

"Is that what you went back for in the school?" Dawn said from the front seat. The tenderness in her voice allowed Charley to continue.

"Yes. It's all I have left of them. No other pictures. It was all lost when I went into foster care. I can barely remember what they looked like."

Sorrow bit her to talk about it. It stung in a new and different way. But it also felt reverential—like she was honoring her parents with it.

"I'm so sorry, Charley," Henry said. His voice was gentle.

It was all she needed. Just that.

He placed his hand on her shoulder.

She didn't draw back.

CHAPTER 114

"We're here," Thom said.

The tree line had cleared and was replaced by a long run of cyclone fencing with warning signs hanging every few feet. Several large cranes protruded into the sky and held large metal crates in their hydraulic grasp.

Thom slowed the truck.

A large sign hung on the side of the fence with block letters on its face.

"Kayville Waterfront and Shipping Yard," Henry said. "That's where we are?"

"It's east," Dawn said. "We're at the water's edge."

Thom dimmed the truck's lights.

"Remember," he said, "the Nekura are most active at night. Be careful."

Henry wasn't sure if they had crossed through the Veil or not. It didn't seem like it—especially compared to their experience at the volcano. Although, creating a tranquil night could be Nekura trickery.

The truck approached an entrance gate at a slow roll. The gate was closed, with two fenced partitions on wheels meeting in the center. No guard building, no cameras.

Thom put the truck in park. "I'm going to go open those gates," he said. "Henry, once I open the gate, you pull the truck in and I will close it behind you. We want things as undisturbed as possible."

"I'll get the other gate," Dawn said.

"I can get it," Thom said.

"No, let me help you."

"You don't need—"

"I'm going to."

Thom didn't argue anymore. He reached into the backpack and grabbed his gauntlets and slid them on.

Thom and Dawn hopped out of their seats and walked up to the gate. A padlock hung on a chain at the gate's center. Thom lifted the chain with one hand and with his other hand he created an arrow of light. The arrowhead penetrated the lock, and it split apart. The pieces fell to the ground, and he began to unwind the chain from the gate.

"Thom," Dawn said, "did you tell them? While I was asleep?"

"Tell them? Tell them what?"

"Don't play ignorant. You know."

Thom grimaced into a scowl. "No, I haven't. I meant to but I—"

"Thom, we talked about this! You have to."

"I know! But I want time to explain, to make sure they, and especially Henry, understand." He unwound the chain in silence.

"We don't have time," Dawn said. "You should tell them now, before we go into this."

"Right now?"

"Yes! What if they find out, but not from you? You would be shattered."

He scowled again. He pulled his side of the gate open and Dawn slid her side on its wheels the other way. Thom waved Henry through the gate. They slid the gate closed and Thom rewrapped the chain. It looked undisturbed, except for the missing lock.

"Thom, they need to know about you."

He shut his eyes and exhaled. "What if they don't understand? Right now they're frightened. Should I add to it?"

"You act like it's so monumental, who you were, as if that were the main attraction," she said. "But you forget the point."

She walked into his space and demanded him to look at her. She squeezed his hand. "The point is not who you were, but who you are now," she said. "The reason to tell them is to show what it means to be the man you are."

He smiled and his features softened. "You're right. I'll tell them once we get parked and figure out our plan of attack. Thanks, babe." He stared into her eyes, the eyes he finally could remember from long ago. "How are you this amazing?"

"Easy," she said. "I'm a creature from another world." With that, she bopped away, back to the truck.

CHAPTER 115

An enclave of large stacked canisters lay just ahead on their right, a U-shaped entry that provided significant cover. Thom backed the truck into the opening and they hopped out.

The dockyard was massive. Large stacks of corrugated metal crates were littered throughout the yard. The crates were innumerable, some stacked in pairs and others stacked in giant pyramids. Large orange cranes with enormous arms and cables stood like giants, unmoving in the tranquil night.

One building stood out among the crates and was only several hundred feet away. It was open at the bottom and was elevated with exposed support joists. The small structure at its top seemed to be a building intended for occupancy, with vents and windows. There was an entry point with a small enclosure at the top, a stairwell that allowed access to the open flat roof.

"That is probably the administrative building," Thom said. "It's in an elevated position so the administrators can survey their employees' work.

Otherwise, they would see only as far as the stack of containers outside the window. We can get a better look from up there."

A black metal staircase rose on the side of the structure. Thom crept forward and then waved for the rest to follow.

Climbing the stairs took a couple minutes.

At the top, Thom slung his backpack off his shoulder and squatted down. He pulled out a pair of binoculars from the zippered compartment. He looked around the docks with a slow, sweeping pan.

There were so many containers. Henry guessed upward of two thousand.

"Is this where the furnace is?" Charley asked.

"I hope we don't have to look through every one," Henry said.

"Shhhh," Thom said. "We will see."

Dawn tapped Thom on the shoulder. "There," she said and pointed out toward the water's edge.

The shadows under the moonlight did not seem right. They appeared at incongruent angles and they didn't stay still under the steady moon. They moved with intent, disappearing from sight, betraying the senses.

"Hmmm," Thom said, "there are a handful of Gremlins with a few Bludgeons down there." He continued the panoramic sweep with the binoculars. A minute later he stood up and looked at the others. He frowned. "There are roving sentries everywhere. Many on the ground but some on container stacks as lookouts. This place is crawling. Luckily, I didn't see any people here tonight." He looked into the distance again. He looked back to Dawn, eyes set.

"You all need to stay put," he said, "I need to go take care of some business."

"Thom, you don't have to do this alone."

"No," he said, "they need you." He pointed at Henry and Charley.

"Don't you think you should talk with everyone?"

"Yes, I should. But not now—not with all the Nekura here. Something is going down. I promise we will all talk as soon we are safe."

"You promise?"

"I promise."

Dawn sighed.

"Talk about what?" Henry asked.

"Soon," Thom said. "Soon."

CHAPTER 116

Thom rummaged through his backpack. He moved aside the pistols and the *Book of the Salients* and pulled out his long black coat. He put on the coat and snapped down on the collar, pulling it tight against the back of his neck. The coat covered his gauntlets, but still he traced his fingers over them ceremoniously. He stretched and flexed his fingers inside the thin metallic apparatuses.

He zipped up the backpack.

"You're not taking your pistols," Henry said.

"Too loud. This needs to be done silently." There was an edge in his voice. "No guns right now." He turned to Dawn. "And that means you, too. Your shotgun will give away our location. I will signal when I'm ready for you. You won't miss it. Until then, stay put. All of you."

He crouched down on the edge of the administrative building and surveyed the landscape. Then he stood up and walked back toward Dawn and pulled her close. He kissed her in a long, lingering embrace. It felt awkward for Henry to watch.

Their lips parted.

"I promise," Thom said.

She nodded.

Thom climbed on top of the stairwell enclosure. He pointed his arm toward a stack of containers a little lower and away from the Nekura. With his other arm he pulled back and his blue bow formed, but its blue light was barely visible. He pulled his arm back even further, and a large, long arrow shaft formed as he did.

The arrow shot out of the bow and soared through the air toward the distant freight stack. The arrow sailed with a blue tether line on its tail. It spooled out of his gauntlet with an endless line of blue light. The arrow struck home in a container.

Thom tied the end of the tether around one of the ventilation pipes on the roof until it was taut. He swung his bow up and grabbed it with his other hand. He dropped off the ledge and zipped into the night, suspended from his bow. A moment later, the faint blue line evaporated.

"He looks so good when he does that," Dawn said.

"But why would you let him go off alone?" Henry said.

"You've never seen him on a hunt before."

"You used to hunt the Nekura?" Charley asked.

Dawn nodded. "We had some family reasons."

A brief glimpse of blue light flashed in the distance and then was gone. Henry wondered if he'd really seen it.

Dawn smirked and sat down on the rooftop. She held out the binoculars.

"Get comfy, because the show is about to begin."

"But Dad said that you were the one who was . . . I don't know, like our secret weapon or something. Shouldn't you be the one to do this?"

She shook her head. "He's always doing that, embellishing." She patted the ground next to where she was sitting and Henry and Charley sat down. "Have you ever wondered what a nightmare is?" she asked. She stared into the night. "Why you've been having them recently? The

Salients used to say a nightmare was a walk through the shadowlands of the Nekura. To dream a nightmare was to breathe their ash into your lungs while your mind slept. To flit away to dark realms. But what terrorizes a nightmare? When the monster under your bed is falling asleep and hears things that go bump in the night, what does it fear will come out of its own closet? What is the nightmare's nightmare?"

Another faint, nearly imperceptible spark of blue light in the distance. It was gone immediately.

"They fear your father—the man they knew as the Mastodon."

CHAPTER 117

He stalked them.

It had been a long time since he had been on a hunt.

Thom stood over the ashes of the Nekura he'd just banished. Muscle memory returned and instincts flooded his mind. He darted between the dark corners of the containers. His movements were invisible and he delivered quick, silent strikes.

He had to make his way to the water's edge. He moved along a container with his back tight against the metal corrugated surface. He slid into a narrow passage between two large stacks and shuffled forward. A small group of Nekura walked in front of him, patrolling. Two Bludgeons led and two Gremlins followed.

He slowed his breathing and stood still. The plan came instinctively to him—his mind was supercharged with the Light's connection.

Another narrow entrance between two containers was on the other side. He waited until the last creature, a spiky and moderate-sized Gremlin, lined up with the entrance.

A splayed arrowhead would do nicely.

The silent arrow ripped through the night and pierced the Gremlin. The momentum of the arrow carried the Gremlin off its feet and into the distant small corridor.

The Gremlin in front turned around. It jumped back, startled that its counterpart had vanished. No ash, no smoke, no anything. It looked around with brisk, snapping movements. Its fear was rising. The two Bludgeons walked on unaware.

That was just the separation Thom needed.

The Gremlin turned back to the Bludgeons ahead and pointed behind it with a clawed finger. It never had a chance to speak.

Another silent arrow sped through the air with a blue tether line on its end. The arrow penetrated the Nekura through the chest and silenced it. With a swift tug by Thom on the tether, the second Gremlin flew back toward him in the shadows.

The two Bludgeons walked on without notice.

Snaking through the shadows, Thom moved ahead of the lumbering, slow gait of the Bludgeons. He ducked into a container with its door propped open. He waited for them to walk by.

The first Bludgeon continued on, unconcerned. As the second Bludgeon walked by, Thom jumped behind it and wrapped the bow of blue light around its throat. The bow strangled the creature and crushed down on its short, stubby neck. It backpedaled. Thom led it silently back into the container, and they disappeared. Ash and smoke filled the container. Thom stepped out and eased the door shut, hiding the Bludgeon's remains.

The last Bludgeon finished its patrol route and turned around to head back. No other Nekura followed. There were no signs of struggle, no ash or smoke to signal their demise. Just a vacant and quiet dockyard.

The Bludgeon walked back, turning its head right and left. Its rocky mouth was open in apprehension. It spun in circles, looking all around.

But it never looked up.

Thom jumped down from the top of a container with an arrow in his hand. He drove the arrow into the center of the Bludgeon's flat head, and it never made a sound.

The creature began to decompose. Thom threw open the edge of his long coat and enveloped the smoke, holding it inside. He went down to his knee and encased the ash. With a quick, smooth motion, he swept the ash back into the dense shadows of the containers. He had to hide it from the moonlight and the Nekura lookouts. Any rising plume would signal his presence.

He spun with his coat edge extended, and the smoke dispelled into faint wafts in the shadows, dissipating into the night air.

CHAPTER 118

Another contingent dispatched. No alarms were raised, no guttural war cries of the Nekura. Everything remained hushed. Thom was nearing the water's edge.

He stuck to the shadows. He crept along, eyes darting to the elevated positions of the lookouts. He could not take them out quietly, so he avoided their gaze. They were large Bludgeons and they would make a large plume of smoke when destroyed. It would be a death knell to shoot them on the elevated ground.

Thom waited for the closest lookout to turn around.

An open container lay in the distance. He could hide in there.

He emerged from around the corner.

Three Gremlins stood in his way. He hadn't seen them.

The Gremlins noticed him but took a moment to register that he was barreling toward them. They drew up the talons on their hands and prepared to sound a warning cry.

Thom jumped into the air with his bow turned sideways and level to the ground. Three arrows appeared, notched in place, and he released them. The blue shafts of light tore through the air and sunk deep into the foreheads of the three Gremlins. They collapsed to their knees, muted, and began to disintegrate.

He had to act quickly now.

Using his momentum from the jump, he rolled into a somersault and tumbled forward. As the soles of his feet landed back on the ground, he held the hem of his coat and spun in a circle. Like a sail on a sailboat, the coat's edge billowed out and filled with night air, forcing the smoke further into the recesses of the container stacks and dispelling it into fine, unnoticeable wisps.

He ducked into the open container and took a few heavy breaths. Still no alarm had been sounded.

That was sloppy. He chastised himself for nearly compromising the mission.

He had been careful at the start—using barely visible blue arrows, zip-lining away from lookouts, doubling back to retrace his steps.

If he had enough time, he could take out every Nekura one by one.

But that wasn't the mission. He needed to see what the Nekura were doing at the water's edge without alarming them. The Nekura were pregnant with deceit at every turn. He needed to see their plans without them knowing he was there. This was the first time since the Nekura had resurfaced that they hadn't beaten him at every turn. This time they were unaware of his presence.

Good.

He had to get to the water's edge. If they had already found the furnace . . .

He didn't know. It just wouldn't be good.

CHAPTER 119

The faint form of a Bludgeon moved in the distance.

It navigated around a corner and out of sight before Thom could move on it. He left the container when it was safe and followed the Nekura's trail.

He was almost to the water's edge.

The breeze flowed more freely as the stacks lessened. He turned around the corner where the Bludgeon had disappeared.

The Nekura were dense. Multiple Nekura milled about in general clamor in various groups, some small and some large. The area appeared to be command central.

A group of large Bludgeons stood in a clustered circle further off, nearly at the end of the dock. The large, rocky creatures were agitated. They shoved each other in frustration and yelled in throaty, gurgling tones. Thom wasn't close enough to hear anything. But with an improved vantage point . . .

He had to be twice as cautious now with the increased swarms.

Wait for the right moment.

The cluster of Bludgeons growled, and their griping intensified, drawing the attention of all of those around.

Now!

He bolted to one of the remaining container stacks closer to the grouping. He ran on his toes to silence his steps. He ducked around the corner.

He paused. Still no war cries.

He looked at the metal poles used to lock the crate in front of him. He clambered up the poles like they were rungs on a ladder.

The stack was four containers tall. When he got to the top, he stayed on his belly to keep his appearance unseen. He slid forward with a military crawl to the edge of the container and peered down.

He gasped.

CHAPTER 120

On a large wooden table in the center of the Nekura huddle was a giant picture. A cloaked man stood tall in the center of the picture, with a nondescript face, holding a hammer to the side, and a thin ribbon trailed from the hammer's shaft.

The Hammer of Andelis.

Charley was right. The dream she and Henry had was really no dream at all. The Nekura had the same picture as the one that appeared in the book.

The Bludgeons grumbled at each other and continued to shove. They pointed at various locations on the picture. They seemed to be using it as a map.

Charley might have told them east, but they couldn't know anything more without her glasses. The details perceived by the Light were lost to them. They hadn't won yet.

But the Nekura were still closer than he had hoped. He wondered how they would exploit the furnace if they got it. Henry had tried to use the

Light for his own purpose and had been burned because of it. Surely the Nekura weren't that imperceptive.

Thom's thoughts seized in his mind. All his attention turned toward something else.

A large Bludgeon walked out of a line of containers at the edge of the docks. One feature made this creature distinctive from all others.

It had a half-severed arm.

CHAPTER 121

The Bludgeon's right arm hung halfway off its torso in a garish presentation.

It was the same one—the one that had tracked Henry and Thom shot.

But why was it here? Why would the tracker stop tracking? The Nekura wanted the furnace, but Henry was the key. They still didn't have the furnace, so they still needed Henry. It made no sense that the Nekura suddenly stopped tracking the one with the answers.

Thom tried to recalculate.

Something was wrong.

If the Bludgeon from Henry's bedroom was here, then something had changed.

What was really happening? Was there something else all along?

He had to get back to his family. He couldn't dive headlong into the unknown with the Nekura.

He and his family could figure out the next step together, just like they had with the picture. He eased himself backward on his belly toward the metal apparatus to climb down.

He froze.

A sudden snap of blue light ripped through the air and crackled. One of the Bludgeons split in half.

The blue light was the end of a whip.

The remaining Nekura shrieked in defiance. Some scattered and others charged forward toward the light. Pandemonium ruptured from them all.

Thom looked up. The Bludgeon with the half-severed arm was fleeing. It used its arm like a hydraulic piston, launching itself forward in bounds. It was nearly out of sight.

He wanted to pursue it. Grab it. Throttle it and make it talk, find out what it knew. Then grind it to powder for what it had done to Henry.

The remaining Bludgeons from around the table charged toward the source of the blue light. Thom looked back and saw the Bludgeon with the half-severed arm disappear.

He scowled.

Let the Bludgeon go. He had to prioritize his family.

Thom ran down the container and jumped into the air.

The element of surprise was gone. He had to take out the Nekura scouts.

He twisted in the air like a corkscrew and unleashed four arrows in successive timing. The arrows bolted away, shot in a laser line. They bloomed out in every direction like a blossoming firework-flower of Nekura death.

The four lookouts on the container stacks couldn't react in time. The arrows sliced through them with surgical precision. They withered into four decrepit piles of ash, with smoke billowing up like a signal fire.

A signal to all the Nekura that Thom had returned to the war.

Thom landed with a crunch of the ground beneath him. Fine cracks appeared on the concrete dock under his weight, but he felt no pain. The Light—it was cranking him higher.

He stood and sprinted toward the Bludgeons.

CHAPTER 122

Henry stood back to back with Charley.

Several piles of ash were already collected in front of them, like tombstones of the recently deceased. Smoke rose from each pile and made it difficult for Henry and Charley to see the two remaining Bludgeons and the cluster of Gremlins.

Charley set her feet and snapped her whip like a lion tamer. She pulled back and cracked again, over and over, fending off the wild animals. The Bludgeons grimaced and kept their distance. Henry covered her from behind.

He saw something from the corner of his eye.

A Gremlin reeled back with its talons to rip open their legs. Henry jammed the end of his staff down into its paltry abdomen and crushed it.

He'd barely seen the creature. It felt like the bo had leapt into it.

The Gremlin collapsed under the blow and its arms went limp. Henry threw the end of the bo forward and launched the Gremlin like a giant hockey puck toward the Bludgeons.

Then the Bludgeons made a loud, guttural call.

The two Bludgeons began dripping lava from their mouths. Molten, steaming secretions fell and chewed the ground into divots. The Bludgeons heaved back, as if taking a large breath, heads pointed upward. It was the same posture of the Bludgeon at the volcano top. Henry had stopped that one in time—but he couldn't stop two at once.

Henry grabbed Charley and yanked her to the side. They dove to the ground.

Two expansive streams of lava burned through the air at the place where they had been standing a second earlier.

He tried to get back up but tripped over Charley's feet and landed on top of her. He scrambled but couldn't set his feet. Charley tried moving but was pinned underneath him.

The Bludgeons wound up again.

The acid was going to smother them.

Two arrowheads burst through the foreheads of both Bludgeons. Each creature went slack, and the lava oozed out of their mouths like a tepid stream. They fell to the ground and vaporized.

The remaining Gremlins screamed when the Bludgeons fell. They retreated into the night with screeching defiance.

Thom stormed forward. "What are you doing here? I told you to stay put! You could have been killed! Now our surprise is gone and we don't know what the Nekura are doing. They were looking at the same picture from the book. I don't know what—"

"Dad!" Henry shouted.

"What?"

"Mom told us to. She said we had to tell you that the Fracas are here."

Thom stiffened up. He looked around with darting glances. "What?" he said, suddenly different.

"The Fracas are here."

Thom's face drained to plaster white. "We have to go. Now!"

CHAPTER 123

"Where's your mother?" Thom said.

"She said she was going to stay at the lookout so we had a safe exit," Henry said.

A sigh of relief. "Good job, babe," Thom spoke into the air. "Come on! We must get back to the administrative building. We can zipline down to the truck from there."

Thom charged through the container stacks with cavalier strides, unleashing arrows of blue light without ever stopping. Resistance was minimal on the return trip.

The exterior stairwell of the administrative building came into sight. They were nearly there.

"We have to get out of here," Thom said.

"Why, Dad? What are the Fracas? Can't we fight them?"

When Dawn told Henry about Thom a Nekura hunter, Henry had been impressed. This sudden change in Thom didn't jibe.

Thom paused. "No, we can't," he said. "The Fracas are spindly, sore-covered creatures with dislocating joints that allow them to contort.

Their sores release noxious gases that can incapacitate you if you get close to them. They can penetrate unsuspecting areas to sneak up on you. They travel in large packs and attempt to overwhelm by sheer number. If you see one, you can guarantee twenty more are with it. And it only takes one getting close enough and then," he shook his head, "then you're done."

Thom did another visual sweep. "That's the Nekura's insurance policy here—they brought the Fracas. We have to get your mother and leave immediately."

"What about the furnace?" Charley asked.

"We'll figure it out. But we need to regroup."

Thom turned the corner and led them down another aisle of containers, then around a second corner. The path was straightaway to the administrative building, and a clearing lay in front of them.

A creaking sound broke the night. Metal against metal.

Henry looked up to his left.

A Bludgeon stood on top of a container stack. It pulled down on a long black pole stuck into door of the giant shipping container. The Bludgeon wore an evil smile, its large shark-like teeth exposed.

The door of the container flung open. Diseased-looking creatures fell out in a shower onto the ground. They landed in a sickening thud just behind Thom, Henry, and Charley.

The monsters had nearly translucent skin, covered in scabs and open wounds. They continued to tumble out and formed a giant mountain of flesh.

Then they started to move. They twisted in awkward, terrible ways, heads bending more than humanly possible, and moving their dislocated joints back to anatomic. A shrill cry emanated from the first one. The others joined in chorus until the whole dock was abuzz with the Fracas' call.

It was feeding time.

Thom's eyes went large as saucers.

"Run run run!" he screamed.

CHAPTER 124

Charley and Henry sprinted to the external stairwell of the administrative building.

They had to get Dawn. Henry flew up the stairs, leaping two to three stairs at a time and Charley staying with him every step.

Henry looked back on the ground. Thom stood still.

He notched five arrows into his bow with a single draw. The arrows flew into the mound of undead flesh, and several small groans came back. A few Fracas teetered and toppled.

Other Nekura had a demonstrative display of turning to smoke and ash, but the Fracas slowly decomposed. They simmered as the Light destroyed them, like a wet log on a fire that sizzles as it's consumed.

Thom loosed another charge of five arrows.

And another.

More groans. But the Fracas poured out faster from the container than Thom could notch the arrows. The Fracas mountain was growing. And moving.

Thom turned and fled after Henry and Charley.

The horde pursued him. Fracas crawled on all fours and some galloped in awkward, sideways movements, their joints sliding and popping in deformation.

Henry couldn't pause to observe. He raced to the top of the building with Charley.

It was vacant.

A moment later, Thom bounded up the stairs. "Where's your mother?" His voice was frenzied. "We can't go without her!"

"I don't know! She said she would be here."

"Look," Charley said. She pointed to the door of the stair access that led down into the building. "The door is open. I don't think it was before. Maybe she went in there." Charley ran to the door.

Henry bolted after her.

"Wait!" Thom cried.

Charley was already inside the stairwell. They had no other option now—they had to follow her. "Mom, where are you?" Henry said.

The stairs from the rooftop ended in a moderately sized office. No one was there—no administrator, no night watchman, no late-night receiver for shipments.

And no Dawn either.

Thom ran in behind them. "I locked the door. That will only buy us a minute or two."

Henry began to panic.

Where was his mother?

"She's not here," Thom said. "Now we have to get out somehow."

Irregular thumping sounds started above them. The Fracas were already on the roof. They would be down the stairs soon.

"There must be a secondary exit. Fire code would require it. Maybe a drop-down ladder. We just have to find it."

The banging on the locked stairwell door echoed through the small office like a bullhorn.

The Fracas had broken through.

Thom pointed to a door at the end of the room. "There!"

Thom reached the door first. He spun around. He pulled back an arrow in his bow and pointed it toward the stairwell.

Charley and Henry ran toward the door.

"Quick," Thom said, "find the ladder!"

The Fracas poured down the stairs. Thom shot three arrows in succession past Henry, but only managed to hit one Fracas. It grunted and collapsed on the stairway in a heap, momentarily stemming back the tide of the coming horde.

Henry ran through the door and looked around.

His heart plummeted to his stomach. He felt sick.

Thom backed up through the door and shut it. He locked the door and turned around. "Have you managed to—" Thom stopped mid-sentence.

Henry and Charley stood transfixed.

They were in a small bedroom the size of a studio apartment. It was a call room for the night watchman. There was a twin bed, a couch, and tiny kitchenette. No windows. No ladder.

No exit.

CHAPTER 125

Thom had sealed their doom.

His decision to run through the door had cost them their last few seconds.

He'd said he would protect them.

He failed.

Henry and Charley paced the room. They looked for something. Anything.

They found nothing.

Then the clawing began. It was a crazed, wild scraping on the door.

Henry and Charley said nothing to each other. They understood their predicament. Their whitewashed, slack faces said it all. Thom's words still hung in the air. "It only takes one getting close—then you're done."

He had stolen their courage, dismantled them.

The Fracas' panicked mauling shook the doorknob, and the door
heaved on its hinges.

Thom wished he had his pistols. He left them in the backpack for
stealth and speed. So much for that. If he had his backpack, the situation might be different.

There was no point in wishing. He didn't have it.

That's right—

He failed.

The thought blistered his mind with accusation.

Thom looked back to Henry and Charley. Charley sat on the bed,
resigned. Henry sat down and put his arm around her. They barely moved.

They were preparing themselves for their fate. Volition gave way to a
silent, unspoken abdication. This was the end of the road.

Henry looked up and locked eyes with Thom. A small tear rolled down
Henry's cheek, eyes large and terrified.

"Dad . . . I don't want to die."

An image came like a flood to Thom.

The memory of Henry lying on the bed in the center room blazed in
Thom's mind. Nearly dead, incapacitated for days, Henry fought to stay
alive while the frenzied Nekura clawed at the door.

"No," Thom said.

In his mind, he stood in front of it. The dam.

He could see the dam again.

It was a place he erected years ago, where thick walls had been built
for safety, and heavy doors were locked and bound for fear of ever being
reopened. It was a place of distant burning that could spark a small ember
into a raging inferno. It had been hidden away.

"No!" he yelled at the rattling door.

He had been scared to go to the dam again. He told himself he
couldn't. But the Light would not be hindered—it was leading him back
to this place. His memory reached to a somewhere long ago.

The forgotten was being called out.

"NO!"

The dam burst open.

Thom walked forward and took a huge breath. He unlatched the door and threw it open.

CHAPTER 126

Henry saw Thom reach for the door. "Dad, no!"
Fracas gushed through.

The first three Fracas jumped right at Thom.

He met them with a giant arrow in mid-pitch, a huge bolt of blue light he threw forward like a javelin. The arrow impaled them and they sailed away and stuck to the far wall.

Thom sprang backward.

Fracas squealed and pressed forward, but in the eagerness of their appetites they smashed against each other and fought to be the next ones in.

They were bottlenecked at the door. They could only come in a couple at a time.

Thom notched two fresh arrows, knocked down two more Fracas. He jumped forward and kicked the door closed again. The door latch engaged.

He generated a new cluster of arrows in each hand and buried them into the wall next to the entrance. The splayed arrowheads pointed out and glinted—an awaiting death trap.

A spindly creature burst in and flew at Thom's face.

Thom anticipated it, arrow in hand.

He threw an uppercut through the spindly, sore-covered chin with the arrowhead. It went through the head of the Fracas and stuck in the ceiling. The creature hung limp, like it was dangling from a gallows.

Two more Fracas jumped into the room. Thom's bow instantly relit in his hands. With a mighty sweep, he launched the Fracas into the arrows protruding from the wall.

Skewered, they began to sizzle.

Two more handfuls of arrows appeared. He jammed them into the door, creating a spiked transit-way. Thom kicked the door closed again, and more Fracas were impaled on the new arrows.

The Fracas hung like decrepit trophies from the wall, from the ceiling, from the door—a mausoleum of macabre taxidermy. They slowly decayed and smelled like sulfur. The pile of dead Fracas was growing bigger, and black smoky tendrils snaked off it.

Yet for all this, the Fracas were still persistent.

They poured in.

But Thom was glowing.

He would not relent.

Thom sprang forward. He broke off the door handle with a downward smash of his bow, and the metalwork fell to the ground. The small hole from the door handle became a gateway of death. He crouched and streamed glowing arrows through the hole in furious succession.

Then a tethered arrow flew through the hole of the closed door with an unfurling blue line behind it. The line tugged on the other end with pierced Fracas.

Just like fishing, Thom had caught something.

He ripped the line. Avulsed it. Three Fracas were tethered on the other end and flew forward to open the door again with their dead weight.

It was a dance. He moved with the door, flinging it open, slamming it closed, impaling Fracas on its every movement.

An arrow released to the right, inside the room. Thom barely gave it a glance. It sunk into the Fracas squeezing with dislocating joints through the ventilation system.

Thom bolted forward, shoulder-checked the door. It couldn't close because of the growing mound of dead Fracas. The entrance was only a foot wide.

He launched two arrows into the ceiling, two into the floor. The stems of the arrows held the door tight against the growing mound of the dead Fracs, barricading the entryway nearly closed.

The arrows tightened the funnel.

The Fracas streamed into the narrow door jamb.

They streamed into arrow after arrow, into a flurry of deadly light.

Thom held up his bow and tightened his grip. He brought it down in a huge, over-the-top blow. It crushed the Fracas slinking underneath the disintegrating corpses. It was the cymbal clash at the end of his symphonic performance.

Then, the song was over, the dance was done.

Rotting Fracas corpses adorned the room. Nothing else moved.

The cold fear in Henry's neck stopped. He gazed at his father.

Thom had stood against the entire horde of Fracas with nothing more than his connection to the Light and a hinged door. He had become a one-man wrecking crew, insatiable, unstoppable.

Thom turned around to Henry. Veins bulged and his face was red, contorted with pain. He went lax.

Then he exhaled.

He collapsed unconscious to the floor.

CHAPTER 127

Thom lay in a heap on the ground. He didn't move.

No way that just happened.

His dad had held his breath the entire time.

Henry didn't dare move either. Moving might break the spell that Thom created. What if the fumes of the Fracas still lingered?

He hoped his dad wasn't dead.

Henry had watched it all unfold. The ethereal blue of Thom's Salient markings had never glowed that brightly. The cords of light shone through his coat in luminous intensity.

Why didn't his dad unleash that before? They could have avoided all of this.

But something told Henry that he knew the reason why.

His dad had transformed.

Something inside him had not just bent. It broke right off.

The blue glow from inside his dad's coat faded and the bow in his hand disappeared.

Thom groaned.

Henry was getting accustomed to surprises with the Light. But he had never seen anything like this.

His dad had stemmed the tide.

CHAPTER 128

Dawn crept through the quiet dockyard.

She felt terrible sending Henry and Charley off together into the night. She'd made a split-second decision.

The trauma of leaving Henry alone in the safe house seared her mind.

But they were not in the safety of the center room anymore. Fracas stalked the night.

Henry wasn't alone this time, either. Thom could protect him better than she could. He was with Charley, too. And he was connected with the Light.

Thom would have never approved of her decision. But then again, Thom wasn't here.

She had seen a lone Fracas amble away from the administrative building in its nauseating gait, joints slipping and bones tumbling over themselves. It moved in a different direction than Thom had gone earlier, into the darkened distance among high stacks of containers that cast deep shadows on the dockyard's surface.

She knew the Fracas and how they acted. The worst was to be caught off guard by them.

She had to catch them off guard instead.

It was a deadly game of cat and mouse, and she desperately felt the need to be the cat. She had been batted down like a ball of shredded yarn, the cat's plaything. No longer.

Now was the time for her to be the cat.

The lioness.

Uncaged.

She stuck to the shadows. She darted from hiding point to hiding point, running on the balls of her feet. She placed her back against one of the containers and stood still. She caught her breath.

Right now, the element of surprise was on her side, but she had her shotgun ready to use if necessary.

She wished her hair could glow like it had done at the safe house. She tried summoning it up inside her. She thought of the emotional turmoil she'd been through. She thought of what had happened to Henry. She thought of what could happen if the Fracas found her family.

None of it worked.

She clutched the shotgun tighter in her hands and felt the cool of the steel, the familiar curvature of the stock. She might not be able to command the Salient remnant inside of her but she could still take care of business.

A large ship sat in a cargo-loading slip, awaiting unloading when the sun broke the night. It stood like a quiet mountain floating on the water, a giant monolith of unmoving steel. Multiple cranes lay dormant in the night, their massive frames and cables soaring into the air with claws closed and still. She wondered what she would find inside that large ship.

The Fracas disappeared. Dawn moved up, creeping through the yard, darting between shadows.

She stopped. A giant Bludgeon turned the corner in front of her. The large black frame of rock blended into the night, but the glint of its white shark teeth betrayed its presence.

Dawn ducked behind an opened container and waited in the shadows. She saw it approach her position.

It was going to cross her path.

She made a single knock on the outside of the container's metal frame.

The Bludgeon's attention immediately piqued. It looked at the open container and bared its teeth. It moved with arms out, its massive rocky hands ready to crush. Its eyeless face was trained on the container's opening. The Bludgeon walked inside to trap its prey.

Perfect.

Dawn crept around from behind the container.

The hunter became the hunted.

She walked inside and eased the door closed.

The closed cargo container concealed the devastating shotgun blast that ripped the Bludgeon apart. The night sky never saw the light, never heard the explosion. The only evidence of the event was the ash-filled smoke that rose upward when Dawn walked out of the container.

Killing the Bludgeon had cost her valuable time. She couldn't afford that luxury again.

She had to find the Fracas and assault its nest before they all awakened for their feeding frenzy.

CHAPTER 129

Dawn neared the large cargo ship.

She looked for the Fracas she'd seen earlier but couldn't find it. She was getting frustrated at its disappearance but she relied on her contingency plan to move toward the cargo ship. Something told her that the Fracas nest was aboard that ship.

Her thoughts drifted to Henry and Charley again. She hadn't heard any clamor so far. That was a good thing. Thom was skilled at stealth and could conceal them from prying Nekura sight.

The idea of stealth danced on her brain. The moon rolled out from the clouds again and the moonlight played on her silver hair. She grabbed a strand of her hair and looked at it.

The moon had always done that and she felt it was symbolic. The moon was the light of governance in the dark night sky, and when the moon was out, it displayed her Salient connection to the Light amid the sea of Nekura darkness.

Except she had forgotten all of that. Her hair had stopped its moonlit glow. For years she had let her connection to the Light slip, unaware that her hair no longer glistened in the moon's reflected silver presence, and eventually forgot that it ever did.

But now, after a long separation, she returned to the Light. She had abandoned it for convenience and an unanticipated, voluptuary burning. But she had been stirred again.

And her hair glistened more each night under the open sky.

It presented a problem for her now, trying to remain unseen. She reached into her pocket and pulled out a black knit hat that Thom gave her for her birthday. She was thankful she had it.

Another Bludgeon appeared. It was large and lumbered away from her. Its right arm dangled from its black frame.

That was the Bludgeon Henry described! Her desire for secrecy gave way to resolve. She could not let this one escape. She had already lost the Fracas into the night's shadows.

She sped forward.

The Bludgeon darted away and moved into a clearing of containers adjacent to the ship. It stopped and turned around.

The Bludgeon made a gurgling sound deep in its throat. Acid filled its mouth and steam rose as it arched backward. The creature lurched forward.

The stream of acid spewed out of the Bludgeon's mouth. It flew left of Dawn's position. She dodged it easily with a side-step to the right. The acid fell to the ground, bubbling and crackling, and corroded the ground into shallow channels. The Nekura reeled back again for a second attempt.

It missed left again.

Dawn dodged it easily again with another side-step to the right.

The Bludgeon was too far away for Dawn to reach it with a shotgun blast. She advanced, but the Nekura withdrew a couple steps and jostled to one side.

Just then, she heard a sound in the distance.

"Run run run!"

It was Thom's voice.

She was too late.

The Fracas had found them.

She turned back to the Bludgeon with renewed vigor. Thom's cry, the emotion in his voice—it drove her forward. She felt her hair start to lift off her neck. She felt her steps become lighter.

The spark was igniting.

CHAPTER 130

Dawn flew forward.

The Bludgeon took one step backward and stopped. The steam from its mouth subsided.

It didn't move.

She was glowing brighter. The Bludgeon didn't care.

With each stride forward a new thought broke into her mind—a new question that unnerved her.

Why wasn't it moving? Why wasn't it still trying to burn her with acid from its bowels?

She landed a few more strides.

The Bludgeon remained motionless, anchored in place, almost like . . .

She suddenly stopped.

She was being baited.

She spun around in a circle.

Dawn perceived it now—she was being corralled. Like a wolf jockeying witless creatures, it coerced the sheep forward, nipping at them until they were where they needed to be.

She spun around again, looking. There was nothing around her except the Bludgeon.

Its face parted into a wicked smile, rows of razor-sharp teeth displayed in pleasure. Dawn had played into its hands and she needed to run.

But a mechanical grinding had already begun.

The large steel claw of the crane opened above her. From their opened cocoon, Fracas fell in cadaverous rainfall to the ground. They thudded on the concrete, and gases expulsed from their sores into an asphyxiating cloud.

They landed on her. They landed around her. The noxious fumes incapacitated her in seconds.

CHAPTER 131

Henry sat at Thom's bedside in the small room. He hoped Thom would wake up soon.

Thom was breathing. He lay still on the bed. The gentle lifting and recoiling of his chest were his only movements.

Charley watched the door. It took several minutes for the Fracas to decompose to smoke and ash. She used a small broom from the room's kitchenette to sweep the remains into a pile and then barricaded the half-functional door with a chair. No more Nekura came for them.

Yet.

"Ughh . . ." There was small movement on the bed, and Thom turned his head to the side.

"Dad! Dad!"

"Hgh . . ."

"Dad, you did it! You beat them!"

"It . . . It wasn't me, Henry," Thom said. He grunted. He leaned up on an elbow and opened his eyes.

"What do you mean it wasn't you? I saw you do it! You are my dad, right?"

"Yes," Thom said and chuckled. "Of course it's me." He laid his head down on the bed again and closed his eyes. "What I mean is the power you're talking about. It wasn't me."

"Why haven't you ever done that before?"

"Because," Thom said, "I went back to a place I was afraid to revisit. I was ashamed to reopen that part of my life."

"Why would you be ashamed? You just wasted three dozen Nekura!"

"It's a long story."

His father looked exhausted.

"Okay, not now," Henry said. "Dad, you need to rest, but do it fast, please? I don't want to stay around this place any longer than we have to."

For the next three minutes, it was quiet in the room except for the faint humming of the radiator. Thom lay with Henry at his side, and Charley stood, leaning against the wall halfway between the bed and the door.

"Thom," Charley said, "what do you mean that it wasn't you?"

Thom mustered his strength.

"There's a story," he said, "that I once heard about someone driving by a farm. The driver noticed a man pumping water with a hand pump in the distance. Intrigued by the hard work and the simple way of life, the driver slowed down to watch. As he watched, he became more impressed as the farmer continued to pump the water without stopping. He pumped on undeterred, unfatigued. Wanting to see the strong farmer closer, the driver approached. The man still pumped the water furiously, with an unreal ability. Pump, pump, pump! When the driver got close enough to see better, he realized that the farmer was a hinged, wooden cut-out of a man. It moved with the water as the water sped out of the spigot. The force of the water is what made the appearance of the farmer move in response. You see, the man wasn't pumping the water, the water was pumping the man."

Henry nodded his head.

"You might think that you are channeling the Light," Thom said, "but it is actually the Light channeling you. That's what happened at the door." He smirked. "I bet you've felt it."

Henry nodded again. Thom was talking stronger than before. With each breath, the sentences became longer. He would be strong enough to leave in a few minutes.

At least Henry hoped.

"I think that's the point of the picture," Thom said. "You know, with Charley's glasses. The point is not the hammer, or the weapon, or whatever. It's also not the man, either. The point is the fire's blazing core, behind the man with his hammer. It's the fire behind him, the thing that pushes him forward. That's the point of the picture."

Henry thought about it. It seemed strange that the picture would have so many different levels, like an onion with endless peels. "You got all that from that one stanza and a picture?"

"Yes."

"Okay." He placed himself under the lesson, like a pupil under his master. His mind felt like it was being stretched, but he would have to do mental gymnastics later. "Dad, are you feeling good enough to go?"

"Just about."

Thom stretched on the bed, and his gauntlets showed under his coat as he yawned. "Ah! I wish I had my pistols with me."

"Why don't you just take them back?" Henry said. "Charley's got your backpack."

Thom's eyes snapped open and he sat up. "Really? I thought your mother had the backpack."

"She gave it to Charley to carry."

"I didn't even notice it," Thom said. "Great!"

Thom looked around the room. "Where's Charley?"

Henry looked to the door. The barricaded chair had been moved and the door stood half-open on its damaged hinges.

"She's gone." Henry looked around the room. "And she's got your backpack."

CHAPTER 132

Charley wandered through the labyrinthine maze of containers. She had no idea which way to go.

Nekura were at the water's edge and Thom had gone initially in that direction. But she had already gone that way with Henry. She looked around at the multitude of directions she could go, chose one, and walked forward.

She had not encountered any Nekura since leaving the administrative building. But if the Nekura were not chasing her . . .

They must be chasing Dawn instead.

The thought made Charley shudder, but it added resolution to her mission. She set out to do what they came here to do—to find the furnace and end this Nekura nightmare. She needed to make restitution for handing the enemy the information right out of the book.

Apprehension ripped through her. She slung the backpack down to the ground and tore it open. The book was still in the backpack.

She closed her eyes and sighed in relief.

She looked down again. Blue light shone through the fabric from the secondary compartment.

It confused her. She zipped up the compartment that held the pistols and the book and unzipped the secondary compartment.

The stone from the volcano top was glowing. Flecks of blue in the stone's matrix glowed like it was radioactive, light emanating from its core.

"That's strange." She pulled it out of the backpack to look at it further but then thought twice about it. The glowing stone would act like a homing beacon in the middle of the night, and the Nekura would find her.

Charley zipped up the backpack and looked around the dockyard. In the distance was an open container. She ran over and sealed herself inside.

She opened the backpack and pulled out the stone inside her new fortified location. The shipping container was pitch black inside, but when she pulled out the stone, it lit up the container like a lamp.

The stone was growing brighter.

She turned it over in her hands. The stone felt different than it had before. It made a faint hum with a gentle vibration on her fingertips.

What did the vibration mean? She couldn't linger, she had to get going. She placed the stone back in her backpack and walked out of the container.

No one was around. The landscape was quiet and empty.

A large crane towered in the distance, close to a giant metal ship filled with cargo. It seemed as good of a waypoint as any. She walked forward.

Something made her feel awkward.

In the stillness of the night, it seemed like things had become ominously hushed. Charley paused.

Something was different. Why were her nerves complaining?

Then she realized. She no longer felt the stone's vibration on her back.

Charley hadn't even known she was experiencing it until it was gone. She had felt the stone's gentle hum through the fibers of the backpack. With her trek forward, the sensation fled from the small of her back.

She lowered the backpack and looked inside it. The stone had stopped glowing and looked as it did when they'd found it.

"What a finicky thing." She glanced back to where she had come from.

She jumped when she heard a metal grating sound in the distance.

She spun around again but saw nothing moving. The crane sat immobilized, an open claw basket at its end.

She thought twice about going in that direction. She was sure she would be walking into peril if she did.

Charley walked away from the large crane and peered into the backpack again. The stone started to glow with a faint blue light. She kept the backpack in front of her as she walked.

The glowing intensified again.

She leapt with realization.

She knew what the stone was doing. The glowing, the vibration—they weren't random or capricious.

The stone was a compass.

CHAPTER 133

The stone grew brighter as Charley walked.

She followed the inexplicable glowing blue stone wherever it led her. It became too bright for her to look at in the backpack. Its brightness might betray her location. She zipped up the backpack and swung it onto her back again.

The humming was more distinguishable now. She felt the stone sing with vibration in the small of her back. She could use the vibration as a tactile guide.

She walked toward a large red container and opened the door to walk inside. She shut the door behind her. The reverberation of the stone echoed inside the metal chassis.

The furnace must be here. The stone's vibration was too intense to ignore.

She looked at the other end of the container with growing excitement. A horizontal lever hung in the middle of the opposite door, ready to be opened like a large steel door handle. She reached for the lever. She was about to pierce the Veil again and move to the other side of reality.

Take a big breath. Be ready for anything.

Charley threw open the door and leapt through.

She stood on the other side of the large red container, in the waterway shipping yard, moon hiding, then bobbing out from behind the clouds.

No one was in the shipyard. Nothing was different—except for one thing.

The stone had stopped vibrating.

Charley took off her backpack and looked in it. The flecked stone sat lifeless, like any other stone. She picked up the backpack and ran back into the container.

Nothing changed. The stone didn't glow again. It lay dormant where it had glowed intensely just a few seconds before.

Nothing.

Nothing!

Charley shook the bag. "Come on!" She groaned in frustration.

A groan replied back to her from the night. It was the distant howl of a Bludgeon. The sound hung in the air and then faded like an apparition. A haunting silence replaced it, and Charley's hair stood on end. She barely breathed.

The night had been momentarily calm. She hoped that she hadn't awoken the storm.

The eerie howl filled the night again but was louder this time. Closer.

Charley bit her lip and grimaced. She had given away her location in a careless moment.

She zipped the backpack up and threw it on her back. She yanked on the shoulder straps and cinched the pack down tight.

Time to run.

CHAPTER 134

Thom and Henry hurried down the external staircase of the administrative building as fast as Thom's legs would allow. He had gained his strength back quickly, but he could have benefited from a few extra minutes of rest.

"Dad, what are we going to do about Mom?"

"We'll find her."

"Do you think she's at the truck? She said she was going to make sure we could escape safely."

"No, she would have driven to get us. Remember how important the getaway vehicle is?"

"No."

"Oh, that's right," Thom said. "You were at the safe house when we raided Middleton High. Let's just say that your mother would have been parked at the administrative building, waiting for us, if she had gone to the truck."

They stood in the clearing of the containers, through which they had fled from the Fracas. The door hung open from a container that crowned the stack from where the Fracas had emerged.

"Wait," Henry said and held his finger up to his mouth. He pointed upward.

"I think the nest is empty," Thom said. They stood still for a moment, watching, listening.

Nothing emerged from the open door.

Thom started to lead them through the stacks but then paused and turned back to Henry. "I don't know which way to go. We're looking for two separate people." He grimaced and looked around.

"This dockyard is so big," Henry said.

"I know."

"I wish we had some evidence that pointed us in the right direction."

"That would help."

"Do you think they're alright?"

"They're resourceful."

Henry wasn't convinced. The presence of the Fracas had unnerved Thom, and that unnerving spoke volumes. However, Henry had heard how Dawn dismantled the Nekura hit squad outside the center room when he was inside. That at least gave him some comfort. Some.

But Charley . . .

She didn't have the Salient heritage that his mother had.

"We have to find Charley first," Thom said.

Henry nodded. The next thought he blurted out. "Dad, what if she's dead?"

"No!" Thom said. He strode up into Henry's face. He wagged his finger like he was scolding a puppy. "No. Look, Henry, she's smart, savvy, and she had an instant connection to the Light, unlike you or even I did. She's come a long way from the girl I carried out of the hotel in a shower curtain."

Henry felt the tension pour off his father. Thom was trying to convince himself also.

"But how are we going to find her?" Henry said.

"This place has been crawling with Nekura since we got here," Thom said. "We just follow the commotion and I'm sure we'll find a girl with a blue whip and large piles of ash around her."

CHAPTER 135

The sweat stung Charley's eyes.

She ran away from the pursuant sounds. She weaved and bobbed through the maze of the shipping yard, a metal labyrinth she was trapped inside.

She didn't know where she was going. She just knew what she was running from.

Charley darted around one stack and leaned her back against it. She needed a moment to recover. She had to catch her breath, and try to think.

Her breathing settled and her heart stopped pounding in her ears.

A small rumbling sound came from the container she was leaning against. She leapt forward. She feared she had run into a Nekura trap.

But the rumbling disappeared when she leapt away.

Charley crept toward the container and leaned forward. She put her ear up against the metal frame.

Nothing.

What just happened? Charley wasn't sure of anything anymore. Maybe she had crossed the Veil to the other side after all. Maybe she was now in a new, sensory-altering mind game.

She pressed her back up to the side of the container as she had done initially. The sound resumed.

She threw her backpack down and ripped it open. The stone was glowing again and vibrating with a faint hum.

She sighed. "Some compass!"

Temperamental stone. Maybe she broke it.

She glanced at her surroundings. No Nekura had found her yet, but she still heard their incessant drone, like an evil cicada-storm swarming around her. She wondered how much longer she had before she was found. The low-pitch groaning of the Bludgeons and the ecstatic chirping of the Gremlins made a terrible combination, a symphony of terror that was—

That's it!

She jumped up.

Combination. The word rang in her mind like a gong struck by a mallet. She looked at the stone in her hands. The search wasn't like following a treasure map to an X at the end. It was like opening a combination lock. It required the right sequence of checkpoints, like a tumbler on a vault's lock required the right sequence of numbers. She had already gone through one checkpoint and that was why the stone had reset—it was leading her to the next entry.

It glowed brighter when she stood back up.

Charley looked at the stack of containers next to her. She had to climb them because the next entry point was up. She stowed the stone in the backpack and scolded herself to be more sensitive to its subtle vibration so she would not have to take it out again. She cinched the backpack down again and began climbing the stack.

The stack was four containers high. The metal rods on the outside of the containers acted like rungs on a ladder. But climbing upward made her more visible.

It didn't take long until she was seen.

Charley glanced down toward the ground and saw Gremlins scrambling to the base of the stack. They had closed in on her quickly.

The vibrating in her backpack became intense as she neared the top of the stack. She flipped the latch on the highest container and the door swung open. It was empty inside, just like the first one. She pulled herself up and saw light glowing in the container, shining through her backpack.

The Gremlins shook the bottom of the stack with growing agitation. Charley's foot slipped on the ledge with the sudden bang and she tottered backward.

"Whoa!"

Charley grabbed the sides of the container and pulled herself forward. She nearly fell out. She looked back down.

Two large Bludgeons were running toward the base of the stack in tandem, like massive linebackers.

She only had a moment before the stack would topple.

CHAPTER 136

Charley charged toward the end of the container.

She had to get through the checkpoint.

Just a few more steps.

The impact struck before she made it.

The Nekura blitz against the bottom of the stack felt like a giant earthquake shook Charley's entire world, and she crashed against the inside of the metal container. The doors of the container flew open with the sudden shockwave, and Charley felt the last step give way beneath her.

She began falling. She was still inside the container, in free fall, helpless to get out.

A new, foreign instinct suddenly commanded her. Her arm was up and pointed skyward through the open doors of the container's opposite end. The blue whip unfurled from one of her gauntlets toward a girder that formed a crane tripod high above her.

The whip wrapped around the girder and tightened like a constricting snake. She yanked down. The pull took barely any strength.

She flew through the container's open doors and into the air. The container crashed beneath her into a pile.

Charley landed on the girder that her whip had wrapped around. She looked down.

She was fifty feet higher.

She was astonished to see the distance she had sailed. She had snapped upward like her whip was a bungee cord.

The Nekura were furious. They threw their arms upward and their commotion increased. They circled the container stack and howled in hatred.

But they couldn't reach her.

Charley smiled down at them. The new instinct from inside the container rushed through her. She ran down the length of the girder and dove off the end.

The whip snapped out of her gauntlet. It sped toward a tall stack of containers in the distance. It snagged the top of one and she tugged down on the line.

She sailed through the air like a bird.

She landed on a stack of containers with a graceful dismount and looked back to the ground.

The Nekura chased after, but the maze of containers prevented easy pursuit. She had left them behind with one swing.

She felt amazing. This new feeling—it was powerful and completely foreign to her as of sixty seconds ago. But now, she felt it surge inside.

It was like the man and his water pump that Thom had described. He'd finished telling the story right as she stole away from the administrative building. "You might think that you are channeling the Light," he had said, "but it is actually the Light channeling you."

Now she was living it.

The vibrating stone had quieted after her swinging through the second door. She was on the right path. She ran off the end of the container stack.

The whip of light ripped her through the sky.

CHAPTER 137

"What was that?" Henry said.

The terrible clanging sound had torn through the still night air. He and Thom couldn't see amid the jungle of stacked containers.

"I think it came from over there," Henry said and pointed. The sound had been a cacophony of crunching metal.

"Is that a good enough signal for you?" Thom said.

"It didn't sound good."

"Let's go!"

Thom charged forward with Henry behind him.

After a minute they pulled to a stop. A large stack of containers littered the concrete dock in a pile. Bent corrugated metal lay haphazardly, like a giant hand had plucked up the containers to let them fall randomly on the awaiting ground below.

Nekura surrounded the debris of heaping metal. Two Bludgeons were caught in the center while Gremlins bounded around the pile. The Bludgeons were irate, yelling at the Gremlins in incomprehensible growls and swatting at them with free arms.

As the Nekura tore into the pile of containers, Henry had the fleeting thought that Charley or his mother could be underneath the rubble.

The two trapped Bludgeons howled in anger when they saw Thom and Henry. They heaved back and spewed large expulsions of acid from their pinned position.

Thom and Henry side-stepped quickly and charged toward the Nekura. Henry created the bo staff out of thin air and held it ready to strike.

He was becoming accustomed to Light's connection. Each time he called upon the Light he felt he was more adept, more proficient than before.

The Bludgeon in front of him launched another stream of acid, destined to coat Henry in corrosive toxin.

Henry raised the bo staff, planted his left foot, and launched the bo through the air like a javelin. It sped toward the Bludgeon and penetrated the flying stream of acid. The liquid separated around it, and Henry stood safely in the wake of his flying weapon. The staff pierced the Bludgeon through its open mouth, and acid dribbled out as the creature decayed into nothingness.

Thom pulled back his hand and the blue bow appeared with another arrow from the endless invisible quiver of the Light. The arrow sank deep into the other Bludgeon's chest and the creature crumpled forward.

"Quick thinking there, Henry," Thom said. "I've never seen anyone do that before."

"Something more than me, Dad. Like you said."

Thom nodded and grinned.

The remaining Gremlins scattered after the Bludgeons were dispatched. Henry took off after them but Thom called him back. "Leave them, Henry. Help me look here. We need to make sure . . ." He didn't need to finish.

Henry drove the end of the bo into the pile and wedged it in. He wrenched backward on the staff like it was a giant lever, and with the power of the Light it moved the cargo containers. They stared down at the bottom of the pile.

Nothing was there.

"I'm so glad that we didn't find them," Thom said. "Not here, at least."

"That means they are still out there."

"But what happened here?"

"They must have gotten away. Some Gremlins ran that way when we first got here." Henry pointed in an unexplored direction that stretched down the water's edge. "We should go."

"Then lead on."

CHAPTER 138

C harley hoped her search was almost over.

She had already gone through two entry points but she wasn't sure how many she needed to go through. Standard convention was three for tumbler locks.

The Light was anything but standard.

She felt the stone's vibration on her back slowly increase. With each turn, with each leap and swing from the whip, she stopped to make sure that the stone still led her. She knew one thing about navigation—trust the instruments.

Charley stood on top of a crane and surveyed the landscape. A large pyramid of containers rose in front. It was made up of more than three dozen individual cargo units, each stacked on top of the other in clusters of various colors.

The stone had led her here.

The second entry point had been at the top of a stack of containers. The top of the pyramid would be a good place to start looking for the third. It was the most easily accessible option.

Charley found a grapple point and lassoed the whip around it. She swung through the air and flew to the top of the pyramid, landing on the highest container. She let herself down, then opened the container door and ran in. She hoped this one was the answer.

The vibrating continued on her back.

It wasn't the right one.

This process was like cracking open a safe. She would have to try all the containers until she found it.

She dropped down to the second highest row of containers and ran through them. Still nothing happened—the stone hummed without change.

The density of containers increased the lower into the pyramid she went. There were so many possibilities clustered together. She would be a prime target while she searched them since she was no longer running. She picked up her pace.

The light from the stone was difficult to contain now, even with it still inside the backpack. Charley noticed the increased glow as she ran through each successive container. The vibrating intensified and the light refused to be dimmed by the backpack's fabric. It entered a small nova state and she became a beaming lighthouse in the dark of the night.

The light was easily seen.

CHAPTER 139

Charley thought she was inside the sixth container. Maybe the seventh? Still nothing.

She ran out to see a pack of Gremlins charging at the pyramid in ravenous fury. They squawked in frustration, enraged at being outdone. They clawed over one another, fighting to be the first to reach her, like a pack of hyenas racing each other to their prey.

Charley ran through a couple more containers. Still nothing.

Time was running out.

She looked down and the Gremlins were halfway to her position. She ran through the next container closest to her. Still no change. The same vibrating. The same emergence into the dark night without difference.

The same Nekura closing in.

A large Bludgeon stole Charley's attention and scaled the pyramid in leaping bounds. It jumped from one stack of the pyramid to the next and crumpled the cargo containers underneath its weight.

Charley cracked her whip at the large beast but it dodged. She cracked at it again but it flew sideways again. It stood still and waited for another attack.

Charley reared back to snap but paused.

A few moments of devoted attention to one Bludgeon allowed three more to crawl up the sides of the pyramid. Nekura streamed toward her position from the shadows—Gremlins, Bludgeons, and even the twisted, contorted deformities of remaining Fracas.

She was about to be overwhelmed. She wished she had someone else with her right now. She ran through the next container.

Nothing.

She couldn't leave. She had to find the furnace before they did. Everything depended on it.

Like a surging tide, Nekura rose on the pyramid to where she stood.

She snapped her whip downward again, but they retreated only for a moment.

She couldn't buffet the tide any longer.

She reached blindly behind her and her fingers swiped a cargo container's latch. She fumbled with it, the adrenaline making her movements erratic.

She only had time for one more.

She wedged the door open and darted inside. She turned and ran forward.

There would be a swarm of Nekura waiting on the other side.

This was it. The end of everything.

The furnace or the Nekura.

Victory or death.

She set her face, pulled back her whip, and charged forward through the container's back-end door.

CHAPTER 140

The door flew open.

The Nekura were waiting on the other side. An acid bath poured from the mouths of several Bludgeons and sped into the open container like an erupting geyser. The putrid liquid seared the door and corroded the frame into rivulets of molten metal that ran down the pyramid. The container entrance corroded, then imploded like a shriveled balloon.

The Nekura cheered. Their hunt was over.

The steam faded. The air cleared.

No one was there.

There was no corpse on the ground. No bagged animal from their hunt.

The door of the container swung on damaged hinges and showcased its empty contents.

Gremlins opened the door at the container's other end. The Nekura looked blankly at each other through the hollow corridor.

The Bludgeons let out a terrible howl.

CHAPTER 141

Henry heard another sound.

An awful howl, like a pack of giant mutant wolves wailing at the moon.

"Dad . . ." Henry looked at Thom.

"That's our cue!" Thom said.

They sprinted in the direction of the sound.

Another clue, another signpost to the direction they needed to go.

The horrible sound filled the night air with evil, and Henry's hair stood on end. It fueled him forward, urging him to get there, and it sublimated in his mind. It was not a victory cry he heard—it was a cry of intoxicating fury. The Nekura were outraged.

That was a good thing.

Thom charged in front of Henry. A small spark of hope burned brighter, lifting them out of desperation.

Charley and Dawn were still out there. Fighting. Thwarting. Refusing to give in to the darkness.

They were not overcome.

Henry's legs thundered against the ground in full sprint, like pistons pounding inside an engine to redline.

"Don't worry," Henry said through heavy panting. "We're coming."

CHAPTER 142

Charley ran her hands over her body.

No burning acid. No liquefying pain.

She was alive.

And the dockyard had disappeared.

She was in an expansive building with large marble pillars that supported high walls. Torches interspersed between the pillars cast a warm, receiving light around the chamber. The walls were made of stacked stone, the work of a skilled craftsman. The room felt like a sacred stage, peaceful after the stirring chaos that drove her here.

She had crossed the Veil.

This time felt different than at the volcano. There, it had felt dizzying. Here, she felt soothed—the kind of calmness experienced underneath a heavy blanket, coaxing the restless sleeper to be still and dream.

Charley swung her backpack around. The sudden movement felt unnatural here, under the vaulted ceiling. She unzipped the backpack and pulled out the stone. The stone pulsed with a peaceful, rhythmic light, growing and dimming, as if finally contented.

She walked forward. The large room crested, like she was walking up a hill, and at the end of the chamber she saw a pair of rustic wooden doors. The immense doors hung by metal brackets and rivets. She reverentially pushed on one of the doors, and with modest effort the door swung open.

The corridor was dark. She drew back into the room from where she came and grabbed one of the torches from the wall. The torch cast light into the new corridor and glowed with reflection upon the hard, polished floor. The light from the torch jumped to all the dry torches and spread through the new room, alighting them with unbidden flame.

The light wrapped at the end of the corridor in a round atrium. Small pillars adorned the perimeter, connected by arches between them.

Something was in the middle of the atrium.

CHAPTER 143

Charley couldn't tell what was in the middle of the atrium. She walked forward, her eyes locked.

The center platform of the atrium was raised into a dais. A pedestal rose in the center with a glass container on top.

Her vision narrowed. She no longer noticed the pillars and their elegance, or the stacked stones hewn with precision craftsmanship, or the torches and how they burned without ever-dripping wax, or how they spontaneously lit in the first place.

What had captured her attention was the glass case with a blue glow inside.

Excitement grew and she moved faster toward the dais.

She also didn't notice the large group of stacked stones on her right side, how it was the only section without a torch mounted in its center. She didn't notice how the stones gently rumbled as she walked past. They slipped loose in silent motion from the wall and gave birth to another presence in the room.

The stones pulled out into a mass, a giant cluster, cut out from the wall like pieces removed from a masonry jigsaw puzzle. They formed a head, legs, arms—a living creature of stone.

The integrated stones of the giant creature moved over each other in quiet motion. The creature filled the room, its headstone a few feet from the top of the vaulted ceiling.

It noticed Charley and began to move behind her.

It closed in on her.

The creature raised up a stone fist. The fist grew in size to a massive anvil on the end of the creature's hand.

The strone fist would crush her to powder.

CHAPTER 144

C harley stopped staring at the glass case and looked down to the polished floor. A large inkblot of darkness filled the floor. That's strange.

The light from the torches had dimmed. The darkening around her looked like a massive shadow.

Her transfixion broke. She heard it now—the gentle grinding sound behind her, like a car driving down a gravel road.

She whirled around.

A massive rock creature stood in front of her and enveloped the height of the room. An enormous stone hand, the size of a school bus, was raised above her.

It came down in a furious blow.

Reflexes ignited inside her. She jumped backward into a series of successive back handsprings.

The giant fist crushed the polished floor like a small meteor. Broken segments flew upward from the pulverized crater. Tremors vibrated through the floor and made Charley's legs wobble.

She was no longer in the creature's striking distance. For the moment.

The monster was a humanoid mold of countless stones, held together by invisible sinews and threads.

A massive Nekura. It must have followed her here.

She would have had better luck with the sea of Nekura on the dockyard than this one.

She could try running. Maybe she could grab what was inside the glass case, but the creature would block her exit through the doors. She would never get out.

There was no sense trying to talk to it. It had no mouth or ears—it was just a being of stone. Besides, there was no reasoning with the Nekura.

She could try to fight it and look for a weak spot.

That was ridiculous.

But she needed the furnace. She could not give in.

Victory or death.

Charley materialized her whip and reached her arm back into a ready position, the living blue cord of light wrapping around her. But the whip didn't dance or twist like it had always done. It lay dormant, like a piece of painted blue rope.

Something else caught her eye on the ground in front of her. She glanced down.

Her heart sank.

CHAPTER 145

The rock creature stood over her backpack.

The pack had fallen off Charley's shoulder during her handsprings.

And she hadn't shut the zipper the last time she opened it—the blue speckled stone had skidded out of the backpack and lay halfway between her and the rock creature. The stone pulsated blue light like a heartbeat.

The *Book of the Salients* had also scattered of out of the backpack. It lay only a couple feet away.

Charley gritted her teeth in frustration. Now she had multiple items to retrieve, some dangerously close to the rock monster. But she needed to get them all. The furnace, the backpack, the book, the stone—everything.

She would not leave without fighting this monstrous Nekura to its death. She would turn it into the largest ash heap yet and fill the whole chamber with its smoke, or die trying.

Charley cocked the whip back and waited for the creature to attack. But it didn't.

The rock creature noticed the whip. It noticed the blue-speckled stone and the book that slid from her backpack. It paused, and the large stone that made up its head tilted, like it was thinking. It took a step back from its aggressive posture and stood upright, its headstone nearly touching the vaulted rock ceiling. Its anvil hand regressed in size.

There was strained silence that seemed eternal in length. Charley and the rock creature faced each other, unmoving, unsure of what should happen next. Then the rock creature took a large step forward and bent its hulking frame of stone, down to one knee.

Surprise, confusion, and relief all swirled inside Charley. She kept her whip at the ready. With surprising dexterity, the rock creature picked up the blue-speckled stone and reached out to give it back to Charley. It dropped the stone into her cautious hand.

The rock creature bowed its head to her.

The immense creature had moved from aggression to conciliation. She looked at the stone in her left hand and her whip of light in her right.

She understood.

It was a sentry. This creature wasn't a Nekura—it was a guardian. Charley's possession of the stone and the whip had recast her presence—she was connected to the Light.

The great rock creature stood up from its bended knee. With several steps backward it went toward the section of the wall from where it had emerged. A silhouette of earth carved out from the wall stood ready to receive it. The creature slid into place, and only a smooth wall remained, with stones stacked on each other, just as a mason would have placed them.

Charley stared at the seams of rocks. She couldn't tell any difference between that wall and the rest of the stone walls throughout the corridor. The whip vanished from her hand.

The guardian had just bowed to her in deference. After the swarming Nekura nearly enveloped her at the docks, she had found a creature here that was willing to help her.

It struck her as odd, for a moment, that she had fretted at all about the Nekura.

She chuckled out loud. Just this one creature would have been enough to decimate the whole legion of Nekura on the other side.

The creature hadn't spoken, but Charley felt as if it had.

She was never as alone as she thought.

Not all was lost.

She grabbed her backpack and collected the book and stone. Thom's pistols were still inside. This time, she made sure to zip up the compartments. She slung the backpack over her shoulder and made her way to the dais.

Time to see what was in the glass case.

CHAPTER 146

Charley walked beneath the archway formed by the pillars. The inside of the atrium was well lit, more than the rest of the chamber. The glass case was tall and thin and glinted with light along its gentle, flowing contours.

As Charley approached, she realized it wasn't a glass case.

It was a vase.

Floating upright in the center of the vase was a flower. It had blue petals, with a single thread of silver running through its stem, which shimmered. It was beautiful—a solitaire in the soft light of the room.

Etched into the glass vase was the same intricate symbol as the one on the spine of the book. Charley reached out to take hold of the flower. She cringed, waiting for the burn.

It lifted into her hands.

No burning. Just warmth, tingling her fingertips.

It was a tulip in full bloom. She brought it closer to her eyes. Fire burned in each petal, rolling and lapping upward. The internal peals of flame were enough evidence.

She had found the furnace—a perpetually burning and self-sustaining gift of the Light.

Now the remainder of the lyrics made sense as Charley tumbled over them in her mind:

> *Not burnished bronze nor smelter's ore*
> *Is the fire's blazing core*
> *In weathered lands on distant shore*
> *Fire reaches, wanting more*
> *From dancing flames, the skies adore*
> *The rising fire they implore.*

The fire in the song wasn't the sun, it was the flower under the sun. The flower rises and reaches toward the sun's dancing flames in the skies. And here she was on the distant shore, staring at soft petals hiding the fire's blazing core.

Charley opened her backpack. She had nothing to put the flower into, so she gently placed it inside the backpack and lifted the pack onto her shoulder. She turned to walk out.

She stopped to look at the wall barren of a torch. She placed her hands on the rocks, feeling them beneath her fingertips. They felt no different than ordinary stones. Charley looked up the course of the wall. She wasn't sure, but she felt an attempt was worth the effort.

"Thank you," she said.

A gentle vibration returned under her fingertips, just like the speckled stone had vibrated in her backpack.

She was not alone.

The doors on the far side of the chamber had shaken closed with the thunderous strike of the rock guardian. She ran up to the door and pulled it open, then ran into the other room.

It was dark and she couldn't see. She created her whip of light to illuminate the room.

She stood inside a small metal container made of corrugated steel.

She'd crossed back through the Veil.

Time to find the others.

CHAPTER 147

Thom and Henry arrived at the wreckage.

What used to be a large pyramid of containers was now in shambles. Torn and rusted corrugated metal was strewn everywhere. Shrapnel flew in chunks as the Nekura ripped the containers end to end. Gremlins tore through the metal with their sharp claws and Bludgeons dissolved it with acerbic vomit.

They were furious, like a pack of rabid animals that had lost their dinner among the reeds. The Nekura clawed and fought against one another in crazed agitation.

It was pandemonium.

Henry was relieved to see it.

Thom drew back his arms and his bow appeared. He aimed it at the sky and unleashed a hailstorm of arrows among the frustrated Nekura.

The arrows rained down, and the remaining Fracas fell to the ground in the assault. Smoke and ash rose from their decaying corpses in Nekura funeral pyres.

"That's it, the last of the Fracas," Thom said.

"Do you think that's really all of them?" Henry said.

"Not a chance."

"But are we clear for now?"

"Clear."

"Then let's go! We don't have a moment to lose."

Thom and Henry charged forward.

The remaining Nekura, already manic in rage, stampeded toward the two intruders. The chirping Gremlins charged ahead and the Bludgeons bellowed out angry howls as they followed.

Henry followed Thom close into the fray. Thom created his bow, and it grew larger than his body. He dashed forward and turned it sideways to use it as a battering ram. He smashed four Gremlins backward, pinning them against the container's metal, and they fell lifeless to the ground.

Henry threw his bo staff along the ground to the right. It twisted in circles like a typhoon and flew into a pack of Nekura and severed their legs. Smoke and ash poured onto the ground from their bleeding limbs. In a few moments the top halves of the Nekura disintegrated as well.

The bo disappeared beyond the Nekura, and Henry summoned it again in his hand, where it materialized out of nothingness. That was one of the best parts of the gauntlets. He could throw his weapon and immediately manifest it again. His connection to the Light was deepening.

Thom and Henry stood back to back in the center of the swarming Nekura. Thom fired arrows and Henry struck and parried with his bo staff with advancing skill.

The Nekura pressed in on them.

Thom and Henry pressed back.

The night became alive with the shrieks of the Nekura.

Suddenly, the Nekura stopped.

CHAPTER 148

All the Nekura stood straight up, silently responding to something. Thom and Henry stood at the ready, their postures still guarded, their weapons still drawn.

All at once the Nekura turned to the coastline. Their attention was demanded elsewhere. Without a sound they flew toward the water's edge.

"Look, Dad, they're just . . . leaving."

"Hm," Thom said and rubbed his chin. "That's strange." He shook his head. "I don't like this."

"They just turned and ran," Henry said. "Something doesn't feel right."

"I agree."

"What do you think?"

"I think we need to find your mom and Charley and leave."

"We should start by looking through this scrap pile. The Nekura were frantic about it until they left."

Thom and Henry ran to the disarrayed pile of containers lying on the ground. They started to search through the wreckage. Henry used his bo staff as a lever to pry the containers up.

"Do you see anything?" Henry asked.

"No."

"Keep looking. We have to find what they were after."

They looked through the pyramid of containers, opening and closing doors. Charley and Dawn were still missing.

"I'm sure we've searched through this entire pile," Thom said. "I think I've personally looked through every container twice."

"I know. I've looked under every piece of metal. The girls aren't here, and neither is the furnace."

"But why were the Nekura so insistent on tearing this pyramid apart?"

Henry hopped down from the container he stood on. He opened its latch and swung the door open, using the light from his staff to illuminate the inside of the container.

It was barren.

With a sigh, Henry closed the door. He glanced around the wreckage, wondering where to go next, but took a step back when he heard something inside the empty container in front of him. It was the same one he had just looked in.

The door burst open and Charley ran out.

Seeing her was like seeing an apparition. Henry was dumfounded.

Charley flung herself into Henry and hugged him.

"Henry! Thom!" she said, "I found the furnace! I was in a large stone room with pillars and torches and it was in there!"

Henry processed the information, scrolling through hidden databases he didn't know he had. "That's the Narthex of Light," Henry said. He surprised himself. "I know it. I think it's one of those implanted memories. You got the furnace?"

Charley grinned and nodded.

She took her backpack off and set it on the ground. She opened the zipper and reached in to pull out the delicate blue tulip.

"Whoa," Henry said. His eyes drunk up the image. He watched the fire lap inside the petals, and it felt like the flames leapt through his eyes and scorched his mind. Something felt different inside him, like something had unlocked, or maybe burned away. "It looks like the flower is burning on the inside. Dad, what do you think? Dad?"

Thom was gazing at the shoreline where the Nekura retreated. They had all vanished. He looked stoic, staring off at the water.

"Do you know where Dawn is?" Charley asked Thom.

"I think so." Thom's voice was ominous.

"Is she in trouble?" Henry asked. Panic rose in his chest.

Thom didn't answer. He just hung his head.

Henry looked at the soft blue tulip in his hand. A shred of ice nestled again in the base of his skull.

He couldn't afford that price—not if the price for the furnace was his mother.

Thom set his face and began walking to the edge of the water.

"Come on," he said. "This isn't over yet."

CHAPTER 149

They entered a clearing among the containers with a large, open crane basket above.

Something lay on the ground in the middle of the clearing.

Charley saw it first under the cresting vestiges of the moon's light. "Oh no . . ." She ran into the clearing.

Henry ran to Charley and looked down. Cold fear washed over him like a waterfall. He silently pleaded into the night air.

"Please no . . . please no . . ." The tears that stung his eyes should have been hot, but they were ice on his cheeks. He bent down.

He picked up Dawn's shotgun from the lifeless concrete deck.

Henry turned around and held it out to Thom.

A look of horror passed Thom's face.

Thom grabbed the shotgun and seethed. "This will not end like this," he said. He turned to Charley and handed her the shotgun. She cinched the weapon through the twin straps of the backpack. It stuck out sideways and held to the small of her back.

"We have to find her," Henry said.

"I know," Thom said. "But how did they catch her? They should have never been able to get close to her."

The cloud covers passed and the moon shone in the night sky, its pale complexion bright in the darkness. With the added light, Henry saw it—adjacent to where the shotgun had lain—indistinct threads of green rising into the air.

Thom bent down on his knee next to the green vapor and leaned closer. An arrow appeared in his hand. He pointed the arrowhead down and scraped the concrete. He brought the arrowhead up and looked at it. A faint tinge of green slowly sizzled on the tip. With his other hand he wafted some of the vapor toward him.

He coughed and hacked. Even the scant amount nearly choked him. He regained his breath and spat on the ground. "Fracas!"

Dawn's disappearance had always been real in Henry's mind, but he'd chased it away with the thought of reunion.

Thom stared at the stained ground.

"We always returned to each other," he said. "All those years, all those voyages into the darkness—we always came home. We built a life apart from the Nekura to find peace." Thom's voice shook with emotion. "But now we're back in. We dove in headfirst. I just hope we haven't broken our necks with the dive."

CHAPTER 150

Henry felt the hope of his mother's return sink in the depths of his soul.

The memories of his life with his mother were being scrubbed away. In a way, he knew it from the start but refused to believe it. Now the token of the lone shotgun realized his deepest fear.

Dawn Murphy had been taken.

"But you stopped the Fracas at the door," Henry said, "I saw it!" He pleaded into the night air, trying to convince reality that it should have acted otherwise. "You killed them all!"

Even as he said it, he knew it wasn't true.

There had been more.

Thom's arrow brightened and the green secretion crackled away. The arrow disappeared from his hand.

"I should have known," Thom said. "There's always more."

A large grinding sound echoed through the night. It was the same sound Henry had heard earlier.

He jumped and looked around, his bo in a ready position.

"Henry!" Charley said.

He followed the sound of Charley's voice. She sat in the operator's seat of the large orange crane. She worked the lever for the giant mechanical arm, and the large grinding sound returned to the night. Henry saw the crane basket open above their position, like a giant serpent's mouth releasing death upon them.

He understood how the Fracas got close. They cascaded down upon his mother.

"The fumes are pungent," Thom said. "They are still fresh. She wouldn't have been taken long ago."

"Where did they go?" Charley asked, returning from the crane.

"The water's edge."

Henry didn't hear anything else. He couldn't contend with the nausea he felt. The dizziness. The apprehension.

She was gone . . .

Thom had said Henry didn't have to worry because Dawn was with him. She was a Salient.

But that didn't mean anything anymore. Not even a Salient had stopped the Nekura. What hope did he have?

His legs buckled. He collapsed on his knees.

He couldn't do this. He just couldn't. Anything, anything but her.

The memories flooded him. Her smile, her kindness. She had always been there for him.

She wasn't anymore.

He couldn't live without her.

He squinted his eyes until they hurt. He wanted to scream into the night. This was the one thing he couldn't give up. His mind reeled. What the Nekura would do to her, the darkness they would smother her in . . .

His mother . . .

Gone.

All was lost.

CHAPTER 151

Thom led them toward the waterline.

He stood at the dock with his toes on the edge of the concrete.

Henry followed like an invalid. He could barely walk. He looked into the gently rolling water, belying the evil that disappeared somewhere in its vast array. The water bled indistinctly into the distant, dark horizon.

"Dad, what now?"

"They went to the other side," Charley said. "I'm convinced of it. After just passing through it, I know the feeling. They fled back through the Veil."

Henry kicked a small stone on the concrete surface down into the waves, which lapped the sides of the steel-encased concreted dock. The stone sank into the water and vanished. It never made a splash. The waves received it as if unaware, without sending ripples or lifting sprays of water.

Thom frowned. He glanced at Henry and Charley. "See you on the other side," he said.

Thom jumped into the water.

He disappeared in the same way as the stone. The water swallowed him as if it had better business and would not be agitated by its intruder.

Charley looked at Henry. She half smiled and lifted her eyebrows. She leapt into the water and disappeared the same way.

Henry was alone.

He felt increasingly nervous. Neither Thom nor Charley resurfaced in the water. The other side of the Veil was disorienting. If they jumped in the water and time sped away like it had at the volcano, they could drown in a second.

Henry breathed harder. He looked down into the water's vacant surface.

He needed to find his mother.

The thought was enough.

He took a giant breath and leapt.

CHAPTER 152

Henry never got wet.

He jumped through the water and felt the surface tension of it break.

He fell from a ceiling and landed in the middle of a room. He landed on his side on a stone floor. Pain shot through his ribs.

Thom and Charley stood waiting.

"Aghh . . ." Henry said. "Are you both alright?"

"We're fine," Charley said.

Henry sat up and held his side. "You didn't crash-land?"

Charley helped him up. "I've done this Veil-hopping a couple more times than you."

Thom watched the door at the end of the room, which was at the top of a small flight of stairs.

The room was dimly lit and large stones formed the walls in deep, murky tones. The air was dank and musty, and coolness crept into Henry's bones.

Henry looked up. In the center of the ceiling a whirlpool of dark water swirled above him, suspended in the air. The water churned without falling to the ground.

"Dad, where are we?"

"Charley was right," Thom said. "We're on the other side."

"These stones," Charley said, "this building . . . It's all ancient. It feels like a dungeon."

"It's not a dungeon," Thom said. "It's an entry point—a staging ground for moving across the Veil."

Thom walked up the small flight of stairs to the doorway. Charley and Henry followed.

Through the doorway, they walked into a hallway made of the same kind of stones. They entered a portico—a chamber with four passageways, each leading in a different direction, like at the center of a compass. Each passageway was made of a stone-worked arch with a dark hallway beneath. The room felt abandoned.

"Three choices," Charley said. "We walked out of this one." She pointed backward. "There's no sign of which way to go."

"Go down the one on the left," Thom said.

"How do you know?" Henry said.

"You go down a small flight of stairs and then come to a branch in the hallway. Go to the right, and then the corridor will curve and ramp downward. There's a door at the end. It should be where your mother is held."

CHAPTER 153

Henry squinted at his father. There was silence. Thom stared ahead, no object in view. His shoulders slumped.

"Dad," Henry said, "how do you know all this?"

Thom took a breath, but his voice seized in his throat. He paused and collected his composure. "I've been here before."

More silence.

Thom snapped out of his reverie and looked at Henry and Charley. His face was pained. "Be quick. You need to save your mother. I know you can do it."

Henry nodded.

"Lead the way, Henry," Thom said.

Admonition refocused Henry. He took off through the entryway on the left and ran through the dark corridor. Charley sprinted behind.

"I have to take care of family business," Thom called over their shoulders.

"Family business," Henry said and agreed. They needed to put the family together again.

Henry led the way down a set of stairs and came to the break in the hallway. He ran through the hallway on the right. The corridor was long and winding. It curved to the right and angled downward, descending further into the bowels of the strange building.

The directions were exactly as Thom said.

The doorway at the end of the corridor was made of thick wood gathered together by metal piping worked through the frame. It was more ornate than anything Henry had seen so far. The door hid something significant on the other side.

A maximum-security prison cell—that would be significant. Henry pictured a dank and solitary cell where Dawn would be confined behind iron bars.

Henry turned. "Dad, you were right. What do we—"

Henry's mouth fell open. Fear rose.

"Henry, what is it?" Charley said. She turned around also.

Thom was gone.

CHAPTER 154

"Where's my dad?" Henry said.

Panic piqued.

He didn't have his mother. He didn't have his father.

He felt it creep back—the premonition of dread that had wormed its way into the deep places of his heart. The ice in his skull.

He couldn't do this alone.

Charley grabbed him by the shoulders.

"Hey . . . hey. Look at me. I know, I feel it also. But you have to think, Henry." She shook his shoulders. "Think! Things are different now. The Light, your connection to it—I've seen what it does. I've felt how it changed me. Your dad trusts us if he left us to do this. I'm different now. You're different now."

Henry broke his gaze. Her words tumbled in his mind. She paused, waiting for his gaze to return.

"And if I've become convinced of one thing," she said, "it's this—you're not as alone as you think."

Her words were balm to his battered soul. She was right. Things were different.

Charley needed him.

His mother needed him.

He nodded.

Charley released him. She put her ear up against the door.

"I can't hear anything," she said. "It's too thick."

Charley pushed against the door and it slid open. She crouched down and peeked inside, with Henry looking above her.

It wasn't the prison cell he expected.

The room was a large rotunda. Long benches faced away from them in regular intervals, some within a few feet of the doorway. The long benches had rigid, upright backs. The room was empty.

Henry and Charley snuck into the room and moved behind the closest bench.

From their new position they saw other benches stretch the length of the room, uniform and facing the front. Structural pillars supported the room's ceiling and gathered in a central spire. Ragged tapestry the color of crimson hung above each archway, with strange symbols written—or splattered—on the tapestries in black. Above Henry and Charley, in the center of the room, was a large metal chandelier. It was made of black coursing iron, with charred stumps of candles dotting its edges. At the front of the room was an elevated platform, like a stage with several broad, shallow steps leading to it.

The room was not designed for holding prisoners.

It was an amphitheater. It was designed for spectacle.

A door to the right burst open. A horde of Gremlins, Shades, and Bludgeons poured in with a din of commotion.

Henry and Charley dropped to hide behind the high-backed benches.

There must've been fifty Nekura that entered the amphitheater. Or more. A mob of darkness.

They all streamed into the front benches but none sat down. They buzzed too much in agitation. There was a chorus of cheering directed toward the door where the Nekura had come in.

The last Nekura to enter was a large Bludgeon. A half-severed arm hung from its torso, with its knuckles dragging on the ground. It left a trail of rocky, blackened ash in its wake. Its teeth shown in a broad and terrible grin. It took center stage, with clamorous ovation.

Slung over the shoulder of its other arm was a figure, incapacitated and limp like a rag doll.

Henry's mother.

CHAPTER 155

H enry didn't know what to do.

The ice in his skull was a drill press.

The Nekura touted his mother like a victory trophy in a circus of darkness.

But fifty Nekura against the two of them? Even with their weapons of Light they would be ripped to tatters from claws or dissolved by acid.

He had to think of something.

The sight of his mother in the clutches of the Nekura clogged the gears of his mind with thick emotion. He tumbled over his thoughts, tried to align them, but kept winding up at the same place.

His mother was as good as dead.

He glanced over his shoulder.

When was his dad was going to show up? Why wasn't he here yet? His father would come, just like at the university laboratory.

Henry looked back to the stage.

Faint tendrils of vapor and scrapes of green decorated the Bludgeon's onyx frame. Henry feared what the wounds meant—the Bludgeon had beaten off the Fracas to preserve Dawn for its dreadful playtime.

The Bludgeon lowered Dawn from its shoulder and used its moribund arm to take off her black hat. Her silver hair spilled out and hung toward the ground.

The throng of Nekura hissed with the revealing of her hair. They clawed at the air toward her. They crowed and squawked. They were ready for the main event.

The Bludgeon grabbed Dawn by the hair and hoisted her upward, dangling all her weight from the silver threads. Her body swung like a pendulum in the Bludgeon's grasp.

The horde of creatures climbed over each other and filled the air with demands for execution.

The Bludgeon held her like a bagged animal caught in the wild that it planned to fillet and eat. It was a display of power.

For the first time, Henry heard the Bludgeon speak. The slow, vitriolic voice resounded through the room, the word it spoke lingering in its acid-filled mouth.

"Salient."

It was a curse word.

The Bludgeon's face turned into a scowl of hatred. The Bludgeon thrust her forward, extending her to the mock jury to present her for her crime. The crime of being a Salient.

The Nekura went berserk at the showmanship. The Bludgeon had acted as prosecutor and judge. The jury passed its sentence—immediate death.

The smile of malevolence returned on the Bludgeon's face. The Bludgeon raised its good arm into the air, and its hand changed into a long black spike, flashing in pale reflection.

The Bludgeon pulled back to impale the incapacitated woman.

CHAPTER 156

This couldn't be happening.

The spike thrust forward.

It stopped midway, immobilized. The Bludgeon grunted. It looked up at its paralyzed arm.

A band of blue cord wrapped around its arm, held like a grappling. Charley held the other end of the taut whip from the center of the room and dug her heels into the ground, pulling with all her weight. She was several rows of benches in front of Henry.

Henry was shocked. She had never been this . . . this . . .

Daring.

Bold.

Shame draped over the fear in his heart. He sat ruminating while she had moved to save Dawn. And Dawn wasn't even Charley's mother. She was his.

The courage he imagined he had flitted away.

Charley snapped the whip, and the motion threw the Bludgeon into a spin. Dawn fell to the ground in a heap. The Bludgeon crashed into the wall at the front of the stage. It staggered, smoke and ash pouring from the gouges on its spiked hand.

Time stood still. The Nekura gawked at the intruder, stunned in disbelief. Their fun had been interrupted.

With searing vengeance, the Nekura surged toward Charley like a tidal wave of darkness.

Charley tossed and snapped her whip to maintain distance. She spun the whip in circles in front of her like a lasso, but in a matter of seconds she was surrounded.

CHAPTER 157

C harley had no idea what she had been thinking.

She didn't have a plan. She just knew that those dark creatures couldn't destroy Dawn.

In a flash, memories with Dawn crashed into Charley's mind. The long-road treks. Meals at the safe house. The battle at the high school. Their late-night conversation.

Charley remembered seeing the stars with Dawn that night. She also remembered what it meant to be taken. Maybe the Nekura weren't going to kill Dawn. Maybe they were doing something worse. Charley didn't understand what it meant to be a Salient, but Dawn was one of the very few people who had ever showed her true kindness.

So she acted.

Come what may, if Charley was going to die, this was the way she wanted her death to happen—making her life count for the sake of someone else.

She fended the Nekura off, spinning her whip in front of her. She dispatched some that dared to get too close.

She fended them off.

Until she couldn't.

The circle of Nekura tightened around her like the cinching of a belt, squeezing until she couldn't breathe.

There were so many.

Some of the Gremlins peeled off from the pack. They left her alone.

They found something even more delightful.

The Salient woman lay on the floor unconscious. The Gremlins stood over her and indulged in their gloating. They spat at her and waved angry claws over her.

One Nekura swiped at her hair with its razor talons. Several silver threads were cut while other strands were yanked out. In squeals of rapturous delight, the Gremlins ravaged her head.

CHAPTER 158

It was desecration.

It was a moment that could never be unseen, forever imprinted on Henry's soul—the Nekura tearing at his mother's silver hair while Charley was swallowed up by a deluge of Nekura.

He was terrified. Uncertain. Frozen.

He tried to muster his strength. He stood up from his hidden position in the back of the room, where he cowered in the shadows beneath a crimson banner.

"Stop!" His attempt felt like a dream where he tried to yell but couldn't. The feeble, quivering voice betrayed his fear.

The Nekura paused and looked at him. Renewed smiles flashed.

They sprang toward him.

He had just offered himself as another plaything before the main event.

Henry manifested the bo staff in his hands. It felt like a pole of lead. He knocked down a couple Nekura with sideways strikes, but others swarmed him instantly.

His mind was fractured. The darkness pressed in upon his soul. He couldn't shake the picture in his mind.

A third Gremlin lunged toward him.

Henry realized the feint too late.

Like a kamikaze, the lunging Nekura flew into the end of the bo to protect two other Gremlins that charged underneath. Each one swiped its talons at Henry's outstretched arms.

His two metallic gauntlets fell to the floor with a clang. Electrical impulses flickered and faded out, severed by the Gremlins.

His bo staff immediately disappeared.

He was a dead man.

CHAPTER 159

The Nekura seized Henry.

One Bludgeon grabbed his arms and another one held his legs. He hung between the two like a prize boar from a successful hunt.

The Nekura marched him toward the front of the room.

With their attention divided, Charley fought off smaller numbers of Nekura. The commotion with Henry's capture bought her a brief moment of reprieve. Charley snapped her whip upward and snagged one of the metal arms of the black chandelier. With a forceful tug, she flew up and landed on one of its large, swooping arms.

The pack of Nekura that had surrounded her became disinterested. They disbanded and went to revel in Henry's capture.

As Henry was carried to the front, he saw the Gremlins had returned to their game, clawing at Dawn's head. He saw the detailed abuse of his mother.

He could do nothing.

Despair flooded him. He yelled at them in bitter anguish.

"Stop! STOP! Please, stop!"

But the Nekura did not stop this time. They continued their desecration, delighted to disgrace the Salient before her death.

Sweat and tears mixed to sting Henry's eyes. He thrashed in the Bludgeon's arms to no avail. He was thoroughly bound.

His mother was captured.

Charley was alone.

His father had vanished.

The Bludgeon with the half-severed arm had recovered from the slash of Charley's whip. The Bludgeon looked at its long, obsidian spike, and scarred grooves now covered what used to be its good arm. The hulking creature bent over into Henry's face and leered. The pungent, acidic odor of its breath made Henry gag. It spoke with scathing hatred.

"Death to the Light."

The Bludgeon took up a ceremonial position between the two Nekura who restrained Henry and called to the raucous crowd. The clamor turned into cheering again.

All Henry's hope disappeared. Resignation took him.

He waited for the final blow.

He couldn't fight anymore without the Light.

CHAPTER 160

In a small corner of Henry's mind—a thought whispered.

He was connected to the Light.

He had lain in a bed for days without any weapons or gauntlets, but his father had said that the Light carried him through that time. It had seared his hand, but it had also knit him back together.

He glanced up at his exposed wrist from underneath the Bludgeon's large black hand. He saw the dark navy inkblot under his skin.

It looked different. It felt different. The large inkblot was a sign that he had been changed by the Light. He had been given over to it. The deep blue discoloration on his hand was not really a scar.

He was branded.

A marked man.

He never thought of it before now. The gauntlets did not create his connection to the Light, they merely displayed it.

It all suddenly made sense. Like stagnant, articulating gears that surged to life under the power of an engine, a glimmer of hope surged in his frame.

He whispered into the air. "Please, help me."

He heard something sizzle. It sounded like grease flash-frying on a stovetop. The large Bludgeon holding Henry's arms groaned and dropped Henry to the floor. It shook its hand and bent over in pain. Then Henry's legs dropped also.

Henry landed on his back. He couldn't see what was happening. He rolled and looked at the Bludgeon. It yelled in agonizing pain and held an injured hand, pouring smoke and weeping ash to the floor.

Thom wasn't there. No arrows flew through the air; no shots were fired by percussion pistols.

Henry looked at his hand.

It was glowing.

CHAPTER 161

The navy inkblot on Henry's skin ignited in color and surged with iridescent illumination from deep inside.

Henry scrambled to his feet. The light grew in magnitude and became a violent, irresistible blue color that traveled up his arm.

The horde of Nekura backed away and held up their arms to shield their faces.

Then the light dove through Henry's arm into his chest. The blue light flared into a blinding nova state and absorbed the whole room.

Moments later, the light dimmed. Henry looked down.

Blue flames consumed his seared hand. The flames licked up his arm past his elbow and danced, fueled from the burning light under his skin. The fire singed away the sleeve of Henry's athletic jacket and bared his skin all the way up to his shoulder.

He was on fire.

It didn't hurt, but his hand burned with surreal intensity.

He felt different, like he was alive for the first time. It was like the difference between seeing a beach on a postcard and feeling the warm breeze on his face, the sand scrunched between his toes, the sting of salt-water air in his nostrils.

Everything was different.

The Light called to him.

Henry held his flaming hand above his head. The Nekura didn't move.

He squeezed his hand shut. The bo appeared without gauntlets, without clamoring, without effort. It just appeared.

The Nekura staggered backward.

He was connected to the Light.

But it still called to him. Something else, something more.

CHAPTER 162

He felt the surge all through his body.

In the moment, the Nekura faded from his vision. The stage, Charley on the chandelier, his mother—they all disappeared.

It was just him, holding on to the staff.

The staff of Light.

Events cycled through his mind of all that had been thrust upon him.

He had left school, forfeited his chance at the scholarship, and couldn't even go home anymore. His future was gone.

His dad had left him. His mother was nearly dead. Charley was alone. His family was gone.

He had nothing anymore. Everything he cared about had been taken from him. He was an empty hull of a man.

Except one thing remained—the secret insanity, the monster buried deep inside.

But the Light still connected to him. It wanted him.

If the Light wanted him so bad . . .

Fine. It would have him.

Henry squeezed the staff tighter until his fingers hurt. He held it above him, his hand burning brighter. He heard the Nekura howl—the distant, lonely howl of a Bludgeon. The one he heard before. It cried in anger. The volume rose and pierced Henry's ears.

The voice told him to let go.

He squeezed the bo with all his strength.

The howling roared louder.

It said let go!

Pain seared his hand again. Blinding pain, which took his breath. He nearly buckled.

No. He would hold on.

He no longer held the staff up. The staff held him. He held on to it like it was the only rung between him and a fall into the black, eternal abyss beneath.

His hand throbbed.

The howling Bludgeon screamed in his mind.

Let go, Henry Murphy.

His eyes were on the flame.

He would not let go.

He would never let go.

The Bludgeon shrieked like a banshee. It was close. Henry looked down.

The shriek had come from him.

CHAPTER 163

The Bludgeon's face—the one from his dream world—crowed on Henry's stomach again. But this time it didn't laugh. It roared. The flame from Henry's hand flared again, and the Bludgeon screamed in agony. The brighter the flame grew, the more the Bludgeon wailed.

The fire crackled and burned. It was eating up the Bludgeon.

It gave one final cry. A bitter, horrible scream of pain.

Then it was snuffed out.

The face of the Bludgeon went lax on Henry's abdomen and began to fade away.

The howling subsided. Ash fell from Henry's stomach. Then, for the first time, his ears were unstopped. He heard a lullaby.

The face of the Bludgeon was singing. It sung a gentle, sweet song with a simple tune that made him drift on melodic fantasy to a place of simple cares, green hills by a river, a small ship docked at a pier, and picnics with chocolate éclairs. He unwound; his muscles loosened.

He nearly let go.

Then he quickly squeezed the staff with his hand and the blue flames jumped again.

The Bludgeon's face wiped away from his belly.

The lullaby disappeared.

The Nekura's song had been there all his life, but he never knew it. All along, the call of the Bludgeon had been a saccharine lullaby instead of a howl. It hadn't stalked him in the night—it had cooed him by night. Slowly, drifting, snuggled into his blanket, less awake, until . . . he would let go.

Let go and forget what really mattered.

He now saw how easy it was to slip. How his parents had succumbed to it. How it was the Nekura's fault, but it was more his own fault for ever listening to their song.

A dawning conviction flooded him.

It was a conviction to not forget. To never fall asleep to that lullaby again. To cherish what he had been given without taking it for granted, and to take off the mantle of self-autonomy and its insatiable hunger. To actually see the world—past the abstractions and recycled philosophical monologues of the day and existential dead-ends. No longer would he try to manipulate to fulfill his own ends, like he was a spoiled toddler throwing a tantrum because he'd been given milk instead of juice.

He had life. Rather, he didn't have life.

Life had him.

He was a part of it, and it surged through him by no prowess of his own. He resolved to stop demanding it be just so, as he would dictate it to be. He resolved to know why it was so.

Then he saw it. Life—it fathomlessly opened before him, like a curtain being drawn back on the face of infinity. Life was not the dreamy picnic by the river, but the river itself coursing its way to a vast, glittering ocean beyond, full of immeasurable possibilities, grand questions, and immense power. He had been so concerned about the lullaby's picnic, concerned about the nature of his tiny ship, that he thought himself satisfied on a small, muddy river even though an expansive ocean called him forward. The lullaby sung him to sleep, beside his docked ship, face-down in the mud.

Life was about the ocean—not only his tiny tugboat bobbing up and down, but everything that floated upon and swam below and soared above that immense ocean. The telescope of his ship was now turned outward, beyond the ship's own confines, and instead of looking inward upon his dull and excessively self-absorbed life, the lenses saw purpose and meaning.

He saw it, finally, the ocean that is life.

He dove into it.

In an eruption of fire and fury, a fountain of piercing light shot from the staff. An enormous rectangular hammerhead with mitered edges appeared on its end. A long banner unwound beneath the hammerhead, a beautiful royal red color with silver threading and a crest emblazoned on it in rich detail, like a coat of arms.

Henry's mouth fell open. His whole body tingled.

It was a strange feeling—humble honor instead of surging pride.

He didn't deserve this.

But still, he held it.

The Hammer of Andelis.

CHAPTER 164

The scene of the stone amphitheater reappeared around Henry. Dawn, Charley, and the mass of Nekura came back into vision. The Nekura all reeled backward. Their eyes had widened in horror and they resumed their chorus of hatred. This time, it was directed at Henry.

Some Gremlins fled through the door. None dared to get close to the stage.

Henry readied his feet. He saw their faces. They knew what he held.

More Nekura turned and ran away.

The Bludgeon with the half-severed arm pointed at Henry with its burnt spike and howled.

Henry roared and sprang forward like a puma. He crashed into the center of the horde, with the hammer swinging in an arc over his head. He slammed it down.

The floor shattered into a crater, and broken shards flew upward. A shockwave rippled throughout the room with a low, baritone sound. All the Nekura fell to the ground, a dozen turning to smoke and ash from the shockwave.

Henry leapt and swung the hammer as easily as his bo staff. Like swinging a golf club, he propelled a large cluster of retreating Nekura through the air into a mass of intertwining smoke and ash that landed on the far wall.

Henry swung back the other way and sent another cluster flying. He marshaled forward like a hunter beating back a jungle's vines, each swipe of his machete carving out another hunk of path. Back and forth, hack and slash, he cut them down.

Two Shades charged at Henry, enormous heads bobbing and leaving peels of skin in their wake. They slashed with razor fingers glowing red hot.

One Shade got too close.

Henry grabbed the Shade's razored arm with his burning hand. The Shade screamed as the flames eagerly poured off Henry's hand onto it. The blue flames drank up the Shade and enveloped it like dry tinder. It screamed and ran a few steps before it collapsed into a pile of burning blue ash.

The other Shade ran away shrieking.

Henry looked around the room. They were gone.

"Henry!" Charley yelled from the chandelier. She pointed behind him. He spun around.

The Bludgeon with the half-severed arm stood over Dawn, unconscious on the ground. It was rearing back, mouth dribbling acid.

It would cover her in corrosive death.

Henry pulled back the hammer like a spear. He felt the poise, the strength, the balance from the Light. He stepped forward and hurled it.

The hammer flew forward like a rocket.

It smashed the head of the Nekura with a devastating crunch. The Nekura flew backward and its acid spewed safely away from Dawn. The large Bludgeon slammed against the wall like an airborne cannonball.

The half-severed arm ripped off completely, and the hammer left a cra-
terous hole in the low, flat, dematerializing head of the Bludgeon. The
hammer disappeared out of the Bludgeon's ashen cadaver and reappeared
in Henry's hand.

A loud reverberation echoed through the chamber with the impact,
the staccato note at the end of Henry's new song.

No more lullabies.

CHAPTER 165

Charley rappelled down from the chandelier by her whip.

What just happened to Henry was unbelievable. She paused for a minute, still suspended above the ground.

Maybe it really was unbelievable. Was this more Nekura deception?

"Are you alright?" Henry asked.

"Me? What about you? Your hand is on fire!"

Henry held his hand up and looked at it. He lifted his eyebrows. "You were right, Charley. You're never as alone as you think."

She smiled. He had heard her.

His words alleviated all her doubts. She landed on the floor and walked up to him.

He looked taller. His face was the same but he looked more mature, catapulted forward by the Light. His voice seemed different. Deeper? Maybe he was just more confident. Maybe—

"No, I mean it," Henry said. His insistence drew her attention back. "You were always right, even from the beginning. I didn't listen." He paused. "Wasn't loyal. Changed. You said it, but I didn't believe it and almost lost everything. I'm sorry for being hateful and aloof and jealous and all those terrible things inside. I wish I could say it wasn't me. The truth is, it was me. All of it."

He hung his head.

Silence.

He lifted his head and looked at her, then gave a soft, pleading smile. "But that Nekura part of me is being burned away."

The sudden, genuine tone in his voice was unexpected. He seemed not just aware but dismayed about his failures. His confession was an abrupt emotional maturation—the ability to look inside himself and actually understand faults without dressing them up, rationalizing them away, or blaming them on anyone else that happened to be present.

Her own fears had become ordered and not inexplicably dominant or inordinate in degree. The same happened with Henry and his failures—they had become ordered, perceptible, and declared for what they were.

He was coming clean.

His confession imploded the façade—the façade of a smiling face that covered up the swirling turmoil of marginalization and slow decay that compromised everyone she met.

Charley smiled. "It's okay, Henry. I just . . ."

No one had ever been so honest with her. So . . . true.

She reached forward and hugged him. He returned her embrace and the flames of his hand didn't burn her. They only felt warm and gentle upon her back.

"Come on," she said and stepped back, "let's get your mom and get out of here!"

CHAPTER 166

Henry ran to his mother.

She lay unmoving on the ground, except for the gentle rise and fall of her chest with her breaths, which came too scarcely. Charley got down on her knees and pulled Dawn's head onto her lap.

She didn't look good. She was beat up, bruised, and most of her hair had been ripped out.

"Dawn," Charley said.

No answer.

"Dawn!"

Charley tried shaking her shoulders and pinching her skin. She was comatose.

Charley leaned over and put her ear on Dawn's chest. "Henry, she stopped breathing!"

Henry frowned and bent down on his knees also. "I don't know if this is going to work," he said.

"What?"

The Hammer evaporated from Henry's grasp. He clutched Dawn's throat with his burning hand. The flames lapped around the edges of Dawn's neck. A burning, sizzling sound gurgled from Dawn's throat.

Suddenly, Dawn gasped. A large cloud of green, putrid gas and smoke billowed out from Dawn's mouth. The gas still burned in the air, a kaleidoscope of color turning from green to blue.

Dawn breathed again. She opened her eyes and looked up.

"Henry, you did it!" Charley threw her arms around Dawn. Henry sat back and sighed in relief. He relished the moment.

She would be okay.

She almost wasn't. But she was now.

Dawn bolted upright.

"The Fracas! They're right—"

She stopped and took in her surroundings. Large clouds of smoke swirled around piles of ash strewn throughout a room of crimson banners.

Her eyebrows knotted together. Charley answered it before she could ask.

"Henry took care of them."

Dawn saw him now, sitting next to Charley, his hand on fire. "That's amazing," she said.

"It doesn't hurt."

She smiled. "You look great, Henry."

Henry frowned. "I wish I could say the same about you." His voice quivered. "They ripped out your hair." He couldn't say anything more.

"Oh, they did?" She said it with surprising levity. Dawn stood up on her feet, wobbling, trying them out again. Once she had her balance, she whipped her head around like a fashion model selling a line of shampoo. Immediately, her hair bounced out of her scalp in full volume, beautiful, silver with brunette streaks underneath.

Henry nearly fell over. "I thought the damage was permanent."

Dawn smiled. "I'm full of surprises."

CHAPTER 167

C harley produced Dawn's shotgun from where it was slung between the backpack straps. Dawn took it back and racked the slide.

She looked around the room and counted all the ash piles littered about the chamber.

"You did this all with your hand and the bo staff?" Dawn asked.

"Actually . . ."

The Hammer of Andelis appeared in his burning hand.

She was more surprised to see the Hammer of Andelis than Henry with a hand on fire. She stared at the hammer, eyes wide, mouth open.

"So, you have the Hammer of Andelis," she said. "I confess that in all my years I never saw it. I began to think it was just a legend. The Light and its countless surprises," she said, shaking her head. "It is a formidable weapon, surging with the Light's power. Its full name is 'The Hammer of Andelis, the Breaker of Night.'"

Henry felt the power, but he also felt the responsibility. He nodded.

"Where is your father?"

"I don't know."

"You don't know?"

"No. He left us right before we came in here."

She drew back and gawked. "That doesn't sound like your father. It sounds completely opposite of him. What happened?"

As Henry and Charley described everything, Dawn's concern grew.

"He said he had some family business to take care of," Henry said, "right before we ran in here. I thought he was going to help us rescue you."

Blood drained from Dawn's face. She looked around the room and realized where she was. "Oh no."

"Do you know what's happening?" Charley asked.

Dawn turned back to them in a panicked voice. "We have to run. Follow me, because your father is in trouble."

CHAPTER 168

Thom had not wanted to leave them alone.

He hated to do it. He castigated himself as he ran down the hall.

He had chosen the hallway to the right once he sent Henry and Charley down the hallway to the left. But if he did not take care of this problem now, it would follow them forever.

Thom raced down the hallways that he knew all too well. The bleak décor and oppressive shadows followed him, and he used an arrow in his hands to light his way. He arrived at a stairwell and ran up the large, smooth stones to the grand entrance doors at the top.

This was it.

He opened the doors and walked into a giant rotunda. The large, circular room was akin to a ballroom—but no one would have reason to be happy here. The walls rose into the air, several stories high, and collected in a vaulted ceiling. The architecture was brick and hewn stone, like the remainder of the castle, with gray color and long, leering shadows. At the opposite end of the room was a large staircase that led to a catwalk that encircled the rotunda. In the center of the room was a sanctimonious stone circle built into the floor.

"Show yourself!" Thom's voice ricocheted through the room, ringing in his eardrums as his call chased itself into the dark emptiness.

Thom walked into the center of the room. He looked to the elevated catwalk and litany of doors around the rotunda. Various pathways merged into this room, resulting in a network of corridors, like a giant black heart with its blood vessels streaming off to provide darkness wherever it was needed.

"Show yourself!" he called again. "I know you're here."

A gentle chuckle came, almost indistinct. It was a voice that Thom had not heard in many years. One he had gladly forgotten. It came from the left, from the balcony above him.

It made his blood curdle to hear it again.

"Welcome home, brother."

CHAPTER 169

Thom was indignant that the man still called him "brother."
From the shadows of the balcony, the man appeared and
ambled to the staircase, sauntering as he went. He had brilliantly black hair slicked back and a handsome face, with a sharp nose
and a thin, wide smile and perfectly straight teeth. He wore a red regal
gown draped over him like a carapace, embroidered with black and gold
stitching. He was a mixture of sullied refinement.

"I trust you've had safe travels," the black-haired man said.

"No thanks to you."

"No, no, no, you misunderstand me," the man said. "Let me clarify.
I trust you had safe travels because you are standing here *alive*." He spat
with disgust.

Thom shook his head. "Why are you doing this, Carl?"

"Why am I doing this? Why did we do anything, Thomas? Because
we needed to for a grander plan. I need that furnace, brother, so you can
hand it over and be on your way."

"What exactly is your grander plan?"

"Certainly more than what you plan on doing with the furnace, hiding it away under lock and key."

"You think you're going to exploit the Light?"

"Oh yes," Carl said. He crested the first step of the staircase, acting like a deity descending to adoring throngs that are much to his dismissal. "Yes, you don't even know. That's how it is with you—small-minded and myopic. You can't even see what you've got when you clutch it in your sweaty hands."

"What is that supposed to mean?"

Carl descended the staircase opposite of Thom one slow step at a time, savoring each moment.

"Don't you remember, Thomas? All that you and I had together? We were brothers fit to be kings! You were in charge of legions of Nekura, given your special . . . skills. But you threw it all away for that little family and your droll connection to the Light."

"It's so much more than that," Thom said. "Connecting to the Light is what saved me. It gave me purpose."

"Oh, let me be clear. I have purpose."

"Not like I do."

"You poor, misguided soul!" Carl sang with a patronizing voice and walked down the last step of the grand staircase. "Power is purpose. It is meaning. The more power, the more freedom. You know they made me sole commander after you left. And your little family—that's your meaning?"

"Family is everything to me."

"Liar!" Carl stormed forward. "You left me. You left your family."

"Don't turn this back on me."

"You left me alone. We were family long before you ever met that Salient. I had your allegiance first. I was entitled to it."

"You squandered that allegiance. You dragged it through the mud."

"You betrayed your family! You betrayed me."

CHAPTER 170

"Y ou betrayed me!" Thom thundered back. "You think I'm ignorant of what you were up to? You were jealous of my authority as commander. You plotted to kill me and usurp my position. You just confessed how consuming your quest for power is. What about those family ties, brother?"

"A mere trifle, an informality," Carl said with a wave of the hand.

His air of pretense was stifling. Carl's condescending tone and his twisting of the situation was maddening. He was trying to goad Thom.

"I would never have been able to usurp the mighty creature of Nekura legend," Carl said. "You know they still whisper legends about us? The Half-Bloods, born of human and Nekura blood. We were children of privilege."

"It wasn't privilege," Thom said. "It was exploitation. They didn't care about us so much as they cared about what our dual heritage would offer them. They used us so they could get to what made us special."

"I made them special!" Carl entered the circular space in the center of the room and paced with Thom, each of them circumscribing the other. "All those Shades," he said, "they all trace their ability to shape-shift back to me. I was the one who taught them, who drew it out of them. After you left, after you rejected us all, I took up the mantle. They honor me with a new title: the King of Onyx."

"You're no king, Carl," Thom said. This was his chance to knock his brother back by attacking his festering, overgrown pride. "I would know—I've got the same parents. And look at your kingdom! Is this the heritage you want—a legion of half-alive demons that kidnap and extort children? And you're so proud." He let the sarcasm drip in his voice.

Carl's face contorted with anger.

"That's why I left," Thom said. "I regret the things I did. But instead of reveling in my wrongs, I changed."

"And that little whelp of a Salient took you in? She's controlled by the Light. You want to talk about exploitation? That Light of yours only uses Salients to achieve its own end. You are connected to it through her, so you are just as much a pawn as she is."

"The Light is my own," Thom said, "my own repose. I'm not riding the coattails of another person. And my wife, whom you will apologize to when she arrives here, never forced anything on me. I chose the Light— just as I chose to leave you behind with your illegitimate promises."

"Enough!" Carl's voice echoed off the chamber walls with unnatural force. The ground shook beneath their feet and several chamber doors opened. Legions of Shades poured into the room from the tunnels.

"So," Thom said, "you've turned our throne room into a gladiator pit. So be it!"

CHAPTER 171

Thom threw off his long coat. His gauntlets showed beneath the cuffs of his shirt.

He drew in a breath. Blue arrows formed in each hand. The snaking, subdermal artwork on his chest lit up and glowed from beneath his shirt.

The Shades swarmed Thom.

Thom danced and twirled with the arrows like they were pointed swords. He dispatched Shade after Shade as they charged toward him. They never got close.

Carl stood at a distance. He ceased the influx of Shades with a simple call and put his hand in the air.

"Bravo! Bravo!" Carl clapped. "Such a display!"

"What's your game, Carl? You and I both know I can do this all day."

"Ah, I just wished to evaluate your capabilities. We both know you lost something when you gave up your Nekura heritage. You were half-blooded—two separate halves. Now, you're only one. One-half that is. You're limited, half a man. You surely can't handle . . . me."

Carl threw his regal cloak to the side, just as Thom did his coat. He took up a fighting posture across the circle.

The lies Carl spoke made it difficult for Thom to focus. Carl's ability to twist the truth was dizzying. If Thom could just get his brother to listen for a moment . . .

Maybe he could try. One last attempt, despite all the times previous, one last attempt to reach his brother. Diplomacy could be the answer if both sides were willing.

Thom and Carl faced each other, brother against brother.

The Light against the darkness.

CHAPTER 172

Henry followed Dawn up the stairs with Charley behind him.
He had not broken stride the entire way.
She'd said his dad was in trouble.

He ran without the hammer. It was too large for the narrow hallways.
He could call on it anytime he needed.

The large double doors at the top of the stairs were cracked open.
Dawn stopped and held out her hand across the doorway. She peered
inside, then held a finger up to her lips.

"Shhh," she said. "He's safe. Watch for now."

Henry looked through the narrow opening. His father stood in the
center of a circle in an expansive room. Another man stood across from
him. He didn't look like a Nekura. His face was polished and pale—like
a mausoleum.

Each of them were focused on the other, muscles tightened. Thom
looked ready to pounce. He held his arrows ready.

"Mom, who is the—"

"Shhh. Watch."

CHAPTER 173

"Carl, please, listen to me," Thom said. "Give up this life. It leads nowhere. I was in it, I know it, and I know life on the other side. It is far better."

Thom dematerialized the arrows and put his hands up. His gesture was a white flag, a moment to put down arms and attempt something more reasonable.

Henry was confused. Why was his dad surrendering?

"I don't want to fight you," Thom said. "We could be restored—together. I was half Nekura also, but the Light could burn away the Nekura blood in you, just like it did me. You can connect to the Light, just like I did. Please, Carl, I'm trying to help you—you're my brother. You're family. It's worth it."

Henry was aghast.

Brother? Nekura blood?

He immediately denied what his father had said. It must be one of the Nekura's lies to throw Henry off balance. He looked at his mother, desperate.

She held his gaze. "You know your connection to the Light? How it changed you—made you something different?" She pointed at Thom. "It did the same for him."

Dawn turned back and watched, leaving the conversation at that.

His father—half Nekura. The same blood coursed in Henry's veins, mixed with his Mother's Salient spark.

But that meant that the Nekura vision on his belly had been . . .

Real?

Carl laughed with derision.

"Oh, how the mighty have fallen! Behold, the mighty Mastodon! Now pleading with his brother to give up and play nice. I don't want your charity, and I will certainly not give up my crown as the King of Onyx." Carl clenched his fists as he spoke. "Do you want to help me? You helped me when you led your Salient wife into my trap so she could be slain in my own house. You'll find her carcass in the Crimson Sanctuary. And now I will help you, too—by ending your miserable existence!"

Carl began to change. His face contorted, his eyes bulged, and he grew in size. His frame enlarged and his clothes ripped to tatters. Thick, oily hair covered his face and ran down his body. He put his hands on the ground and claws replaced his hands and feet. His nose narrowed to a point with crooked whiskers, and his face showed reddened eyes and white pointed teeth.

The man had turned into an enormous rat-beast. It was a grotesque transmogrification, and the beast's size was impressive, twice as big as Thom.

The Rat swung his tail around. On the end were imposing barbs that looked like they had been taken from a medieval torture device.

Carl breathed hard on Thom, the barbed tail a foot away from his face.

Henry felt crazy. He had to help his dad. And now that he had the hammer, he could.

"Mom, we have to do something! That rat is going to kill Dad!"

"Wait," she said. "He has to do this. He needs it, for his own sake."

She squeezed Henry's hand tight but kept her eyes on Thom. "Please, Thom. Remember." She closed her eyes and whispered the words.

Thom appeared unfazed. The Rat pointed its hideous tail at him with imposing threats, but Thom did not seem imposed upon. Carl's voice spoke again, this time a gravelly sound from deep inside the Rat.

"You can't beat me! You're nothing now. You're half a man and you lost your ability as a Half-Blood." He drew back his tail to strike. Thom didn't move.

The Rat's tail sped forward to skewer Thom.

CHAPTER 174

Two blue arrows flew up and crossed in front of Thom's chest. The arrows penetrated the tail, and the spiked end hovered inches from Thom's body.

The Rat grunted in pain.

"I tried to give you a chance," Thom said, "but you wouldn't listen. And I have to thank you, too. For all those years, I thought I truly was only half a person. But I realized something back at the docks—when the protective dam I erected in my mind broke loose, and I returned to the place I said I would never go again. I realized that the Light took all of me, not just some of me. It even took the dark and shameful corners of my past that I regret. I am connected to it completely, every last part of me. You said I've lost something. You're wrong."

Thom threw the tail with the arrows to the side.

"I've been reclaimed."

He held up his bow in the air with both hands and split it in half. Two individual arrows formed in each hand, one from each half. The markings on Thom's arms and chest screamed in light. He pulled the arrows down to each side of his body. The light grew out of Thom's chest and took form in front of him. From each side of the circular pendant inscribed in his skin, a projection grew. They looked like sharpened horns.

No, they weren't horns.

They were tusks.

They grew bigger, and light shot outward from Thom, stretching into an outline of a massive mastodon.

The giant creature stood over Thom, with its enormous tusks jutting out. The animal was a tracing of light, transparent and outlined in a brilliant blue perimeter, like a projection of a pencil sketch.

Henry thought the Rat had been big, but the Mastodon towered over the Rat.

Rather than transforming himself, Thom stood in the center of the Mastodon with an arrow in each hand. The man inside was still the same.

Thom took a ready position inside the projection. The Mastodon readied itself also, following Thom's motions, as if he were controlling it by the thin wires of a marionette.

Thom called out from inside the creature.

"You came looking for the Mastodon. You invaded my house, assaulted my son, abducted my wife, and tried to undo my life. You've made your final mistake, Carl." Thom pointed his arrow at Carl, and the Mastodon brandished its tusk and dropped its front leg with a thunderous boom. "You called down the thunder—and now here I am!"

The Rat seethed and pulled back on its haunches. It foamed at its mouth, spittle flying.

"No! I will bury you with my own hands!"

The Rat charged in for the first blow.

CHAPTER 175

Claws extended, froth pouring off its sharp teeth, the Rat leapt into the air.

The Rat dove for Thom inside the creature.

A quick toss of the Mastodon's tusk blocked the Rat and threw creature to the side. The Rat clambered to regain its footing. It charged forward again.

The Rat was faster than the Mastodon. It jockeyed for position and came in for quick strikes.

But the Mastodon was far bigger. And more powerful.

They fought and parried, blows followed by counterblows, and every move Thom made his blue creature followed. Each time Thom struck forward with the arrow in his right hand, the Mastodon struck with its large right tusk. Left arrow, left tusk. When Thom ducked, so did the behemoth. He was a virtuoso of movement.

Henry's fear was replaced by astonishment. The fear of his father being overpowered changed sides in his mind—the Rat had seriously under-estimated its opponent.

Thom struck with a quick flurry of jabs. The Mastodon responded with successive, forward strikes with the tusks that acted like spears. The Rat retreated, spun around, and leapt again.

The Rat was infuriated at its own inability.

As many times as the Rat struck forward with its barbed tail, the Mastodon knocked it away with its impenetrable tusks, like an irritated horse swatting away flies with a quick and dismissive flip of its tail.

"I will finish you off," the Rat said. "You will be nothing but a stained memory."

"At least I'll be remembered. I'm sending you back to the darkness. You will be lost in the Void forever."

"You can't beat me!"

"Watch me."

"I've grown stronger. More powerful. You can't—"

The Mastodon blared a concussive blast from its trunk, sending out a sound of ten thousand trumpets that shook the whole chamber. Henry felt the vibration travel up the soles of his feet, and it shook his skull on his spine.

"Stop running your mouth, Carl. Nobody likes the sound of your voice except you."

"It's the last thing you will ever hear."

CHAPTER 176

The Rat's rage grew wild.

It's strategic fighting vanished. The Rat fought like a rabid animal with flailing attacks. The Mastodon stood its ground. It would not be corralled by the smaller creature.

Then the Rat got too close.

Thom threw his arms up in the air. The Mastodon threw itself up to its back legs and stood with all its weight on its rear haunches.

Its front legs became massive levitating pillars. They imminently hovered.

The Rat clawed to get away. It darted just beyond the Mastodon's legs as they crashed down with devastating force. The decorative floor underneath was crushed to gravel.

The Rat dove forward between the tusks while the Mastodon leaned on its front legs, but then the Rat froze in mid-air.

The Mastodon's trunk curled around the Rat and held it tight. Thom held both arrows in front of his face, like he was doing a pull-up. The more Thom pulled down, the tighter the Mastodon's grip. The Rat clawed in wild disarray but couldn't escape.

The Mastodon squeezed with a vice-like grip on the Rat. Ribs cracked underneath the Mastodon's overpowering strength, and the Rat gasped for air.

The Rat went limp inside the trunk.

The Mastodon threw the Rat across the room, where it hit the wall with a crunch. It landed in an unmoving pile.

Thom opened his hands. The arrows dissipated and the enormous Mastodon retreated into a flurry of light that rushed back into the pendant inscribed in his skin.

He looked to the side wall.

The Rat did not move. The oily brown hair retreated and gave way to humanlike skin. The Rat had shrunk in size and Carl's face re-appeared. He didn't open his eyes or move. He wasn't breathing.

Thom stood still and hung his head. He walked over to Carl's unmoving corpse and notched three arrows into his blue bow, then pulled back. He knelt down to point-blank range.

Thom grimaced. "I'm sorry, brother," he whispered. A tear rolled down his cheek. He turned his head away. He couldn't watch.

The arrows sunk into Carl's chest.

CHAPTER 177

Henry leapt in the air.

"He did it!" He ran out into the room. "Dad!"

Thom jumped. He smiled when he saw Henry and sighed in relief. His posture relaxed and he ran to meet Henry in the middle of the circle.

"Oh, Henry!" Thom said. His voice was drained and he looked weary, full of somber dissonance. "You made it. You're okay."

Henry threw his arms around his father. Charley came up and embraced him also. Thom squeezed them with strong arms.

"Dad, that was amazing! So that was the Mastodon? Why didn't you do that earlier? I didn't know you could do that!"

"I didn't want to leave you, Henry. I hated myself for leaving. But my brother . . ."

"It's okay. You were right. The Light protected us."

"Is your mother alright?"

"For sure."

Thom looked to Dawn, who still stood at a distance at the double doors. She nodded slowly.

Thom sighed. He opened his mouth, then closed it again and looked away.

"What is it, Dad?"

With a long drawn breath, Thom began to tell them everything.

CHAPTER 178

D awn leaned against the entrance of the stairwell.

Finally, it was all coming out.

No more secrets, no more hidden past, no more previous life. Now, there was just life.

This was the moment for Thom to open up his secret past. It was a moment for them—Thom and Henry, even Charley. She knew better than to intrude on it. They already knew her history.

She smiled. Letting the truth out felt good. It was like when she would garden in her yard and become filthy, but cleansing at the end meant the work was complete, culminated by the debris falling off and no longer clinging to her body.

Thom was coming clean.

She soaked in the moment.

But a catch appeared in the corner of her mind. Something didn't seem right. She tried to think of what still pestered her.

It wouldn't be long before any remaining Nekura became aware of her family's presence here. Maybe that was what she felt. The Nekura would try to trap them from crossing the Veil by blocking their exit from the room with the swirling whirlpool in the ceiling.

No, she wasn't fearful of a scuffle with a few more Gremlins or Shades. Fighting them was the price of doing business on this side of the Veil.

A chill lurched down her spine, an icy finger tracing a rivulet from the nape of her neck down to her waist. The cold embraced her, pressed in on her.

Suddenly, it was hard for her to breathe.

She gasped.

She clutched her chest. She almost fell to her knees.

Her lungs were in a vice.

She held on to a pillar.

She knew this feeling.

The darkness.

Like when She and Thom had fled as refugees. And when they drove by their house.

A domino effect had started—with Carl's demise, the evil that had infused him became threatened. It swelled and bristled in retaliation.

The evil wasn't here yet. But it was coming.

Her feeling was precognition, like when the pressure drops and the leaves in the trees still their rustling, almost unnoticeably, right before a tornado rips the landscape to tatters.

Henry and Charley were safe with Thom. They needed this moment. She would not sacrifice his confession again. That sacrifice had been given too much already. His confession would never come if they kept waiting for another time.

But she—she had to get them out of here.

She ran down the stairs.

She would clear them a path.

CHAPTER 179

"It was something hidden away, long ago," Thom said, "something that I felt ashamed about for years."

"Why were you so ashamed?" Charley asked.

"Yeah, Dad, you could have just been the Mastodon from the beginning."

Thom shrugged his shoulders. "You would think so, but there is something to be said for the journey along the way. The Mastodon was from my previous life, from my time as a Half-Blood with the Nekura. It was used for terrible things. When I left the Nekura and connected to the Light, I was ashamed of what I had done and I told myself I would never be that creature again."

Thom focused in on Henry and released him from his embrace.

"I buried my past deep for many years. That burying, that willful negligence, is what allowed me to begin to forget in the first place—to forget who I was, how I changed after my connection to the Light, and to forget to warn my family of the dangers of the other side." He looked at Charley, then looked back at Henry. "But it's what you said, Henry—it's reclaimed. Even leftovers from a previous life. I thought that when the Nekura part burned away, there were only charred remnants left. That wasn't true. Even what was broken and wrong in the past can still be sewn together for something good. The Light filled up all that emptiness. The Mastodon isn't new, it's just renewed."

Thom let his arms fall from Henry's shoulders. He shifted his feet.

"I'm not sure if any of this makes sense," he said.

Henry smiled and held up his scarred hand to his father. The navy stain transformed into iridescent blue fire, flames jumping upward.

"Whoa," Thom said.

Henry nodded. He saw Thom's knowing eyes and nodded back. He didn't need to say anything more.

Henry had been reclaimed, too.

Like father, like son.

The flame in Henry's hand diminished and his skin turned back to a murky midnight color.

"Carl held a vendetta against me for years," Thom said. "He hated me because I left the Nekura. Actually, I think he always hated me. Leaving the Nekura gave him the opportunity to nurture his hatred until the seed grew into full, all-consuming rage."

Henry and Charley nodded.

"With him gone, things should—"

Thom choked and gagged mid-sentence. His eyes went large in pain and surprise. He couldn't breathe.

The Rat's barbed tail exploded through the center of Thom's chest.

CHAPTER 180

Henry and Charley jumped backward.

Carl appeared in human form, with the Rat's long tail and its torturous end filling Thom's chest. Thom collapsed to his knees.

Henry was transfixed, overwhelmed by the instant horror of what he saw.

His father . . .

"But I saw you die," Henry said to Carl. "The Mastodon crushed you!" Henry shot a glance to the far wall. The remains of a large Shade lay there, with three arrows sticking out of its chest, decomposing to ash.

"Oh, just a little sleight of hand," Carl said. "I switched places. When I realized I could not outpower him, I would outwit him instead. It's all deception, dear nephew. Have you not figured that out by now? After all your brushes with the Nekura, you're still just as dimwitted as the rest of your family."

Henry took a step forward, but the tail whipped upward and dangled Thom in the air like a marionette.

"Ah ah ah. He belongs to me," Carl said. "And he always will. He will always be Nekura." Carl's tone softened. "But you always knew this, Henry. There is Nekura inside him and inside of you."

Henry remembered the Bludgeon's face. On him, inside him.

"It wants to have you, Henry. So give into it. Don't be like your father here," Carl said. He paraded his victim around like a trophy, lifting him up and wagging him back and forth for display. "In fact, I just saved you from his betrayal. All the years of feigned love and empty posturing! Just for display. He would betray you, because that is what Nekura do. He would betray you all. I just saved you all that time and brought it to a close now—before you lie at his feet, broken and dying, disbelieving that your own father would turn against you."

Henry's hand burned bright with indignation. "No. That part of me has burned away." The flames leapt upward and consumed his arm, extending all the way to his shoulder. The brightness reflected off Carl's smooth face.

"Ugh, how droll," Carl said and rolled his eyes. The gravelly voice of the Rat filled his human throat. "You wish to fight? Fine. If I cannot sing you to sleep, then I will put you to sleep like a diseased dog."

Henry threw his hand into the air.

He called on the Light.

He felt the smooth shaft of the hammer appear in his hand.

The Rat let loose a terrible, otherworldly shriek, the mixture of a wolf's howl and the caterwauling of a dozen felines in heat. Carl's tail snaked back and forth above him like a scorpion's. The Rat's red eyes filled out his face and gave him a terrible, ghoulish appearance.

"So, you have the Night Breaker," he said. "That hammer is of no consequence to me. You cannot hurt me with it. You cannot bear a true weapon of the Light because you have Nekura blood. The Light would never—"

"Enough!" Henry boomed. "The lies must stop."

Charley nodded. The blue whip of light jumped out of her gauntlet and danced on the floor, leaping in anticipation.

"You want truth?" Carl said and spat. He pointed a clawed finger at Henry. "Here it is: You are abomination, Henry Murphy. You are contradiction. Two worlds that should never have merged."

Henry set his feet.

With a vicious snap of his tail, Carl launched Thom through the air like a rag doll. His body thudded against the far wall and fell to the floor.

Thom was alive, but barely. He rolled over and clutched at the hole in his chest, gaping and barren.

CHAPTER 181

Thom pushed himself up to his knees. He buried his hand deep inside the hollow of his chest. The gaping wound that had been filled with the Rat's murderous tail was now filled with his own fist.

Carl smirked.

"Modern medicine can't save you, brother. You haven't even lost a drop of blood! That's because you've been pierced by the darkness, by the shadows of the Blighted One, and now your soul has been scoured." He said it thrillingly, savoring the victory.

The blue light of Thom's markings throbbed and flickered like a dying light bulb.

Thom looked off into the distance. He slouched forward.

"This belongs to you," Thom said. He sounded delirious. He pulled his hand out of his chest, balled up in a fist. Each word pained him. He teetered. "I . . . will always . . . love . . .you . . ."

He reached his clenched fist out in a feeble gesture. The gesture took the last of his strength. He tottered forward and collapsed, arm outstretched. He didn't move.

Thom Murphy was dead.

CHAPTER 182

"No . . ." Henry said. Tears filled the corners of his eyes. The light faded from Thom and the blue glow beneath his skin vanished.

Carl walked up to Thom with a sauntering gait and leaned over him. He cackled inches from Thom's ear, his voice filled with mockery. "No apologies here, brother," he said. Carl stood up. "And now for the matter of that family you cherish," he said. He cast his attention on Henry and Charley. "Then, the furnace."

Henry looked past the King of Onyx. His gaze was transfixed on his father.

The muscles in Thom's arms failed and his hand slowly opened. A brilliant spark of blue light shone through the opening fingers. The spark levitated in the air.

Carl followed Henry's gaze back to Thom on the floor and the levitating spark. "But the light should have extinguished," Carl said. "The spark should be gone. Unless . . ."

Carl shrieked. He spun in circles, his cool countenance changed into inordinate fear. Henry didn't know what Carl was trying to find. His horrible rat call echoed through the chamber and his face turned ghastly pale.

"No, no, no!" he cried. "Stop it!" He pointed at the spark of blue light. "It must not get back to her!"

Her.

Henry and Charley looked back at the distant stairwell.

It was the Rat's caterwauling call that made Dawn return. Her face was knotted in anger and sorrow. The blue spark of light lifted from Thom's hand and moved toward her, flittering in the air as a butterfly winding its way back to its home.

In his dying breath, Thom gave back Dawn's Salient spark. And if he gave back the spark, then if it returned to her . . .

Carl shouted all the more. "Stop it! Don't let her become Salient again!"

Nekura surged out of the numerous doorways and converged on the small light. Gremlins jumped in the air and slashed at the dancing spark, but their claws but passed through it. Bludgeons belched vomit upon it and tried to smash it between their hands, like squashing a gnat, but the dancing light was undaunted. Shades morphed into the form of Thom Murphy, hoping it would seduce the spark away.

None of it worked.

The spark had been given from one woman to one man years ago as her promise of love and unity, and now it was going back, again given out of devotion for the other. The gift would not be undone.

Dawn threw her shotgun aside and it clanged on the floor. Her face was set with the wrath of an infuriated spouse.

The spark reached her and dove into her chest.

CHAPTER 183

A fountain of light erupted like a geyser out of Dawn. The light ripped up to the top of the room, and rocks fell from the ceiling to the floor. It swelled to unbearable intensity and the Nekura scrambled away in fear. The torrent of light lasted for only a few moments, then it faded.

A new creature stood in the place where Dawn had been swallowed by the Light. A giant creature, several stories tall, stood in the room.

She was the most beautiful and devastating thing Henry had ever seen.

She was a living being of light and flesh. She looked avian, with a long, slender neck and strong shoulders. Her face tapered down to a beak, but it made her seem more elegant, with flowing, curving lines. Her slender and powerful frame was hidden underneath a dark silver cloak bound by a corded sash around her waist. Her skin glowed a light blue tone, like an egg in a robin's nest.

Long, brilliantly sterling hair fell from her head, like silver molten in a furnace that burned with fury. She looked like an angelic bird of prey.

Like waking from a dream, the Salient took a moment to stir. She focused her eyes, set her face.

Sharp, arcing wings burst from her in mighty flares. Their metallic curves ruptured from her back and rose to the sky, like a phoenix rising from ashes.

She'd arisen from the ashes of her husband.

Now there was a price to be paid.

She flexed her wings, and the cavernous room shook under her movement. Her silver cloak rustled with the wind and exposed her feet underneath—powerful black talons with sharp ends.

Terror shook the Nekura from the moment they saw her, but when her massive wings shot skyward, they howled in despair.

She was effulgent in light, mystifyingly beautiful, and uncompromisingly dreadful.

The Salient towered above the Nekura like a heaven-sent sentry of doom. They clawed at their faces and hissed at her with terrible, incomprehensible sounds.

Dawn was unmoved. She looked through the room. Her eyes quickened on Carl, who fled toward the edge of the room.

"Carl Half-Blood, Rat of the Nekura!" The room shook with the sound of her voice. It rang in the corridors throughout the mansion. "Hearken to me!"

The Rat was bound by the command. He couldn't move away. He and the Nekura looked upon her with begrudging eyes. Some withered away from merely gazing upon her presence.

"Carl Half-Blood, Rat of the Nekura!" she boomed again. She didn't open her mouth—the words projected out from her, piercing through body into soul. "Carl Half-Blood, Rat of the Nekura!" she thundered again. "King of Onyx, Captain for the Blighted One, you are a betrayer and a deceiver. Your brother sought to save you and you have murdered him for it."

She spoke the truth, plain and clear, but to the ears of the deceivers, the truth was acid. Moans of pain bellowed from the Nekura, and more of them erupted into smoke and ash in the wake of her words.

"Countless have fallen in your path of ruin. Your lies have caused many to stumble, and you are a worker of injustices."

Carl hissed and his eyes bulged. He sprung toward her to attack. He strafed sideways in a quick zigzag and thrust his spiked tail forward.

Dawn blocked the tail with her left wing like it was a giant, living shield. In a sudden upward thrust, her right wing severed the tail midway down. It was lightning fast, and the blue wing cut cleanly. Ash streamed from the Rat's open wound, and billows of smoke plumed from the stump of its tail.

Carl howled in pain and tried to scurry away.

"You are more a rat than a man. You killed my husband!" Her voice shook his skull. He put his hands to his ears and moaned with the piercings through his head. "Your time as the King of Onyx has ended—and your bloodlust is your undoing!" She surged forward. She skimmed on the floor, wings blown back, the bird of prey about to strike.

Carl cried out in terror.

She enveloped him. Her wings covered him and muted his strangled cries. A sound echoed from within her wings, like the crackling of logs in a fireplace. She flared her wings open wide. Tendrils of smoke coiled upward.

CHAPTER 184

The King of Onyx was no more. A pile of charred ash bowed at Dawn's unmoving feet. A simple sweep of Dawn's arcing wing blew it away.

She looked at the remaining Nekura. "Be gone!" she cried. The mouthless scream shook the foundations of the chamber.

The Nekura fled in command. The room emptied.

Dawn avian image shrunk until she was her normal size. She looked over her shoulder to Thom's unmoving body.

Henry turned around and looked, too. His father was now just a memory.

Memories. The word gnawed Henry's mind.

Thom had implanted memories in Henry, trusting him to know something no one else would. Henry knew more about the furnace than anyone else.

And he knew that the Nekura were after it.

Henry stiffened up.

The furnace—it had been the prize all along, and it still was. It was the thing that made his parents flee across the Veil, the point of this endless chase.

The furnace had scorched his mind when he saw it. Henry glanced to Charley's backpack. He could feel it, even from this distance. He felt like the furnace was burning on the dry tinder of quieted memories. The furnace was the fire to ignite the forgotten.

Henry's eyes darted around the chamber.

The victory was all wrong.

The Nekura could have taken them out earlier. They could have killed them a long time ago.

The Nekura were after the furnace.

Henry's memory shifted gears. Thoughts aligned, powered by the furnace's direction, like an orchestra being arranged by a conductor.

A memory of Dawn's voice: "The Nekura thrive on manipulation."

A memory of Thom's: "It was their grandest scheme—to convince the world they didn't exist."

A memory of Carl's: "It's all deception, dear nephew."

Carl confessed, in a rare moment of truth.

Henry gasped.

If Carl couldn't outpower them, he would outwit them. Henry suddenly feared Dawn never killed him—the Rat was going to try to pull the same trick twice. The Rat would convince them he didn't exist in order to take the furnace!

"Charley," Henry yelled. The hammer appeared in his hand. "Get down!"

Henry swung the hammer with all his strength like a baseball bat. His baseball instincts were innate after so many years.

He was trying to launch something into orbit.

Charley ducked without hesitation. The hammer passed over her head. It connected with something behind her with a colossal crunch.

Carl was indeed still alive, but now his body flew upward at homerun velocity. His human form appeared in the air, transforming out of the shape-shifting mold of the environment that had made him invisible. He nearly pickpocketed the furnace from Charley's backpack.

Smoke streamed from Carl's head. His body hit off the angled ceiling like a pinball and landed in the middle circle. Henry strode up to the King of Onyx.

Carl's teeth were knocked out and his once polished face now looked like a raisin, a wrinkled purple mush, crushed by the hammer blow. Smoke spurted out of him like pressured motor oil.

"Good-bye, uncle," Henry said.

The final blow sent Carl's ash flying throughout the room.

CHAPTER 185

"There," Henry said. "Now, it's over." He didn't move.

"Henry," Charley said, "how did you know the Rat was still alive? And that he was going for the furnace?"

He shrugged his shoulders. "The Light. The hidden memories my dad gave me." He looked at her and held her gaze. "What you said is true, Charley, just in a bad way, too. You're never as alone as you think."

Henry looked at Dawn and choked back tears. "I just want to go home."

"I know," she said. "Me too."

Dawn smiled but started crying also. The terrible cost to return to Salient form bore heavy on her soul.

Even through tears she appeared radiant, a bird-human amalgamation whose skin glowed and sparkled with her connection to the Light. Specks of silver flowed up and down her body like blood coursing through her veins.

"I came back when I heard the Rat howl," Dawn said, "but I was too late."

"No, Mom," Henry said. "I should have seen the Rat before it got Dad. His deception was so strong." Henry hung his head in defeat.

This cost was too great, too much to be demanded.

Dawn pulled him in her arms and reached out to pull Charley in, too. She wrapped her wings around them and hemmed them in. She smelled sweet, like peonies blooming in the late spring. The same wings that had just acted as a cleaving blade were now soft in her embrace. They helped to offer some comfort.

"We should go to him," Dawn said.

It stung afresh to see Thom, lifeless up close.

Thom's body was facedown on the ground with one arm extended, hand opened. Henry went down on his knee and rolled Thom over to his back. The hole carved in the center of his chest was cavernous and the edges were burnt with ash. Charley bit her lip at the sight.

Henry wished the image were just a bad dream—the kind of fevered nightmare he could awaken from like he had done before. But this was real. There was so much he still wanted to say to his father, so much that they had yet to do.

Dawn changed back into human form and her inconspicuous silver hair returned. She bent over Thom.

The torrent of emotion let loose.

She sobbed over him with great, racking sobs. She beat her fists on his injured chest.

"You promised!" she yelled into the indifferent air, "you promised to never leave me!"

She leaned forward, her body over his, and covered his wound. Chest to chest, heart to heart.

"Please, come back to me," Dawn whispered.

He didn't move.

CHAPTER 186

Charley looked away.

She felt she was going to explode. The emotions churned in her and she felt like she had been socked in the gut. She had learned so much, come this far. She disregarded the humming inside the backpack.

But now Thom was dead at her feet. The loss was too much. She could not go on. She had already lost so much, and just as she was getting close to someone—to a family—it was stripped from her.

The vibrating in the small of her back was getting bothersome.

But she couldn't deal with that now. She was buried in thought. Where else would she turn? Why did everyone she care about vanish?

The humming distracted her to the point she couldn't ignore it anymore.

Charley took off the backpack and set it on the ground. A faint glow shone through the cracked zippers. She unzipped the pouch and looked inside.

CHAPTER 187

The blue tulip burned with flame inside its petals. Charley pulled out the flower and held it with delicate fingers. It hummed in her hands.

"Dawn?" Charley said.

Dawn still lay on top of Thom with her head down. She looked up and her mouth opened in disbelief.

"Where did you get that?"

"Henry said the place was called the Narthex of Light."

Dawn sat up on her knees. Charley walked toward her and extended the flower. "I followed the directions from the compass stone."

Astonishment washed over Dawn's face. "Compass stone?"

"The speckled stone, that's what it was. It led me to this. I think it's the furnace," Charley said and pointed at the flower.

Dawn turned the flower over in her hands with solemnity. "The furnace—an always-living, self-sustaining token of the Light imbued into an object to perpetually burn." The words sounded like a recitation.

Henry looked back at Thom.

He was the same color as the gray stone floor he lay upon. An ashen scar spread out from the hole in his chest.

Henry's eyebrows knotted up in the center of his forehead. He looked at the flower in Dawn's hand and the lapping fire in its petals, the glowing warmth alighting her fingertips.

"Mom, do you think—"

He didn't have time to finish.

Dawn lifted the flower high in the air. She ripped her arm down in a blur with enough force to wake the dead. She buried the furnace deep into Thom's chest.

CHAPTER 188

The furnace shattered everywhere. The soft, pliable flower ruptured like breaking glass. Crystal shards flew through the room and landed on the floor around Thom. There was nothing left of it except a million small pieces of glass lying in a halo around the dead man.

Thom lay still. He didn't move.

But the Light did.

In the center of Thom's chest, a light flickered. His chest swelled, first with a small candle's glow, then a large flame.

Then a floodlight.

Then a hydrant of light.

Familiar cords of light snaked down his arms and chest and returned to the place from where they had retreated. The wound in his chest closed, the ashen edges burned away, and new soft skin knit together in its place. His chest sealed shut with vibrant blue color.

Thom opened his eyes. He breathed the air of life again.

He looked at Dawn, kneeling over him with her tear-stained face.

He tried to sit up.

She wouldn't let him.

She bowled him over in embrace. This time, joy replaced sorrow. She hugged him and kissed him and wept over him and refused to let go. He wrapped his arms around her and lay with her, reunited.

He lifted his head to her ear.

"Love is on our side," he said.

For their moment, time stood still.

CHAPTER 189

Dawn helped Thom sit up. Henry and Charley embraced him. "You promised you would never leave me," Dawn said, "and I'm making good on that promise."

He smiled at her and wiped her tears away. "I'm here now," he said. He looked down at his chest. Instead of a pendant inscribed on his skin there was now a large inkblot of dark blue scarring. "What did you do to me?"

"It was the furnace," Charley said. "It brought you back to life."

Thom touched the large scar with his fingertips like he was checking to make sure it was real.

"Are you okay?" Dawn said. "I'm still worried about you."

"Yeah, I think so," he said. "It's just that I've never died and come back to life before." He smirked. He looked back to the inkblot on his chest and then to Henry and his hand. "We're quite a pair now, aren't we?"

Henry nodded.

"The only thing," Thom said, "is that we don't have the furnace now. But neither do the Nekura."

"We should celebrate that," Henry said. "More root beer floats?"

Dawn and Charley helped Thom to his feet. Thom looked at his family and smiled.

Then his countenance fell. His eyes shifted and deep lines furrowed in his forehead. He opened his mouth, but only silence hung instead of words.

"What is it?" Dawn asked.

Thom shook his head. He grimaced. "Later."

"If it can wait, good. We need to leave. Do you remember when we went by our house after the high school? I felt that crushing pressure on my—"

"That's enough for me," Thom said. "Let's move!"

CHAPTER 190

Henry floated up in the water.

When he surfaced, he was just off the shoreline of the docks, splashed by the waves. Charley and Dawn swam in front of him toward the access ladder on the side of the docks. Thom's head popped up through the water behind him.

They made it through the Veil. Relief came over Henry.

Henry swam the rest of the way to the ladder and clambered up. Dawn and Charley stood in front of him, dripping water on the concrete docks. Thom climbed up behind them.

It was cold. The autumn night air on the water's shore wrapped them in a chill in their dripping clothes.

There were no signs of Nekura. All was still except for the blustery breeze.

"I'm freezing," Charley said. "Let's get out of here!"

They ran back toward the truck in the enclave of containers.

Home. It was on Henry's mind. It beckoned to him. Warm clothes. Full plates. Sweet sleep. No more nightmares. No more lullabies.

It started to rain. He was already wet from seawater, but the rain refused him warmth.

"We're almost there," Henry said. He pointed to the administrative building. The Fracas' remains had disintegrated and washed away in the rain. "Come on!"

Henry turned around. Thom stood still.

Dawn turned around and stopped running. "Thom, what is it?"

He stood like a statue with his head hung. It felt like ages before he looked up. The strange silence was unsettling.

Charley and Henry walked back and stood next to Dawn.

"Dad?" Henry said, "are you alright?"

Thom pursed his lips. He looked up with an expression of pain.

"Thom, what's going on?" Dawn said. Her voice was higher, more urgent.

"I'm sorry," Thom said, "I have to do this."

In the blink of an eye Thom held three arrows in a bow, parallel to the ground like a crossbow. The arrows were pointed at each one of them.

CHAPTER 191

Henry's fear surged. Betrayal? The last words of Carl flooded back to Henry and stained his psyche: *Once a Nekura, always a Nekura. He will betray you.*

Henry's hand burst into flames. He tried to call upon the Hammer of Andelis.

His attempt was too late. The arrows flew, each one singing through the rainy night. They plunged into the foreheads of their three targets.

Pain erupted in the center of Henry's forehead. He collapsed to his knees. He couldn't move.

The arrow burned with intense fury, but Henry didn't know if it was his skull or his mind that was riven. How could his father betray him?

He heard Carl's words again in his mind, taunting him—*before you lie at his feet, broken and dying, disbelieving that your own father would turn against you.*

He was paralyzed. He felt like all his nerves had been severed. His vision faded and unconsciousness loomed in front of him.

He tried to ask why.

For heaven's sake, why?

They had just won. They were supposed to enjoy happily ever after. He would scream if he could, but his tongue was thick and numb. Only something unintelligible murmured out.

"I'm so sorry," Thom said. The blue bow disappeared from his hand.

Dark ash coated Henry and he felt hot, rising smoke swirl around his head and choke him.

He drifted away into the black.

CHAPTER 192

Henry awoke with a start.

He wasn't dead.

He was no longer at the docks. He was in the blue candlelit room of the safe house. He was dry, warm, and in a different pair of clothes.

He looked around the room and saw Dawn and Charley. Each lay on cots in the room, also covered in generous blankets. Henry heard their rhythmic breathing and sighed in relief.

It wasn't betrayal? But why—

Thom opened the door to the room holding a wooden tray and a bowl of hot soup. Henry jumped at the sight of his father. Thom set the tray down on the table. "Oh, Henry," he said and sat down and embraced him. "I'm so glad you're awake."

Henry didn't say anything. He wasn't sure if he could.

"I thought the effects would have worn off sooner," Thom said. "I wanted to be here when you woke, but I guess I'm late," he said. He sounded like the same father Henry had always known. He smelled the same.

"Dad, what did you do?"

Thom sighed. "You've been asleep for three days."

"Didn't I already do that?" Henry shook his head.

"You would think the first time was enough."

"What happened?"

"I think it would be better to show you."

Thom got up and left the room. A minute later he returned with a cream-colored canvas sack. "Look at these," he said.

Thom pulled out a heap of clothes. They were stained with a ghastly amount of black ash, stuck to the clothing in chunks. They reeked of smoke, and the whole room smelled after he pulled them out.

They were Henry's clothes.

Thom put them back in the bag and threw the bag outside the room. The blue candlelight sizzled in defiance and grew brighter until the Nekura smoke burned away.

"That doesn't make sense," Henry said. "I don't remember any Nekura covering me in ash. And it should have washed off after all the rain."

"It didn't wash off because it wasn't ash from the Nekura," Thom said. "The ash was from you."

CHAPTER 193

"Mine?" Henry said.

Thom nodded. "When I died, I had a brief moment away from my body. When I woke to life again, I saw things different. It allowed me to see something else the Nekura hid from us."

"You've got to be kidding. And you had to shoot me in the head?"

"I'm sorry, Henry, it was the only way I could free you from it."

"So, you weren't trying to kill us?" Henry needed to hear his father say it.

"Kill you? Not at all!" He put his arm around Henry and pulled him close. "Never ever," he said. Thom paused. "Those are the lies of my brother. It's like a snake when its head is cut from its body. Although it is dead, there is still poison in the fangs. My brother may be dead, but we still have to remedy his poison."

Henry nodded.

Thom continued. "I only used the arrows of the Light to break the Nekuras' hold. When they struck, thick smoke and ash poured off each one of your heads."

Dawn groaned and rolled over. She opened her eyes. "If you meant to kill us, I'm going to take back that whole furnace-in-your-chest thing I did for you."

Thom went to her bedside and leaned over to kiss her. "I'm so glad you're awake," he said. "Sorry that it had to happen that way."

Charley woke up also. She rubbed her droopy eyes and propped herself up on an elbow.

"Thom, what were you talking to Henry about?" Dawn said. "I only caught pieces. Something else the Nekura hid from us? They've already taken so much."

"I know," Thom said and nodded. His voice caught in his throat. "I know." He held Dawn's stare. "We forgot about *him*."

Dawn looked back blankly. "Who?"

Then, her eyebrows darted high and her eyes swelled to saucers. Horror painted her face. Thom held her in his arms and she buried her face in his shoulder. Her chest heaved with silent cries.

Henry was confused. Dawn had just watched Thom die. What more could evoke such tortured emotion?

Charley leaned over to Henry. "Henry, what's going on?"

He shook his head. "I don't know what—"

But suddenly, he did.

Henry's heart sank like a lead weight to the soles of his feet, and drilling nausea gouged his stomach. His skin went cold. He braced himself with his arm to not pass out.

He knew it. He understood.

The extra bed in his bedroom. The extra dresser for clothes.

He turned and looked at Charley. His voice was tight and he thought he would choke on his own throat.

"The extra room, the extra food, the extra gauntlets . . ." he said and hung his head, "they weren't meant for you."

Dawn pulled back and looked at Thom. The words pained her to speak. "What have they done with him? Where is our other son?"

EPILOGUE

The man had dark-brown hair slicked back and he wore wire rimmed glasses. A blue vest hung open from his shoulders. He approached the throne that was covered in shadows. A voice spoke from the blackness.

"Is that the form you have chosen for the other side?"

The man nodded.

"What news do you bring?" the shadows asked.

"The captain is dead. Sent to the Void."

A guffaw came. "He was a pompous fool, calling himself the King of Onyx. Of course he's dead."

"Of course," the man nodded. "He showed no discretion."

"Did we obtain the furnace?"

"No, but we have these." The man held out his two hands and opened them. "Empty shards from the furnace, and hair from the Salient woman taken from the Crimson Sanctuary."

"Hmm," the shadows said. "It did always present a problem, how we would eventually remove the Light from the furnace. How convenient that they have done it for us."

"Yes, your Darkness." The man bowed.

"What of the Murphy sons?"

"The eldest now fights alongside his parents with the Hammer of Andelis. The younger one is still maintained, although the Mastodon has become aware of his presence."

"The dual heritage of these children provides me with rare opportunity," the shadows said with wicked satisfaction. "The Mastodon and his rebels are of no matter, even with that accursed hammer. Our plan moves forward. With the pieces you have brought me, we are closer now than ever before."

"Then I will give direction regarding the detained child. By order of the Blighted One."

"So be it. We will have our own light. Then nothing will stop us."

END BOOK ONE

ACKNOWLEDGMENTS

I would like to first thank my wife and family for their tireless support during this lengthy writing project. They know me best, love me best, and have given me encouragement even when the going was slow. I am truly blessed to count them as my own.

A big thank you goes out to Ross Browne and his team at The Editorial Department. Ross has put together a spectacular group of professionals. John Marlow, my developmental editor, gave tremendous insight and assistance during the story crafting process. Jill Twist, my copyeditor, was vital in creating a polished, publish-worthy final edition. I would not have created such a work without their careful eyes, insightful thoughts, and commitment to the work.

Thank you to the cover designer, Andrei Bat, courtesy of 99Designs. His technical skill, responsiveness, and vision breathed a portrait of the story onto the cover. He is an amazing artist. Thank you also to the typography and layout specialist, Predrag Markovic, also courtesy of 99Designs, who helped me to create a beautiful presentation. A big thanks also to Colleen Sheehan from Ampersand Bookery, who perfected the layout and ebook files when the time crunch was on.

I would also like to thank Brandon Macier, a dear friend, who has helped me with production and marketing. From creative graphics to business essentials and beta reading, he has been with me each step of the way.

Other production specialists that have helped me along the way include Bernardo Cruz, Randy Dissmore with cello piece creation, MARKISS courtesy of SoundBetter with music production, and Stephen Bertalan with video production for marketing trailers. Thanks to all of you.

Most importantly, thank you to my LORD and Savior, Jesus Christ, for whom this story is created and to whom it leads. May the pages of fiction reveal truths in the real world around us.

ABOUT THE AUTHOR

Joseph T. Humphrey is a premiering author of contemporary fiction for young adults with adult crossover appeal. He loves a good thriller with complex, cerebral plot lines and plenty of action. And he loves his heroes to be heroic!

When Joseph is not writing, he works as a board-certified emergency medicine physician, although he wishes he could be out slaying minions of the darkness with the characters in his books. He lives in Illinois with his fabulous wife, who gave him inspiration for his story. He also served as a flight surgeon for the U.S. Navy, but even more perilously, he is the father of two young boys.

Joseph is also a Christian thinker and speaker—he loves talking about Jesus Christ and the Gospel message. He tries playing the banjo when his lovable Goldendoodle allows him a break from the constant petting. He likes baseball, loves the Avengers, and hunts for the best donuts shops across the country.

Website: www.JosephTHumphrey.com
Twitter: @JosephTHumphre1

CPSIA information can be obtained
at www.ICGtesting.com
Printed in the USA
LVHW091636011121
702141LV00012B/265/J